THE
LAIRDBALOR

THE LAIRDBALOR

KATHLEEN KAUFMAN

Kathleen Kaufman

TURNER

Turner Publishing Company
Nashville, Tennessee
New York, New York
www.turnerpublishing.com

The Lairdbalor

Cover artwork: Isla O'Neal
Cover design: Maddie Cothren
Book design: Glen Edelstein

Library of Congress Cataloging-in-Publication Data

Names: Kaufman, Kathleen, author.
Title: The Lairdbalor / Kathleen Kaufman.
Description: Nashville, Tennessee : Turner Publishing Company, [2017] |
    Summary: Seven-year-old Jamie falls down a very long hill into a nightmare
    world where nothing is familiar except the Lairdbalor, his personal
    bogeyman come to life.
Identifiers: LCCN 2017007610 (print) | LCCN 2017031667 (ebook) | ISBN
    9781683365891 (e-book) | ISBN 9781683365877 (paperback : alk. paper)
Subjects: | CYAC: Monsters--Fiction. | Nightmares--Fiction. |
    Anxiety--Fiction. | Fear--Fiction. | Horror stories.
Classification: LCC PZ7.1.K377 (ebook) | LCC PZ7.1.K377 Lai 2017 (print) |
    DDC [Fic]--dc23
LC record available at https://lccn.loc.gov/2017007610

9781683365884

Printed in the United States of America
17 18 19 20 10 9 8 7 6 5 4 3 2 1

To Robert, who knows how much I love him.

"... no, it were being too familiar even to let his bones lie there, — the home, this, of Necessity and Fate. There was there felt the presence of a force not bound to be kind to man. It was a place for heathenism and superstitious rites, — to be inhabited by men nearer of kin to the rocks and to wild animals than we."

Ktaadn Part 6 – Henry David Thoreau

THE
LAIRDBALOR

ONE

CUIDADO. That was the last word that Jamie remembered. As he pulled himself out of the bramble at the bottom of the very long hill, he rubbed his forehead, which was growing a sizeable lump. *Cuidado.* It had been printed on the small yellow sign at the top of the hill; there had been other words as well, in English and in Spanish, but Jamie had only been interested in the Spanish, so he really had no idea what the others had said. As he pulled a thorn out of his arm, he imagined they must have warned against going too close to the edge. Not caring to understand and having far too much fun in his seven-year-old way—walking just close enough to the edge of the walkway so that his mother made that sucking-in-her-breath noise and then reached out to pull him away by the back of his shirt—he had utterly ignored the rest of the warning. Now, sitting in an increasingly damp patch of dirt with a burning sensation rolling down his right side and thorns in every inch of exposed skin, he imagined that he had been properly warned about walking—skipping, really—too close to the edge of the path.

Slowly and not without pain, he looked up the mountainside, expecting full well to see his father crashing down the brush after him, his mother at the top yelling his name. It was awfully quiet for all that, though. In fact, as he strained his neck to look up the hill,

Jamie realized that all sound had stopped. No birds; the buzzing of insects was absent. Panicked, he patted his hands against his ears—had he gone deaf? Had he hit his head? In the hospital drama that his parents liked to watch at night, people were always hitting their heads and ending up in the emergency room. No. He heard the pat against his ear, hesitated a moment, and then called out: "Momma! Daddy! I'm here!"

Nothing. No tall figure crashing through the brush after him; no sight of his mother in her blue knit skirt with the tiny ducks around the edges. Nothing at all. The hill even looked different. Back at the *Cuidado* sign, the pine trees provided the only green, and dead shrubs and grass created a carpet of brown, scratchy needles. But here, as Jamie pulled still more thorns from his shin and forearm, the grass still grew. The bottom of his pants was wet, as though he were sitting in a puddle. When he shifted to the side, he realized that the slightly marshy ground was soupy and soft wherever he moved. Green bushes lined the bases of gigantic trees. A patch of sunset-colored flowers popped out from underneath a raspberry bush. Up the hill, the green continued—but how could that be?

Jamie knew he hadn't blacked out. Last year, he had fallen from the monkey bars during the annual school fitness test. He had landed square on his back, and the next thing he remembered was a circle of people overhead and Mr. McCallahan's burrito breath in his face. But Jamie remembered this fall. He had grabbed one of the dying berry bushes on his way down. He'd seen his mother's face, contorted in a scream for a split second before the branch tore away in his hands and he tumbled farther down. He remembered the thorns—he'd seen them coming, the bright colors of the roses standing out defiantly against the dead hillside. He remembered thinking what a perfectly horrible thing was happening and how utterly helpless he was to stop it. He had covered his eyes and clenched his teeth. In his parents' hospital show, they once had a patient who had been blinded by a fall off a ladder into a rose bush. The episode had been titled "Let Down Your Hair," for reasons Jamie had not understood; when he tried to ask about it, his mother had shushed him and ordered him to go brush his teeth. But he thought he might understand now. Maybe if he had had longer hair, it would have caught on the thorns and kept him from falling quite so far. Maybe the hair would have acted like padding, like the poppy bubbles in packages, and kept him from going blind. In any case, he could see just fine, so maybe the hair had nothing to do with the thorns at all.

He looked up at the sky, flinching slightly at the sting in his neck. The perfect blue was interrupted by a cloud shaped like a bunny. As Jamie watched, the bunny cloud stretched its front paw, lifting its butt into the air. Jamie almost laughed, it was so funny. Then, with one graceful movement, the cloud bunny hopped toward the sun, dissolving as it moved. Jamie closed his eyes and then opened them again. That was impossible. He must have hit his head, like in the hospital drama when a man had forgotten his name after getting knocked out. Jamie must have forgotten he'd been knocked out; he must also have forgotten that cloud bunnies didn't exist.

He needed to keep his feet on the ground. That's what his teacher, Ms. Hamilton, told him. Ms. Hamilton put red X's through the drawings of unicorns that he added to his spelling papers. When Momma had asked him what he learned, he repeated all the things she wanted to hear: the spelling words from the impossible list, the confusing difference between the long and short hands on the clock. However, it wasn't the entire truth. Jamie had also learned that unicorns don't belong on spelling papers and if you want to use counters for a math problem, they better not be little drawings of gnomes, because little drawings of gnomes will get your paper covered in red X's. Jamie had learned to become boring.

Sitting at the bottom of this impossibly big hill, his gray sweatpants getting wet around the bum (Jamie liked "bum" better than "butt"; he had seen it in Daddy's copy of *Hitchhiker's Guide to the Galaxy*), looking at the sky now empty of cloud bunnies, Jamie felt a stab of panic followed by an emptiness in his stomach. Quite beyond his control, his lip began to twitch and his eyes filled with tears. Jamie hated crying, but he supposed it didn't really matter now; no one was around to see him. Momma would have pulled him into her arms and stroked his hair—he loved that. Daddy would have given him a big bear hug, knocking the breath out of his lungs—he loved that too. The realization that no one was there to do either made the tears well up even faster, until they ran down Jamie's cheeks.

Then Jamie realized with a jolt that his orange backpack was missing. It had been strapped to his back when he fell down the hill. He had carried it to the Getty that day, his most prized possessions in it. There was a piece of smooth pink rock that Daddy told him was rose quartz; Jamie supposed it was magic but hadn't been able to get it to actually do anything magic yet. The backpack also held an ever-changing collection of leaves and sticks—just the interesting ones though. The most important item, however, was Bilbo. Bilbo was a stuffed rat with a long tail that Jamie liked to wrap around his fingers while he thought about things that needed understanding. Much of Bilbo's fur had been rubbed off over the years, so he appeared to be a patchy gray color now, not his original tawny brown. Bilbo was brilliant. He knew all the answers to the questions that Jamie asked. He didn't speak, exactly, but Jamie could read his thoughts, and he supposed Bilbo could do the same to him. There were rules though: Momma said Bilbo was not to go to school and unless they were at home, Bilbo had to stay in the backpack.

But now Bilbo was gone. Jamie looked back up the hill hopelessly. Although he knew it to be impossible, it seemed to have grown steeper in the last few minutes. No backpack, no Bilbo, no magic rocks. Nothing. Jamie started to cry for real now, the sobs impossible to contain. In a sudden rush, Jamie felt all the painful places all over his body. There were still more thorns stuck in his back, in places he couldn't reach, and when he tried, his left wrist felt like he had been given the mother of all Indian burns. Momma got mad at him when he called them that, and the memory of her rebuke made him howl even louder. His head hurt, the knot on his forehead aching all the way down into his teeth.

With a terrified start he realized that his loose bottom tooth was missing. Missing entirely. Gone. It had been barely wiggly; there should have been a good week left before it fell out. The fairy people brought him presents when he lost teeth: shiny stones or little amulets. The other kids at school talked about getting money. Jimmy Farrell had even bragged about getting a whole five dollars for his front tooth. Jamie's mother had told him that Jimmy's fairy must be too materialistic and that he should never be jealous of someone over money. Jamie didn't mind; he preferred his little gifts. Once he had found a little golden pendant with an angel imprinted on the side. He kept it next to his bed. It felt good to rub the outline of the wings when it was dark outside and he heard noises he couldn't explain, noises that even Bilbo didn't know about.

The tears slowly dried up, and the foreign sound from his throat trickled to a whimper. An overwhelming tiredness overtook Jamie. His arms and legs felt like chocolate pudding, so rich and overladen they could hardly move. Some distant memory warned him not to close his eyes. On his parents' hospital show, he had once seen a woman with a concussion—a bad bump on the head, which was exactly what Jamie had. He couldn't quite remember why closing his eyes was bad, but the television doctors had all been quite concerned with the patient and her concussion.

Concussion or not, Jamie could not keep his eyes open. The patch of bright-green grass next to him was lined with soft dark moss, and it all smelled like the lavender lotion his mother wore. With little hesitation, he laid his head down on the fragrant green pillow and closed his eyes. The smell of lavender surrounded him, and he could almost feel his mother's fingers in his hair.

TWO

JAMIE found himself walking through a dense forest. The trunks of the great dark trees stretched so far up that he could not see the tops. Sunlight was obscured by the thick mat of leaves far above. The ground was a maze of emerald-colored ferns and spots of bright flowers. Jamie looked down and saw he was walking along a path of sorts. Square stones lined the path. Looking back, he saw that he had evidently come quite a long way already, and the path ahead stretched even farther into the wood. Kneeling down, Jamie examined the stone in front of him. As big as a baseball plate, it was a dark-gray stone covered in a thin layer of moss, underneath which Jamie could see a pattern of strange lines and curves. He traced it with his fingers. He crawled forward and examined the next stone; a different pattern this time, like a symbol. Jamie knew he should feel afraid, but a milky calm rushed through him. Rising, he walked down the path, careful to stay on the stones. He didn't know why, but he felt stepping off the trail would be a very bad idea.

"I think you're about ready now."

The voice coming from the depths of the trees and ferns made him jump. He looked for the source of the voice, but nothing stirred.

"About ready? Yes? Over the shock of it all?"

It was a chirpy, not-too-high voice with a hint of an accent, like Jamie had heard when his parents watched BBC.

"You can wake up now. I think you're just about ready."

Jamie shook his head, straining his eyes to see into the darkness. He tried to call out, but his voice wasn't working. With effort that caused the back of this throat to burn, he broke through the calm only to emit the tiniest of gasps. Jamie shook with frustration.

"Come on now, it's not all that upsetting. Just wake up. No need to be so dramatic about it."

With a start, Jamie opened his eyes. He flew up, all the painful parts of his body crying in protest. No forest, no strange stones, and no voice. He was still where he had fallen; the emerald moss held an imprint of his head, and the grass was crushed from the weight of his body. The sun hadn't moved in the sky, so Jamie guessed he hadn't been asleep too long. He winced at the soreness in his knees, which was notably more pronounced than it had been before his nap. His blue sweatpants were caught up about midshin. Jamie tried to tug them down, but they didn't budge. His long, baggy T-shirt, with the Ninja Turtle flashing the peace sign, now seemed tight. Pulling his arms back and looking down, Jamie saw that it was up to his belly button. There was a terrible pressure on his toes. Jamie pulled off his sneakers and socks and jumped back—huge feet exploded from his size 1 shoes. They were at least two inches longer now, and his toes were red and angry from their confinement. In fact, all his joints ached. Jamie stood up, and his head bumped on a low-hanging branch. How tall had he actually become? Was he a giant now? Like Gulliver in the story Daddy had read him?

"No. You're just a bit older, and with older comes taller. Don't they teach you basic science where you come from?"

The voice, the one from his dream, surprised him so that he fell back onto his green grassy bed.

"Who are you? Who's there?" Thankful his throat worked this time, although it shook a bit, Jamie continued, "Where am I?"

"Where are you? Why, you're here. Isn't that obvious?"

The voice seemed to bounce all around him, coming from one direction and then another.

"Where is here? Where are Momma and Daddy?"

Jamie's voice still shook, but he felt a bit numb now. He wondered if he was in shock. Shock was something that the patients in the hospital show experienced a lot. It meant that they didn't feel everything they ought to, because feeling everything all at once would be too much.

"You're not in shock," the voice said. "I rather expected you to get a bit smarter with age, but looks like not. Too bad, that."

Now Jamie was insulted. He was plenty smart: he was the first in his class to read chapter books; he knew a lot of things, medical things from the television; he could even do multiplication and spell the names of all the Greek gods.

"Well, I stand corrected. Plenty smart indeed, aren't you."

"How are you doing that?" Jamie asked crossly. He stood back up, the soreness only increasing.

"Can't really say. Must be magic."

Something furry brushed past his bare feet. He looked down to see a tawny rat, its long tail wrapped around his body. The rat stood up on his hind legs, regarding him with shiny black eyes. Involuntarily, Jamie jumped back. The rat remained on his haunches and then turned away dejectedly. A sharp realization came over Jamie. It seemed impossible, but a lot of things seemed that way right about now.

"Bilbo?" he asked hesitantly.

The rat brightened up, dropped to all fours, and padded to him, standing again at attention. The more Jamie stared, the more he saw the familiar markings, even down to the little twist at the end of Bilbo's tail from where he had accidentally been caught in Momma's vacuum cleaner.

"But how? Where are we?"

Jamie knelt down and, with a shaking hand, stretched out his arm. Bilbo climbed right up and scurried to Jamie's shoulder, where he nestled in, his sharp claws digging a bit at Jamie's skin.

"I take it you don't talk, then?" Jamie asked, not really expecting an answer.

He reached up and with one finger stroked Bilbo's soft fur. It was just as it had always been, although now he felt the muscle and bone underneath. Oddly, this seemed perfectly natural, as though Bilbo had never been any other way.

"We need to get out of here," Jamie said to no one in particular. He turned to face the hill and took one painful step up the incline.

"No way out if you go up. You have to go through."

The chirpy voice echoed around him. Jamie felt Bilbo turning in circles on his shoulder, as if he, too, were looking for the source.

"What I mean is, you have to go through to go up. Going up takes you down, and down takes you to . . . well, you don't want to go down."

Jamie shook his head. "Through what? Where are you?"

"You saw it before. The wood. You must go through the wood if you're to go up. Best to start before dark. You don't want to be out in the dark."

Jamie realized that the light had dimmed considerably in the time he had been standing there with Bilbo. He also realized his shirt was dreadfully uncomfortable. He stroked Bilbo and gently lifted him out of the way while he tugged the T-shirt over his head. He leaned down as best he could, Bilbo climbing onto the back of his neck for balance, and rolled his shrunken sweatpants up to the knee. They were tight around the waist, but not too bad. It was odd to be standing outside without his shirt—Momma would say it wasn't appropriate. She allowed him to run around in just his shorts only when they went to the beach. They had a neighbor who never wore a shirt; sometimes he even walked his big dog around the neighborhood not wearing a shirt. Momma always shook her head when she saw him. "Not appropriate," she'd say.

Jamie had never really known what she meant, but now he saw the word quite clearly in his mind and understood. No one else walked around without shirts where they lived; there was an unspoken rule that the neighbor was breaking. It wasn't anything Momma, Jamie, or Daddy could call the neighbor out on, but it was something that he should have just known. Jamie stood for a minute in this strange, green, dimming place, very proud of himself for figuring that out. However, while he wasn't sure if Momma would consider his shirtlessness appropriate right now, it was rather necessary.

Jamie looked around; the sky was growing even darker.

"I don't know who you are or why you keep talking to me, but I need to go home."

Jamie glanced over at Bilbo, perched on his shoulder. The rat was nervously licking his tiny paws, rubbing them together in a compulsive gesture that Jamie understood entirely in that moment.

"Go through to go up doesn't make sense. I came down the hill—I'll go back up."

Jamie waited for a response. Hearing none, he turned to face the slope. It was difficult to make out the details, but no matter; he would take it a step at a time. He was barefoot, shirtless, and had a very real stuffed rat on his shoulder. With a deep breath, he took a step up the incline. So far, so good, he thought. The mossy ground provided a soft carpet for his bare feet, and the hill wasn't nearly as steep as it looked. He walked easily, not even needing to grab the small shrubs to steady himself.

"Not so bad then, right, Bilbo?" Jamie said.

The rat was now wrapped around his neck, little claws clinging to Jamie's hair, which he realized was longer than he remembered. The tickle of it on the back of his neck was unfamiliar. Momma had recently tried to cut Jamie's hair herself. The result had been a close cut with electric clippers to mask where she had miscalculated what she was trimming. Jamie had cried, but his daddy had told him to cheer up, it was only hair, and from now on they would go to a professional. Jamie realized now that Daddy was trying to tell him that Momma wouldn't be cutting his hair anymore and he would get to go to a barber like all his friends. He wondered why that hadn't been clear before. Just a few hours ago, Jamie had imagined a professional as someone like his school principal. Mr. G was the tallest man Jamie had ever seen, and he always wore a suit. As Jamie walked, he shook his head at how foolish his assumption had been.

He had no idea what would happen once he reached the top. Would Momma and Daddy still be there? What would they say about his sudden growth spurt? Or Bilbo? It had been an overall terrible afternoon, but having Bilbo alive and well, sitting on his shoulder, clinging to his too-long hair, was magnificent. Jamie continued climbing up, up, up. It was difficult to tell how far he had gotten—the light was nearly extinguished, and the stars were beginning to appear. How that was possible, Jamie didn't really know. Night never seemed to fall quite so fast, but then again, he had never been stuck at the bottom of an impossibly steep hill before. Lots of things that had previously seemed impossible had proven themselves very possible indeed today; the rapidly encroaching darkness seemed like the least odd of all of them. Up, up, up, Jamie continued to climb. Bilbo made a clicking chatter noise in his ear.

"I can't understand you, Bilbo," Jamie replied. "You'll have to learn to talk, like the animals in Narnia."

Jamie knew only one of the Narnia books; Momma had read *The Lion, the Witch and the Wardrobe* to him before bedtime. It had been scary in parts and confusing in others, but he greatly liked the idea that animals could talk just like people. He wondered if the book would make more sense now. Everything seemed clearer now, all manner of things that he had previously been confused about. Last week, for example, Momma had been upset with him. Jamie had wanted to take his collection of lizards and snakes to the grocery store, and Momma had said no. The idea of Momma never letting him take his lizards and snakes anywhere ever again was horrible, and it had made Jamie cry buckets—so much so that Momma had made him go to his room until he calmed down. He had worried that maybe Momma was planning on taking the lizards and snakes away for good. Now, with his taller legs and longer hair, Jamie was a bit embarrassed. Of course it would have been foolish to take all the lizards and snakes to the store.

Jamie needed to calm down right now. He continued to climb up, up, up, but he didn't feel as though he were going any higher. He must be, though; he was walking forward, and the incline was making the new muscles in his calves ache with the effort. However, he had the sensation that you get when you walk up the down escalator. There was no moon, and the night was dark, darker than Jamie had ever seen. He was used to seeing the lights of houses, office buildings, passing cars, and planes. But here, at the bottom of the very steep hill, Jamie saw nothing but the useless light of stars. But oh, what stars they were—bright white and larger than he was used to. As he trudged upward, he tried to find the patterns that Daddy had showed him. He didn't see the three bright stars of Orion or the handled cup of the Big Dipper, but maybe the stars were different here. The night had become rather cold, and Jamie shivered even though his exertion was making him sweat.

Bilbo chattered again in his ear, but Jamie, annoyed, ignored him. Suddenly, there was a sharp sting on his earlobe, and a drop of warm liquid fell to his bare shoulder. The pain radiated from his ear to the whole side of his face, and he instinctually reached up to smack the offending biter away. Bilbo ducked right in time, scurrying up Jamie's hair. Jamie stopped in his tracks, feeling slightly dizzy, though whether from the blood or the sudden halt of motion, he could not tell.

"Bilbo! You bit me!"

He was more shocked than angry. The reality of being bitten by a previously stuffed rat was almost too strange a thought to process. Jamie squinted into the perfect blackness in front of him. He couldn't see a thing—the darkness seemed thick as custard. As he waved his hand back and forth, it grew too dark to make out his fingers.

Something stung his left shoulder. He started to scold Bilbo again but realized quickly that it wasn't his rat; it was some kind of insect. It hurt too much to be a mosquito—a hornet maybe? Before he could even rub that sting, another lit into his bare leg. Jamie squealed, jumping backward. Another and another, over and over. Jamie smacked futilely at the invisible attackers. Bilbo, panicked, clung to Jamie, burrowing into the hair at the back of his neck. Bilbo's clawing hurt, but in comparison to the rain of fire that was bouncing off Jamie's skin, it was the least of his problems. The bites swelled; the pain rose to intolerable levels and then broke like a wave across his body. Over and over the bites came, and Jamie realized he was screaming, a high, frantic noise that was utterly unfamiliar to him. He tried to run up the hill, but the thick night pushed back like a scene in a nightmare as Jamie pumped his arms and legs hopelessly, never gaining an inch.

All of a sudden, the ground heaved. Small rivers of sensation were followed by pinprick stabs into the bottom of Jamie's feet. While these hurt significantly less than the bites, their sheer quantity made them equal partners to his misery. Exhausted, Jamie covered his head and dropped to his knees, the pinprick pain attacking his knees and shins. The assault from the air continued without reprieve. Jamie sobbed, not caring who might hear. He wanted Momma and Daddy, he wanted to be home, he wanted dinner and a bath, and he even wanted his botched haircut back. He wanted to go back to the moment he saw the sign. *Cuidado.* He wanted to step away from the edge instead of dancing closer. He even wanted his stuffed rat back. The frantic, clawing creature that was trying to bore a hole into his head was not the same Bilbo he loved.

"Warned you. I said you didn't want to be out in the clearing after dark. I told you that you couldn't go up, but you didn't listen." A gentle clicking sound followed the admonition.

Despite himself, Jamie cried out. "Help me! Help!"

"Oh, okay, since you asked so politely."

The voice held a hint of sarcasm, but Jamie saw a faint green light to his right. It appeared to be coming from within a thick wood. He thought of his dream and involuntarily shook his head.

"Suit yourself. Although much more of this and you'll be food for the gnights. You know their arrows are poisoned, right?"

Jamie ached all over; the continual assault on every surface of his skin was too much to bear. Bilbo yanked his hair hard. With a deep breath, Jamie scrambled toward the green light. As he ran, the pinpricks followed, driving deeper into his bare feet. The stings pelted his back. Jamie ran on clumsy legs, stumbling through the trees. Tripping over a stepping stone, he careened forward, his hands and wrists absorbing the full shock of the fall. The green light was coming from a small lantern that now hung right over Jamie's head. A small candle burned inside a golden cage. Around him, Jamie could see dark mossy trees, too tall to see the tops. The air smelled faintly of decay, although in a not-altogether-unpleasant way, like the smell of a newly sown garden. The biting and stinging stopped. He sat up, rubbing his arms. On his skin were a thousand tiny pinholes. What appeared to be a stinger stuck out of one of them. Jamie squinted as he pulled it out. On closer inspection, he saw it was a tiny arrow, its miniscule feather fletching neatly lining the rear of the shaft. Bilbo, who had calmed down considerably, crawled out of Jamie's hair and padded down his arm, perching on his wrist, examining the miniature arrow.

"Gnights are nasty little buggers if they catch you out after dark. Tried to tell you, but you seemed so intent on doing things your way."

A slender boy with olive skin and hair the color of polished oak stepped from behind a tree. He wore a simple tunic of unbleached cloth. As he stepped closer, Jamie saw that his overlarge eyes were the same mesmerizing, gleaming wood color. His voice was deeper than it had sounded from the meadow, lyrical as though everything he spoke were words to a song.

Jamie stuttered, his voice unsure. "Who are you?"

The boy took another step forward.

"My name is Feidlimid. You've nothing to fear from me. I'm not carrying a quiver of poisoned arrows. You're Jamie and Bilbo."

Bilbo leaned forward, sniffing the air. Feidlimid's mouth twisted up into an amused grin. Jamie rubbed his head.

"Where is this place? What's a gnight?"

"All in due time. You should come with me—the others are waiting, and we're still too close to the clearing for my taste." He took the golden lantern from the tree branch. "C'mon then."

Jamie sat stubbornly on the ground. His legs felt like a block of swiss cheese, tiny holes lining the surface. Feidlimid stared at him for a long moment.

"And what do you plan on doing here? I told you, if you want to go up, you have to go through. This way." He indicated the dark path into the wood. "This way is through, which leads to up, and up is where you say you want to go, yes?"

"I was going up. I was walking up the hill. Why would I go with you?"

Jamie's voice was strained and barely controlled. He knew he sounded like a child, but he was sick of not knowing what was going on. Bilbo jumped from his hand and ran down the stepping stones toward Feidlimid, stopping to look back at Jamie.

"Fine. Leave then." Jamie sniffed.

Feidlimid stared at him.

"You think you were going up, do you? I can get in a fair amount of trouble for doing this, but I suppose you're not going to move yourself from that spot until you know for sure. Here, look."

Feidlimid came back down the path, standing right on the threshold of the meadow. The darkness was far too thick to see into. Jamie stood next to Feidlimid and realized they were nearly the same height—an odd discovery that delighted him for no real reason.

"If I show you that you are exactly where you started, despite all your walking, will you come with me? Trust me a bit?" Feidlimid asked, staring Jamie square in the face.

They were inches apart, and Jamie was momentarily lost in the woody depth of Feidlimid's eyes. They were too large to fit his face, and in this close proximity, they filled Jamie's entire field of vision. He nodded slightly.

"Fine. Look."

Feidlimid reached up to the dark sky and plucked one of the bright stars from its post. Jamie gasped as Feidlimid opened his palm to show Jamie an impossibly bright diamond the size of a pebble. Without warning, he tossed the pebble into the clearing, and for a moment the whole space was illuminated as though it were day. Jamie saw clearly the hollowed-out space where he had slept, the green carpet of grass. It was all the same. He also saw thousands of tiny specks charge toward the glowing pebble, which quickly faded, taking the scene with it.

Jamie was speechless. In a day full of impossible things, this was, so far, the most impossible of them all.

"Are you coming then?" asked Feidlimid, already moving effortlessly down the path.

Jamie nodded and followed, Bilbo scurrying up his leg. Jamie placed the rat back on his shoulder, stroking his soft fur, a talisman as they entered the wood.

THREE

THE stepping stones were the same as in Jamie's dream. Each was etched with a different symbol. As he followed the point of light emanating from Feidlimid's lantern, he tried to make out what they were. Swirly gray marble peeked out from underneath the mossy grime. The markings were no more than a series of lines and slashes. He glanced behind him as they marched. Without the light it was difficult to be sure, but the stones seemed to disappear once he was a few steps past them. Jamie shook his head. Impossible, another impossible thing. He imagined that he would eventually wake from this dream; his mother would gently shake him, and he would snap awake. Maybe he really had fallen down the hill and was lying unconscious at the bottom. Maybe the police and the firemen were looking for him right now. Maybe he had been found and was in a coma. Jamie knew about comas from the hospital show. Daddy had explained that they were nothing more than a really long nap that you can't wake up from. The thought sent a wave of goose shivers downs his arms. What if he stayed like this forever? What if he grew up like this—immobile in a bed, with people coming and going, machines beeping, and dying flowers filling the windowsills?

As if reading his thoughts, Bilbo rubbed his small head against Jamie's ear—a comfort. Jamie ran his finger down Bilbo's soft back, and the little rat arched in appreciation. Jamie didn't know where people in comas went. Maybe they all went here and were simply in a different part of this strange forest; maybe they had their own places, a meadow for some, a balcony overlooking the city for others. Maybe some were sitting in their own living rooms, watching all the comings and goings. Jamie decided that of all the options, the one he was in didn't seem so bad; his skin still itched from the attack in the meadow, but he imagined that pain was nothing compared to the terrible loneliness of being unseen in your own house. Maybe he would go on this adventure and then wake up, or maybe he'd wander forever. Maybe he was dead.

Jamie had never really considered what dead was. Daddy said it was when you didn't need your body anymore and got to choose whether you were reborn or whether you stayed in the otherworld. The otherworld was a place where everyone's imaginings all collided—that was what Daddy said. A place where your imagination mixed with everyone else's and everything was possible. Jamie had asked why someone couldn't just go back to their body then; if everything was possible, why couldn't you just leave and go back home? Daddy had been silent for a long minute before he finally asked, "Why would you want to?"

Daddy had made it sound like when you were dead, you chose where you were. This made Jamie feel like maybe he wasn't quite dead yet, since he never would have chosen to be attacked by whatever Feidlimid called those little creatures. He never would have chosen a name like Feidlimid either. It sounded like the scientific name for an insect, like the earwigs that hid in the crevices of the porch swing on Jamie's back patio. Unless . . . unless this was the *other* place you could go when you died. He didn't know much about hell, and Daddy had said it didn't even exist, but Jamie couldn't help but wonder. When he had been much younger—although given his newly large feet, he couldn't say exactly *how* much younger—he had read a book about a god named Ganesh. It was meant to be a children's story, as indicated by the bright drawings, but it told the story of a baby boy whose very presence had angered the gods so much that they turned his head into ash. He hadn't read on to find out how the headless little boy ended up with an elephant's head, but he imagined that it had involved surgery. Surgery was very serious, and it often led to people dying.

Jamie continued down the mossy path, following the bobbing candlelight before him, trying to remember how his mind had wandered to the story about Ganesh. It was funny, but now he realized what Daddy and Momma had been trying to tell him when he had been so upset over the idea that a little baby's head could just be dissolved into ash. Daddy had said it was metaphorical and not meant to be taken literally. That statement made absolutely no sense to Jamie at the time and had only upset him more. But now, with his long arms and legs, Jamie thought he had an idea of what that meant. Ganesh's head hadn't actually been dissolved into ash—that was just a way of telling a story. Maybe they were trying to say that even gods can lose their tempers; maybe they were trying to show that even when the worst possible thing happens, there's a solution, albeit a strange and decidedly inconvenient one. Jamie wondered what it would be like to have an elephant's head. He imagined it must be very heavy—after all, elephants were much larger than humans. With a sigh as he brushed a dark, leafy branch from his path, he thought that was probably metaphorical too, although of what he could not figure out.

In any event, Jamie wondered if he might have ended up in hell. And if he had, he wondered if it was literal hell or metaphorical hell. He wondered if it made a difference which hell he was in when he was stuck following a strange-looking boy through a dark forest with a previously stuffed and now very much alive rat sitting on his shoulder. If he were in metaphorical hell, he was still very literally dead, and that thought brought him little comfort. Jamie found himself wishing someone would just dissolve his head into ash and get it over with.

"Not to interrupt, but you have quite the dark side, don't you?" Feidlimid commented, not looking back. His voice bounced around the trees like it had when Jamie had been sitting in the clearing.

"Stop that! Do you know everything I'm thinking all the time?" Jamie asked, his voice edged with frustration.

"Of course! Most of the time it's just not interesting enough to pay much attention to, but this bit about heads made of ash and elephants was rather intriguing. Can I ask, why do you think you're dead?"

Jamie thought of his body lying in a hospital bed, machines making his chest rise and fall. He sighed.

"Why else would all this be happening?"

"Why? That's the wrong question. Sometimes there's no *whys*, just *is*. You fell, and quite a long way too. There was no reason, it wasn't anyone's fault, but you can't expect to fall such a long way and have everything remain the same, can you?"

Feidlimid glanced back and flashed a grin. His teeth were perfectly white, and they caught the faint light from the stars overhead. It wasn't just the tint of them that disturbed Jamie, though—they were all neatly pointed. Before he could examine further, Feidlimid whipped his head back around and continued on down the path.

"No time for all this, whatever you might think you are. You are going to miss the last ferry. No time to waste."

THE ferry was a tiny rowboat tied to a dock post. No one was waiting for them, and Jamie wondered how this could be the last ferry when it was apparently the only ferry. He also wondered if this really qualified as a ferry at all—it was just a rowboat at the end of a very mossy lake, in the center of which was an island with a wooded area like what they had already walked through. Feidlimid paused on the shore, looking back at Jamie.

"Here you go. On out to the center."

Jamie shook his head. Alone?

"No, I will be with you," answered Feidlimid to Jamie's unspoken question. "But I must caution you, there is little I can do to protect you as we cross, so it is a bit as if you were alone."

"How is this getting me back up the hill?" Jamie muttered as Bilbo adjusted himself on his shoulder.

"It's not." Feidlimid looked surprised. "It's helping you get through, and you have to get through before you go up. And you'd best get going—there are plenty of things in these woods that would be pleasantly surprised to find you, all pink and tasty such as you are."

With that Feidlimid flashed a smile full of pointed teeth. Jamie shivered involuntarily.

"Oh, I'm the least of your worries. My kind aren't prone to eat clumsy children, even those that tumble unannounced into our backyard." Feidlimid waggled his eyebrows over his golden-amber eyes.

Jamie planted himself on the shore and faced the strange creature.

"None of this is real anyhow. None of it. I'm going to wake up and find myself in bed, or the hospital, or maybe at the bottom of a very real hill that I can simply walk back up." His voice was cross. He was starting to feel sleepy again and hungry, his stomach clenching and growling, punctuating his increasingly sour mood.

"Well, if none of it's real, you have nothing to lose by getting in the boat," Feidlimid replied, nodding toward the pathetic little craft.

"But I do. I do. It's my dream, and I should get to decide what I do, not you, and not you." Jamie directed the last bit crossly at Bilbo, who was scratching at his ear as if he could pull Jamie on board the tiny boat.

"Let me ask you something," Feidlimid said as he circled Jamie slowly. "Do you remember how you got here, to this exact point?"

Jamie nodded, confused.

"Have you ever had a dream where you remembered all the details of how you got from place to place?" Feidlimid asked.

Jamie thought for a minute.

"I suppose not, I just kind of . . . "

"Ended up there, right?" Feidlimid finished Jamie's thought. "You see, dreams are different that way. Time doesn't exist in dreams, so it doesn't take any time to go anywhere—that's why you never remember all the comings and goings. You don't wake up older, you don't get injured, and you aren't in any danger."

"But I did!" Jamie exploded with frustration. "I did wake up older! I fell asleep back there, and now nothing fits and my hair is too long and I have no idea how it happened! It has to be a dream, otherwise it's, it's . . . "

"Impossible?" Feidlimid finished. "You did dream back there in the clearing, and a hella dangerous place to take a nap it was too. But your dream was different, right? You moved without knowing how, you lost time in your dream, but not out here—when you're out here, you are in the greatest danger. You have no idea the creatures that run these woods. I brought you down a path my people laid out before time began. It's older than these woods and all the dangers in them. It's the only way through unless you want to be eaten up by any manner of foul monster." Feidlimid flashed his pointed teeth again and gestured out into the darkness. "You can hear them if you listen closely—they crowd the path, waiting for some foolish somebody to step off, to decide this is all a dream and run into the darkness. Just because you can't see the monsters, it doesn't mean it's not dangerous, Jamie."

Jamie listened closely. Bilbo stopped tugging on his ear and froze in place. Jamie could hear a scratching just beyond the tree line. Jamie felt the nauseous weight of uncertainty in his gut.

"You want to know why you're older?" Feidlimid asked. "Why your hair is too long and how you grew out of your clothes?"

Jamie nodded miserably.

"Our worlds are not the same. They're connected by the mist, but they exist in different planes. You had the misfortune of tumbling right through a portal. There aren't many anymore, but you managed to find one. You grow older faster here, Jamie. Our world spins faster than yours, so our years are shorter. As long as you're awake, you're fine. But when you sleep, time catches up."

Jamie shook his head, overwhelmed.

"You're saying every time I fall asleep, I grow older? But . . . but how old will I get?" His voice was shaking despite his weakening stance that this was all a dream.

Feidlimid nodded. "Every time. How old? I don't know. My people live long lives—maybe you will too, maybe not. Best not to sleep, especially in these woods."

Jamie nodded again. When he was very little, his grandmother had forced him to take naps with her. He had to lie down on the white quilt with the tiny knobby balls of string. Grandmother would lie down next to him and immediately fall asleep. Jamie didn't sleep, though, and Grandmother's stale breath would cover his face. He imagined that breath as a foreign invader in his body, permeating every cell, making its way into the liver and spleen he had seen in her ancient illustrated book that sat on the dusty shelf, filling his lungs. He imagined his body getting older with Grandmother's every exhalation—her age, the mold and crust of her rusting up his body. Jamie would try to hold his breath as long as possible to prevent the contamination. It never worked. He could never not breathe long enough, and he always gave in, inevitably when Grandmother would release a giant sigh. For an eternity he would lie there, imagining the decay of his insides, wondering if time was speeding up, if his childhood was disappearing. He tried to tell Momma once, and she looked at him oddly. After that, he never napped with Grandmother again. Instead of the white knobby quilt, he was made to lie down on the scratchy sofa that felt like it was made of old rucksacks. He didn't sleep there either, but at least his insides were safe from the aged air. The fact that Momma seemed to believe him validated his fears. He wondered how many years he had lost already, how much of his insides had been rotted away.

Feidlimid's revelation made sense to Jamie. The solidification of an idea into a belief, an unknown into a truth, spread through Jamie like a warm light. Even if this was just a dream and he would wake up later in bed or attached to a litany of wires and tubes like in the nightly hospital show, Jamie felt his gut settle. The fear of his new long legs and arms, his curling hair, dissipated. He knew how to defeat this. He would simply stay awake and get back before he lost any more time, before he crossed the invisible barrier into adulthood.

He met Feidlimid's golden eyes. The creature was staring at him curiously. Jamie was confident that Feidlimid had been privy to all of Jamie's thoughts and wondered why he didn't comment. Whatever the reason, Feidlimid stood silent and then crossed to the boat, taking a seat on one of the wooden planks that served as seats.

"As I said, the last ferry leaves soon—any minute, in fact. If you want to be on it, you'd best board," Feidlimid said softly, his voice gentler than before.

Jamie nodded.

"What's on the other side?" he asked, his voice small.

"Someplace else."

"Somewhere safe?"

"Perhaps," Feidlimid said with a bit of sadness in his overlarge eyes.

"I don't have much choice, do I?"

Jamie could clearly hear the scratching and rustling on either side of the path now. He even caught sight of a patch of thick black fur and the tip of a very sharp claw. Bilbo tugged on Jamie's ear again, hard enough to draw a bit of blood. Jamie winced and stepped carefully into the boat, fearful of what might be in the water.

"How do I row?" he asked Feidlimid, whose great amber eyes stared at him.

"Don't worry about that. The ferry knows the way. Don't touch the water, and remember—it's important to be afraid."

The boat sat on the shore. Jamie felt a jolt of panic. What if it didn't move? What if those things in the forest found him? He shook his head, fighting a wave of sleepiness that clung to the back of his eyes. The boat started to move, drifting out into the calm lake. There was no disruption in the water—it was as though the ferry was floating above rather than gliding through the silky surface. Jamie stroked Bilbo's head; the little rat leaned into his touch, curling up on his neck.

"Do you remember our nightmare, Bilbo?" Jamie whispered.

In response, Bilbo buried his tiny, wet nose into Jamie's neck. Jamie stroked his fur. The nightmare happened most every night; sometimes a reprieve in the shape of a dreamless sleep would be granted, but not often. Jamie was walking across a broad field, the grass cut too short, dying in places. In the distance was the outline of a soccer goal. The light was growing dim. A sun was setting, too large and unnaturally orange to be the sun in the waking world. It took up the entire sky, and its heat was oppressive. Jamie knew that it was futile to keep going, that it would all be over soon, but he had to get the attention of the boy walking a distance in front of him. The boy wore white pajama bottoms and no shirt. His feet were bare. Jamie tried to cry out to the boy, but his voice was silenced, emitting no more than a squeak. He tried to find something to throw at the boy, but there were no rocks or sticks. The enormous dying sun grew lower in the sky, the fatalistic light spreading. This must be what it is like to get caught in the ovens, Jamie thought, like the herds of people forced into the fire at gunpoint in Daddy's history books. They wore tattered pants and stars on their arms. They walked as if already dead. Jamie became aware of the weight on his own arm. He looked down at the star emblazoned around his child-sized bicep, the weight of it pulling him forward. Jamie called again to the boy in front of him, his voice defying his efforts, the blanket of heat descending even lower.

Suddenly, the boy stopped, turned around, and stared at Jamie. He had the same curly blond hair and bright brown eyes that greeted Jamie in the mirror each morning. He had the same small mole on his neck, the same faint scar on the underside of his chin. Jamie stared at his own face in the dying of the light. As the dead sun collapsed on the horizon for the last time, a wave of fire roared toward him. Jamie's twin gave him a small grin as the tidal wave hit. His hair, arms, white pajama pants all caught fire, and his skin melted; the familiar features dissolved, the grin the last to go. The strange word was etched into a patch of dirt, always the last image that Jamie saw before he woke. The word was nonsensical and at the same time frightening. It appeared in a different place in each nightmare, scratched into the ground, painted on a wall in rough print, sometimes it glowed from a pattern set by the stars: L A I R D B A L O R. At this point Jamie would always wake up, the memory of the horror tugging at the dawn, making him jump up and run to the window to make sure the sun was the proper size and shape.

The ferry continued on, the night growing darker as they moved from the shore. No moon in the sky, only the stars, which seemed increasingly near. Jamie looked about, confused. The shore of the little island had seemed so close before he had stepped into the boat, but that was when he could see where he was going. Feidlimid's lantern did not share its light with the darkness. Bilbo was pulling on Jamie's hair nervously; instinctively, Jamie reached up and ran his finger down Bilbo's back, gaining no comfort from the action. Only gentle ripples in the water indicated any movement. Jamie still had no idea how they were moving. There were no oars, nothing inside or apparently outside to propel them forward. Jamie realized what it was that seemed too oppressive: there were no insect noises, no birds, and certainly none of the sounds that Jamie was used to—cars passing, occasional planes overhead, muffled voices from the street—just perfect, crushing silence. Even the water made no sound as it moved. The silence was deafening. Jamie reached over the side of the boat and splashed a bit, just to make a sound; as he reached, Bilbo bit into his earlobe hard, hard enough to draw a drop of blood that dripped onto Jamie's shoulder. Feidlimid stared at Jamie in silent agreement with Bilbo. Jamie felt a rush of frustration and fought an irrational urge to splash again, out of pure spite.

"Bilbo!" Jamie moaned. His voice broke the silence, although it brought no comfort, feeling out of place, alien in the blackness. "You must find another way to communicate!" he muttered, already regretting the intrusion he had made into the night.

Without warning, something broke the water's glassy surface, sending ripples—small at first, then stronger, harder—against the side of the boat. Jamie's heart raced, and he was so afraid he held his breath, as though not moving would make him disappear. The sleepiness was gone, the memory of his nightmare was gone; gone too was his desire to crack the stillness of the night. He wished more than anything that the mysterious ripples would disappear. Daddy read him a story once about a boy who could make himself invisible—it turned out that the boy was a wizard and had special powers. He could stand next to an umbrella stand, and if he was very still, he would appear as one of the umbrellas to the average passerby. Jamie had wondered what kind of house had a whole stand dedicated to umbrellas and how many umbrellas any family would really need; nonetheless, he would have liked to have turned into an umbrella in this moment, or any object that no one wants to harm. He thought of Feidlimid's response; he had said "perhaps," he *perhaps* was going somewhere safe. He also, perhaps, was floating toward something horrible. Or, perhaps, he was lying in a bed, near death and experiencing the last explosion of his brain synapses. He rolled that last thought around for a moment. He would certainly feel cheated if his last visions of life were as terrifying as this moment was.

"For in that sleep of death, what dreams may come . . . "

A barely audible whisper carried across the ripples. It moved like a breeze, swirled around him, and moved on; the words hung on his flesh, sticking like a layer of perspiration, although the night was not warm. It was neither low nor high. Jamie couldn't even be sure that he'd heard anything. The cadence was like a dream. Shaking his head, he tried to defy the lethargy that enveloped him, soaking his limbs in blackness. Jamie felt Bilbo trembling as he clung to Jamie's neck.

"Come, love, don't shake so. You've suffered a thousand natural shocks, you need a rest. Come, *bhalaich*, end the heartache . . . "

The night grew thick, weighing down on Jamie like a stifling quilt. He remembered the rancid age of his grandmother's breath creeping into his pores; he felt the thick pudding immobility of his legs. He saw a flash of images: In place of Feidlimid, the boy sat in front of him, white pajama pants glowing in the perfect night, and stared at him with empty eyes. Jamie opened his mouth, but the sound was strangled. At his neck, Bilbo grew rigid. In a panic, Jamie reached up, but the fur was already stiff, the life beneath it leaking out into the darkness. The boy reached one pale hand toward Jamie as his face began to melt, the familiar features running into each other like hot wax. Jamie tried to scream but could only stare as the outstretched hand dripped creamy, pale flesh onto the bottom of the ferry.

"This calamity of so long life . . . "

The voice bounced around Jamie's ears, the air a breath like the dying sun of his nightmare. His skin dried up; he looked down in horror to see flakes of it blowing away in an invisible wind. The wretched creature in front of him laughed, the jaw falling away with the effort. Jamie's hands withered. He saw the bone poke out from the mass of pink tissue, the blood a dried reservoir scattered like the makings of a child's craft. Still the creature in front of him laughed. It had no face—the head had melted into the torso, which was like a bit of wax thrown into an immense fire. Down, down, down it dissolved until all that was left was a scrap of white pajama material. Jamie's hand flaked away to the bone, and he clenched his digits, the bone screeching against bone, a sound that made the hackles rise on Jamie's neck.

"Silence!"

The great voice boomed over the water. The ripples stopped as fast as they had begun. Jamie's hand snapped back to whole, the skin untouched, the horror in front of him gone. On his neck, Bilbo madly wrung his hair, life restored to his dead fur. Jamie let out the scream that had been stifled, and it filled the darkness, a cry of one so lost he no longer had the will to even begin to look for a way home.

Abruptly, the ferry struck ground, lurching Jamie forward. He scrambled out, not caring what was on the shore as long as it was away from the water. He lay facedown in fine, muddy sand, his breath heaving. Bilbo scrambled off his neck, apparently just as glad to feel land under his paws.

"You'll want to be coming along—as soon as you've got a hold of yourself, that is," Feidlimid said.

Feidlimid waited on the shore, looking out across the water. Jamie pulled himself up, Bilbo jumping back to his post on Jamie's shoulder. He motioned out to the lake, which was so dark it was impossible to even tell it existed.

"That voice I heard? What I saw? Was it . . . "

"Real?" Feidlimid replied. "Very. And while it's easier to get at you on the water, it's not so much a challenge off of it, so we'd best get moving."

Jamie shook all over. His legs were weak, and he realized the blue sweatpants were tighter around the waist and legs than before.

"Oh no," he muttered.

"Yes, it took a bite—that was unavoidable. Not a big one, and not so much that you can't walk, so let's go on, shall we?"

Feidlimid turned, dark-oak hair creating a curtain around his form. With sudden confusion, Jamie realized that Feidlimid was not really a he any more than a she. Whatever it was—it was somewhere in-between, something not human—Jamie's inability to define it was increasingly frustrating.

"You can call me whatever you like, it's all the same. 'He' will do if you are itching for a label, but my kind doesn't put much mind to such matters," Feidlimid replied to his unspoken query. "Come now, just a bit farther from here, but we simply must get away from the water. It's full now, but that won't last. I interrupted its game—that won't go unnoticed."

As Jamie followed with unsteady steps, he felt new muscles in his arms. His chest felt wider, stronger. His hair fell down his back now, sticking in unpleasant clumps. Feidlimid led them down a path of mossy stone like the one across the lake. In this moment, Jamie didn't even care about getting back up the hill. Momma and Daddy were lost to him, and he simply wanted to survive. He realized that he was taller than the creature in front of him. Just a short while ago, Feidlimid had been his height; now Feidlimid reached about to his shoulders. Jamie looked down to see the blue sweatpants tight against his thighs, more like shorts now. He took a deep breath, trying to control his panic.

"What is *it*?" Jamie asked in a small voice that sounded unnaturally deep to his own ears.

"All in due time. Not my place to tell you, and besides, you'd really rather not know while you're still so close. Trust me on that."

The lilting voice danced in front of him, and even though Feidlimid held a lantern, light seemed to emanate from his entire body, his dark hair catching the light of the stars.

Confounding—that's what this was. Jamie didn't need to puzzle the word out much now. It had been an answer to the crossword puzzle that Daddy had been working on one morning. To Jamie's eyes, crossword puzzles were terribly dull things meant to keep adults from falling asleep when they were doing absolutely nothing. "Confounding" had been the answer to eleven down: "Word for a vastly confusing mystery." Jamie had been confounded by Daddy's explanation of the term at the time, but now it seemed entirely appropriate. The safety of the idea that this was a dream had disappeared quickly on the boat. He had no desire to dream ever again; in fact, closing his eyes to blink was as much as he could bear. However, if he wasn't dreaming, and if he wasn't wired to machines in a hospital room, he had to accept the pure confounding nature of his circumstances. As he stepped carefully along the mossy stone path, he wondered if he ever did found his way home, would his parents know him?

He had seen a movie with Momma once where a little boy, older than Jamie was then, had wanted to grow up. He had made a wish on an entirely creepy game at a fair and woken up as an adult. Jamie had cried until Momma turned the movie off. She had held him in her arms, the scent of lavender and soap permeating his senses. She sang quietly in his ear until he calmed. Truth be told, he had cried a bit longer than needed just to hear her voice and smell her peppermint-scented breath.

Hush, little baby, don't say a word.

Momma's gonna buy you a mockingbird.

Would she know him now? He was too big to fold into her arms and hide in her long hair. He was too old to do many of the things he had been capable of only a few hours ago. There was no hill anymore, no way to climb out of this. He had to, as Feidlimid had instructed, go through, although he wondered now if he would be welcomed when he got there.

"How old am I?" Jamie asked, the question startling him. He hadn't meant to say it aloud. His voice cracked slightly, caught between the child's tone he was used to and something else he dreaded.

Feidlimid glanced back but kept walking.

"I'm sure I don't know. How old were you when you fell?"

"Seven," Jamie answered hesitantly.

"Well, strictly speaking, you're still seven, although a rather large seven if I do say." He giggled lightly, the sound bouncing off the misty leaves on either side. "You'll need to ask these questions when we arrive. I'm not the one to know such things."

"Where am I going?" Jamie asked, not really expecting a straight answer.

"To the Elder. They're deep in the forest, away from the water, away from the one whom you met on the lake. Not that it's bound by the lake, but it does seem to be a preference—tonight anyhow." He hopped lightly over a broken stone. "Jump over that one, the surface is cracked. The outside gets in in that spot, and you don't want any more of the outside, I'm guessing." Again, he giggled.

Jamie wasn't sure if he was laughing at him, but the sound irritated him despite the musical ring. Nonetheless, he jumped clumsily over the broken step and felt a rush of cold air and the bristles from the snout of some animal. He looked at Feidlimid, who stood, hands on hips, waiting for him.

"Told you."

Feidlimid turned abruptly and continued skipping down the trail. Jamie scrambled behind. He wasn't used to his awkward new gait—he had always had excellent balance. In fact, he had been the only boy in the entire class who could walk across the balance beam in gym class. They didn't always have a balance beam, just that one week. Jamie had wished it could stay forever; it seemed to be the only thing he was good at in gym. As he stepped onto the next stone, his ankle twisted, throwing him forward. He flailed at the branches that loomed in on him from either side, trying to grab anything that might break his fall. He hit hard, his left shoulder absorbing most of the blow. It wasn't the hard rock of the path that crushed against his face, but the soft, fine soil from the forest. Jamie had a long moment for the smell of the rich earth, scented just slightly like the pipes his grandfather used to smoke, sweet and stifling, to fill his head. In the next moment, though, he remembered all the warnings—the feel of the bristly fur, the sharp claw. He tried to pull himself up, but his shoulder screamed in protest. He reached for Bilbo, and with a jolt realized that he wasn't there. Jamie was all alone; Bilbo was lost in the woods, dead already, perhaps. He looked back, but the trail was nowhere to be seen. How could that be? He had only fallen a foot at the most—he should be right next to the path. Confounding. That was the word for this place. Except confounding implied innocence, the idea that not knowing something was no more a bother than forgetting the name of your favorite flower. This type of confounding was much worse—nothing made sense, and everything led to something more horrible than the last horrible thing.

In the dark, Jamie heard a deep, snuffling breath. It huffed out hot, foul air that struck Jamie like a wave. Jamie thought of the bristly fur, remembered the glimpse of the sharp claw, and seized in fear. He had nothing to protect himself from whatever monster stood only feet away. He reached a shaking hand into the darkness, brushing past prickly leaves and branches. The snuffling breath was closer this time, the air heavy with the rank smell. Jamie felt a thin line of urine run down his leg and, ashamed, his cheeks burned with embarrassment even though there was hardly anyone who would see. He would die in a confounding woods, at the mercy of a monster he couldn't see, and he had peed himself. He didn't know what was worse.

All of a sudden, a wet snout pressed against his leg and a head full of scratchy bristles rubbed against his knee, like a cat looking for attention. The creature snuffed again, and again the bulky weight of the head rubbed his knee. Jamie reached down and felt coarse, spiky bristles beneath his fingers. The snout shot abruptly upward. Jamie jumped back and lost his footing again, falling directly on his bum, the pain in his shoulder shooting into his chest. Confounding.

The foul-breathed creature was directly in his face—Jamie could see its tiny, hooded eyes staring into his. Surprised, he saw it was a pig of some sort. He could make out dark-brown or black bristles and a pink-and-black speckled snout. It stared at him for a moment and then rubbed its blockish head against Jamie's good shoulder. Instinctively, Jamie placed a hand on its back and stroked with the grain of the bristles. The creature gave a pleased snort, knocking Jamie back with its breath, and then turned abruptly and ran off in the opposite direction.

Jamie pushed himself back up on his feet. It hadn't killed him—in fact, it hadn't seemed like it even wanted to. Feidlimid had made it sound as though the creatures off the trail were all monsters. The pig creature was certainly odd, but "monster" seemed a bit strong. Jamie looked around, suddenly keenly aware that he was being watched—and not by a large pig. He rubbed his arms, remembering the gnights. This time he wouldn't be able to get away; they'd eat him alive.

"Lost your way a bit, did ya?" a teasing voice, high as a birdsong, sang out.

"Where are you?" Jamie asked defensively, turning in circles, seeing only thick growth and darkness.

"Right here, silly." The singsong voice danced in front of his nose.

Jamie squinted, and in the dark he saw something like the huge flying beetles that buzzed around his backyard. This shape was the same, and the faint starlight reflected off a green-blue metallic surface, wings humming faster than could be counted. The body was oblong, like the beetles, but skinnier and longer. It moved closer, and Jamie saw two large, glassy black eyes. The stir of the breeze caused by the ever-moving wings whispered against his face.

"See me now then, do ya?" it asked.

Jamie squinted. The tiny mouth was almost too small to see, but indeed, the sound had come from this insect.

"What are you?" Jamie asked, incredulous. Like the pig creature, it seemed to have no intent of harming him—he wasn't even sure it could, but he'd doubted the gnights too.

"What am I? You don't know? My name in this world wouldn't mean much to you. My kind live here in the forest. What do you call those that live in the forest in your world?"

The little creature buzzed around his head. Jamie held out his hand, and it landed. When the wings came to an abrupt stop, Jamie could see they were a bright sunset gold.

"A fairy?" Jamie said. "But fairies are like little people with wings and faces."

"I have wings and a face," the beetle creature answered.

"Yes," answered Jamie slowly, a small smile tugging at his mouth. It was nice not to feel that he was in mortal danger for even a small minute. "But fairies are supposed to be like little people. You're not a little person. You're more like a beetle."

"Huh. Well, maybe I'm not what you'd call a fairy then, or maybe your idea of what fairies are is entirely wrong. Or maybe you've spent your entire life underestimating beetles. I mean, really, when was the last time you talked to one?"

The smile that Jamie had resisted broke over his face.

"We don't really talk to beetles where I come from, at least the grown-ups don't. I've tried, but they've never answered. I've never even seen a beetle who was a fairy before. You're a bit of both, I suppose—a beetle fairy."

"Grown-ups? You look pretty grown-up to me," the voice sang, each word its own melody.

"I wasn't this old when I fell. I slept, and then the boat . . . I'm older now. Feidlimid told me . . . " Jamie trailed off, unsure of what to say.

"Feidlimid?" the beetle fairy replied, indignant. "That's your problem right there—you've been with the wood elves. That sort will scare the skin right off you. Bet he told you all sorts of things, didn't he? The horrible creatures, the man-eating monsters. He did, didn't he? That's why Bolly shook you up so, isn't it?"

"Bolly? The pig?" Jamie asked, his brain still processing the term "wood elves."

"Well, a hog to be precise, but I don't think Bolly'll take offense to being called a common pig. Harmless as they come, all the hogs are. The woodies have created quite the mythology about them—and about us too. Did he warn you about us?" The beetle fairy's voice was hopeful.

"About beetle fairies? No, he didn't say a thing," Jamie answered. When he saw the tiny antennae droop slightly, he lifted his voice a bit, not wanting the little thing to feel bad. "However, he did save me from the gnights. Are you related to them?"

"Oh dear no," the beetle fairy answered. "Nasty little buggers, them. Not so much after you get to know them, but I doubt you want to take the time to do that. They're not entirely a bad lot, just protective of their space and sage and oak, I tell you. They do hate the Elvin folk."

"Look . . . " Jamie was worried about Bilbo, and the thought of that creature from the water finding him again made shivers run up his spine. "I don't know what to call you."

"Mallorie." The effervescent wings fluttered with pleasure as she spoke.

"Mallorie, I had a friend with me, a rat. He's gone now. Do you know if he's around here? Also . . . there was a thing on the lake. Feidlimid said we had to get away from it or else it would find me in the woods."

"A rat? Haven't seen one of them—might still be on the path. It's right over there. You can see it if you try."

Mallorie pointed to an open spot in the brush. Jamie squinted, shaking his head.

"You have to really try. Focus on your friend if it helps." Mallorie took to the air, flying to the open nook. "Here, look again."

Jamie squinted again, focusing on the feel of Bilbo's soft fur. Suddenly he saw the mossy green stones, and on the one nearest to him was Bilbo, standing on his hind paws, sniffing the air. Feidlimid stood impatiently next to him, his dark-oak hair pulled back from his face. His mouth was open as though he were calling out. The sound was muted, but Jamie could see two rows of sharpened teeth, and he shivered.

"Bilbo!" Jamie called out, but there was no response from Bilbo, who continued sniffing the air and then hunkered down, frantically cleaning his paws.

"He can't hear you from there," Mallorie stated. She buzzed in Jamie's ear, the vibration from her tiny wings making it hard to concentrate. "They have this path all sealed up. Think it's going to protect them, they do. Funny that, thinking something could do that."

"Protect?" Jamie asked, turning his head as Mallorie lighted on a tiny branch on the edge of the trail. "Protect from what? That thing that attacked us on the water?"

"That and other things," Mallorie said, her singsong voice sounding the tiniest bit dissonant. "From some things there is no protection. In any regard, this path is a bit like . . . what is it they say in your world, holding an umbrella in a hurricane?"

"I've never said that," Jamie retorted. He wasn't even sure what a hurricane was, although he imagined it was very nasty.

"Well, I believe some in your world say it, and it means simply that sometimes there's no safe place, so best to learn how to properly be afraid." Mallorie buzzed closer to the trail. "Enough of that. Let's get your rat over here, shall we? Or do you want to go back to the trail? You won't hurt my feelings either way, but I'm telling you, wood elves never do anything out of kindness, and you might want to consider what they use all those gnashy teeth for at the end of the day."

Jamie stared at her. It hadn't really occurred to him to ask why the wood elf had been helping him. He'd been too busy thinking he was dead or in a coma or perhaps knocked unconscious at the bottom of the hill. He still wasn't entirely convinced these things weren't true, except the memory of that thing on the ferry was too wretched not to be real, so that meant everything else had to be real too. But he hadn't asked why this creature with its overlarge eyes and sharpened teeth was leading him through the forest. He was suddenly and pointedly frustrated with himself. The first thing Momma and Daddy had told him about being out and about was not to talk to strangers, and here he went wandering off with them at the first opportunity.

"How do I know you're not out to hurt me too?" Jamie asked Mallorie.

"Hurt you? What in the world could I possibly do? I have more reason to fear you than you me—one swipe of that rat-catching hand, pardon the expression, and I'd be dead." Mallorie stared hard at him.

"The gnights were smaller than you, and they hurt."

Jamie's voice shook. He wasn't used to being defiant, even to a beetle fairy.

"I bet they wouldn't have been half so crabby if you hadn't had a wood elf near. There's a lifetime of stories as to the blood between those two, I tell you."

Mallorie's singsong voice was slightly mocking, and Jamie's head began to pulse with the start of a headache. When he had a headache at home, Momma always gave him a cool cloth for his forehead. He felt very alone.

"I need to go home, and I need my rat," he said miserably, feeling like a baby, a lump in his throat making the words uneven.

"Ah, there now . . . no need to be so sad, love. We can get Bilbo to ya, or you back to him. But I tell you the truth when I say the teeth on this side of the path are a bit less gnashy." Mallorie hummed softly, like a lullaby. "In any case, it's easier to go through the break, unless you want to tear a hole through the skeen again. But I imagine that didn't feel too good the first time, did it?"

Jamie looked at her questioningly.

"The break, where you felt the outside leaking through? Bolly ran under your legs there, gave you a right good start." Mallorie flew back a few yards. "Unless Bilbo's as clumsy as you and likely to fall right through the skeen." She giggled. "I think not though. Clumsiness is not a trait I associate with rats, only overgrown little boys." With that, she flew a few feet away and turned back. "Here."

Jamie followed her to the spot where he'd broken through from the path, stepping over rocks and prickly ferns. Bolly came barreling back from the opposite direction, stopping where Mallorie was paused. He snorted a sort of greeting.

"He likes you," Mallorie chirped. Turning to Bolly, she said, "Not that you'll be much help here, you know. But nice to have you along all the same."

Bolly snorted a reply.

At the break, Jamie could clearly see the wood elves' path. It was as though a rip had been made in fabric, or a piece of wallpaper was torn away to reveal the underneath, only this was living and breathing. Fascinated, Jamie waved his hand into the other space, but he was caught by a powerful suction and struggled to pull back. In his ear, Mallorie buzzed impatiently.

"Careful, you! You'll go popping right back on the path, and then what will become of ya? You have to be careful! Now, is there a special name, a call, a song that Bilbo would recognize? Something that would make him come back here?" Mallorie asked, lighting onto Jamie's still-outstretched arm. "Oh, smoke and birch—this will really burn the woodies up good. They do hate to be interfered with." With that, Mallorie dissolved into laughter, flying in hysterical loops.

"I'm not doing this to help you 'interfere' with Feidlimid—he saved me on the water. I don't know what to think, but I don't like being stuck out here. I want to know what to do."

Jamie's voice cracked, the uncertainty of the moment almost too much, and a trickle of snot ran from his nose. He didn't know who to trust: Feidlimid, this little beetle fairy, or neither of them? He kept hearing Feidlimid's "perhaps." Was Feidlimid trying to warn him that he was headed to somewhere not so safe? What was at the end of this confounding path anyhow?

"He told me I needed to go through to go up, and up is where I fell from and where my parents are. They must be looking for me, and I don't know how they'll know it's me, especially if I stay here any longer . . . " Jamie looked at Mallorie, his voice full of frantic energy. "I don't know who to trust, you or the elves! I just want to go home!"

"Come, child, it's not that bad. I know, I know—the wood elf told you he had the only way to get back, didn't he?" Mallorie stopped her lazy air circles and lit on Jamie's hand. He raised it to his eye level, and he gave a small nod. "Well, there are many ways through, and not all of them have a 'perhaps' at the end." She fluttered her tiny wings as if to emphasize her point.

"Confounding!" Jamie exclaimed, the word uncomfortable in his mouth. "Can all the things here just know what I'm thinking all the time?"

"For the most part, yes," Mallorie answered, as though puzzled by Jamie's question. "Except perhaps Bolly, and even then he probably has a right good mind as to your disposition."

Jamie leaned close to the skeen again. Feidlimid was pacing; Bilbo was still on his hind legs, sniffing the night air. Suddenly Feidlimid snatched up the little rat and, his face contorted with frustration, threw him against the skeen. Bilbo bounced off the invisible layer surrounding the path and lay still where he fell.

"Bilbo!" Jamie shouted.

Feidlimid tilted his unearthly face to the sound, a small smirk on his pale lips. He grabbed Bilbo's limp form off the ground and held him high, squeezing much too hard. Bilbo bucked in his hand, awakened by his will to escape.

"Oak and fire!" Mallorie exclaimed. "Damnable wood elves!"

Jamie pressed his face up against the skeen, trying not to hyperventilate. Bilbo squirmed and wriggled, straining his tiny head to bite Feidlimid's hand, but it was just out of reach. Feidlimid shouted something Jamie couldn't hear, but when his perfectly sharp teeth lowered to Bilbo's head, Jamie screamed in fear. Without thinking, he shoved as hard as he could against the skeen. He felt pressure, and an unworldly outline of himself invaded the path. Feidlimid threw his head back and laughed, and Bilbo suddenly went limp. Jamie screamed again and pushed with the full force of his body, even though Mallorie was madly buzzing in his ear, yelling at him to stop, and he could feel Bolly's rough coat rubbing his legs, presumably to throw him off balance. No one is any good, thought Jamie, and the thought hit him like a knife to his chest. Mallorie, Feidlimid, Bolly—the whole lot of them are rotten, Jamie thought viciously as he pushed harder still, feeling the skeen stretch to the point of ripping. No one was helping him rescue Bilbo; no one cared. The momentum of his anger propelled him back through the skeen, and he tumbled onto the mossy green stone path. The tear hung there in space, a hole to the out, the ragged shreds of the skeen hanging like a wound.

"Give him here!" Jamie ordered.

Feidlimid released his grip. Bilbo dropped from his hand to the ground.

"No!" Jamie shouted, scooping him up.

The little rat lay loosely in his hand. Jamie felt all over for a heartbeat, not really knowing where to look or if he'd even feel it.

"A mess you've made, haven't you?" Feidlimid said crossly, hands on his hips, eyes narrowed as he surveyed the damage.

"You've killed him! Why? He didn't do anything!" Hot emotion rushed through Jamie. "I fell! It was an accident, and it wasn't his fault!" Jamie's anger formed a clot at the back of his throat.

"Oh, what a lovely little window! I love what you've done with your little tunnel. Better watch out—all sorts of dangerous elements will come barging in and destroy this . . . what do you call it? Mold?" Mallorie fluttered in the in-between of the woods and path, her lyrical voice taunting.

"Shut it, fatum," growled Feidlimid.

"Shut it? The hole you mean? Sorry, can't do that. I suppose you'll be in a right lot of trouble for this, won't you, Feidlimid?" the little beetle fairy continued, her voice rising and falling as though she were speaking to a very small child. "What to do, what to do?" She buzzed around Feidlimid's head, making the wood elf bat at his ears.

"Shut it, all of you!" Jamie cried. He collapsed on the stone path, Bilbo in his hands.

Feidlimid waved his small, perfect hand up and down the length of the tear. It began to knit itself back together, the seam becoming invisible in seconds. He left a tiny hole at the top.

"There you go—out, fatum," Feidlimid growled.

"I come and go as I please, thank you very much," Mallorie replied, stopping her torment and buzzing down to Jamie's eye level. "Now, what's going on here?"

"He's dead. Bilbo's dead." He barely choked the words out. He didn't care if he looked like a baby. He held out the limp body of his friend, the fur still soft.

"Let me see here." Mallorie lit on Jamie's hand and leaned over Bilbo's still form, pressing her effervescent body to his chest. "Oh now, he's all right—he's still ticking in there, anyhow—just stunned is my guess. Give him a bit. I bet he'll perk right up."

Jamie looked at her, wanting what she said to be true.

"You're sure? You heard his heart?"

"Well, I'm no expert on rats, but there's something like a clock in there. Come on back with me through the break. I'll take you to a place to rest up a bit—"

Mallorie was cut off by Feidlimid, who sealed the tear with an angry swish of his hand.

"Oh, a place to rest, is it?" he snarled. "Jamie, you want to go home, yes?" Feidlimid waved away Mallorie, who had taken to dive-bombing his dark hair. "Well, I'm leading you out, but she"—he batted at the tiny beetle fairy with both hands—"she is leading you in. There's a difference."

Jamie shook his head, not knowing whom to trust. Feidlimid had proven that his sharpened teeth were a distinct extension of his personality. But he had a point—Jamie wanted to get out, and Feidlimid had said he had to go through to get out, not in. But then again, Feidlimid was a wood elf, so maybe he'd lied. Likewise, Mallorie had seemed awfully excited to bother Feidlimid, and Jamie had a sinking feeling in his gut that she was using him as a way to bait the wood elf. He stroked Bilbo's soft fur. The little rat still didn't move. Jamie thought with a bit of a shock that maybe Mallorie had just told him Bilbo was all right as a way to get him back into the woods. He needed Bilbo to bite his ear and pull on his hair. He needed someone to tell him what was the right thing to do.

Making decisions terrified Jamie, even the little ones. Each decision was always met with a wave of fear, and even the simplest things could set it off: Momma asking what he wanted for dinner, Daddy asking what book they should read at bedtime. Momma had tried once to get him to order his own meal in a restaurant; Jamie knew what he wanted, but the words wouldn't come out, only a stream of tears—tears like a baby. The familiar lump formed in his throat. He wouldn't be a baby this time, he wouldn't. He would make the right decision.

"What if you don't?" a rumbling voice hissed in his ear like a roll of thunder. "What if they both want to eeeeat yooooou whollle?"

Jamie shivered.

"Go away!" he murmured, trying to turn off the sound.

"Go awwayyyyy," the voice mocked. "Go ahead, Jamieeee, cry like a baby—except you're not a baby anymore, are youuuuu? Got a bit older? Lost a biiiit of tiiiime." The thunder rumbled low and steady in Jamie's ear.

"Go away! Go away! Go away!" he shouted, struggling to keep his voice steady. He cupped Bilbo to his chest with his free hand, his fingers wrapped protectively around the little rat.

"Liiitttle friend, liiitle friend, wake up liiittle friend. Seeeee youuuu sooooon, Jamieeeee."

The thunder rolled to a stop. Jamie found himself crouched on the path, covering his head with one hand, Bilbo wrapped in his other at his chest. Mallorie perched on Feidlimid's shoulder, both creatures staring at him. Feidlimid's mouth was slightly ajar.

"We need to get off the path," Feidlimid stated.

Mallorie buzzed down to Jamie, landing on his knee, staring at him with her unblinking black eyes.

"I'd say so. You all right in there, love?" Her voice rang like a lullaby.

Jamie could hear his mother singing in the far, far distance, *Hush, little baby, don't say a word . . .* and collapsed into tears.

"You heard it, didn't you?" Feidlimid asked. "I knew it'd have your scent, what with the lake and all. I knew it was taking too long, and then all this nonsense with the path." He glared at Mallorie.

"Don't go looking at me!" The beetle fairy was indignant. "You sealed the other hole, yes? The one he fell through in the first place?"

"Of course I did, you little worm," Feidlimid snapped. "He must have gotten through the break."

"Seal the break," Jamie said in a voice that was almost inaudible.

"Oh look, he lives!" Mallorie buzzed closer to Jamie's face, staring directly into his eye, and then she backed up and returned to his knee. "A grand idea that, grand, but it's impossible. The genius wood elves built their sacred path, placed before time began, la la la, on a fault line. No sealing a fault line, hence Bolly and I slip through when we want. But so can others—the one that seems to have taken a shine to you for one. So what now?" Mallorie demanded, flying up to Feidlimid's eyes. "Your secret, oh-so-sacred shrine safe enough for him? You want to be the one who brought the Lairdbalor home with ya?"

"The Lairdbalor?" Jamie shot to his feet, blood rushing to his head, making him dizzy enough to fall again. He swayed in place for a moment, waiting for the fog to clear. "What did you call it?"

"You know the one we speak of?" Feidlimid asked cautiously.

"No. I mean, I don't think so, not a person. I know the word." Jamie rubbed his forehead with his free hand, dots of static still dancing in his vision. "I see it in my dreams, nightmares, letters written on a wall or in the dirt sometimes. I don't know what it means. I've never known."

Feidlimid and Mallorie exchanged a glance.

"No wonder," Mallorie hummed. "It tracked you from your world. Didn't have to look too hard to find you in this one . . . " Her melodic voice trailed off.

In Jamie's hand, Bilbo suddenly squirmed and lifted his small tawny head. Jamie looked down to meet his gaze, tears welling in the corners of his eyes.

"Oh thank god, Bilbo!"

The rat cautiously put his weight on all four paws and arched his spine. He was unsteady, but very much alive.

Jamie swiveled to face Feidlimid, his fear and grief suddenly turned to anger.

"You tried to kill him!" Jamie spat at him. "Why? He didn't do anything. He's my friend, and you said you wanted to help us get home, so why?"

Feidlimid growled, and his voice, once so gentle, now sounded like shattered glass.

"I don't owe you explanations, human. I'm told to bring you back, you disappear from the path, I do whatever needs to be done to bring you back on it, yes?" He paused. "Besides, he's fine."

"You could have just come after me. I just fell, and it wasn't on purpose after all," Jamie sputtered.

"Can't, can't, can't . . . " Mallorie sang as she buzzed in Feidlimid's ear, making the wood elf smack at his own head angrily.

Mallorie deftly avoided the blows, timing her movements so Feidlimid kept hitting his own ear. "Can't leave the path, can you, wood elf?" She abandoned her sport and flew to Jamie and then hovered in the air in front of him. "You see, love, your volatile friend there has to stay on the path at all times. Ugly what happens if they leave it, isn't it, Feidlimid?" Mallorie dissolved into a fit of giggles.

Frustration welled up inside Jamie at these two smacking at each other, Mallorie giggling, while Bilbo stretched uncomfortably in his hand. He spat out the words, the anger alien to his own ears.

"He's little, and you almost killed him!" He spun to Mallorie, who was buzzing near his ear. "And you! Were you ever trying to help me? Or just trying to mess with him?"

"A bit of both, if you want the truth," Mallorie hummed. "I rarely get the chance to so perfectly harass. You can't really blame me." She flew in lazy circles in the space over Jamie's head.

Bilbo crawled up Jamie's arm and resumed his post on his shoulder. Jamie breathed a sigh of relief at the familiar weight.

"You through?" Feidlimid asked, his voice flat, the question aimed at Mallorie as much as Jamie. "I suddenly have a very vested interest in getting you back to your world, as it seems that you have been marked—why, I couldn't say. But one who is marked gets too much attention, and we like to not have that kind of attention, if you catch me."

Jamie nodded, the venom gone. His hands were shaking at his outburst. He was terrified of Feidlimid, but Mallorie was just playing a game. The clot of frustration returned to the back of his throat as he realized he had no idea who to trust—neither of them if he had the choice, but that he did not have.

"We have a problem," Feidlimid continued. "If it can find you on the path, then it's not really the safest route, is it? You might be better off in the woods after all. At least it might provide a bit of confusion."

"Do I hear you right?" Mallorie dive-bombed Feidlimid's head, making the wood elf duck. "Was I right after all?"

"Shut it, fatum," Feidlimid growled. "I still need to bring him back, at least to the next Holding—I'm under word from the Elder—but I'm going to recommend that he go to the Burg. He'll need a guide to get there."

He looked pointedly at Mallorie, who buzzed right up to Feid-limid's eyes. Jamie could see all the muscles in the wood elf's slim arms twitching at the instinct to smack the tiny insect.

"The Burg? Well, well, well, I've seen everything now. I thought your kind had written off the Burg?"

Feidlimid growled at the beetle fairy.

"None of your concern, fatum. You want to help the boy? Stay with us till the Holding, then lead him out. The faster the marked one goes back to his world, the better off we'll all be."

Mallorie answered by buzzing up the path, pausing only to look back, hovering in midair.

"You coming?" she sang, her voice a lark's song in the night.

FOUR

JAMIE trudged along the path. Mallorie was so far ahead that she blended in with the darkness, making her presence known only when she buzzed back and circled Jamie's ear, and then she quickly disappeared again. Several times she swooped at Feidlimid's head, but the wood elf was on a mission. He ignored the distraction completely. Feidlimid's voice and demeanor had changed. Gone was the playful creature that had first led Jamie down the path; he had now very much taken charge, did not look back, and did not pause. It occurred to Jamie that while Feidlimid had seemed like a kid when they'd first met, now he was more like a sir. Jamie had known both girl and boy sirs, so he figured that might be a better thing to call him—sir. Daddy said that anyone, boy or girl, who was in charge was a sir. Jamie had suspected that there was more to that explanation than Daddy had let on. In fact, as he marched down the path of mossy green stone laid before time, he realized that a great many things that Daddy and Momma had tried to explain had been missing important components. Jamie understood why: He was a little boy—at least he was then. He dared not think what he was now. But you can't tell a little boy everything, at least that's what the adults thought; little boys—and little girls, perhaps (Jamie hadn't understood much about little girls before he fell down the hill, and the last few hours had made him understand even less)—won't understand.

It's rather backward, thought Jamie crossly as he remembered Momma explaining why he couldn't have a playdate with his friend Bryan. Bryan was a boy in his class who always seemed to be in trouble, and he desperately wanted to come to Jamie's house. One afternoon, as Momma had arrived at school to collect Jamie, Bryan had loudly asked if he could come to Jamie's house. Momma had told him that they were going out of town for the weekend and maybe some other time. Jamie had been utterly confused; only the night before, Momma and Daddy had been saying they wanted to sleep all weekend (which sounded perfectly terrible to Jamie), so where would they be going? Later, Momma had tried to explain to Jamie that Bryan's feelings might be hurt if he knew she just didn't want him to come over to their house. It was odd that now—in his much, much-too-small sweatpants with his long, clumsy arms and legs and his tangled hair—he understood what his mother had done. He thought back on it and could see the indecision, the fear in Momma's eyes when Bryan asked to come over. She had just blurted an answer. Now Jamie understood what it was to blurt, but it hadn't made much sense at the time. Jamie assumed that adults blurted answers quite a lot, as they were expected to tell the truth but at the same time expected to never hurt anyone's feelings, and it didn't seem like the two things were possible. Bryan was a bit of a problem, though, and Jamie wouldn't have wanted to see him tromping through Momma's garden or breaking his favorite Egyptian god statues that he got in his Christmas stocking last year. Maybe it was okay to say they were going out of town; maybe it was okay just to say no. Jamie didn't know, but he expected it was a very grown-up problem to have.

"It's not, you know."

Mallorie buzzed past Jamie's head and landed on the shoulder that wasn't occupied by the sleeping Bilbo, who had fashioned a nest out of Jamie's too-long hair.

"Not what?" asked Jamie crossly, for he was still annoyed at her using him as a way to play with Feidlimid.

"Possible to tell the truth without hurting feelings."

Mallorie flexed her wings. From the corner of his eye, Jamie saw a flash of sunrise orange.

"Then what's the point?" Jamie muttered. Things are a lot clearer when you are too young to really think about them, he thought.

"There isn't a point, not really. It's just the reality of it. You either become a person who doesn't care if you hurt feelings or you become a liar, or maybe you become both. It's no different here, if you were thinking that humans had cornered the market on confusing reactions." The beetle fairy giggled.

"Cornered the market?" Jamie wondered. "What does that even mean?"

"It's when . . . well, I'm not really sure actually. It's a human saying. I figured you'd know." Mallorie settled down, pushing a clump of his tangled hair into a makeshift bed.

"How do you know human sayings?" Jamie asked, wondering if he'd get hurt feelings or a lie as an answer. "It's not the first time you've used one—you said something about an umbrella and a hurricane earlier."

"I come and go as I please. Most of us do, except the wood elves and others like them. I'm in your world the same as I'm here, you just never noticed," Mallorie whispered in his ear.

"But you don't talk in my world, I know. I tried to talk to bugs, and cats, and dogs, and the neighbor's bunny rabbits. They never talked back, never even once," Jamie stated.

"Can't speak for cats, dogs, and rabbits, but when it comes to beetles, or beetle fairies, you weren't asking the right questions. Simple as that." Her voice was very soft now, barely perceptible. "Now let me be a bit. It's a long walk once we get to the Holding."

FEIDLIMID marched on. Jamie's legs grew numb, and weariness sank into his bones. He pondered different ways to ask for a rest, expecting the same answer to all of them.

"No," Feidlimid answered all the unspoken questions with one word, his voice final.

"It really was an accident, you know," Jamie muttered, trying to catch his breath. "I tripped and fell through the path or whatever you call what's covering it."

"I am aware," Feidlimid stated, his voice devoid of emotion.

Jamie shivered. Feidlimid's moods changed like the amber wood tint of his hair and eyes.

"Why are you taking me to the . . . the . . . " Jamie struggled to find the word they had used earlier.

"Holding," Feidlimid filled the gap. "Why? Because I was told to. And don't bother asking why was I told to, I just was, and I don't question the ones who tell me things. You could take a cue."

"What's the Holding?"

Feidlimid sighed as he realized Jamie was not so easily deterred.

"It's a watchtower. I suspect they won't want you to go all the way to the keep, at the center. I suspect they will agree with me and let the little worm on your shoulder take you to the Burg. The Holding is a place for us to keep a watch on the forest. It's as safe as anything ever is."

Perhaps rang in Jamie's ears.

"What are the Burg?" he asked, unable to swallow the question but knowing that he should. The icy fear of being passed off to creatures even more terrible than the wood elves was almost too much.

"Twig and twine, child, you *are* seven, aren't you?" Feidlimid's voice softened by half a degree. "It's easy to forget—you've outgrown yourself."

The familiar lump rose in Jamie's throat.

"Don't go crying again," Feidlimid said, his voice a full half-step nicer than it had been since Jamie had met him at the clearing. "The Burg are creatures like me, only a little different. They live closer to your world, where the mist is quite a bit thinner. They have very different lives, and that breeds quite a lot of anger sometimes."

Abruptly, he stopped walking. Jamie almost ran into him in his surprise.

"I might as well tell you here so you don't go blurting out something inappropriate when we reach the Holding," Feidlimid continued, his voice soft. "You'll have trouble seeing that the Burg and us are related—we're two ends of a very long spectrum, if you can understand that."

Jamie shook his head, frustrated with all the words and things he still didn't know, even though so many other things had become clear. Tears threatened to fall again.

"None of that now." Feidlimid rolled his eyes, but his voice remained soft. "A rainbow has two ends, yes?"

Jamie nodded.

"And then there's everything in the middle, yes?"

Jamie nodded again, glad to finally understand someone's explanation.

"Well, the Burg are on one end of the rainbow, and we are on the other. We're in entirely different places, but by and large, we're made of the same parts." The wood elf examined Jamie for a long minute. "That make sense?"

Jamie gave a small nod.

"I'm not used to talking to children. Before you came along, I hadn't actually seen a real human child in many years."

He turned and started walking again.

Jamie stumbled after him. Encouraged by his tone, he asked, "You said I fell through a portal. Am I the only one who's done that?" His question sounded naïve to his ears, but he had to know. If he was the only one to ever fall down the hill, then how could they be sure they knew how to get him back?

"No," Feidlimid said carefully as the path turned sharply to the right. "There have been others. There are more portals from your world to ours than you would believe. Occasionally, it happens that one of your kind ends up here."

"You said you hadn't talked to children in a long time. Were the others, the other ones who fell, grown-ups?" Jamie asked cautiously, trying to edge his way into his real question.

"No, usually children, like you. The grown ones from your world don't usually last too terribly long in ours; too much to believe, too much to trust. You're different from the grown ones, you and your kind. It's easier for you—I couldn't say why. It's not a thing I know much of, but the elders do, and I know what they have told me." Feidlimid hesitated. "I don't say this to scare you, but if you had been a grown one, you would most likely never have left the clearing you tumbled into, where I found you. You'd still be there, thinking you were dead, losing your ability to listen to yourself, to determine what is real. Children are different. You listen to yourself. I'll never understand your kind and its backward way of growing up."

"What happened to the grown-ups who did end up here?" Jamie asked, his voice a whisper. His arms and legs felt strangely insulated, like they were made of marshmallow puff.

"They died," Feidlimid answered simply. There was no malice in his voice, but the straightforward answer sent a shiver up Jamie's spine. "They died sitting in place or they died climbing a hill they couldn't climb or they died fighting a cloud of gnights. But every time, they died. Remember, time works differently here, Jamie— you're already much older than you were when you arrived. The good bit is that you have quite a ways to go still, and unless It picks at you more, you aren't likely to sleep—too afraid, am I right?" He looked over his shoulder to see Jamie's nod. "That's what I and the little fly on your shoulder meant: you have to learn how to be afraid properly. It's good and right to be afraid to sleep here. Listen to that fear, and obey it. The grown ones from your world have such an idea about being afraid, as though it's something that needs combating—a monster out to kill them—when it's rather the opposite. Fear is what keeps your heart beating. It's what keeps you from making all those small, deadly mistakes. It's what keeps you on the path when keeping on the path is the best way to be." He emphasized that last point, and Jamie felt a small wave of chagrin.

"So the grown-ups got too old?" Jamie was struggling to understand even as the fear that Feidlimid spoke so highly of made his heart race.

"That and other things. But yes, getting old was part of it," Feidlimid responded. "You didn't really explore that clearing you fell into, and a good thing too. A few feet from where you landed, you'd have found the frame of the one who fell before you."

Jamie struggled to understand this. "The frame?"

"The frame, yes, the hard bits under all that skin—frame." Feidlimid's expression indicated that Jamie was clearly the dullest boy he'd ever encountered.

"Skeleton," Jamie said proudly, pleased that he had figured it out. He had seen many skeletons in the medical TV show at night. Suddenly it hit him what Feidlimid had been trying to tell him. "There were bones in that clearing? But who . . . "

"Couldn't say—before my time. I only know the stories, and all they say is that a grown one of your kind ended up in the clearing, tried for days to walk the hill, curled up to sleep in the brush, never woke up. Some say the gnights finished it off, some say the grown one lived in the clearing for a good long time—as long as our time would allow, that is. I couldn't say. But you can see why I was so insistent on getting you on the path. To stay in the clearing would be your death. You can't go forward while you're standing still."

Jamie shivered. A thought occurred to him.

"How did you know I was there? Was there some kind of alarm I couldn't hear?"

Feidlimid laughed, the chords trilling through the forest, the sound so unexpected that Jamie jumped.

"No, we have less mysterious ways when it comes to communicating out here. Look up."

Confused, Jamie stopped and looked up at the night sky—so many stars, they crowded the space. Suddenly, a dark shape swooped over his head. He ducked instinctively, and Feidlimid snorted again.

"Bats. They've been there all along. They report back and forth, share anything of interest. Remarkably reliable, incapable of lies— makes them rather hard to get along with but quite the quality for a good messenger." Feidlimid paused, looking back at Jamie. "Come on then, almost there."

FIVE

THE Holding was nothing but a collection of sticks stacked up to the level of the trees. Jamie was utterly disappointed; he'd had an image of a medieval tower, turrets for the archers lining the top, a grand balcony wrapping around, and perhaps a drawbridge and a proper moat with crocodiles in it, waiting to eat the prisoners who tried to escape. But this—this looked like a blind beaver had tried to build a dam and stopped halfway through. Feidlimid stopped before the collection of sticks and broken tree branches and looked back.

"Best wake your passengers," he said wryly, eyeing the sleeping creatures on Jamie's shoulders.

Jamie gently stroked Bilbo's spine until the little rat stirred and stretched, and then he poked Mallorie gently, careful not to touch her gossamer wings.

"Just grand, isn't it?" Mallorie swooned.

Jamie glanced at her suspiciously as she flew to the edge of the Holding, hovering. Jamie knew what this was—he had talked about it with Daddy many times. Sarcasm. He breathed a sigh of relief that he had remembered the word. Sarcasm was saying one thing and meaning another. Jamie had asked if it was like saying he wanted broccoli for dinner but really wanting chocolate peppermints. Daddy had said it went beyond that, and Jamie hadn't understood. He knew sometimes Daddy and Momma said things that made no sense, so he had figured that sarcasm was something grown-ups said when they didn't want kids to understand. But like so many things, Jamie could now understand what Daddy had meant: it went beyond not wanting broccoli. It was calling a pile of sticks in the middle of a forest grand without even a hint of a different meaning in your beetle fairy voice.

Jamie, proud of his deduction, replied with more sarcasm. "Oh yes, just grand. I bet this took you a long time to build."

Feidlimid narrowed his eyes at him, considering his words. "You aren't seeing it, are you?"

"Of course he's not, of course, of course, of course," Mallorie trilled as she flew in loops up the length of the heap.

"What? What am I not seeing?" Jamie asked, alarmed.

"Anything of value here," Feidlimid responded, his voice ice. "Well, no matter, it's better on the inside anyhow."

He motioned to Jamie to follow him; Mallorie landed on the end of a protruding stick and shook the dust off her wings. "I know, I'll wait here." She sighed. "If I don't see you in a bit, I'm going back through. There's another break at the top of this marvel."

Jamie shook his head. He strained he eyes at the structure; it still just looked like a mass of forest waste.

"You're seeing it with your grown-up eyes," Feidlimid said, and he placed his hand on an outward-leaning stick. "Grown eyes wouldn't see it as much. Too bad you're not seven anymore. It's really something."

Jamie glared, and Feidlimid looked pleased with himself. More sarcasm, thought Jamie bitterly, and what a terrible thing it is too.

"Never mind, though," Feidlimid said as he stared at the mass, apparently waiting for something to happen. "It's the inside that's really impressive, and no amount of grown-up can mask that."

A rustle of activity inside the mass of sticks and leaves spewed out a cloud of dust that flew straight into Jamie's face. His lungs felt like they were coated in glue—he tried to cough but could only produce a wheeze. Feidlimid gave him a backward glance.

"Oh yes—you should probably duck."

His voice was cold and amused.

Jamie spat out black spittle. His chest burned.

"What . . . what is that?" he managed between wheezes.

"Dust," Feidlimid answered sharply. "Or don't they have dust in your world?"

"That wasn't just dust—" Jamie began, but Feidlimid interrupted.

"Duck," he said simply.

Jamie fell to his knees just in time as a cloud of smoky particulates shot out from the cracks in the Holding. Feidlimid placed his hand on a particularly large leaf and closed his eyes.

"It's all very dramatic, isn't it?" Mallorie squealed. For once she did not sound as though she was trying to rile up Feidlimid—she sounded as though the odd display in front of this wretched-looking mass of nothing was actually dramatic and wonderful.

Jamie looked at Feidlimid again and shook his head—maybe he really did have grown-up eyes. It struck him that this was how his parents must have seen all the things he thought were so wonderful. Even Bilbo, back in his stuffed-rat days—did they simply see him as a shabby bit of nothing? When Momma watched him set up kingdoms with his Lego men and multicolored blocks, did she see how magnificent they were? Did she see the ancient temple he was building or just a pile of useless sticks and terrible dust? Jamie felt betrayed, and very grown-up.

All of a sudden, the stick pile began to shake and the outlying debris fell to the ground, revealing an entrance of sorts. Mallorie sighed in admiration and clung to her branch. Feidlimid entered the chamber and motioned for Jamie to follow. With a deep breath, he ran his finger down Bilbo's back, as the little rat clung to his hair, and stepped inside. He had to duck—the passageway was built for someone Feidlimid's size, the size that Jamie used to be. Unaccustomed to his new height, he bumped his head brutally on a tree stump. There was no light, save from the outside, and as Jamie moved forward, that disappeared as well. He glanced back and saw the sticks back in place, guarding the door. His bare feet, which had thus far been spared too many cruelties of the forest floor, were poked and prodded at every step by sharp rocks and bits of sticks. At one point something bit his big toe, and he cried out in surprise. Feidlimid glanced back impatiently. Jamie scrambled to keep up—he did not want to be stuck here, not alone.

As they wound down the long corridor, Jamie wondered how this was possible. From the outside, the Holding had looked no deeper than a few feet, but they had been walking several hundred yards now with no sign of stopping. When they turned a corner, Jamie said silent thanks for the amber glow in the distance and promptly stubbed his left foot against a bramble-covered branch. He swallowed his cry, somehow sensing that whatever was at the end of this path didn't appreciate or sympathize with his discomfort.

Jamie had two distinct memories of pain. In one, he had a splinter in his hand, and he wailed and cried. He couldn't guess how old he was, but he remembered the sturdy comfort of Momma's arms as she lifted him from the floor. He remembered being carried, his uninjured hand tangled in Momma's hair. He remembered burying his face in her neck and breathing in the scent of her lotion and skin. He had almost forgotten about the splinter, especially when Momma started singing to him.

Hey Jude,
Don't make it bad
Take a sad song and make it better . . .

She hummed the melody as they pulled the splinter out with a pair of baby-pink grabby things that he would later know as tweezers. She blew on his hand as she washed his wound in the sink. Momma carried him back to the sofa, where he remembered falling asleep to the sound of *Hey Jude* deep in her throat and the sweet smell of her neck.

That was the first memory. The second memory was a splinter of the same ilk. He wailed his pain and waved his hand. Momma rushed by, ignoring him. He wailed louder; again she rushed by, not looking down. In his frustration and fear that he might have suddenly become invisible, Jamie stood up—he had no context for his actual age, but the act of standing seemed a monumental feat. He stood and stepped in the direction that Momma had last rushed by. He screamed, the effort making his throat ache like it was on fire. Finally, what seemed like a lifetime later, she reappeared, stopped in front of him, and pulled him into her arms. This time, though, there was no comfort or soft songs. She rushed him down the hall and plunked him on the bathroom counter. Puzzled, he had stopped crying. Where was the song? Why didn't she care? He quite forgot about his injury until she rather roughly assessed his hand and then assaulted it with the baby-pink tweezers. Jamie had screamed his protest, the effort making his face feel hot and uncomfortable.

"Honestly, kiddo, it's a splinter—you'd think you'd lost a limb."

With a quick and very dry kiss to his forehead, she had unceremoniously plunked him back onto the floor and rushed back to whatever was so important. Jamie had been so depressed about the whole affair that he hadn't even bothered to cry.

With his new grown-up eyes, Jamie could see that a time comes when you're too old to cry about a little splinter and too big to fall asleep in the crevices of your mother's neck. Still, he preferred the first memory.

As he mused about the two splinters, Jamie stepped squarely on some sort of spike that jutted right out of the ground.

"Ouch! Yeooow!"

He couldn't help the outburst—there was sticky warmth on the bottom of his foot, and he realized that he was bleeding. Bleeding, and there was no one to clean it and put a Band-Aid on, no one to apply the antibiotic gel. Daddy called the gel "mishap" and made it himself in the kitchen with handfuls of herbs and oils. Momma used it on her lips at night. Jamie didn't know what it really was, but he knew in this moment that he desperately needed some mishap. He yelped in fear, stumbling into the wall of the corridor. Feidlimid turned sharply and growled, his pointed teeth catching the faint light from the end of the passage.

"Shut it, boy."

He hissed the words, a feral, rattling sound. Jamie momentarily forgot the pain in his foot as he decided that this was very much more like the second memory, the one he did not prefer. He stumbled after him, even though his foot became increasingly slick with the inky substance. The pain brought tears to his eyes, but he was determined not to be a crybaby, not this time. The light was getting closer—maybe, Jamie thought, they might have some antibiotic gel. He wondered what an antibiotic was anyhow, and how it was better than the stabbing pain in his foot. He'd never asked Daddy, and now he wished he had. Another wave of utter misery washed over him, and he forgot his injured foot. Daddy and he had been making a game together. It wasn't finished yet, and Jamie supposed it never would be now, especially since he was overgrown and probably too big to play it anyhow. It was a board game. Jamie had drawn the board on a large piece of poster paper using a ruler that Daddy had given him to keep the lines straight. It was an adventure game. In it the little pieces—tiny, flat marbles from Momma's junk drawer—moved around the spaces and had different adventures for each place they landed. Jamie had lots of ideas for adventures; most of them involved lizards. In his best handwriting, he was writing the different adventures down in his composition book. He had felt very grown-up having a composition book. Now he wondered if, wherever and whenever Daddy was, he was still working on their game. Jamie reached up and let Bilbo nuzzle his finger. He was queasy, his foot was beginning to throb, and a couple of times he nearly lost his balance due to the slippery stickiness coating his foot. By the time they reached the opening of the passageway, Jamie struggled to stay upright. His head was pulsing in the same way as his foot, his stomach dropped, and suddenly he didn't care one bit about upsetting Feidlimid. He concentrated for a minute, finding the corner where the passageway opened into a larger room. His vision swirled—all he could take in was light and several figures, each just reaching his shoulders, moving toward him. With a concerted effort, he slumped to the floor, using the wall against his back as a guide; he was not going to fall and lose Bilbo again. Bilbo turned frantically in circles on his shoulder—his tiny paws pulled on his ear—and Jamie let the darkness wash over him in a wave.

SIX

"BERRY and bush, Feidie!" a deep voice echoed in Jamie's ear. "You brought him back half dead!"

The effort to open his eyes made the world spin. As Jamie cracked his right eye just enough not to vomit, he found himself eye to eye with a pair of gold-and-green-speckled hazel eyes as big as saucers.

"Not quite half, if you ask me," the voice behind the eyes responded. The creature had a milky voice, smooth and level.

Jamie opened his eyes a bit wider and saw four wood elves, each with slightly different coloring, staring at him. Feidlimid stood away from the others, hands on his hips, lips pursed over sharpened teeth. In a rush of panic, Jamie reached up to feel for Bilbo. The adrenaline made his head swim, but the feeling abated as he felt the familiar silky fur. The little rat burrowed into his hair.

"It's hit some sort of artery, or maybe a vein." The hazel-eyed wood elf was intently studying his foot. "That's what you have, right, human? Arteries and veins?"

"I guess so," Jamie murmured. That sounded right; he had heard those words on the nighttime hospital show, but he didn't really know what they were. "I need the antibiotic gel and a Band-Aid." His foot was still throbbing, and his head felt as though it were tied to a string floating a few feet above his body.

"Move aside." ·

A ruby-eyed wood elf with fire-red hair pushed its way through the others. It wore a dark tunic like the rest, but around its waist was a small pouch made of forest-green leaves.

"The lot of you is useless, you know." The voice was rough, as though all the words were caught in the back of its throat. "The human is bleeding."

Jamie saw the looks of confusion on the others' faces. Feidlimid rolled his oak-dark eyes and walked to the other side of the room, which Jamie realized was rather small.

"Blood is—oh, how to describe it—it's as though all your insides were a liquid, and then that liquid had to keep moving all about your body all the time or else you would sleep. That cover it?" the ruby-eyed wood elf asked while leaning over Jamie's foot, examining it.

"That's not really what blood is," Jamie muttered, trying to make sense of the wood elf's explanation. "It's like a juice that runs through our arteries and veins and keeps everything from getting dry."

The head of fire hair raised for a minute and stared at Jamie with its unnerving and utterly unreadable eyes.

"Hmm. Interesting. I'll ask you to repeat that a bit later so I can write it down in my book."

As it spoke, the wood elf dug through the small leaf pouch. It then pulled out a stack of deep-green leaves and, with startling efficiency, began to bind Jamie's foot. The bleeding stopped; the pulsing pain subsided.

"There you go."

The wood elf tucked the extra leaves back into the pouch and then reached farther in and pulled out a book too impossibly large to have come from the small pouch. It struck Jamie as funny that, of all the things he had seen today, this was the most unbelievable. The cover was made of some sort of wood bark, and the pages looked like pressed leaves and flowers. The wood elf removed a long twig, sharpened at one end.

"Now, tell me again—blood is a juice that keeps your insides from getting dry?"

"I . . . I think so," Jamie stuttered.

The wood elf nodded and began writing madly.

"What is that?" Jamie asked, his head clearing.

"Something I'm working on."

The creature finished its writing, closed the book, and held it out for Jamie to see. On the cover in ornate lettering was written: *Things About Humans.*

"We so rarely get to actually speak to one—usually I have to rely on the bats, and they bring back such baffling reports. You'll pardon me if I ask you about a few other things." The wood elf's eyes flashed with excitement as it flipped through several pages in the book, stopping long enough to wrinkle its tiny, perfect nose. "Tell me, what is 'confounding'? The bats said you kept repeating it a while back. Is it something inside your skin? Is that confounding?"

Jamie shook his head. The others were leaning in close, hanging on his words. Feidlimid had even skulked a bit closer, although he was clearly not as impressed with things about humans as the others of his kind were. An odd thought struck Jamie, one that hadn't bothered him until this minute.

"Are you writing your book in English? How is that you all speak English? And Mallorie, how does she . . . "

At the mention of Mallorie, Feidlimid flashed his teeth at him. Jamie shrugged and stopped his query.

"What I mean to say is, how is it that we all understand each other?"

The ruby-eyed wood elf looked at Jamie, its face perplexed.

"I'm not sure what 'English' is, but I'm delighted to be speaking it. I'm not really the one to explain about understanding—the Elder will do that, momentarily."

It was Jamie's turn to be perplexed. "You're not the elders?"

The creatures erupted in giggles.

"Of course not," tittered the hazel-eyed wood elf. "The Elder will be along soon, no hurrying."

"What do I call you?" Jamie asked. They seemed so different from the cryptic and vicious Feidlimid; they seemed curious, friendly even.

"I am called Suibhne," the ruby-eyed wood elf replied, and indicating the hazel-eyed creature, it said, "and this is Seisyll. That," Suibhne said and pointed to a mossy-eyed wood elf with short cropped hair the color of newly turned earth, "that is Ninian, and finally"—pointing to the last wood elf, who stood a bit away from the others—"that is Morcant."

Morcant nodded a greeting. Its skin was a muted gold, dark against its molten-gold eyes. Morcant's hair was a shade some-where between, shorn close to its head except for a long shock springing from the top that flowed over half its face. Jamie smiled, and Morcant nodded back.

"As I was asking," Suibhne continued, "confounding—"

"What do your names mean?" Jamie interrupted, which he knew was terribly rude, but he couldn't resist. Something about this hollowed-out room . . . He felt himself losing his manners and even whatever it was that made him not just blurt questions. He wondered for a terrible moment if he had become a grown-up, and like Momma, if he would continue to blurt out questions.

"Our names," replied Morcant, its voice molten like its eyes, "are from the old language in your world. They are from a time when the mist was thinner than it is now, when you didn't have to tumble down a very big hill to cross the threshold."

"As I was asking," Suibhne interrupted, sounding slightly irri-tated. "Confounding. Can you tell me what it means? The bats had no idea."

Jamie smiled again. His foot injury seemed years away, and the dizziness was entirely gone.

"Confounding. It means something that is very confusing, something you don't quite understand no matter how hard you try—that is what I think it means. But . . . " Jamie struggled for the words. "It's more than that. It's not just a word—it's a feeling, like when you don't understand something so much that it makes you want to cry."

The wood elves themselves looked utterly confounded. Suibhne scribbled down something in the book. "What is 'cry'?"

Jamie had just started to answer when he was interrupted by a great rustling, leaves and sticks shaking from the sides of the walls.

Suibhne quickly shoved the book and twig into his (Jamie decided that Suibhne must be a boy, based mostly on his rough-sounding voice) impossibly small pouch. Leaves flooded in from the top of the structure, and as Jamie looked up, he saw it went higher than he would ever have thought possible. The wood elves shuffled to the walls, clearing the space in the middle. Jamie pulled his knees to his chest, afraid the entire structure might be collapsing. Feidlimid stood at his side. He leaned close to Jamie's ear and growled.

"None of your foolish talk now. You can't go babbling on with the Elder like you did with the young ones."

Jamie looked at the other wood elves, all standing together, staring up at the shaking walls in anticipation. Young ones? Like kids? How confounding—they looked exactly the same age as Feidlimid. No wonder they were nicer, he thought nastily, glancing up at Feidlimid, hoping he caught that thought.

Jamie had been in many earthquakes, and he knew what to do. This earthquake wasn't much different. Even though he'd never had to deal with sticks and leaves falling on his head, he still knew it would stop in a short moment, and then everyone would go about the business of cleaning up. Until then, he did exactly as Momma had always told him—he stayed put and covered his head with his hands. Feidlimid looked at him with cynical amusement. Jamie closed his eyes, not only so he could pretend that Feidlimid wasn't staring at him, but also because the dust from the walls was stinging them.

Finally, the shaking stopped. When Jamie opened his eyes, he saw a passageway had opened up on the other side of the small room. In the doorway stood another wood elf. Even though this creature appeared no older or younger than the others, Jamie knew instinctually that this must be the Elder. The Elder's eyes were a perfect, unpolluted white, the white of clouds on a sunny day. They seemed to be in constant motion, as though they were masking a real sky. Jamie was mesmerized. The Elder's hair was shorn in the same way as Morcant's, one long, silky piece hanging down to its chest, highlighting its extraordinary skin. A perfect shade of darkest night, it seemed to catch the light and shine not unlike the glow from a star emanating from its velvet surface in miniscule bursts. The total effect was almost too much to take in. It wore a tunic like the others, but instead of earth-toned rough cloth, the Elder wore silken layers of fabric that seemed to change color as it moved—one minute, it was shifting shades of sunset gold, then another step brought a roll of lapis blue. Jamie opened his mouth, but no sound came out. He hugged his knees tighter as Bilbo stood on his shoulder, front paws in the air, straining for a closer look. The other wood elves bowed their heads and stood silent.

"Suibhne," the Elder spoke, its voice the sound of an ancient river, at once familiar and comforting but simultaneously unpredictable. "Suibhne, turn to page forty-three in your book."

Suibhne pulled *Things About Humans* from his pouch and flipped through the pages. He looked up at the Elder for further instruction.

"Go on, read it." The Elder was encouraging in a way that reminded Jamie of Daddy.

Suibhne straightened his back, obviously proud to have been chosen for this role. "Humans rely on hospitality and will not discuss matters of any importance without it. Before you can conduct business, you must first spend between ten to fifteen minutes discussing such mundane matters as family, weather, and athletic events. This is also the time when humans serve refreshments, such as tea, coffee, or wine." Suibhne looked up from the book, ruby-red eyes glowing with pride.

"Refreshments it is then," the Elder replied, giving Suibhne an approving nod. "Jamie, would you like a wine?"

Jamie was so shocked that he couldn't answer—first, to be addressed by this creature that was the single most important thing in the world as Jamie knew it; second, to be offered wine. Wine was something grown-ups drank in odd-looking glasses a little at a time. Jamie had been allowed to try a sip once out of Momma's glass, and it had tasted like dead things and dirt. Jamie had spat it out, and Momma and Daddy had laughed. Confounding.

On his shoulder, Bilbo let out a tiny squeak. The Elder listened intently as though Bilbo had delivered a sermon.

"I see. Add that to your book, Suibhne, as a footnote. Children do not customarily drink wine. That's certainly changed." The Elder nodded to Suibhne as he scribbled the footnote in the book. "You see, Jamie, much has changed in your time since we last had a guest. Do pardon our manners. Perhaps some tea then?"

Jamie nodded. He didn't really drink tea either—it was, strictly speaking, still a grown-up beverage—but he was sure it had to be better than wine.

"Good, good."

A wave of the Elder's hand, and a long table made of dark wood appeared, benches on either side. On top of the table sat eight ivory-and-rose-colored china cups in saucers, a matching teapot in the middle.

"Come, everyone, we will have tea and talk of mundane matters for ten to fifteen minutes." The Elder nodded encouragingly at Jamie. Bilbo jumped from his shoulder and ran to the table, where he sat on the dark wood surface in front of a teacup and saucer. "Excellent. Come, everyone."

Jamie forced his legs to move. Bilbo's actions were as surprising as the entire scene. He sat on the long wooden bench next to Bilbo, who looked back at Jamie, his tiny black eyes gleaming. The other wood elves took their places as well. Everyone at the table seemed entirely mystified by the setup—all except Bilbo, who looked, despite being a rat, completely at home.

"Morcant, would you serve?" the Elder asked gently.

Morcant nodded, her dark-gold hair catching the light, which Jamie realized had no actual source—no lamps, no torches, nothing. Morcant, Jamie decided, must be a girl because her voice was nicer and her hair too interesting to look at. Feidlimid cast him an exasperated look, and Jamie knew that he'd heard that thought. Jamie realized that the wood elves didn't deal with things like girl/boy, but his brain desperately wanted to make them one way or the other.

"It's perfectly all right, Jamie," the Elder said. "Morcant is not insulted that you think *her* to be a girl any more than Suibhne is to be a boy—whatever makes you feel more at ease. I believe there's something in the book about that. Isn't that right, Suibhne?"

As Morcant carefully poured hot, dark liquid from the teapot into each cup, Suibhne flipped through the book until he found the page he was looking for.

"Humans like to have a place for everything. For example, the human way is customarily to keep their food in a different room, and even in that room, it is customary to keep items separated in an order that seemingly makes little sense."

Suibhne looked up, proud again to have found the passage.

The Elder looked thoughtful. Her brow (Jamie had decided that she must be a girl; not just a girl, but a full-grown woman— her voice was too smooth and her manners too nice) wrinkled slightly and then released back to perfect smooth skin.

"Suibhne, I feel that last part is a bit nasty. Just because we find it to make little sense doesn't mean it doesn't make sense at all. Let's cross that last bit out, shall we?"

Suibhne nodded rapidly, using the sharpened twig to mark through the passage.

Morcant sat back down, her face expressionless. The other wood elves, with the exception of Feidlimid, looked excited and expectant. Feidlimid looked ready to burst with frustration. Jamie suspected that he had no patience for hospitality.

"Well then, let's have tea," the Elder said with a wave of her hand.

Jamie lifted the delicate teacup to his lips and sipped carefully, cautious not to burn his lips. The liquid met his tongue and assaulted his taste buds. It tasted like overripe apples and the corners of dark rooms. He fought the urge to spit it back out. The Elder regarded him as he carefully put the teacup back down.

"Interesting. Perhaps I should have gone with the wine after all. Well, no matter. First, you may call me Elisedd. Your question to my young ones was a good one—you asked what our names meant. They have all been used by your kind at some point, although in the old times. Their meanings have changed with the ones who used them. Now they are simply points of reference, and they could be anything. Indeed, we often change them, don't we?" Elisedd nodded to the others, who met her eyes with utter admiration; even Feidlimid seemed to let loose his annoyance for a moment. "Keeping with the spirit of mundane matters, what does your name, Jamie, mean?" Elisedd cast her cloudy eyes on Jamie, who wanted to both shrink away and at the same time run straight into them.

"Um, I don't know. My granddad, Momma's daddy, he was named Jamie," he stammered.

"Very interesting, very interesting." Elisedd nodded, even though Jamie knew perfectly well it was not. "You had another query, did you now?" Elisedd continued. "You wanted to know about the understanding? Yes?"

Jamie nodded eagerly, unsure of how to actually say his question. There was a boy in his class at school who spoke only Spanish, and several others who spoke both Spanish and English, and still another girl who spoke a language called Farsi, which Jamie thought sounded very fancy, much fancier than English. But what he found confounding was the fact that he couldn't understand the children who spoke Spanish, and Farsi sounded like a murmur of sounds, not actual words, so how was it that all these creatures—elves, beetle fairies, monsters—all spoke English?

Elisedd nodded even though Jamie hadn't actually articulated his thoughts. Next to him, Bilbo was happily lapping up the horrible tea. Jamie grimaced.

"Let me ask you something, Jamie," Elisedd's voice filled the room, gentle and powerful. "When you speak your 'English,' do you have to think about it?"

Jamie shook his head, his voice stuck in his throat.

"When you hear English, do you have to think about understanding it?" Elisedd asked.

Again, Jamie shook his head, confused.

"When you have a dream, do you understand what everyone says or writes in it?" Elisedd continued, the young fairies around the table hanging to her every word. She didn't wait for Jamie's response. "This world is closer to your dreams than it is to what you know as your waking life. We exist somewhere in between— it's why, as Feidlimid told you earlier, the grown ones do not fare so well here. The Oidhche is what they used to call it long ago, a place somewhere between sunset and sunrise." Elisedd paused, staring deep into Jamie's eyes, and his head felt light, like before he passed out. "In your waking world, you would not understand us—you would probably not even see us, at least in the way you do now, even though we can go back and forth quite easily. It's because you're in the in-between, the Oidhche, that you hear your 'English'; if you were a different type of human, you would hear something else. Does that make sense?"

Jamie nodded, although it was still quite confounding. He forced his voice from his throat. "What do you look like in my world?"

Elisedd smiled, revealing her razor-sharp teeth, and a chill settled over Jamie's skin.

"Child, you should feel lucky you do not know." She let the moment sit.

Bilbo looked up from his tea, and Elisedd nodded in his direction.

"Yes, quite time. Have we had enough mundane chitchat?" Elisedd asked, looking around the table.

The others didn't respond, only looked expectantly at Elisedd. Feidlimid looked like he was about to burst.

"Feidlimid, would you like to fill us in on why, exactly, you brought this human child to one of your kind's most holy places even though you know him to be a direct danger to all we hold dear?" Elisedd's fluid voice took a sharp turn away from the nurturing mother and into something far more dangerous. Its tenor changed the entire atmosphere of the room, and the other wood elves leaned forward, their eyes shining.

Feidlimid started to reply, his face pure shock. Elisedd cut him off.

"And please tell us, why did you allow him to mark my house with his blood? And in that action, marking Suibhne, who touched that foul poison?" Although perfectly pitched, her voice held an undercurrent, intense and unmistakably deadly.

"Feidlimid."

Elisedd bared her razor-sharp teeth. The other wood elves directed their stares to her, disconcerting and unblinking.

"I was told to bring him back—I was ordered to!" Feidlimid's voice shook with fear; gone was the haughty frustration he had shown since Jamie had fallen off the path.

"He is marked. You knew that, and you still brought him in this place." Elisedd turned to Jamie, and now dark clouds moved lazily across her cloud-white eyes. Jamie thought he might wet himself again, the potential shame of which was forcing his nails to dig into the palms of his hands. "Jamie, you need to tell us your dream. The bats said you mentioned dreams in which you saw the name of the one who hunts these parts. Dreams in which you saw its name, the Lairdbalor."

Jamie managed a nod. He glanced at Feidlimid, who looked stricken.

"I have a lot of nightmares. They're mostly the same, but a couple that happen more than the others."

"How often?" Elisedd interrupted.

"I . . . I don't know, when I'm really scared," Jamie stuttered. Streaks of electricity passed through Elisedd's eyes, and as her skin caught the spark, a constellation of light flashed. "There are two, sometimes I hear it, like a chant, I'm in a field and the grass is broken and dead, it scratches my ankles and feet. I hear voices around me chanting the same word over and over but no one is there, I can't see anyone, but it's the same word, over and over. In the other dream where I see the name, I'm walking through a city, but there's been some kind of war. Everything is broken. The buildings are all torn down, there's no lights anywhere, it's night, and I'm all alone." Jamie looked around the room. The young wood elves fixed their eyes on him, their faces frozen in calm fascination. "I keep walking because I feel like someone, something's behind me, and I need to hide, but there's nowhere left that's safe. I look at the broken walls around me, and on them is written that name—Lairdbalor."

"What then?" Elisedd asked steadily.

"Usually I wake up, but sometimes I keep walking, and I see it written everywhere, on the ground, the walls, signposts."

Jamie's heart raced. He had never thought the dream meant anything, but now he knew he had been terribly wrong; it meant everything, and he had ignored all the warnings. He felt as though he were at the edge of a very high cliff. Elisedd nodded as though she agreed with his internal panic.

"Have you told any of your kind about these dreams?" she asked, the great river voice still steady, but tense.

Jamie stammered a bit.

"Y-y-yes—I told Momma, but she said it was just my worries and it didn't mean anything, that the Lairdbalor wasn't real."

Jamie's skin felt as though it were made of ice. He was filled with a steadily growing horror that Momma had been wrong, that the Lairdbalor was very real, that the horror of his dream, the fear in all his nightmares, was real. The boy with the melted face existed, the fire, the burning city—all these things were real, and Jamie was powerless against them. He felt suddenly betrayed. Everything Momma and Daddy had told him was wrong. The nights when Momma had sung him back to sleep, the times when Daddy had let him crawl into their grown-up bed and sleep because he was scared, all false, a lie. They should have told him; they should have told the truth. The realization flooded Jamie, and as he stared desperately at the wood elves, he understood why the river of Elisedd's voice was now the crash of waves in a storm. He understood how terrible it was to know things and how impossible it was to go back to how you were before. His long hair and arms suddenly seemed fitting—he wasn't a child anymore, and that realization was terrifying in its implication. Bilbo looked at him, his small head cocked. With a single fluid motion, he jumped from the table to Jamie's shoulder, burrowing in the hair at his neck. Jamie flexed his fingers, the frozen stiffness evidence of his guilt, the end of his naïveté.

The wood elves stared at him, their unfathomable eyes unblinking and unknowable. Elisedd turned to Feidlimid, whose dark eyes were closed. He was murmuring what appeared to be a prayer. Jamie was confused—prayer seemed a very human thing to do.

"Hoping in vain for a power greater than yourself to provide safety is not just a human thing, Jamie," Elisedd said, her voice rising and falling, the undercurrent of a never-resting roar. "And Feidlimid is right to be afraid. Now, what to do with you." She turned her terrible gaze to him, and the young wood elves followed suit.

"Will I get to go home?" Jamie asked, his voice trembling.

Elisedd looked at him oddly, the dark storm clouds rolling past in waves.

"Home?" she asked. "Back to your world? Of course not, dear child. You were never meant to go home. You are marked; there is no home for you. You belong to the Lairdbalor, and your flesh may provide us with a bit of peace. Perhaps your presence here, as faulty as it is, is not—what do you say—the end of the world?"

Jamie's body went numb. Ice spread from his fingertips to his gut. His head filled with static, a block against the growing realization of what Elisedd was saying. He was marked for the Lairdbalor, and he was never going home. The tears that had soaked his face dried up, and he started to shake; at his neck, Bilbo was madly wrapping Jamie's hair around his paws, his wet nose poking into the back of his ear.

"Now child, don't fret so," Elisedd rumbled. "You will be leaving this place. We will not harm you; we will not need to. You will be found soon enough, and we can only hope that when you are, the stink with which you have polluted our temple will have waned. Perhaps the Lairdbalor will be so full that he will overlook the stain you have laid here. Perhaps."

"Why can't I go home? The Lairdbalor was just a dream there. I can leave your world and go home, and we can all forget, can't we?" Jamie's voice cracked, the words tumbling out in a panicked rush.

"Have you ever asked yourself how it was that you came to fall down that very large hill, Jamie?" Elisedd asked, her voice barely a whisper, the whistle of the winter wind.

Jamie shook his head.

"It was an accident, I was playing and—"

"And nothing," Elisedd cut him off. "You fell through a portal to your world. What do they call it, Suibhne?"

"A coincidence. They call it a coincidence," Suibhne replied, his eyes rapt on Elisedd.

"Yes, thank you." Elisedd looked at Feidlimid for a long moment. "Quite the coincidence. Now, what to do here."

Feidlimid looked up, his voice steady.

"I was ordered to bring him to the Holding. The bats sent word—I was ordered."

Elisedd considered the statement.

"Yes, I suppose you were. However, you know the consequences of bringing one who is marked to our Holding."

Feidlimid shook his head violently.

"No. I didn't think it really existed. They talked about the marked ones only in stories, we haven't seen one such as him since, since . . . "

"Yes," Elisedd cut him off. "It's been many, many years. The last one was back when children drank wine. And I think we all remember how that turned out, don't we?"

The younger wood elves snickered, the sound ominous and dark. Feidlimid looked around desperately.

"But it wasn't my fault—what was I to do? Leave him in the woods? I would have been punished! I had to fight to keep him with me. He fell from the path, and he nearly followed the fatum straight away! I fought to keep him with me—I was ordered!"

"Stop!"

Elisedd rose from the table, knocking the delicate rose teacups to the ground, the china shattering on impact. Elisedd waved her great hand and the table disappeared, as did the benches and the broken dishes. Jamie found himself on the ground, too stunned to care. The young wood elves clustered together, watching with rapt eyes, their sharpened teeth bared. Feidlimid fell back, and as he tried to stand, Elisedd held out her ebony hand, the skin twinkling with a thousand night stars. Feidlimid was caught in an invisible grip that he struggled against, but he was unable to move.

"Enough!" Elisedd bellowed. "You brought such a one as can destroy our entire kind! You should have removed him straight away, but instead you listened to the fatum. You brought him here. You have put us all in danger! I have no more use for you."

With that, Elisedd made a sweeping motion with her hand, and Feidlimid's slender neck split in two. Jamie shrieked and shrunk back against the wall, Bilbo cowering in his hair. From the split there was no blood, not that Jamie expected any—instead, a putrid gray sludge bubbled. Jamie watched as Feidlimid's already tiny form dried up, the gray sludge seeping into the dirt floor.

"Drink my children, before it's too late," Elisedd said softly.

With that, the young wood elves descended onto Feidlimid's rapidly disappearing body, their sharpened teeth tearing into his skin, lapping up the life that flowed forth. It smelled of ash and things long buried. Jamie stifled a scream, squeezed his eyes shut, and covered his face, searching for something familiar, anything: Momma singing, Daddy typing on his computer, the sound of grown-up television while Jamie played in the bathtub with his plastic dinosaurs. He clung to these memories, all the while horribly aware that he was as far away as he could be from that world. He pictured his parents—how long had he been gone? Had it been months? Years? Were they still looking for him? He tried to remember the feel of Momma's fingers in his hair, the bear hugs from Daddy that knocked out his breath. Nothing could cover the stench of the dying wood elf. Jamie opened his eyes, and there was nearly nothing left, only the stain of what had once been on the dirt floor. The young wood elves were searching the ground for any missed drops, their faces black with filth.

Elisedd stared straight at Jamie. The dark storm clouds had passed, and the clouds that floated through her eyes were soft, her voice a perfectly pitched river, gentle and rhythmic.

"It's time to go, Jamie. I will give you something to cover yourself—if the Lairdbalor sees you as a gift from us, then we are likely to gain his favor. Morcant will see you to the door."

Jamie looked around wildly. Morcant bared her gray-stained teeth, the shimmering gold of her skin muted with Feidlimid's remains. Jamie shivered.

Elisedd held out a small bundle of clothes.

"The last one of your kind left these here. He didn't need them anymore, did he, children?" The young wood elves snickered again, the sound winding its way around the oddly lit cavern. Jamie didn't move. "Take them, child—they are the only comfort we can offer."

With shaking hands, Jamie took the bundle blindly. Choking back his helpless misery, he pulled off his torn, tight sweatpants and replaced them with soft leather riding pants, a coarse dark-brown tunic, and matching boots that miraculously fit his enormous feet. As horrible as everything was, Jamie was relieved not to have to face whatever was outside in his underwear. Bilbo settled in on his shoulder, and Jamie stood.

"Enough then. Morcant, take him to the threshold, close the path, and instruct the bats to keep watch." Elisedd turned to Jamie. "Your time will not be long, I am afraid. I must thank you for your company. You were very polite about that tea— wretched stuff."

Jamie could only nod. The stain that was all that remained of Feidlimid had shrunk to a few discolored spots on the ground. Morcant wiped her face on the back of her hand, walked to the opening where Jamie and Feidlimid had entered, and looked back, her luminous gold eyes wide.

"Come, then," she said, before disappearing down the corridor.

As they walked, Jamie stared at the back of Morcant's head. He realized how naïve he had been. It wasn't a "she" any more than Feidlimid had been a "he." They were things, monsters; they were the stuff of the nightmares that woke him from his bed screaming. They were the creaks on the floor in impossibly long nights; they were the doubts that crept up in the corner of his mind, the ones that told him he was never safe, that there was no protection. Suibhne's book had been right, in a way, Jamie mused as they walked on. Humans do like to put things in their places, and he had been trying to see these creatures as humans like himself. He knew where they fit now, and it was far beyond the ways he knew of categorizing life. They were a part of the darkness, the somewhere beyond.

Morcant turned its head slightly, never breaking its gait.

"We're nearly there—that is, where I leave you. You should hope the Lairdbalor comes for you quickly. There are a million forms of misery in the woods, and each one of them can smell you, Jamie. Pray for it all to end quickly."

Jamie straightened his back. He was tired of fearing these monsters. If they were going to kill him, they would have done so back when Feidlimid was split in two. He was tired of their cryptic talk, their saucerlike eyes, and their way of never saying what it was they actually meant.

"I'm not afraid of you any longer, wood elf, so you can stop trying to scare me."

Morcant chuckled, a low, dark sound.

"Such bravery—so sad it's to be so short-lived."

"What happens when you leave the path?" Jamie asked boldly.

"What?" Morcant seemed genuinely startled. It stopped walking for a moment and then hurried forward. "What are you asking, human?"

"Mallorie, the beetle fairy, she said you can't leave the path—ticked Feidlimid off something wicked. Why can't you leave the path? What happens to you? Is it like what happened to Feidlimid—who you all killed just for doing what he had been told to do?"

"Killed. You know nothing of our world, child," Morcant growled. "What happens to us if we leave the path is none of your concern. You are meant to feed the one who stalks our world. You are food for the night, nothing more."

Jamie could see the light from the forest up ahead, and he was seized with an impulse born from the knowledge that he was likely to die no matter what he did. As they approached the light, Morcant raised its hand, and with one graceful flick of its wrist ripped open the invisible skin that separated the path from the forest. Jamie knew he was to walk through the opening, and then it would be sealed. Instead of complying, he took a deep breath, felt for Bilbo, who was holding tight to his hair, and ran as fast as he could straight at Morcant. He barreled into the creature with the full force of his tall new body. Unsteady on its feet, the wood elf teetered at the edge of the tear, its large golden eyes terrified. It reached to Jamie, but he pushed as hard as he could with both hands, and the wood elf flew out into the forest. Jamie stepped through after it, the act of leaving the wood elves' lair a relief. He smelled the familiar scents of the forest around him and felt safe for a moment, a small smile playing on his lips at the absurdity of the feeling.

SEVEN

JAMIE looked around him. He knew Morcant had to be close—most likely it had run off or turned to a puddle of gray sludge on the forest floor. Behind him, the tear remained. Elisedd won't like that, Jamie thought wickedly. He felt giddy, like he'd had too much sugar. If he was really going to die out here, if this was really it, then he wasn't going to spend any more time crying and wetting himself. He was going to be a hero, like Harry Potter or Bilbo Baggins or even King David from the children's Jewish Bible that Momma had read to him. He'd liked the Bible stories, but when he'd asked Momma what smiting was, she'd stuttered a bit and told him it meant to be in a lot of trouble. Jamie had an idea now that she had been too afraid to really tell him. He couldn't blame her; after all, he had been seven. Whatever smiting was, he was pretty sure it was happening to him right now, and he was rather glad he didn't know what it was when he was seven.

"Strictly speaking, you're still seven."

The lyrical voice buzzed in his ear, the tiny wings creating a breeze in the still air.

Jamie's heart lightened. "Mallorie! You're still here!" Aside from Bilbo, he had never been so happy to see a creature alive.

"I am—in there a long time, you were. I didn't go too far, but I heard you crashing about over here and thought I'd come have a look. Looks like you have yourself some new coverings. I'll never understand the appeal, but good on ya."

Mallorie buzzed around his head, landing on a stick right at eye level.

"Mallorie, look." Jamie paused, wondering how to explain. "Feidlimid, he . . . I mean . . . he's dead. The Elder, Elisedd, killed Feidlimid, and the others drank his blood, or whatever that was that came out of him."

Mallorie cocked her tiny head, beady eyes unchanging. "I could've told the wood elf that'd happen. Never hear it from me though. They call us 'fatums,' so high and mighty they think they are."

"It's not just that—I'm marked. They sent me out here—the Lairdbalor—they said I'm marked!"

The words tumbled out in a jumble. Jamie knew he wasn't making much sense, and now everything the wood elves had said seemed a bit ridiculous.

"It's not ridiculous," Mallorie interjected. "They're quite right. He will find you, but he'll have his fun with them first. That's the part that they miss—he loves a good game, he does. It buys you a bit of time, though not much."

"You mean, there's still a way?" Jamie asked in a small voice. He reached up to where Bilbo perched on his shoulder and stroked the rat's back.

"All gloom and doom, aren't they?" Mallorie chirped. "Abandon all hope, no way through, don't leave the path or the Lairdbalor will find you." She paused. "Any of this sound familiar?"

Jamie nodded, his impending death feeling not quite so desperate.

"There's still a way," he repeated.

"You still might die," Mallorie chirped. "But then again, so might I, so might us all. No matter in worrying so about it. Come, the wood elf was right about one thing—you're best off with the Burg." She took off from the branch and flew into the woods and then turned, hovering in midair. "You coming?"

Jamie paused, an unsettled pit in his stomach.

"Why are you helping me? What's in it for you? The wood elves said I'm marked, they said he'd come for me, that I would be food for the night. Why are you here?"

Mallorie laughed, a lilting sound that echoed off the leaves, a sound far too loud to have come from her tiny body. Jamie reached up defensively to Bilbo, who had already scurried into his hair. Jamie could feel him at the nape of his neck.

The laugh became a roar. The bright colors of the beetle fairy's wings lost their light and became as black as the night around them. The dot of bright color and light shrunk until it sank into the darkness, and only the laugh remained, now a cackle, surrounding them, swirling like a wind. Jamie thought he understood now what a hurricane was—the gale force winds wrapped around his head, wailing deafeningly in his ears. He fell to his knees, clutching his hands to his ears. The sound increased in fury and then broke in a snap. Jamie was left alone, Bilbo clinging to his neck, and only a soft breeze rustled the leaves.

Jamie, shaking too hard to stand, leaned his back against the nearest tree, a cold sweat collecting on his face. Bilbo crawled out from his hair and gently perched on Jamie's knee, staring him in the face. Jamie looked at the little rat, the tawny fur fastidiously clean.

"What are we to do?" Jamie asked in a whisper.

Bilbo stared back, equally lost. Suddenly all the bravado of pushing Morcant into the forest, the grand talk back in the Holding—all of it left Jamie feeling like he was about to vomit. He wished more than anything that the real Mallorie would show up; she'd lead them through the forest to the Burg. Whoever the Burg were, they had to be better than the wood elves. Jamie shuddered and looked around. Morcant was somewhere out here with them. It had seemed like such a big idea, revenge—a way to show that he wasn't just food for a monster, that he had a real bite. Now he was left with the reality that Morcant was somewhere in the forest, in whatever form their kind took when off the path. Jamie remembered Elisedd had told Jamie he was lucky he did not know what they really looked like.

"Oh, Bilbo, what have I done?" Jamie murmured.

Bilbo crawled back up Jamie's arm and took his position on his shoulder, leaned over, and gently bit Jamie's ear.

"I can't, Bilbo—I don't know where to go."

He looked at the tear in the skeen, the gaping gash between the wood elves' path and the forest. He didn't know where to go, but he had an unmistakable urge to get as far away from that path as possible. He stood up quickly, fighting the instinct to flee into the woods head-on.

"Something's here, Bilbo, something's here," he murmured.

Jamie took one step away from the tear, fighting the urge to break into a full run. All he needed was to fall down another very long hill and break his legs. Walk slowly, he thought as he took another deliberate step. But a roar from the wood elves' path broke Jamie's control. A cloud of debris flew through the tear, and Jamie heard screams. Once, when he was very small, Momma and Daddy brought home a bunny rabbit. They set the tiny bunny up in a hutch in the backyard. Jamie remembered being too little to even pet the creature without help. Sometime in the night, Jamie had been awoken by a scream. A raccoon had broken into the hutch and ate the bunny alive, and the tiny, helpless creature had screamed as it died. Jamie had never forgotten the sound of those screams, inhuman and full of the darkest desperation. He heard them in his nightmares; they echoed in his head. These were the screams he heard coming from the wood elves' path.

Fighting every instinct, Jamie stepped toward the chaos and looked through the tear. The Holding, so magnificent in the wood elves' estimation, had been flattened—the sticks and branches lay in disarray, and behind it, the mossy stone path continued on into the forest. None of the wood elves were in sight. As Jamie stared in disbelief at the flattened remains of the Holding, he saw the source of the screaming. Gray sludge, like that which had bubbled from Feidlimid's neck, seeped from under the wreckage. Jamie's stomach seized in a sickening turn as he realized the creatures had been crushed and the screaming, so like that of the dying bunny, had been theirs. He stepped away from the tear in the skeen, not sure what to do, what to feel. They had sent him out to be killed by the monsters of the forest, but as Jamie leaned against a tree to keep from passing out, he realized he was most likely the reason they were all dead. He kept hearing Elisedd's unearthly voice: he was marked, he stained their Holding with his blood. He did this, he was the reason they were dead. Jamie could still feel Suibhne's leaves on his foot, and he wondered if the book was in the wreckage—and what was in it. On his shoulder, Bilbo raked his tiny claws down Jamie's earlobe.

"I know, Bilbo, I know. I don't want to." Jamie craned his neck as far as he could to look at Bilbo. "I'm scared," he said simply.

Bilbo nuzzled his ear; Jamie leaned against the tree, the shaking in his legs subsiding bit by bit. If the book was indeed all about humans, maybe it had something in it about how he could get home. And what about Mallorie—except it hadn't been Mallorie, had it? Jamie looked around wildly.

"Mallorie! Mallorie!" he called out in vain, not caring who heard him. Since most of the creatures seemed to be able to read his thoughts anyhow, he figured shouting wouldn't much matter.

There was no answer from the forest, not even the chirp of night insects that usually filled the air back home. Jamie straightened his back; he could either wait here in the forest to die alongside the wood elves, or he could try everything he knew to get home. Holding his breath against the smell of ash and rust, he crossed back onto the path and walked across the decrepit remains of the wood elves' proud Holding. He hadn't been able to see the beauty of it, and Jamie wondered if that was because of his grown-up eyes or because it had never been beautiful. A grown-up would have lied and said it was, even though it all looked a mess of wood and dirt. It was a small comfort that he wasn't quite so big after all.

Jamie felt disconnected from his body, his senses on high alert. Every snap of the twigs under his feet, the stench in the dense air, it all rained down on him with no reprieve. Jamie's heart beat faster and faster. When that happened at home, Momma made him do breathing exercises, which as far as Jamie could see were designed to make him feel even dizzier. Momma said they would help him calm down. Jamie had never believed it, but in this moment—while he walked across the corpses of the wood elves, surely within sight of a creature that had marked him and followed him from his world to another—Jamie couldn't see the harm in trying. He breathed in, imagining a golden light filling up his chest. He held his breath like Momma had said to do, and then he let it go out his nose, imagining dark smoke rolling out his nostrils. His heart reacted by beating even faster. Jamie could feel it in his throat, threatening to break through the skin. Jamie had a wild thought: if he could push his way out of the wood elves' path, then what was to stop his heart from tearing through his throat, his red blood mixing with the silver-gray mud beneath his feet, his body deteriorating? Perhaps here, where time was fast and slow, it would disappear in a matter of hours; maybe it would take years. Jamie stopped, paralyzed by the musing. Bilbo bit his ear hard. Jamie yelped.

"Fine," he muttered and kept walking slowly forward, looking for anything that could be Suibhne's impossibly large book or impossibly small pouch.

What if the Lairdbalor were here right now? It had to be near; certainly it was what had caused this. What else could be responsible? Jamie shut his eyes, trying to block out his thoughts, trying to slow his racing heart. Even if it were here, what could Jamie possibly do about it? The dark musing actually made the palpitations that threatened to crack his ribs slow a bit. Jamie opened his eyes and stopped in his tracks. On his shoulder, Bilbo turned in nervous circles.

"Why did the wood elves bring me this far in the first place, Bilbo?" Jamie asked softly. Something else had to be at play, something other than just the Lairdbalor.

"I should already be dead," Jamie said aloud, the realization washing over him with giddy confidence, like he'd felt before he'd shoved Morcant into the forest. "I should already be dead!" he shouted to the dark sky. Bilbo nipped his ear, but Jamie ignored the little rat's warning. "Come and get me! You know exactly where I am! C'mon!"

Jamie felt wild. He let out a mad giggle and spun in circles like he'd done when he was little, back when he was really seven and not this overgrown thing with too many thoughts in his head. He fell to his knees on the rubble and started digging in the wreckage, looked for anything that resembled Suibhne's pouch or the book itself. Maybe the book was in shreds; maybe it was a puddle of gray mud. He didn't care what happened. He felt the exhaustion of the long walk down the path, the nervousness, the terror, all of it weighing down on his chest. *Peine forte et dure.* The phrase popped into his brain. He couldn't remember why he knew it— something Momma had told him, maybe? No, it was a brand-new thought, a piece of knowledge all his own, something he hadn't learned from Momma or Daddy, something that was all his own. But from where? Jamie stopped digging, placed both filthy hands on the stones and twigs, and closed his eyes. He cleared his mind, and from the darkness he could see the impossibly large book. It lay open, and on the page the words were written. *Peine forte et dure: a method of extracting the truth from a human in which heavy objects such as stones are placed on the chest.* Jamie opened his eyes, the invisible stones on his own chest weighing him down as he began to dig, the vision of the book driving him forward. As he dug, his hands bleeding from a thousand tiny cuts, he felt the forest just outside the path. He saw how thin the skeen of the path really was, and he heard the buzzing of the forest creatures. The noise was deafening—Jamie couldn't believe it had been silent before. In his mind's eye, he could see the book buried a foot or so below where he was digging, stained with Suibhne's gray mud, and it held all the answers to all things human.

Jamie threw rubble in a mad cloud around him. Dust filled the air, and Jamie was fascinated to see it trapped by the skeen. The air inside the wood elves' path, he realized, was its own entity; the nonporous skeen prevented even the air of the forest from entering the space. Of course, it was entering it now—the tear through which Jamie had shoved Morcant swayed in the night breeze. An odd thought hit Jamie. He stopped digging and looked up at the sky. Even though it was partially obscured by greenery,

Jamie was pretty sure there was no moon here, only stars. Jamie remembered Feidlimid pulling one down and tossing it like a pebble; it had been the single most magical thing he'd ever seen. He felt like he'd lived a hundred years in this seemingly endless night. Why wasn't the sky lightening? Shouldn't daybreak happen soon? Jamie had spent hours and hours in this world, and he'd walked for what seemed like an eternity—surely it was near dawn by now. There was, however, no sign that night would ever end.

The wood elves' book called to him again, and a stabbing pain behind his eyes directed him to the disrupted earth. Jamie tore at the ground, pulling up masses of sticks and twigs. Finally, a corner of the wood-bark cover was visible. As Jamie had predicted, it was covered in the ash-scented mud. He pulled the impossibly large book free and gingerly wiped it as clean as possible with his hand and whatever leaves he could find in the wreckage. He sat, staring at his find, not daring to breathe.

"It's not your fault, you know," a voice twittered in his ear.

Jamie jumped, stifling a scream. Bilbo ran down Jamie's arm and under his tunic. Jamie felt his scratchy paws on his hip and instinctively cupped his hand over the little rat, blocking him from whatever might have found them.

"It's not," the voice insisted. "Truth be told, the woodies had this coming for a long time. They were using you—big lot of good it did them, eh?"

"Mallorie?" Jamie asked.

The beetle fairy landed on his shoulder. Jamie craned his neck to see it, gave up, and then looked down at the sodden book.

"You sound awfully surprised! I said I'd wait, didn't I?" Mallorie replied, her voice slightly annoyed.

"I saw . . . " Jamie started, unsure of how to proceed with his question. "I thought I saw you right as I left, but it wasn't, I mean, I think it wasn't . . . It, whatever it was, got darker and darker, all the way to black, and then it disappeared."

Mallorie crawled around the cover of the book, inspecting the surface.

"Bogle. It was a bogle you saw, it was." She tittered. "They are quite upsetting, but at the end of the day, love, rather harmless. Well, in this world anyway—in your world, they're actually rather dangerous. Here they can only prattle on in their way, and when they tire of their game, they move on."

"What are they in my world?" Jamie asked, fascinated even though he knew he didn't have time for all this.

"Oh, what do you call them? Ballybogs? Is that right? Sound familiar?" Mallorie asked.

Jamie shook his head. Mallorie perked up.

"I know—in your world you call them the bogeyman. Not a creature I'd want to ever see. Suck the marrow from your bones they will, and have for many of your kind, especially the young ones."

"But the bogeyman is a story. He's not real. It's just a way to scare kids . . . "

"It's good to be scared, Jamie," Mallorie interrupted. "And make no doubt about it, the bogeyman is very real. Terrible things happen to children in your world, even more so than here in ours. Terrible things. The bogeyman doesn't take any mind to the form he chooses—it preys on the moments of quiet, looking for any crack, any break in the mist. All the times when something happens to a child that no one can make sense of, when there is no one to blame, no reason for the harm, he lives in those moments."

Jamie absently stroked Bilbo through the rough fabric of his tunic. Last year, a little girl on the next block was stung by a wasp while playing in her front yard. Jamie had been stung three times last summer; on him, the stings swelled up and hurt like the devil, but Momma put baking soda and vinegar on the spots and they went away. The little girl on the next block fell down dead before her dad even knew what had happened. Momma had told Jamie the girl was allergic. They had brought over a bag of lunch meat and sandwich rolls for her parents, who looked half dead themselves, as people milled about their house, dropping off bags of food and vases of flowers. Jamie had not understood what the lunch meat and flowers were supposed to do for them—they obviously needed everyone to leave, because no one likes to cry when people can see. Jamie was only seven, albeit a rather large seven, but he at least understood that. The bogeyman. Was it that? Or just a wasp?

"Just a wasp?" Mallorie trilled. "Ever wonder how that wasp found that little girl? Some of your kind go their entire lives without ever being stung by a wasp, but that wasp found the one little girl who was liable to drop dead before anyone could look up to see she'd fallen. That's the bogeyman, love."

"The bogle in the forest—it's not like that in this world?"

Mallorie laughed. "Not by half. Some things, here in this world, are far more dangerous than in yours, and some are the other way 'round. The bogles are the other way 'round. In your world, that little forest bogle you saw could be a fever that takes a child's sight or a too-large bit of dinner, waiting to lodge in a child's throat. But here, love, it's distilled a bit. Don't pay it any nevermind."

Jamie looked at the book.

"Is the way to get home in this book?" he asked the beetle fairy.

"I'm sure I don't know," Mallorie replied. "But I'd not read it here if I were you. The ones who did this are sure to come back—perhaps for this book you found, perhaps not—and I'm sure I wouldn't want to be around when they did."

Jamie nodded. The beetle fairy was right—he needed to go back through the skeen and read the wood elves' book in a place that wasn't thick with the acrid smell of ash and burning rubber. He stood slowly, his hands burning with a thousand cuts from his mad scramble at the floor. Bilbo scurried up his chest and resurfaced through the neck of Jamie's tunic, resuming his post on Jamie's shoulder. Mallorie buzzed back to the tear, waiting.

Jamie paused and considered the little beetle fairy for a minute. "How do I know you're not a bogle?"

Mallorie laughed, a natural trilling sound.

"I suppose you don't. I suppose everything I just told you could be a lie. But you're starting to feel things for yourself now—you've been here long enough, after all. You tell me, am I a danger to you?"

Jamie considered the question. He could hear every sound in the forest, the hum of a thousand wings, the scratching of countless insect legs on the leaves and undergrowth.

"I suppose you're all right," he said simply and followed the beetle fairy back through the tear.

"What happened to Morcant?" Jamie asked as he crossed the threshold into the forest.

"Oh, that?" Mallorie buzzed circles around his head. "You'll see soon enough. Remember what I said about the wood elves and time?"

Jamie nodded.

"Well, let's put it this way—that path is the only thing that keeps the woodies safe from themselves. In any case, nothing to worry about yet. You did a fine job of malafoostering, although considering the woodie would be a puddle of mud if you hadn't, I'd consider you two even."

Jamie took a few steps into the forest. He felt a million years away from the moment, not so long ago, that he fell down the very long hill. It wasn't just his overgrown body—his eyes saw things differently, his ears took in the sound around him more sharply, the colors looked richer. The air was tinged with all different scents: the ash and mold from the wreckage of the Holding, but beyond that, he could smell mint, lavender, and the earthy scent of the forest floor. He looked at the book for a minute and then tucked it under his arm and looked at Mallorie.

"If we should get some distance from this place, which is the best way to go?"

"Depends on what you want," the beetle fairy replied in a lyrical voice, flying in circles around him. "Through there"—Mallorie flew to Jamie's right—"you'll find the caves, but I don't know if you want to find the caves. Through there"—the beetle fairy looped to the left—"you'll find water, but I don't know if you want to find water."

Jamie sighed and pointed straight ahead.

"How about there?"

Mallorie landed on a branch at Jamie's eye level.

"Well, that's in-between—don't know if you want to find the in-between."

"Yep, that's exactly what I want," Jamie answered, assured he wasn't going to get a straight answer from the beetle fairy.

"All right then," Mallorie answered and started to buzz away.

Jamie had begun to follow, when a low chanting came from the direction of the wood elves' path. He turned around as Mallorie came shooting back.

"I suspect I know who that'll be," Mallorie whispered. "Get down, for sage's sake! Don't move. Tell your rat to stay still, hold your breath."

Jamie dropped to his knees and crouched behind a large green fern as best he could. Bilbo dove back under his tunic, scratching Jamie's chest as he clambered down to his hip. Through the tear in the skeen, Jamie saw a procession of tall figures, even taller than he was now, wearing long dark capes and cream-colored tunics. They walked silently in a single line, and although their lips didn't move, a low chanting emanated from them all the same. Jamie didn't understand the words, but it sounded eerily like the recording of monks that his teacher liked to play as the class practiced typing the alphabet. In class, it always made Jamie feel calm, and it did the same here. He knew he should be afraid—there was probably good reason that Mallorie had told him to be still and stay unseen—but Jamie felt no threat from these creatures. From his shadowed spot in the forest, he glimpsed their faces, each one identical. Decidedly masculine, they had pale skin that matched the glow from the stars in the sky. Their eyes, brows, and hair were inky black. The same neatly manicured beard lined each of their jawbones, leaving the cheeks bare. Some carried black iron lanterns with candles lit within, and some did not. They passed the tear, marching into the wreckage of the wood elves' Holding.

None looked in his direction. Although it was impossible not to see the tear in the skeen, the strange figures seemed to be focused on the path. After the last one passed, Jamie waited a moment before letting out the breath he had been holding. The chanting disappeared into the distance. He looked at Mallorie questioningly. The tiny wings buzzed around his head, and Jamie had to suppress the urge to swat at the air.

"We'd best go—they'll be back, and they were probably looking for that." Mallorie swooped down and circled the book under Jamie's arm. "They're good at finding what they're looking for."

Jamie jumped up, his heart racing again.

"Then why not leave it here? Last thing I need is someone chasing me—someone else, that is. I'll just look to see if what I need is in here, and I'll throw it back through the tear for those . . . whatever they are."

"Dwarves. They're dwarves. They came for the dead—they always come for the dead. This book belongs to their world now, but you seem to think you need it. Quite the pickle, quite." Mallorie landed on a dark-green leaf and shook out tiny wings.

Jamie crouched on the ground as Bilbo emerged from the neck of his tunic. Jamie tried to open the book; there was a strange resistance, as though the bark cover was fighting the motion. Jamie looked up questioningly, but Mallorie offered no explanation. Finally, by bracing himself against the trunk of a small evergreen, Jamie pried the cover from the pages. As it tore away, it emitted a terrible cry, like the screams he had heard as the wood elves died, the cry of a tortured bunny, helpless to fight its own demise.

Jamie shivered but continued. He would take one look, see if the book contained the answer he sought, and then he'd throw it back where it came from. If the Lairdbalor was coming for him, he didn't need any further attention. The scream from the cover subsided to a whimper. Jamie looked frantically at the first page.

It was perfectly blank. He could see where the pulp of plants and flowers had been pressed to make the paper, but no words or letters appeared. Jamie's stomach sank. He flipped further and further into the tome. Nothing on any of the pages. He looked frantically at Mallorie, who stayed perched on the leaf, tiny black eyes unreadable.

"It's useless!" Jamie cried. "But I saw them reading from it. I saw writing in it in the Holding. I saw Suibhne write in it, I *saw* it."

"Huh," Mallorie trilled. "Quite the pickle. If you throw it back for the dwarves, you might lose the only chance you have to get home—if, in fact, that's even in that book. If you keep it, you might be taken by the dwarves even before the other has a chance to come looking, and be assured, he is looking. Quite the pickle."

Jamie stood. "Morcant, the wood elf, can read it. She read it before. How do I find her?"

"I'm sure I don't know. I wasn't here to see her ejected from their oh-so-important path. No idea which direction the woodie went. Surprised at how fast it was, all things considered . . . " Mallorie replied tauntingly.

In the far distance, Jamie heard the dwarves' chanting. They were coming back. For a split second, he saw the scene as he would have before the fall down the very long hill. Dwarves were supposed to be short, ugly creatures that lived in mines; empty books were entirely useless, especially those void of pictures, and even more especially those that screamed in pain when opened. He was talking to a beetle and his stuffed rat was frantically cleaning his previously plush face. Jamie felt disconnected from his body, as though he were static that hovered near his form but didn't actually inhabit it. He took another look at the book, the pages as empty as before. The chanting was getting louder, and he was certain the dwarves would not walk past the tear in the skeen this time. He was also sure that he needed to find Morcant, and he was positive that he couldn't stay where he was.

"Mallorie, what's safer? Water or caves? Quick!" Jamie demanded.

"No more in-between, is it then?" Mallorie flew to the left. "I'd take my chances with the Asrai if I were you. Water might mask your smell, which is considerable."

"Fine," Jamie muttered and ran after the beetle fairy, his heart in his throat.

EIGHT

THE forest was thicker than it appeared, not that it mattered to Mallorie. Jamie lost sight of the little beetle fairy after a while and just blindly plunged forward, a new collection of tiny scratches and scrapes collecting all over his face and hands. He was immensely grateful for the clothing that the wood elves had given him—at least he didn't have to go through this in the remains of his shrunken, little-boy sweatpants. As he half-ran, half-walked onward, Jamie's mind returned to the scene in the Holding. The Lairdbalor would be after him, they'd said, and according to them, Jamie should be dead already. Looking around at the thick growth, Jamie realized that any number of things could be watching, stalking, waiting for him, and he would have no idea. There was absolutely no way to safeguard himself. Maybe the Lairdbalor was playing with him, waiting for him to get good and tired; maybe the Lairdbalor was an entirely different kind of monster. Jamie wondered what had been responsible for destroying the Holding. He had figured it was the Lairdbalor, but the farther he walked, the more he wondered. What was he to know about who was after whom?

He paused against a tree, out of breath, his muscles and torn skin aching. He thought of the fake Mallorie—what had the beetle fairy called it? A bogle? He closed his eyes and saw the face of the little girl, the one who died from the wasp sting. He remembered her quite well despite the fact that he really had been seven, actually six, when she had died, and he had never played with her. Her name was Chloe, which sounded like a fancy type of cloud to Jamie. If Mallorie was right, the very same thing that killed Chloe existed in both worlds, but here it was an annoyance, a trick. If he ever made it back home, he wondered if anyone would ever believe him about this. Momma had cried over Chloe, which confused Jamie quite a lot. She didn't know Chloe at all—she didn't even know her name, she'd had to ask Jamie. Jamie didn't understand grown-up crying. They seemed to cry over things they couldn't see more than the things they could.

"Are you coming?" Mallorie buzzed in Jamie's ear. The tiny voice held an edge of annoyance.

"Yes, I'm just—"

Jamie was cut off by rustling behind them. He shoved the book under his other arm and ran as fast as he could through the forest. Bilbo clung to Jamie's hair, the familiar pull a comfort. Mallorie's wings whirred near his head. An unexpected tree branch jutted out in front of him. Jamie tried to duck but grazed the top of his head; blood dripped down the side of his face, its warm stickiness an altogether too-familiar sensation. His vision went black and then turned into fuzzy gray dots. Jamie lunged forward, hoping for anything to break his fall. To his surprise, he felt a wave of soft silk, as though he were running through a clothesline hung with freshly laundered sheets. His body relaxed, but as his vision cleared he saw he was falling, not into a pile of soft laundry, but face-first into a bramble patch. Jamie screamed, an inhuman sound that echoed the cries of the dying wood elves. An absurd thought raced through his head that he was becoming part elf, part boy. He covered his face with the book, holding it in front of him as a sort of shield; at his neck, the pressure of Bilbo's grip released, and Jamie knew the little rat must have jumped away. Good, he thought. Bilbo shouldn't have to go like this. It all happened in the smallest fraction of a second, yet the moment seemed to move like one running through water.

As the first bramble reached his eyes, Jamie snapped awake. He was no longer falling—he was lying on his back on a concrete slab.

His clothes were gone, and he felt icy roughness against his bare skin. His embarrassment was only a secondary response; the first was utter paralysis. Jamie tried to move his arms and found them bound to the concrete surface, by what means he could not tell. The sky was still pitch black, but now he could see stars, more stars than he ever thought possible. They seemed to be chanting to him, low and soft, a rhythmic cadence. With a sick drop in his stomach, Jamie realized that the book was gone. It had perhaps held the only way to get home, and now it was gone. And if Jamie wasn't mistaken, the impossibly plentiful stars were getting closer and closer, and louder. He could make out a word here and there. He remembered what the wood elf had said about understanding and wondered if it were true in all ways of life. If he let go of his inability to understand, maybe he would simply start to know. The thought was so nebulous that it seemed to float out of his head and up to join the ever-encroaching stars.

The steady beat of the chant was closer still. Jamie heard a few words.

SEISMIC CAREFUL WONDROUS CARROT SATCHEL PEANUT

It didn't make any sense, but Jamie had spent enough time at the bottom of the very large hill for that to no longer be alarming. He tried to move his arms but found them still bound flat against the cold slab on which he lay. In a growing panic, he thrashed his legs like a dying fish on land only to discover them in the same plight. He stopped abruptly as the chanting grew louder, the low voices melodic and synchronized. His limbs went involuntarily limp; he tried to move, but his muscles and joints became heavier and heavier, as though pressed by a heavy pillow, the oxygen slowly being pressed out of his lungs. Jamie's breath was quick and shallow. He fought the urge to panic—not because he thought that staying calm would benefit him, but because there was no place for his panic to go. He knew instinctively that, should he allow himself to really feel that panic, he would choke on his own breath and, like Feidlimid, dissolve to nothing more than a puddle of gray mud, the remains of a life.

ALACRITY DIDACTIC ELIXIR ENIGMA CONFOUNDED
CONFOUNDED CONFOUNDED

Jamie opened his mouth and tried to cry out, but his voice was frozen like the rest of his body.

CONFOUNDED CONFOUNDED CONFOUNDED

Louder and louder still. Jamie looked around madly—he saw the green cover of the forest, the glow of the stars beyond. But as he stared straight into the night, the blackness began to overtake the green. With barely contained terror, Jamie realized he was growing blind. His vision narrowed rapidly to a pinhole in each eye, and then it was gone, replaced with velvet blackness, complete and terrifying in its finality.

CONFOUNDED CONFOUNDED CONFOUNDED

An icy point poked into Jamie's gut—a fingernail or perhaps the blade of a very sharp knife. Jamie buckled away from the sensation, lightheaded with fear. There was a sickly, warm sensation of fresh blood flowing from his belly. The icy point continued upward toward his chest, slicing him up the center as it went. Jamie felt no pain, only the pin trickle pressure, the blood gurgling up over the sides of the split. His skin fell to either side, the night air rushing into his open stomach cavity. He ceased to breathe. The utter terror was too unreal, too horrible—his chest ached from air deprivation, but the sickly sweet flood continued to pour from his body.

CONFOUNDED CONFOUNDED CONFOUNDED

The chant was now so loud that it rang in Jamie's ears; all the night sounds of the forest were drowned out in the din. Still the icy point continued upward, clear to his sternum. With alarming clarity, a multitude of light points of pressure prickled amidst the flow of blood from his gut. With even more horror, he felt his insides untangled and drawn out of his abdomen. He felt the resistance of organs long rested in their rightful places, the tear of the cartilage as they pulled away, the blood continuing to pour from his body.

I should be dead, Jamie thought as he gasped for breath, his body lighter as his kidneys were pulled from his body and dropped onto the forest floor. I should be dead, I should be dead, I should be dead.

"*Foisich!*"

The tenor voice rang through the night. It seemed to come from everywhere all at once. Immediately, the icy pressure released from Jamie's gut. The chanting cut off like when the needle on Daddy's old record player suddenly ripped away from its target groove. The ebb of blood ceased, and the sticky warmth dissipated. His skin became tighter and tighter still as the wound closed; Jamie wondered what had become of his insides. The blackness opened to a pinhole and then widened back to the starry night sky.

"*Folbh!*"

The voice had the tone of a brilliantly polished brass instrument. Jamie's muscles and joints regained feeling, the pressure lightened. His voice returned, and Jamie let loose with a wild cry, the sum total of his terror.

"*Clos*, little one, *clos. Gabh d'anail.*"

The resonant tone moved around him like a swarm of insects. Jamie's panic subsided, his lungs filled once again with air, and he gratefully breathed in and out.

"*Cus nas fhearr*, little one—now open your eyes."

Jamie started to protest that his eyes were open, but suddenly he realized that he was still blind. The night sky split open, a seam unraveling down the middle, the forest and stars falling to either side like a drapery pulled aside to let the light in. Jamie squinted from the glare of a brilliant light beyond the façade—an apparent sun, although he felt no heat. The restraints on his arms and legs released, and in shock he pulled himself into a fetal position.

"*Tugainn. No feagal*, little one, *no feagal. Slàn*, now *tugainn.*"

Somewhere, deep in his body, Jamie understood the strange words. He sat up, the fear that had so paralyzed him washing away. He stood and reached for the golden sky. In an instant, was pulled upward, like a magnet flowed from his fingertips. He was pulled through the remains of the night forest, away from wood elves and beetle fairies and impossibly long hills from which there was no going home. He felt warmth on his face and forgot to worry about Bilbo or Mallorie or the remains of his body that lay on the forest floor. The gnawing panic that had encompassed his heart melted away—his parents, his overgrown arms and legs, his too-long hair, his mind that knew too much too fast, his eyes that had already seen far too much to be seven years old. Jamie didn't care in this moment what it was that spoke the strange language or what had split the world in half, revealing this golden atmosphere. The air was thin and crisp on his face. I must be outside the entire world, Jamie thought as he sailed still farther up, and farther still. He stopped abruptly, floating in the light, his weight perfectly suspended. Jamie looked around—he was wearing his clothes again; maybe they had been there all along, he couldn't say. He laughed aloud. He'd never felt so light.

A nervous child—that was what the doctor called him. Momma had taken him to a lot of doctors, and they had called him a "nervous child." Momma and Daddy had begged him to tell them what he was worried about, why he worried. Jamie had no answers—it was like asking someone why they swallowed their food or how they blinked their eyes. Jamie's worries were as much a part of him as his breath. He lived with a weight on his chest built of a thousand what-ifs and not-so-sure impossibilities. He lived every moment expecting what seemed to be inevitable; he slept every night playing out a thousand scenarios. He was a nervous child, but not here—here he was free.

The weight that wrapped his chest in a chronic snare unbuckled and fell away. He watched as a thousand miniscule, angry black flies flew from his head, squeezing through the pores in his skin, each taking with it a what-if and not-so-sure impossibility. He breathed out a cloud of regrets, moments he had held in for so long, unspent consequences that he had waited to come to fruition every night, the stuff of his nightmares. The boy with the melted face smiled back at him in the golden space, his face whole, his ruined eyes intact. He looked peaceful. Behind him Chloe appeared, but not with her face bulging with poison from the wasp sting, not with her tongue swollen and her soft child's skin discolored and bruised from the internal strain of death. She appeared behind the boy, her golden-red hair glowing, her skin a perfect cream, her eyes bright. She smiled. Jamie smiled back. Tears poured down his face, and he was free, free from all the horror.

I must be dead, he thought. The idea was not at all unpleasant. The boy nodded encouragingly. Chloe sailed slowly forward until she was inches from Jamie's face. Her bright green eyes were far too adult for her body. She leaned forward and kissed Jamie on his forehead. Her lips were cold as ice, and as she pulled away, the icy spot stayed, strong as when she was touching him. She stared hard at Jamie and gave him a small nod. With that she turned and took the hand of the boy, the boy who looked so like Jamie had once, back when he had been truly seven. Together, the two figures floated away until they were nothing but particles of the light.

"*Pràmh*, little one, *tùrsach*. It's time to wake up."

NINE

JAMIE jolted upward. He lay on the forest floor, his eyes stinging. "Mallorie!" he cried out, but no answer came. "Bilbo! Bilbo!"

He looked around frantically, the weight of worry back tighter than before, threatening to choke him. No answer, no little rat. Jamie pulled himself to sitting, the frustration in his heart and mind almost too much to bear. He let the tears flooding his eyes fall. They carried the sting with them, and he didn't care about being thought a crybaby, or anything for that matter. He wanted home, he wanted the golden sky, he wanted to be free, he wanted quiet from the noise in his head. He looked up. The night was dissipating, and in its place a pale sunrise leaked through the forest cover. It illuminated a stone path—not like the wood elves' path, though, not like that at all. Jamie couldn't really explain why they were so different; he simply knew they were. Wiping his cheeks with his filthy hand, he stood and started walking, a dogged determination driving his steps. He was tired of being scared, he was tired of the chokehold that threatened to stop his breath at times, and he was overall tired, so very tired. He heard a humming, the same brassy tenor. It was low at first, the melody like a story that Jamie had been told once and then forgotten—the stuff of which lives on the edge of waking and sleep, when dreams take over and twist reality just enough to make it its own nightmare, never knowing what is real and what is not.

Jamie walked carefully along the path, making sure to step only on the stones. He couldn't have explained to anyone else why this mattered, but this one small act of control made his heart slow and his breath deepen. He saw a small cottage in the near distance, shrouded by shadows and things that grew only in the dark of the forest floor. The humming grew louder. The icy spot on his forehead where dead Chloe had kissed him stayed frozen still, the chill burrowing straight to his core. As he walked, Jamie pressed experimentally on his gut; the skin on his belly was taut, but his hand pressed all the way to his spine. The organs—his intestines, kidneys, liver, stomach—all were gone, torn out and abandoned. Jamie grew dizzy with horror; he pressed further, running his hand along his own spine. He pulled back, the icy patch on his forehead intensifying as he approached the cottage. The walls were made of dark wood bark, the thatched roof of dry grass. A small chimney spewed dark smoke into the morning light. Several small, thick-paned windows jutted from the surface like teeth. The domed door was a bit shorter than Jamie was now but would have been perfect for his seven-year-old self, he noted wryly.

He had no choice. His mind was blank, the coldness on his forehead the only indication that he existed at all. He reached for the shining golden doorknob, but before he could turn it, the door popped open. Jamie jumped back; his heart—one of his few remaining organs—felt like it was about to beat out of his chest. The inside of the cottage was something from a storybook. There was a stone fireplace on dark wooden floors. A smallish, round, dark wood table sat next to a stone-lined stovetop, where a kettle was ready to whistle. An evergreen cloth chair faced the fireplace, where some kind of nettles burned, their scent thick in the air. Jamie swallowed dryly as the chair shifted. Its occupant stood to face Jamie.

Jamie was hit with a tidal wave of realization. When you are faced with more horror than anyone thinks possible, there is a moment when all things become reality: the nightmares, the hopes, the fears, and the wonder. All things converge into one, culminating in a creature so great and terrible that it extends beyond your ability to fear it. Fear in itself is a hopeful act—it means that you still cling to the possibility of your own salvation; fear is the realization that this salvation might be out of your grasp. Still, though, you see it and fight for it. It is as much a part of your humanity as is love or sleep or one's unconscious ability to breathe. When we have truly seen the thing from which there is no escape, there is no role for fear.

Jamie realized all this and more as he stared at the creature before him. It stood as high as Jamie's waist, its gelatinous body barely encased in a filthy topcoat, at turns both ridiculous and terrible. Around the area where a neck might have been, a stained white scarf was loosely knotted. On its head an equally foul top hat was perched, hanging down to almost obscure the buglike protuberances that substituted for eyes. Over one, a monocle hung as though by magic, the glass tinted with smoke. But by far the most horrible bit of the creature was its mouth, a slash that ran from one twisted nub of an ear to the other. A half dozen golden tusks protruded from the slit, the sharpened points stained with bronze. It shuffled toward him, a waddle that on anything else would have been comical, but instead, its fishlike body moved as though at any moment it could leap and devour one whole. The creature opened its maw, and any remaining sentimentality for fear was erased. It was hollow. Jamie could see the shell within, all the way down to the bottom, the inside of the cavern tinted bronze. For a wretched moment, Jamie wondered if that was what his hollow torso was now: a bronze cage, ripe for filling. Its arms were twisted flaps of skin wrapped in the filthy topcoat, and they moved in an unsettling manner that suggested they were entirely independent of the rest of the body. With a flourish, the creature gave an oddly graceful bow and motioned Jamie to a smaller wooden rocking chair on the other side of the hearth.

"Tea?"

The brassy voice was both charming and congenial, the voice of a gentleman on Momma's British drama program. Jamie stared incredulously, his body moving of its own accord to sit in the wooden chair.

"Of course, tea—all things are better with tea, even the alarming ones."

Jamie watched, transfixed, as the creature moved to the stove. Its flapping arms deftly poured two cups from the kettle and added sugar and milk from small pitchers on the stone countertop. With unaccountable grace, it crossed back to Jamie, setting his tea on the stone hearth before reseating itself.

"I know you think you might not like tea—I would understand after your last run-in with it. Mine is mite bit better than the wood elves', but then again, they were just doing their best. Never fault a creature that is doing its best, Jamie—remember that. Intention is all we have; it's the best and worst part of our nature. A thing that is truly doing its best—whether it be at tea or other, more lofty pursuits—is, in its essence, trying to reach the divine, and that is nothing to be shamed."

The tone of the creature's voice was so clear that Jamie wondered if it was really speaking. The mouth did not move, not even as it lifted the teacup to its terrible lips and poured the contents into the void that was its body.

"Where does it go?" Jamie whispered, darkly fascinated.

"Where does what go? The tea? The usual places I suppose, same place yours will go if you dare a taste—before it goes cold, that is. We're not so very different, you and I—all men drink tea, and all tea, the great equalizer, goes to the usual places."

Never taking his eyes from the creature, Jamie reached for the cup and took a sip. The sweet, creamy liquid tasted of roses. He realized that it had been an excruciatingly long time since he had had anything to drink. His body clenched and he nearly choked; then, involuntarily, he gulped the liquid, his dry lips demanding more. He looked up at the creature. It was staring at him; one arm flap adjusted the monocle.

"Better, that?" it asked.

Jamie just nodded. Every cell in his body was at full attention, tingling on the surface of his skin.

"Am I dead?" Jamie asked, the words soft.

"Well, yes, in a manner of speaking. But in a manner of speaking, all of us are. Your human body carries in it more dead cells than living ones. Did you know that? The dead skin, the remains of fevers and infections, the waste that sits in your intestine . . . well, used to sit in your intestine." The creature laughed, a sound like a single trumpet note held to its longest extension. It was, in equal measures, the most beautiful and chilling sound Jamie had ever heard.

"But you were always half dead, Jamie. Your kind's fascination with the dead, the stories of those rising from the earth, the spirits—have you ever wondered why there's such a liking to such a dark subject?"

Jamie shook his head. He hung on every word, the icy, tingling sensation on his forehead growing colder still.

"Your kind is half dead already, and you are simply exploring the other side of your potential, your other life, if you will. So when you ask me if you're dead, I have to say yes and no—you are somewhere in between, albeit much more in the in-between than most." The laugh again, the brassy note bringing tears to Jamie's eyes.

"What are you?" Jamie whispered, his voice barely audible.

"You should know, Jamie—you made me. I am as much a part of you as you are a part of me. You've even given me a name. I've been with you far longer than you have been in this place. You have known me for as long as you have been alive, Jamie. I have always been a part of you. I followed you in your dreams. You called on me in every moment where you felt overwhelmed, fearful, and desperate. I am the sum total of your fears, Jamie, the end result of your terrible what-ifs. I live in all the moments when the worst seemed possible. I am what keeps you sane, Jamie, and what has driven you to madness."

A wave of emotion washed over him—not fear, he was beyond that now. It was more of a realization, a reckoning, the point at which nothing could ever go back to what it was. There was no longer a top to the very long hill; there was no more solace in the nape of Momma's neck and the whisper of her voice as she sang to him. There was no safety in Daddy's large hand clasped over his own, and no little rat to burrow in his hair, a touchstone of his old life. All things were dead and, at the same time, terribly and intangibly alive.

"The Lairdbalor," Jamie whispered in a voice too soft to be heard by anyone except the one who sat before him.

"More tea? It's been a long journey, hasn't it, Jamie? A bit of comfort is what you need."

With illogical grace, the creature moved in a single motion off the chair, swooping Jamie's teacup with him, and prepared him another steaming cup of rose-scented tea. Jamie accepted the refill with steady hands. His mind was no longer imprisoned by his skull; instead, it wandered into every crevice of the small cottage. The Lairdbalor resumed its seat and calmly adjusted its monocle.

"Is this real?" Jamie asked, hesitant. His empty gut felt a million miles deep.

"Of course it is real, Jamie. Of course. It is also entirely in your head."

"But how can that be? Both?" Jamie held the earthen teacup, the warmth of the liquid contrasted to the frozen patch on his forehead.

"All things are in duality, Jamie, all things. Every day you lived in your world was both real as could be and also entirely made-up. You simply chose a different backdrop then. Now you are here, in ours. But the ratio of made-up to real is quite the same."

"I don't understand."

The Lairdbalor paused, the bronze-tipped tusks gnashing back and forth as it thought.

"Let me put it this way, Jamie—do you know the word *cuimhne?* Of course you do not. In my tongue, we have two ways of discussing the idea of truth. *Cuimhne* and *firinn.* It's the difference between a place and an idea. You can be in the same place, *cuimhne,* with another and still have an entirely different idea of the truth, the *firinn. Firinn* is different for everyone—we see a single truth in a thousand different ways. We create our own reality; we fill in the rough edges, so to speak. Your *cuimhne* has changed—you fell down a very long hill—but the *firinn* is no less real or true than it was before. It's hard to see now, but you will in time. Do you remember the splinter, Jamie? Think back, you were lingering on it earlier—do you remember?"

Jamie thought hard and then nodded. Two different splinters, two different reactions from Momma. In one, he had fallen asleep in the nape of her neck, a Band-Aid on his finger, perfectly safe; in another, he had been ignored, and he cried himself to sleep while Momma and Daddy rushed about doing grown-up business.

"Yes, Jamie, the splinter. One *cuimhne*, a thousand *firinn*. Your memory of that moment is created from what you knew your world to be. Your mother's memory is created from what she knows, and your father's is a world apart in its own right. So you see, everything is real and entirely created in our minds. This is no different—you are always half in one world and half out of another. You just switched the veil, that is all."

The Lairdbalor looked pleased with its explanation, and it leaned back against the green velvet.

"The wood elves—they said you were going to kill me. The thing on the boat, and on the path—it was you. You were there then . . . I don't understand." Jamie's voice trembled.

"*Sèimhich*, little one, *sèimhich*. I could no more kill you than myself, as you are with me. We are the same, do you not see? The wood elves are another child's *firinn*, and they are afraid of things that we will never have an understanding of. All things in this world are such, Jamie. Nothing exists here that was not the stuff of nightmares or terrible what-ifs. This world is populated with the *firinn* of terror. Have you ever wondered where your nightmares went when you woke? Have you ever wondered how something that felt so real could be chased away by something as simple as the sun? This is the depository of fear. It exists right on the other side of your waking life, and you tumbled right into it. Maybe because of how very afraid you were; maybe you were always meant to be here. I couldn't say. But you're here now, and it's very real and composed entirely of made-up things."

Jamie set his untouched tea down on the hearth.

"I'm not going home, am I?"

The Lairdbalor adjusted itself, the fabric-covered flaps lifting out like terrible stubbed wings.

"That, my dear, is entirely up to you. But you must realize that home is not exactly as you left it. Time is different here—you see the change already. You are half grown, your body closer to that of a man than a child."

"Everything that's happened—the book, the wood elves, the little beetle fairy, my rat . . . " Jamie choked on the barely contained ball of tears in his throat at the mention of Bilbo. "It was all for nothing?"

The Lairdbalor shot forward, the awkward grace of his movement startling Jamie.

"Nothing? *Ist!* Little one, you would still be in that dreadful valley being picked slowly apart by the gnights, wouldn't you? Make no mistake, just because something is imagined, it doesn't make it any less dangerous. No matter if you go back to your world, such as it is now, or if you stay here, you must protect yourself. You nearly met your end back in the forest, and you are more half dead than most as a result. No, your *uidh* is not yet done, and you cannot stay here, not for another cup of tea and never again. Because while I am most certainly not the threat that the wood elves claimed, I am not safe. You must go."

"But why?" Jamie croaked, his voice rough with unspent tears. The monster before him was, next to Bilbo, the only familiar thing in this world. Despite the terror he felt up till this point, he longed to curl into a ball in the wooden rocker and never leave—his arms and legs were already settling, as though they belonged here.

"I am the stuff of your nightmares, Jamie—you have been writing my name on the walls of your fear your entire life. Your anxieties, your worries, all the times you were discounted and your sadness had no place to go, the nights you spent crying yourself to sleep, the nights you woke screaming in your bed, the terrible what-ifs, Jamie, the terrible what-ifs—they are the stuff of which I am made. You made me, Jamie, but I am not safe, not for you and certainly not for others. There is a very real reason the wood elves fear me; your beetle fairies have created their own lore, as have all the other creatures in this world. Everything here, every little thing, every creature in this world was sent here in a child's nightmare. Once here, they grew wild, and now we do as wild things do—we hunt."

Tears ran down Jamie's face—this terrible monster was all he knew in this world, and the horror of leaving it now was more than he could bear.

"No *guil*, little one, no *guil*. You must leave and continue your journey. But know that in this world of uncomforted fear, unheard sadness, in this world there is only one way to live. You need to remember your own *tapachd*, cleverness, Jamie—you must learn to listen to yourself and not let the wave of such great and terrible fears overwhelm you. For in that sleep of death, what dreams may come—do not let them in, little one. Remember, the danger we create for ourselves is the greatest of all. Do not trust in me too much, Jamie—I am but a wild thing, and I will do as wild things do."

Jamie stood with trembling legs, his head racing in a thousand directions.

"But where do I go?" he asked, steadiness returning to his voice.

"I'm sure I don't know. I don't even know what you might hope to find at the end—the world you left has moved on without you in it. But you must keep moving, Jamie, no matter what. Oh, and try to keep what little you have left intact."

The clear tone rang in laughter, the wretched fabric flaps waving back and forth at the joke. Jamie walked to the door; the lip-sized print blazed an icy scar on his forehead. The Lairdbalor moved with an impossibly fluid motion to the cottage door and turned the handle.

"*Curam*, little one, *curam*."

TEN

J AMIE started awake. The sting of a thousand cuts on his face and a very persistent tugging on his right ear forced him to push himself back out of the bramble patch. The effort took every bit of strength he had. Bilbo ran down his arm and frantically chattered at him in some sort of rat-speak. Jamie shook his head confusedly. Panic ran through him like a bolt of electricity—he pressed his hand to his abdomen, terrified to feel the outline of his spine. Instead, however, he felt the familiar weight of his organs, all intact. He breathed a sigh of relief. Mallorie buzzed directly in front of his eyes.

"What was that there? We couldn't wake you. You were muttering to yourself, and you, you—well, take a look at yourself."

Jamie shook his head, trying to clear the fog. He looked around. Where was the cabin? Where was the Lairdbalor? He reached in front of him, and the sleeves on the tunic came to his elbows. There was a painful tightness around his legs and his feet, as though they had been folded in half. He tugged off the soft boots and, with a sinking feeling, saw that his feet were significantly larger than they had been before he had fallen into the bramble patch.

"How long was I out?" he whispered. His voice sounded different. It was deeper, almost unrecognizable. He sounded like his father, and the realization was simultaneously exciting and terri-fying. How old was he now?

Mallorie lit on a small branch, while Bilbo gave up chattering and madly washed his face.

"Light will break soon—look at the sky."

Jamie looked up, jarred by the still-night sky.

"It was daybreak already where I was—I . . . I . . . " He trailed off, not sure where to begin. With a start, he looked around. "The book?"

"It's here," Mallorie answered. "Good thing too—you'd have blinded yourself, you would have."

"The dwarves . . . I . . . I . . . I saw him."

"Who? From what we saw, you saw the ground close-up. You fell and lay there as though you'd knocked yourself clear out for the longest time." Mallorie adjusted her gossamer wings, her voice a bit annoyed.

"No. I saw it—the Lairdbalor," Jamie insisted.

It was impossible for the beetle fairy to turn pale, but Jamie was sure the equivalent crossed Mallorie's tiny face—a moment when the tiny features froze and terror overtook.

"If that's true, love, we need to keep moving. We need to reach the Asrai before he finds you. Maybe the water will mask your scent—you reek of human, you know. Come, you can talk as you move. But trust me, child, move you must. He's looking for you, and he rarely misses his hunt. We need to better hide you—now, move!"

There was a solemn authority in the tiny beetle fairy's voice, compelling enough for the shock to clear and Jamie to stand. Every fiber of every muscle strained in protest. His bare feet felt every thorn, stick, and dry leaf. Jamie looked down at himself. The long tunic was now a shortish sort of shirt; the soft and com-forting pants were like the tights that girls in his elementary school wore—a million years ago it seemed now. He snorted at his appearance. The only option was to pull the clothes off, but then he would be naked. Jamie decided that ridiculous was better than naked, if only so he had a little protection between the sharp edges of the forest and his skin.

A dream or a visit, but not real. It had not been real, at least
not in the way he had presumed. The Lairdbalor had not found
him yet . . . yet. Jamie still tasted the creamy rose tea, still heard the
bright tenor of the Lairdbalor's voice. *I will do as wild things do.*
They hunt—that was what he had said. Now that Jamie realized
exactly what it was the Lairdbalor hunted, a chill ran down his
spine. Without comment, he grabbed the wood elves' book from
the forest floor and plodded forward, adjusting for his new height
and the entirely new level of growing things threatening to hit his
head. He ignored the pain and kept walking. Bilbo scurried to his
post on Jamie's shoulders. Reaching his hand around to his back,
Jamie realized his hair was bordering an absurd length now—it
nearly reached his waist, tangled and full of mats. He must look
like the wild man from the old cartoons he used to watch, the
black-and-white ones, the ones Momma had called "classic" and
Jamie had alternately called "boring" or "scary."

The wild man was scary. The wild man was locked in a cage,
and animals—deer that could stand on their hind legs and gorillas
that spoke like humans—danced around. A marquee sign over
the wild man's cage advertised that he was a freak, a novelty. The
animals danced, dissonant music playing frantically in the back-
ground—rabbits with amusing hats and dogs with too-long tongues
all danced around the cage as though in worship. But Jamie had
known better. He knew they were really taunting the wild man; he
was locked inside, and they were all free. They exacted their revenge
for a lifetime of their ancestors' captivity by flaunting their freedom,
while the wild man sat huddled in the cage, the tinny piano music
playing faster and faster still. At the end, the wild man became
enraged and pulled the bars of his cage apart, scattering the dancing
animals and silencing the music. He stepped into the jungle, his long
hair and scant clothing punctuating his otherness, his inability to
ever fit in again in a world that had decided that he was too far gone,
too strange to ever live in the sunlight. As Jamie clumsily crashed
through the forest, his hair catching the surrounding branches and
his own voice unfamiliar in this throat, he understood what the wild
man had felt in that moment.

The sun broke in the sky, and Jamie felt the beginnings of a sweltering heat. Mallorie buzzed onward, not pausing, all levity gone. Jamie wondered what had become of the dwarves. Before he had fallen forward, he'd have sworn he heard them behind him. Was it all a trick? Another waking nightmare set on him by the Lairdbalor? It said it wouldn't hurt me, Jamie thought, grimacing in pain as he stepped squarely on some kind of pointed root. Wouldn't hurt me, or couldn't? Jamie tried to remember what exactly the Lairdbalor had said and figure out what the difference might even be. If he had, indeed, created the Lairdbalor, couldn't he uncreate him? Couldn't he imagine him gone and it would be so? Jamie was glad for the constant pain in his feet, for it distracted him from his incoherent thoughts.

The Lairdbalor had also said that time kept moving in Jamie's world. Jamie had no way to gauge how old he was now, but if time had moved at its usual pace for his parents, then he had been gone many years. He was nearly grown now, and they had lost him when he was only seven—really seven, not the overgrown seven he was now. Maybe they had stopped looking for him—maybe they thought he was dead. Maybe he was. Jamie paused, out of breath and feet aching, and leaned against a tree. Mallorie buzzed back and hovered impatiently in front of his face.

"You need to listen to me here. The faster we can get you to the Asrai, the safer you will be. How many bites and nips will he take from you out here in the open? You're already too big for your britches, quite literally I might add. Any more and you'll be a grown one, and the grown ones have never fared too well in our world—the wood elves didn't lie about that." Mallorie's normally light voice was laced with annoyance.

"How do you know what the wood elves told me?" Jamie asked, pulling some kind of stinging fiber from his big toe.

"Bats, blabbermouths they are. They tell everything to everyone. Why do you think the woodies use them?"

Mallorie motioned upward. Jamie looked up, and to his surprise, he saw the wide swoop of dark wings overhead, crisscrossing back and forth.

"But . . . but, it's daytime. I didn't think . . . " Jamie trailed off.

"Ah, I see. Are you just now getting wind that things here are a bit different than they were back home? Bats in the daytime the oddest thing you've seen yet, are they?" Mallorie buzzed away, paused, and looked back. "Come, not too much farther. I don't know for sure if the Asrai can help you, but I know out here you're a sitting duck, you are. Come."

The last "come" was less of a request and more of a command. Jamie sighed and followed. He saw a bat hanging upside down from a tall branch several feet above his head. The little creature had beady black eyes, and he would've sworn it grinned at him. Jamie shook his head and kept walking. The sun fell through cracks and crevices in the greenery, burning Jamie's exposed skin where it could. He noticed, with a bit of amusement, that his once-pale child's skin was darker and more freckles had appeared. His exposed arm looked like Momma's shoulders, a constellation of freckles. She had always said he would probably get them as he got older, but if he wore his sunscreen every day, maybe he wouldn't have so very many as she did. Curse of the Scottish, she had said—Jamie had had no idea what she was talking about at the time, but now he thought he rather did. He wondered suddenly what his face looked like and ran his hand over his jaw, pulling back in shock at the feel of soft, downy fur. I'm becoming half rat, he thought irrationally. He carefully ducked around a tangled spiderweb (wouldn't even want to guess what nightmare lived there) and peeked down the front of his tunic. He stumbled in surprise; his chest was covered in brownish-blond hair. I *am* half rat, he thought, the idea oddly appealing. He stroked Bilbo, and the little rat leaned into his touch.

They continued on for what seemed like forever. The sun rose still farther in the sky. Jamie was acutely aware of how thirsty he was—hunger was in there too, but tamped down by the immediate need for water. He found himself craving even the wood elves' dirt-water tea. He felt dizzy. Sweat had run in streams down his face for a time, but eventually it ceased, as though every resource in his body was running dry.

"Mallorie!" Jamie called out. "Mallorie!"

He leaned against a tree, his head pounding. There was no response from the beetle fairy. There was throbbing behind his eyes, not entirely different from before he passed out in the wood elves' holding. He sunk down to the ground, the heat permeating every fiber in his body.

"Mallorie!" he called weakly.

Bilbo perched on his shoulder, washing his face. Jamie realized that if he had had nothing to drink or eat, neither had Bilbo.

"Sorry, Bilbo—it will be pretty awful if after all that's happened, it's thirst that kills us off, won't it?" Jamie said softly.

Mallorie must have flown far enough ahead that she couldn't hear him. Jamie sighed. The crisscrossing dark shapes above him were a contradiction to the bright blue sky. He was struck by a sudden idea.

"Bats! Bats!" he cried out.

The shapes slowed, and a pair of night-black wings swooped lower, the mousy body shrunken and seemingly too small to support the expanse of the wings. It perched several branches above Jamie and looked down at him with glittering black eyes.

"Bats! Can you find Mallorie? I need to rest, and I need water— can you find Mallorie? If she gets too far ahead, I'll lose her for good!" Jamie pleaded.

The bat took to the sky and flew away. Jamie looked at Bilbo, who stared at the sky worriedly.

"Well, buddy, that might be it. I've never sent a message by bat before."

Jamie closed his eyes, his mind swimming, his forehead burning. The strange cold patch of skin where Chloe had kissed him was still a degree cooler than anywhere else on his body. He wondered what he would be doing if he were home. Would he be in high school? Or was he older? High school was a mysterious place. Momma had worked in a high school for a time, but all Jamie had known about it was that there were a great many big kids there and it was a "pain in the ass," according to Momma. Jamie had had no idea what that meant, and Momma had never elaborated other than to tell Jamie never to say "ass." Now Momma taught college kids, and she liked it better, or so she told him. Momma said none of her students were ever in red; they were always green. Red and green was a system that Ms. Hamilton had used. Red meant you were bad, and green was good; you could also be yellow if you were just a little bit bad. Jamie was usually yellow. He hadn't minded, though—he liked yellow; it was a sunny, happy color, unlike red, which reminded him of blood, or green, which was the color of the spots on the bread when it was left out too long.

Jamie's reverie was broken abruptly by a splash of liquid crashing down on his head. He twisted his head upward, just in time to see the shadow of a pair of black wings and be hit directly in the face with cold water. Jamie laughed. He had no idea how it was happening, but he had never felt anything as heavenly. Two little bats descended slowly and gracefully, holding between them a leaf too big to be believed, each side clutched in their clawlike feet. They glided through the air, stopping in front of Jamie, their wings in perfect synchronicity. When Jamie saw the leaf was full of water, he nearly cried.

"Th-thank you," he stuttered.

The bats inched forward slightly, and Jamie gingerly took either side of the enormous leaf, careful not to spill any of the precious liquid. When the bats were satisfied that their handoff was secure, they sailed like tiny night ships into the bright sky. Jamie stared at the water, his hands shaking slightly.

"Bilbo, quick, drink," Jamie urged.

Bilbo crawled lightly down Jamie's arm and dipped his snout into the water, drinking deeply. Jamie joined him, slurping the water as gracefully as he could. Bilbo reached his fill and cupped a drop in his tiny paw, washing his face. Jamie looked up when the leaf was nearly dry. He felt renewed. The water was sweet, as sweet as the honey water that Momma made for him when he was sick. Jamie looked up at the sky, where the dark shapes continued to crisscross back and forth.

"Thank you!" Jamie shouted.

He tilted the leaf and drained the rest of the water into his mouth. The cool liquid worked its way from his chest on down.

Jamie's head cleared. He pushed back his damp hair and wiped his face with the still-wet leaf before setting it down. He pulled a bit of a vine from a nearby plant and secured his hair behind his neck, wrapping the greenery around it like the ponytail holders the girls at school used. A mad buzzing in his ear told him that Mallorie had found him once again.

"All better?" the beetle fairy asked. Not waiting for an answer, she shot forward. "Good, keep going. Almost there. Plenty of water where you're going. Must move, must move."

Jamie followed with renewed energy. Another leaf full of water splashed Jamie on the head as he walked forward, and he waved to the departing bats, who tilted their wings ever so slightly, which Jamie took to mean "You're welcome." The book was tucked under Jamie's arm, and he shifted it to the other side; its empty pages were incredibly heavy. He wondered if it even mattered, if he was carrying it around for absolutely no purpose. Still, he thought, there's a chance—if he could only find a way to read the pages, then maybe somewhere inside was a way home. But home to what? Jamie wiped new sweat from his forehead. If he had to guess, and if the Lairdbalor was right that his fast-growing body was an indicator of time passing in his world, what would he return to? Jamie tried to imagine what Momma and Daddy would look like after all these years. Momma was beautiful. Jamie knew it wasn't just his opinion—Daddy thought so too, and other people, sometimes strangers in stores and clerks behind counters, gave her soft looks. Even a seven-year-old knew what they meant. Jamie took it as a particular point of pride. Her long reddish hair and brown eyes, so much like his own. Daddy looked very different—his eyes were the color of the ocean, and they changed from deep blue to green like the color of sea foam. When Jamie was little, his aunts and sometimes his grandparents used to coo over him and say things like, "What a shame it is, he doesn't have his father's eyes." Jamie loved everything about Daddy, including his eyes, but he was glad he didn't have them. They scared him a bit; the churning ocean blue green reminded him of a storm, as though if you looked into them for too long, they might swallow you whole. No, Jamie was glad he shared his mother's chocolate-brown eyes, deep and dark, comforting like the winter blanket she spread over his bed when it was cold.

Would they look the same? Would Daddy's hair be the same brown black? Would Momma have wrinkles around her eyes like Grandma? Would they still be alive? Jamie shuddered at the thought. He tried to stamp it back down, but once given life, a thought is difficult to put back to rest. When Jamie had been in kindergarten, the father of a boy named Adam had died. Momma said it was a heart attack. Jamie thought now he might know a little what a heart attack would feel like—if it was anything like having your guts pulled from your split stomach, it was surely pretty terrible. Adam was in the other kindergarten classroom, the one next door to Jamie's. Jamie hadn't known Adam, but after the heart attack he became a source of fascination for Jamie. He watched Adam after he returned to class. He didn't seem any different. He still played on the monkey bars and pushed other kids off the mound of dirt on the play yard during the highly disapproved-of game of King of the Hill that they played only when the teachers were distracted. Jamie always thought that if they disliked the game so much, they should have gotten rid of the mound of dirt, as its only purpose in Jamie's eyes was to be shoved off of.

Adam still did all the things he used to before his father died; it was as though the heart attack had never happened. The only indication that anything was different happened one day in May. As everyone was getting ready for the end of school, when summer seemed ready to start any minute, Adam showed up to school wearing a man's dress shirt that hung nearly to his ankles. His eyes were red, and he didn't laugh and shove anyone off the mound of dirt or chase anyone around the tetherball court. Instead, he sat by himself, in his tentlike shirt and with red eyes, on the steps of the school until his kindergarten teacher—a stout woman whose name began with an F—came for him. She put her thick arms around his shoulders and walked him inside, where the principal was holding the door open. The last Jamie saw of Adam that year was through the narrow window on the door leading down the hallway. Miss

F and the principal took Adam to the office, and Jamie had supposed he must be in a large amount of trouble, maybe for getting his shirt dirty.

No one saw Adam for the rest of that week, and by the time everyone returned for first grade, they had forgotten about the heart attack and the overlarge shirt. Everyone except Jamie. Adam was now in Ms. Hamilton's class with Jamie. Adam did all the normal things; he still shoved kids off the mound of dirt and stuck his chewed gum under the desk when Ms. Hamilton wasn't looking. Jamie had desperately wanted to ask him questions, but he didn't know about what. Mostly he wanted to know how he kept on eating his sandwich at lunch and laughing at Ms. Hamilton's terrible jokes and acting so *normal*. Jamie couldn't understand why Adam didn't show up to school every day with red eyes and wearing an enormous dress shirt. But he never knew how to phrase his questions, so he never asked.

Now, as he pushed his way through an impossible forest, Jamie thought he understood Adam a bit more. You kept on acting normal because you had no choice. Acting normal is the only defense to the never-ending tidal wave of grief that comes with loss. Doing normal things, such as eating sandwiches and shoving kids off the mound of dirt, was the only way to keep your head above the ever-surging water that just might drown you if you allowed yourself to show up to school with red eyes and dressed in your father's shirt every day.

Jamie caught the scent of water. The breeze was cool and flecked with bits of moisture. Encouraged, he pushed forward, crashing through a particularly dense thicket and bursting onto a rocky shore. He let out a strangled cry of relief. Mallorie was perched on a branch near his head.

"Told you—almost there I said, and almost there we were." The little beetle fairy stretched her gossamer wings out and then gracefully folded them back in place.

"What now?" Jamie asked.

"Now?" Mallorie replied. "Now we wait. The Asrai come out only at night, which isn't too far off."

Jamie looked up. Judging by the angle of the sun in the sky, he determined it was afternoon.

"Sorry for rushing you along there—necessary though, safer near the water. The dwarves are still out there somewhere, along with a great number of others, and I guarantee they can all smell you a mile off," Mallorie continued. "If I were you, I'd rinse myself off. You stink a bit more than even the average human, and the less scent you leave, the less likely you are to be found. We will have to see what the Asrai have to say about you tonight."

Jamie nodded as though any of it made sense. He did stink, though, that much was true. It was a deeper and more profound stink than he had ever smelled on himself. He smelled like Daddy's gym clothes after he went jogging. He smelled like the towels from the bathroom when he left them in a wet pile all night. He looked down at himself. Every inch of exposed skin was black with mud, and his feet were unrecognizable. Without much urging, he pulled off his soiled tunic, stroked Bilbo's head, and walked into the water. The little rat jumped off his shoulder and hovered by the shore's edge, sipping the clear water before he padded back to the discarded tunic, where he nested and promptly fell asleep. Jamie took a last look to make sure the little rat was safe before he dove under the water. Strictly speaking, he didn't know how to swim, but he figured drowning was the least of his problems at the moment. He flailed a little but resurfaced and turned on his back, thrilled to find that he could float just like his swim teacher, Miss Karen, had always told him. Seven-year-old Jamie had been too frightened to try and had kicked his way back to standing at every attempt. But now, Jamie stretched his long arms and legs as far as they could go, examining the ripple of new muscles. He ran his fingers over the thin hair on his chest and face. He wasn't half rat; now that he was properly hydrated, he realized that he was simply growing hair like Daddy. But unlike Daddy's thick black scruff and chest hair, Jamie's was a fine golden mist. A scattering of freckles revealed themselves beneath the forest dirt. The pants were riding up in the worst way, and after a moment's hesitation, Jamie peeled them off and threw them on shore.

He was never supposed to be naked outside. That was Momma's rule. Never, not even in the backyard when she filled the little splash pool. Even after his bath, he was supposed to wear his fuzzy blue bathrobe from the bathroom to his bedroom. He was certain that she would very much disapprove of this moment of nudity, but considering the circumstances, Jamie was pretty sure she'd understand. He looked down at himself and was rather shocked to find another patch of fine blond hair. He wondered what stories the bats that circled far overhead would spread now. In a moment of sudden, overwhelming modesty, he rolled over in the water and found he could float just as well on his stomach as long as he kept his head propped up.

After a bit, he climbed out of the water and sat on the shore. His filthy clothes lay on the beach. Looking around, he saw several of the large, soft leaves that the bats had used to bring him water. He grabbed a few and clumsily crafted a sort of covering for his lower area. He giggled to himself as he realized he must look like Tarzan from the old cartoons. Tarzan wore the same type of covering, only his was far sturdier. Jamie could hardly walk without his leaf-skirt falling, much less swing through trees. It was no matter, anyhow, as he had no intention of moving. He laid the too-small pants out to dry—he would try to squeeze back into them later.

Mallorie flew lazily inches from the surface of the water.

"What are the Asrai?" Jamie asked.

"Oh, you'll like them, you will," Mallorie answered, the light teasing tone back in her voice. "A pretty lot, if I do say so myself."

"Are they elves? Dwarves?"

"Oh no, child! You think I'd trust you with those creatures? No, the Asrai are a sort of cousin to us fae folk. They have other names in your world, mostly in myth. Not many of your kind have seen the Asrai—they're rather shy and very good at hiding. In your world, I think they're called mermaids."

Jamie's eyes widened.

"Mermaids! But those are just stories!" he exclaimed.

"Are they, now?" Mallorie asked, lighting on his outstretched knee. "I suppose you shall see for yourself before too long, won't you?"

Jamie sighed. He felt as close to relaxed as he had since he fell down the very long hill.

"Mallorie, can I ask you something?"

"Oh, you're asking to ask now, are you? Out with it. If I don't like the question, I won't give you an answer," Mallorie teased.

"It's just about something the Lairdbalor told me." Jamie paused, unsure how to begin. "It said everything here came from nightmares—children's nightmares. It said everything, including itself, was a nightmare. It said I had created it from everything I was afraid of."

"I'm not hearing a question, Jamie," Mallorie said. "Go ahead, ask it."

Jamie took a deep breath.

"What nightmare are you? Is that offensive to ask? I'm sorry if it is." The last bit came out in a single breath.

Mallorie laughed.

"Offensive? No, it's just that not every creature here knows. Not everyone is as self-aware as your Lairdbalor. Us fae folk pride ourselves on keeping our heads clear, so I suppose I have that in common with your monster. I am a rather common nightmare, I'm afraid to admit. It's why there are so many like me here. It's a fear shared by many in your world. I bet if you look at me, you can guess it."

Jamie stared hard.

"I really don't know. No offense, but you aren't very frightening."

Mallorie laughed like tinkling bells.

"Well, not everyone feels the way you do. Many of your kind see a large flying insect, harmless as I might be, and think the sky is falling. I once caused a little girl about your size—your previous size, that is—to run clear down a hill trying to get away from me. She caught her foot in a rabbit hole and broke her ankle. Whenever the hurt caught up with her, she saw me in her mind's eye, but not doing as I really was, buzzing around minding my own—no, in her imagination, I chased her down the hill, I bit and stung. In her nightmares, I flew in her ear and died and she had to go to the hospital, where they pulled out my rotten body with a needle."

"God, that's . . . that's horrible." Jamie shook his head.

"That's a nightmare, love. They don't always make much sense, and the thing that is chasing you is hardly ever the thing you're actually afraid of." Mallorie looked at Jamie for a long moment. "Your Lairdbalor is a particularly nasty one—I don't have to tell you that. It hunts our world, and you being in it makes it particularly dangerous for everyone here."

"It said it couldn't hurt me, any more than I could hurt myself."

"Any more than you can hurt yourself—don't forget that bit, child. Most of the harm that comes our way in this world and yours is self-inflicted. No, we need to get you back home where a nightmare is over when you awake." Mallorie's voice was soft.

"So much seems to go on here that's outside of nightmares. The dwarves, what nightmares are they?" Jamie was not sure he wanted an answer.

"They're all a bit different. You'd have to ask each and every dwarf to find out, and I'm not sure they're all too much aware of their own roots. Not much for talking—dwarves, that is." Mallorie paused. "We may have been created in your world, Jamie, but everything created goes on to create a life of its own. We have our own nightmares here in this world, developed over many, many years. Allegiances, wars, peace, violence—all of it exists here just as it does anywhere else."

Jamie shifted slightly, finding it hard to keep his awkward covering of leaves in place even when sitting.

"Something else the Lairdbalor said. It . . . whatever it is . . . it said that this"—Jamie indicated his nearly grown body—"that this is real, and even if I do get back, all this time has passed and this is really how old I am now. Is that true?"

Mallorie said reluctantly, "I'm afraid so. It has always been that way. Time here moves in lurches and spurts. It slows to a crawl for a great long time and then lurches forward in a leap. It's not like in your world. Your body has had to catch up. But yes, many years have passed since you first fell down that hill."

Jamie felt empty inside, as if his guts had again been ripped out and strewn on the rocky shore.

"If I do get back then—what about Momma and Daddy?"

Mallorie buzzed a little closer, landing on Jamie's forearm.

"I can't answer that, love. I know that if we can get you to the Burg, then you might get a bit of a glimpse. The mist is a bit thinner in places there. You can see in a bit, somewhat like looking in on the wood elves' path, but different. You can't just muscle your way through, but sometimes, you can see. Maybe you'll see something that will make a bit of sense. In any case, there's no life for you in this world, love—you'll keep lurching forward in time like you are, and in a few days you'll be an old man. A few days past that, and your dust will be back in the ground. This world takes a toll on the living."

Jamie sat in silence, staring out at the calm water. Mallorie took to the air and resumed making lazy circles around the surface of the lake. Bilbo curled tighter into a rat ball and slept. Jamie watched his tiny form rising and falling with each breath. What would become of Bilbo when they went back? Rats didn't live as long as people—he should already be long dead. But then again, Bilbo was never a real rat to begin with, Jamie mused. Maybe rats that became real only once they had tumbled down a very long hill could live so long. He showed no signs of aging; in fact, Bilbo seemed like he belonged here.

"Were you someone's nightmare?" Jamie whispered softly, not expecting an answer.

He looked up to see an exceptionally large bat perched on a branch directly over his head. He stared at the creature. Coarse black fur covered its withered body; its impressive, spiny wings were neatly tucked in. It regarded him without judgment, the beady eyes unblinking.

"You spying on me for someone? Can you tell them to bring me some clothes? I'm in a bad spot here," Jamie said quietly, shifting a bit in his leaves.

The bat continued to stare. The sun was beginning to set. Jamie shivered and, making sure to hold his leaves in place, rose

and waded into the water again, drinking deeply to quell the
hunger pains rolling across his belly like a thunderstorm. He
knew that he could live for quite a while without food but
only three days without water. He had learned that from *Survivorman*; Momma liked to watch it on lazy afternoons. Jamie
had been utterly bored with the show at first, but when Survivorman had had to resort to hunting birds and other creatures, he became fascinated. He couldn't imagine having to
kill something and then having to eat it. Wouldn't you just see
its face in front of your eyes the entire time? Jamie had asked
Momma, and she had asked him in return what he thought was
in hot dogs and what bacon was made of. Jamie had felt suddenly queasy and vowed never to eat either again, a resolution
that was quickly broken as soon as he forgot about Survivorman
roasting a dozen baby birds. Jamie remembered now, though;
he thought about it all as he stared out over the water, enjoying
the feel of the cool wetness on his legs. He wondered if there
were fish in the lake and wondered what nightmare they came
from and what would happen if you consumed another's fear.
He could have asked Mallorie, but Jamie wasn't sure he wanted
to know. He might not have a choice if he had to stay here much
longer, and if that happened, he wouldn't want to know the consequences. So he stayed silent, and the bat behind him watched
his every move. Mallorie glided in graceful figure eights over
water that reflected stripes of fire from the setting sun. Back
on shore, Bilbo stirred, stretched, and yawned so widely that
Jamie thought he might turn inside out. He padded down to
the water's edge again and drank and then took to his hind legs
and sniffed the air.

Mallorie landed on Jamie's shoulder, taking Bilbo's usual post.

"Might want to step out of the water now. It's almost time, and
it might be a bit of a shock. Besides, your leaves are falling." This
last bit was followed with a low giggle.

Jamie grabbed at the giant leaves and awkwardly made his way
back to the shore, adjusting his cover. Bilbo hopped over to his
feet and looked up imploringly. Jamie bent over a bit awkwardly

and scooped him up, placing him on the shoulder that Mallorie had vacated. The sun was falling rapidly. Jamie stood, his new height and mysterious new muscles doing nothing to quell his nervousness. It wasn't entirely encouraging that Mallorie seemed to trust these creatures, whatever they turned out to be. Mallorie seemed to love to be party to trouble, and Jamie couldn't help but wonder if he was part of an elaborate game or some kind of sacrifice. He found himself wondering what nightmare the Asrai were made of. Would they have wickedly sharpened teeth like the wood elves? Or death-pale skin like the dwarves? Were they changeable like the bogles? Did they love to incite trouble as much as the beetle fairies seemed to? He closed his eyes against the vision of the Lairdbalor's terrible, empty pit of an inside. Jamie glanced back. The bat was still on its perch, black eyes fixed on him. Jamie remembered a shard of a poem from school, in which a black bird kept saying "Nevermore." Ms. Hamilton had showed them a video—it was animated, but in that scary way that grown-ups seemed to like, everything twitchy and slow. The black bird, a raven, had appeared in a doorway and then on a fireplace, all the while crying out that word, "Nevermore." A deeply unsettling male voice had read the poem, and Jamie didn't remember any of it except that one word: "Nevermore." The bat, still as death on its perch, seemed like the sort of creature that might also croak "Nevermore." But instead it sat in silent, neutral observation.

Mallorie buzzed up to Jamie's ear and sat on his shoulder opposite Bilbo.

"Almost time," she whispered.

"What do I need to know?" Jamie asked, his voice steady.

"Nothing you won't find out for yourself in a minute. It's best if you don't touch them, but if you want to get to the Burg, if you want to figure out that book, they're your best bet."

Mallorie indicated the wood elves' book, which lay on the rocky shore. Jamie wondered if it was worth it or if the book was simply full of nonsense about humans, like their blood was made of berry juice. Jamie sighed. Everything seemed impossible and, at the same time, nothing was out of limits. He was standing in a nightmare with a talking beetle on one shoulder, a very alive stuffed rat on the other, waiting to meet a mermaid.

The water stirred, the ripples rolling softly atop of the surface to the shore.

"Here they come," Mallorie whispered.

ELEVEN

JAMIE took a deep breath and involuntarily took a step backward for safety. Three shapes moved under the surface like dolphins far out at sea back in Jamie's world. One after another, three heads popped up from the water's silky surface. All three were identical, their eyes rimmed with a thick ring of orange red, the color of fire. The pupils weren't a perfect circle but were rather kidney shaped, making them look cross-eyed. Their upper bodies were a combination of scale and skin—patches of uniform silver-gray scale giving way to pale-gray skin, which looked loosely connected to their bodies, floating away and back again. Jamie saw, with some horror, that the patches were gills—gills that lined the length of what would have been a rib cage on a human body. But there was nothing human about the Asrai. Impossibly thin necks widened slightly into gilled chests, which widened still more into fully scaled tails. Their arms were bony and short, ending in clawlike hands, sharpened tips gnashing at the water's surface. Most shocking by far were the faces: the fire-washed eyes lodged in thin faces with just slits for nose and mouth. No ears, only the loose-flesh slits. From their heads grew long black hair, the sort that Momma always pointed out with a jealous sigh. The sort that he imagined in his world would have sailors mistaking these creatures for beautiful women. It fell the length of their bodies and floated on the water's surface; as they moved in place, it swirled around them like a cloud of night. It was mesmerizing. No matter how horrid their overall appearance, Jamie couldn't help but believe they were radiant. His rational mind reeled. More fish than human, they should have sent his skin crawling; instead, he inched toward the water, toward the black hair swirling like a dream he'd had once. He imagined himself surrounded by it, the feel of it on his bare skin. Jamie closed his eyes, moving forward to the water.

"Hello, Jamie," a deep, satin voice intoned. Jamie opened his eyes and realized all three were speaking in unison. "We're ever so glad you've come to us." The slitted mouths didn't move, though occasionally a snakelike tongue darted out and ran the length of the lipless opening. "We have a present for you, something the bats said you needed."

Jamie's heart beat fast, but not in fear—the anticipation of receiving anything from these creatures filled him with a richness he had never before felt, a bone-deep excitement that bordered on nausea. The creature on the farthest right reached her claw hand into the water and pulled out a long sheet the color of the twilight ocean, shades of deepest blue and nocturnal blackness. In the traces of early starlight, the fabric's appearance changed constantly, and Jamie felt an overwhelming urge to touch it, to wrap himself in it.

"Here, Jamie. It is our gift to you. The bats said you were in need of something to cover yourself—a habit, we're afraid, that is of more mind in your world than ours. Take it as a promise."

Their collective voice rippled through the air. Jamie walked forward, his leaves falling away. He waded into the water, not feeling the wet or chill; he felt hypnotized, and the idea that the ever-swirling hair might touch him was overwhelming. He felt rapt and dizzy, fixated on the three ghastly beautiful creatures in the water before him. The one on the end pushed the cloth toward him. It floated across the water straight to Jamie, and without taking his eyes off the Asrai, he caught it and held it to his chest. Even though it was in the water, the cloth was as soft as Momma's neck and perfectly dry.

"Come out of the water, Jamie—don't touch them. Come out of the water," Mallorie buzzed in his ear, her voice firm.

Jamie shook his head, the reverie interrupted. His head was foggy, his movements drugged.

"Told you that you'd like them," Mallorie giggled. "Now get out of the water. Now."

Jamie backed out of the water, looking at the cloth. The blue-black color shifted and swirled; shooting stars swept across it, disappearing into its folds. Jamie held it out, fascinated. He wrapped it around his waist, and it was long enough to make several turns before he tied it securely in the front. The effect was of a long skirt, similar to the ones he had seen on dancers in the drumming class Daddy had taken him to once. Jamie felt instantly more secure. The night fabric rested against his skin and reminded him of being held close to someone, being loved more than one ever felt possible. He looked up at the creatures and, his head slightly cleared, managed to speak.

"Thank you."

His voice was barely a whisper.

"You've come to us for help?"

The voices overlapped, slightly out of sync. The effect was of a choir, each tone accenting the other.

Jamie nodded.

"I want to go home," he said simply, and suddenly he felt very young.

"Dear one, be sure of what you want. Your home as you knew it is gone—is returning to that what you want?"

The Asrai shifted in the water, and Jamie stared at the ripples that lapped the shore. He shook his head, trying to break the fixation.

"I want my parents. I want to see my mother, my father. No matter what's changed, I want to go home." His voice broke with emotion, and tears choked his throat.

"Dear one, dear one, we cannot grant wishes. We can only set you on a path and help you as much as we can so the one who hunts you might not succeed." The overlapping voices echoed around the water, coming from every direction simultaneously.

"Might . . . " Jamie whispered.

"Yes, Jamie, might. I cannot guarantee you will live through the next hour, much less survive the trek back to your world."

A stumped and scaly fishtail broke the surface and then disappeared. Jamie swallowed hard, his throat constricting.

"What nightmare are you?" he asked quietly.

The Asrai dove under the water suddenly. Jamie's stomach sank—they were gone; he had overreached. But they resurfaced, circling each other, their silken black hair intertwining and covering the surface to create a vortex.

"We are the fears of all who want and cannot have. We are the dreams where beauty is discovered to be the deepest horror. We are the truth of what you believe you want. We are the reality behind what you believe to be right and strong. We are the child that cowers in the corner of the darkest closet in the darkest corner of the night. We are the truth, Jamie."

The voices swirled and mixed, a choir that reminded him of everything terrible and wonderful and of how closely connected the two truly were.

"We can tell you the truth too, Jamie, or you can continue on your path and make your way home. We will not harm you." The Asrai slowed, their quiet movement barely perceptible.

"Will the truth keep me from going home?"

"Perhaps . . . perhaps not, dear one. We cannot determine what people will do with their truth."

"I want to go home. I don't want anything that will keep me from it. I want home, and I want my family," Jamie choked.

"All right then, love."

The figures stopped their swirling, lining up in a row. Jamie steadied his gaze, never taking his eyes off the Asrai. They dove under the water and disappeared from sight. Jamie looked at Mallorie, who perched on the tip of his shoulder.

"You're doing well," she said.

Jamie looked to his other shoulder, where Bilbo leaned so far out on his hind legs that it seemed impossible he could balance. There was no movement from the water. He began to wonder if this had all been an elaborate trick and the Asrai were simply gone. Jamie sighed. He was happy, at the very least, to have something besides leaves to wear. Just as he was about to whisper this to Mallorie, the water began to bubble as though a fountain far below the surface were forcing it up. The starlight caught the movement rippling across the surface in small yet powerful waves. The Asrai rose in one fluid motion. The one in the center held a small blue bottle with a cork in the top. She held it out with her raptorlike claws. Jamie took a step toward the water, then glanced at Mallorie, who gave him an encouraging nod. He waded into the water, his wrap floating on the surface, mysteriously dry. Remembering what Mallorie had said about not touching the Asrai, he reached out for the bottle.

He almost had it in his grasp when a great gust of air pushed him forward. His face hit the water, and for a terrifying moment he couldn't breathe and struggled to raise his head. He was nearly chest deep, deeper than he was comfortable. He felt for Bilbo— no little rat. Jamie panicked. It couldn't happen again! Desperately, he looked to shore and saw the tiny figure on the water's edge. Bilbo must have jumped as Jamie fell. He breathed a sigh of relief and started back out of the water. Suddenly, his damp hair was yanked from behind, and his face again plunged into the water. Jamie reached behind himself, inadvertently sucking in a mouthful of lake water, and began to drown under the pressure.

He flailed his arms in a panic. The pressure released, and he resurfaced, gasping and coughing. He heard Mallorie's light voice bark orders, words he couldn't distinguish. Before he could look back, his head was again yanked backward. Jamie reached back and grabbed something that felt like a stick. He yanked, but it was strong, with the cold feel of concrete or some sort of metal pipe. His head propelled forward, but then suddenly it stopped. One of the Asrai appeared directly in front of his face, the fire-red fish eyes wide, the slitlike lips open, baring row after row of razor-sharp teeth. Jamie screamed as the mouth opened impossibly wide. He was sure it was going to swallow him whole. Instead, the Asrai sailed from the water over Jamie's head, so close that the water dripped onto his face. The pressure on the back of his head gave way, and Jamie lurched forward. He swiveled around to see the Asrai devouring a shriveled, wretched creature. Its face, what was left of it, was molten gold, the texture of an apple left far too long in the sun, shriveled beyond recognition. The hair was mostly gone, but patches showed that it, too, had been the color of deepest gold. The arms and legs flailed, but they were shriveled and warped. The entire figure caved in on itself, and now the Asrai ripped strings of flesh from its bones, gray mud streaming down its chin. Jamie scrambled back to shore. He realized with horror that the attacker was Morcant the wood elf. But something had happened to it—the something that Mallorie had spoken of.

"Time catches up with the woodies once they leave their path. That one had been trailing you for some time—part of the reason I rushed you. Even so, that isn't the only one who has your scent, just the one most likely to breach even the open space to get at you," Mallorie buzzed into his ear.

Jamie sat on the shore, his breath heaving. "The dwarves—are they out there too?"

He watched, fascinated, as the other two Asrai joined the first, crunching their way through the thin bones and tearing the paper-thin flesh away in chunks. Bilbo scampered up his arm and onto his shoulder.

"Them and others. Most won't go near the water, for reasons you can probably guess," Mallorie replied.

"Why didn't the Asrai kill me too?" Jamie asked as the remaining silver-gray mud leaked out into the water, pooled for a brief moment, and then slipped beneath the surface.

"You've been marked for the Lairdbalor, love. Most have no interest in getting into a war with that one. No, we will help you as much as we can, and when you are free from our world and back in yours, we will all be safer and your Lairdbalor will once again sleep. Killing you would serve no purpose other than to perpetuate this war." Mallorie fluttered her tiny wings.

"I don't understand anything in this place," Jamie whispered, his voice quivering. He had never wished so hard to feel Momma's arms around him, to hide his head in the soft skin of her neck.

"Like I said earlier, love, not all creatures in this world are blessed with the gift of self-awareness. Morcant thought of nothing but revenge. You exiled it from its world, and it aged two hundred years in as many minutes. The mind ages too, and it saw you as an attacker and did what its deepest instinct said to do—it hunted," Mallorie said softly.

Jamie looked at her sharply. Her words were so close to the Lairdbalor's—*what wild things do*. He wondered if he was a wild thing now too. The Asrai dove back under the surface. Morcant's remains floated across the water as though suspended in oil until the pressure overtook them, and they sank slowly, without even disturbing the surface. Jamie stood, careful not to jostle the shaking Bilbo. One by one, the Asrai resurfaced; once again, they held out the blue bottle with the cork.

"Quickly, Jamie. Others will know what happened here— the bats tell all—and others will head this way sooner than you would like. You cannot stay with us." The dark, melodic voice was insistent. "Drink this, it will mask your scent for a time. You must head to the city. The veil is thinner there, and the one who hunts you will have trouble determining your scent from those of so many who walk the border of our world and yours. You must take this and then go. Mallorie will accompany you."

The clawlike hand held out the bottle. Jamie waded in and reached out. With one swift motion, the Asrai leapt from the water, dove under, and resurfaced directly in front of Jamie. He took the small bottle; it felt like ice. The fire-red eyes regarded him closely. Jamie was paralyzed. Suddenly, the creature took one claw finger and raked it down his forehead. The pressure was light, but he felt the impact reverberate deep inside his skull. A burning cold pierced the skin, the same sensation as Chloe's kiss.

"Let that guide you, Jamie. And now, good-bye. You must hurry from this place. Go to the Burg—they are not like us, but they are also not like other elves of their kind. But do not trust too deeply, Jamie. Never trust too deeply, we are wild things and will do as wild things do."

With that, the Asrai leapt into the water, and Jamie saw a trio of spiny tails disappear underneath the surface. His forehead burned with the cold. Jamie waded out to the shore, his wrap still dry. With Bilbo watching nervously and Mallorie perched on his knee, he uncorked the bottle and drank the liquid. It tasted like it was simply lake water, but it was so cold that it penetrated the core of his throat and all the way down to his stomach. He gasped as it flowed through his lungs and spread out, breaching every particle.

"Well?" Mallorie prodded.

Jamie looked around. He felt no different apart from the icy patch on his forehead and his frozen chest.

"I'm no wiser. Sorry."

"Well, no matter. Perhaps it works with time. We need to leave this place. I can get you to the Burg." Mallorie took to the air, flying along the surface of the lake. "Come, follow me."

Jamie stood frozen on the shore; his legs felt glued to the sand.

"We really must move, Jamie," Mallorie chirped impatiently. "The Asrai aren't known for their false warnings. This way—I'll take you through the caves. It's better than being out in the open."

TWELVE

MALLORIE took the lead, while Jamie collected the wood elves' book from the shore and followed, making sure Bilbo was securely positioned on his shoulder.

The little beetle fairy was moving at a pace that had Jamie jogging to keep up. They followed the lakeshore, the water an unmoving, inky black in the darkness. Jamie wondered how much time had passed in his world; it had been only a bit over a day in this one. He swallowed hard enough to send an ache spiraling down his throat. The sharp stones of the shore stabbed his bare feet, but he hardly noticed.

The shore led through a heavily shrubbed area that forced Jamie to wade out into the water. He hesitated, simultaneously afraid and hopeful that the Asrai would make another appearance. His forehead burned with the cold touch of the Asrai's claw; it seemed to pull him forward as though an invisible string were attached. He shuffled on, out of the water and back onto the shore. Jamie called ahead, desperate to slow the pace but also burning with questions unanswered. "Can you tell me about the dwarves? What are they?"

The little beetle fairy slowed and circled back. "Oh, I suppose we can talk—as long as this isn't some kind of ploy to move slower than you already are." Mallorie's voice was teasing. "What, exactly, do you want to know?"

"For one, dwarves in my world are . . . different. They're short and kind of heavy, not at all like what I saw." Jamie struggled to describe the dwarves he had known of from Momma reading *The Hobbit* to him at bedtime and the ones he had seen in cartoons.

"Wheat and stars, Jamie, they're not fairy tale creatures. Those things don't exist. The dwarves here are made of sterner stuff than your fantasy stories," Mallorie replied, her voice a bit offended.

"You said they took care of the dead." Jamie struggled to remember exactly what it was the beetle fairy had told him earlier.

Mallorie paused. "Yes and no. They *collect* the dead. The dwarves walk these woods seeking dead things. They collect what they find, and then, whatever it is, it travels with them, neither living nor dead but somewhere in-between. They're born of every fear your kind has about death, the horrible things that might happen to them after their bodies have expired—anyone who ever worried that they would live on in a kind of half-life or that the end was as simple as turning off a light. They are made of the fears of those who die with regrets too large to rest, those who fear retribution might be waiting for them."

Jamie swallowed. "Do children have fears like that?"

"Of course, love, of course." Mallorie's voice reminded him of his mother, how her voice became dreamlike when she spoke to him as he was falling asleep. "Children die just like the grown ones in your world. They fear death, as any would. Your kind seems to think that children are incapable of regret or retribution. Children are capable of things greater than your kind could ever dream, Jamie. Never discount a fear simply because it was born from a child. You, love—you created the Lairdbalor. Your nightmares are limitless."

Jamie just nodded. Some children's fears created beetle fairies; his had created the Lairdbalor, a creature that all the creatures created from uncountable nightmares seemed to fear.

"Mallorie . . . " Jamie began, the words sticking in his throat. "Is there something wrong with me?"

Mallorie flew in circles around his head.

"I'm sure I wouldn't know. I don't exactly have anyone to compare you with. You seem to be awfully tall for seven years old, and you walk entirely too slowly. You talk a lot. You also smell. However, you do seem to smell a bit less now—that's good. But I'm not sure that's what you were asking."

Jamie frowned, feeling slightly annoyed by her chirpy answer.

"No, not that. I mean . . . what I mean is, why is my nightmare so much worse than anyone else's?"

"I don't know, love. I can only say this—everyone thinks that their nightmare is the worst of the bunch. The child who created me thought I was by far the scariest creature in the entire world. And as you can see, I'm not frightening at all."

At that, she buzzed Jamie's nose with her tiny wings, making him laugh despite the unsaid words. His Lairdbalor was far worse than a beetle fairy or even a dwarf. It was the thing that the wood elves feared above all others; it was the nightmare of nightmare creatures. Jamie continued on in silence. He was thinking of Mr. Kevin. Mr. Kevin had been sitting on his sofa one day when Jamie had arrived home from school. Daddy had been there too, and Jamie had thought it was funny and also pretty great. Daddy was never home until later; sometimes Jamie and Momma even started dinner without him. But here was Daddy, sitting on the sofa with the soft velvet cover the color of chocolate. Jamie liked to lay on the sofa sometimes and imagine that he was in Willy Wonka's factory and the sofa was a giant bar of chocolate, but one that would never melt, one that was his bed.

As Jamie entered, Daddy had stood up and crossed to Momma. His greeting had sounded weird to Jamie, and they both looked nervous. Jamie wondered if the man on the couch was here for money. He heard Momma and Daddy talk about money sometimes. Their voices got too loud—it made Jamie want to hide. The sight of Mr. Kevin in his blue jeans and button-up green plaid shirt sitting on the couch had all of a sudden reminded Jamie of money and what could happen. He turned to Momma and Daddy, looking for answers. They told him Mr. Kevin was here to talk to him. They said he could tell Mr. Kevin anything and asked if he wanted anything. He wanted milk and a blue popsicle. Despite the absurdity of the request, Momma had just nodded and gone to the kitchen. It was then that Jamie knew something was very wrong. He knew it was an absurd request—under normal circumstances, she would have rolled her eyes and said, "One or the other, kiddo." But instead, she came back with a blue popsicle and a little carton of milk. Jamie took the treat suspiciously and sat down on the couch.

Mr. Kevin had a chart with different smiley faces on it, and he had asked Jamie to tell him how he was feeling by pointing to a face. Even then, Jamie had known it was a stupid thing to ask. He wasn't just one of the smiling or frowning faces, he was all of them, all at the same time—couldn't Mr. Kevin see that?

Momma and Daddy had left the room, but Jamie knew they were lurking in the kitchen, close enough to hear but far enough away to look like they were gone. He felt like he should warn Mr. Kevin that they weren't really gone, that they were spying.

Mr. Kevin came to see Jamie three more times, and each time he brought his chart of faces. Jamie grew tired of trying to explain how he felt, so before what was to be the last visit, he had drawn his own chart. He showed it to Mr. Kevin when he arrived. Mr. Kevin had swallowed in that way that grown-ups do when they are trying not to say something terrible. He had left and never came back. It was fine by Jamie; he hadn't much seen the point anyhow. Momma and Daddy had had another too-loud talk that night, but this time it wasn't about money.

Jamie waded out into the night water once again to avoid an outgrowth of tree branches that blocked his path. The beetle fairy flew ahead, staying just within Jamie's sight. On his shoulder, Bilbo poked his neck with his tiny, wet nose. Now that Jamie was quite a bit taller than before, he understood what the too-loud talk was all about. They had argued about him. Mr. Kevin was supposed to fix Jamie, but he had chased him away with a chart full of drawings that showed the inside of his head. His parents were scared—scared of him. For the first time, Jamie wondered if they even wanted him back. He wondered if he weren't better off here. He would die in a few days—he would grow old and his body would fail. Maybe that was the best thing for everyone. He could stop walking and find something to eat. He could stay here by this lake and listen to the Asrai sing, talk to the beetle fairy and all manner of lesser nightmares. He could let the Lairdbalor finally find him. He could go back to the little cottage and drink rose-scented tea forever. Even the memory of the creature's great empty body and razor-sharp tusks held no horror for him in this moment.

He was walking slower and slower, though Mallorie hadn't noticed yet. Bilbo gave him a worried hair pull. Suddenly, a shape swirled in front of him, the blackness from the sky collecting in one spot, a vortex that sucked all the starlight out of the space. Jamie stopped in his tracks. He couldn't see the beetle fairy ahead of him. Bilbo dove into his hair and hid. The shape kept swirling, slowly forming. It began to walk toward him, gaining clarity with each step. He saw the reddish-brown hair catch the night breeze. The lightly freckled skin was covered with a fuzzy black sweater that Jamie knew smelled of vanilla and cookies. Momma reached her still-forming arms out to him, and Jamie went weak. He fell forward, and the form caught him. Jamie tried to make a sound, but only a choked sob escaped his lips. His mind was in turmoil—he knew that this shadow creature was not really Momma, but it smelled of her. As it lifted him to his feet and he laid his head in the nape of her neck, he had to lean over with his newfound height. A hand circled his head and entwined with his matted hair. Jamie heard himself half sob, half howl, the cry of a wild thing. The grip on his neck grew stronger, pulling him closer, and Jamie struggled to breathe; his face was pressed so close to the pale skin. Suddenly, the vanilla cookie scent became rank; the skin smelled of sweat and heat. Jamie tried to pull back, but the grip around his head became firmer still. Instinctively, Jamie struggled—he reached out, shoving the hand away, feeling panicked and guilty. The arm was too strong, and he choked on his own breath, the overwhelming stench of sweat giving way to the reek of dying things. A million tiny microorganisms moved underneath the creature's skin, eating away the parts that once had made a whole. Now this body was nothing more than a holding tank; inside awaited all that was left of a life. The arm grew suddenly sharp and pointed; the soft fingers became claws that dug into Jamie's skull. He could feel blood running through his hair like a finely coordinated waterfall. He tried to cry out, but the words were absorbed into the rotting flesh. The thin veneer tore away, and Jamie's face was plunged into the sticky network of dissolving organs and skin. Suddenly, the pressure released and he was thrown back. He landed with a hard thud on his back. Madly, he tried to scrape the rot off his face, but nothing was there, just the smoothness of his skin. No blood dripped down the back of his head, no overwhelming scent of decay. Jamie gulped and looked up to see the swirl of black dissolving into a pinpoint of night, a black hole. Mallorie buzzed around its periphery, cursing angrily.

"Bogle," Jamie whispered, his voice ragged.

"Sand and sea, child!" Mallorie hovered an inch from Jamie's face. "Thought you were smarter than to fall for a bogle again!"

"It . . . it looked like . . . "

"Keep your eyes open! It took a bite, it did—look at yourself!" Mallorie finished a particularly venomous cursing streak that involved many words Jamie didn't even know existed while she flew in circles around his head.

Jamie looked. The Asrai's wrap, which before had reached to his ankles, now was midshin. His chest was broader than before, and the golden hair that covered his chest had doubled. His arms were bigger around, and he could feel his hair at his waist. Jamie struggled to his feet and brushed away a tree branch that had previously been safe from his reach. He was shaking so much he thought he might pass out.

"But how . . . I wasn't unconscious, was I? It only lasted a minute, didn't it?"

"It doesn't matter how long, Jamie," Mallorie buzzed in his ear. "All the creatures here, they feed off you. Nasty little bogle—it got quite a bite too. I suppose the good news is that you can't get much taller, can you?"

Jamie looked down at himself. He was taller than even Daddy now. "How much time has passed?"

"I don't know, love," Mallorie answered, her voice soothing. "No time at all in our world, but yours is a bit different. We need to keep moving. We need to reach the caves, and then we'll get you to the Burg, and perhaps, perhaps, perhaps then you will find your way home before your bones become nothing more than the pointy bits in our soil."

THE caves turned out to be a cavern so low to the ground that Jamie had to get down on all fours to enter it. The wood elves' book was entirely too cumbersome to carry through the cavern, so Jamie had fashioned a sort of sling made from a few absurdly large leaves and strips of soft bark. The beetle fairy had impatiently circled his head while he worked; the task was entirely unnecessary in her view. Bilbo worked diligently to chew through the bark and assist where he could.

Now as Jamie crawled through the cave, the book tied to his back, he was grateful that he had insisted she wait for him to finish. The cavern floor was slippery with lake water that splashed around Jamie's knees and elbows, and he was having a hard time not falling on his face. The Asrai's magical wrap stayed dry but tangled on everything. Jamie had finally tied it around his waist, sacrificing modesty for the sake of forward mobility. Mallorie seemed equally ill at ease. She perched on Jamie's head and chirped orders. Bilbo clung to Jamie's hair. Jamie realized grumpily that he was the only one actually moving in the cave; the others were simply riding him like a mule.

There was no light from either end, and Jamie's chest constricted—it was difficult to breathe properly. He had an idea of what this was. Claustrophobia was very common; it wasn't anything to be ashamed of, he simply needed to let people know when he needed space and if he felt scared. That was what Ms. Hamilton had told him as he sat in the school office last April, shaking off the last bit of a good cry. His parents were on their way, Ms. Hamilton had assured him. He was going to go home early, and he could take a long nap and would feel much better.

He had doubted he would ever feel better. He felt perfectly terrible as Ms. Hamilton leaned into his face, her breath a wretched combination of coffee and breath mints, in equal measures appealing and sour. He had closed his eyes and wished for Momma and Daddy, and they seemed to take forever to arrive. The circumstances were whispered to them by the man at the front desk. He was never sure of the man's name but he seemed to know Jamie, and that worried Jamie quite a lot. He worried about what else this man knew about him. He wondered if the man knew what he ate for dinner and why he was afraid to swallow sometimes and why even mashed potatoes seemed like something he could choke on. He wondered if the man knew that Jamie whispered the lines from his book to himself after Momma kissed him goodnight and Jamie was sure no one else would come in the room and wonder what he was saying. *Thank goodness for all the things you are not, thank goodness you're not something someone forgot, and left all alone in some punkerish place, like a rusty tin coat hanger hanging in space.* Jamie couldn't pinpoint why the words made his heart slow down or why they let his chest take in a breath once again.

He had tried repeating the words over and over during the time he was locked in the tiny supply closet. He had gone in after red paint for his project. They were supposed to be painting a picture of where they lived, and Jamie's house wasn't red—it was a rusty brown—but he liked red better, so he planned on painting the walls and windows red. The chimney was another addition. There wasn't really a chimney on Jamie's house, but he liked the idea of one—the idea that you could have a fire, something so wild in your house, tamed like a cat or his terrier dog. The red paint was in the back of the closet, and as Jamie stepped forward to grab it, the door behind him had slammed shut. He had cried out, but all he heard on the other side was giggles. His chest had closed in, he couldn't breathe, and he felt like he might be dying. *Thank goodness for all the things you are not, thank goodness you're not something someone forgot . . .* He'd heard a rustling at the door and

Ms. Hamilton's voice—she was angry. He couldn't properly hear what she was saying, but someone was going to get a time out, he was sure of it. He banged on the door, futilely turning the knob. He choked on his own spit and fell back, coughing so hard his throat was on fire. A shelf full of multicolored chalk fell on him, and in the dark of the closet the thick sticks of chalk felt like worms and snakes. Jamie had screamed and tried to pull the squirming snakes off him. He had felt their fangs sink into his body; he felt himself going numb. *Like a rusty tin coat hanger hanging in space.* The next thing Jamie knew, he was lying on the floor in Ms. Hamilton's classroom, the class standing around staring, their eyes big. Ms. Hamilton had lifted him and carried him down the hallway to the office, and he had lain in the nurses' office for what seemed like forever, stiff as a board, afraid to move lest the snakes come back again. Ms. Hamilton had left to go back to her abandoned class, while he was left with the nurse, who looked like she should be teaching at Hogwarts. Her nose was entirely too long for her face, and her eyes changed color. Jamie found her very unsettling. She smelled of cigarettes that had been sprayed with perfume. Jamie was relieved when Ms. Hamilton had returned to guide him to the bench in the office—coffee and mint were better than perfume and cigarettes.

The man at the front desk spoke to Momma and Daddy in a voice that was supposed to be too soft for Jamie to hear, but he had heard anyhow. It was an accident, he told them. Accidentally pulled the door shut behind him—panicked a bit, that's all, a good scare. Jamie almost broke the illusion that he couldn't hear at that one—*a good scare?* There was nothing good about a scare, why couldn't that man at the front desk see that? He hadn't heard the giggles on the other side of the door, he hadn't been attacked by a thousand snakes, and he hadn't felt himself dying. He knew nothing.

Jamie blundered forward in the cavern. He hit his head on a low rock overhang, sending the beetle fairy into flight.

"Watch yourself, will you!" Mallorie exclaimed.

Jamie was too tired to even respond. It had been over a day

since he had eaten, and even though he was sure he wasn't nearly as hungry as he should be, his limbs felt like they were constructed entirely of Jell-O. *Thank goodness for all the things you are not,* Jamie whispered silently to himself. He lifted his head slightly, Mallorie retaking her perch. Finally, in the far distance, he saw a bit of light. Fresh air swept down the tunnel.

"Thank god," Jamie whispered. "For the record, this is not a cave. This is a tunnel. There's a difference."

The beetle fairy didn't respond, but Bilbo nuzzled his neck in agreement. Closer and closer—the light became more appreciable as night stars got ready to fade into dawn. Jamie sighed. Two nights gone in this world, and how many years had passed since he fell down the very long hill? From the look of himself, it appeared to be at least twenty. Maybe it all would go back to the way it had been when he went home. That wasn't what Mallorie, or anyone else for that matter, had told him, but maybe they were wrong . . . maybe.

Finally, Jamie pushed himself and his passengers out into the night air. His arms and legs gave way, and he collapsed face-first into the damp earth. The lake water had continued throughout the tunnel and formed a muddy pool here at the end. Jamie pulled himself out of the mud and into soft grass and laid his head down again, his limbs trembling with the exertion. Mallorie took to the air, and Bilbo hopped off Jamie's neck and into the grass. Jamie looked up to see the little rat sniffing the air nervously. Poor little thing, Jamie thought.

Jamie lay still, his body more tired than he thought possible. The wood elves' book lay against his back; he shuffled it off onto the grass. He closed his eyes and felt the world start to swim. How long had it been since he'd really slept? Jamie enjoyed the feeling of floating, even though he knew perfectly well what it meant to fall unconscious in this world. He had slept in the clearing back at the bottom of the very tall hill—that had been two nights ago. *Two nights.* He had still been seven and hadn't known any better. He rarely slept well, even when his body was exhausted—his mind would continue at breakneck speed, playing out the horror of his day, the moments of embarrassment, every minute of regret. Not so now; now his mind was entirely free, floating in an inky blackness, like the oil paintings at the museum where he'd gone with Momma. The night sky swirling with muted color, behind it only darkness. He let himself fall deeper into the stillness, his body aching with exhaustion.

THIRTEEN

"GREAT oats, boy!"

Mallorie circled his head. He didn't know why she was angrily buzzing in his ear, and he didn't care. He reached up and half-heartedly swatted away the noise.

"How old exactly do you want to be when you leave this place?" Mallorie shouted, which had the effect of a thousand angry bees.

Jamie opened his eyes. "Easy for you to say—you rode on my head the entire way through that tunnel."

"Nothing to be done about that. You would have had to make your way through with or without us riding on you. Now *get up*."

Mallorie's voice took on a fire-alarm whine. Jamie groaned and sat up, making a quick check to see if his rest had resulted in more growth. He appeared to be no taller, but he wasn't sure how much taller he *could* get. He adjusted the Asrai's wrap and pulled the wood elves' book back over his shoulder. Bilbo crawled back up his arm and into his hair. With great effort, Jamie stood and stretched.

"What's the matter with you, boy?" Mallorie asked, her voice highly annoyed.

Jamie rubbed his eyes with remarkably large hands. He held one out in front of him in the fading starlight, marveling at how grown-up it looked.

"I need to eat," Jamie replied, knowing there was no solution to his problem. "I haven't eaten since before I fell into this world."

The last thing Jamie had eaten was a hot dog bun and a handful of french fries at the Getty. He'd refused to eat the actual hot dog but enjoyed the slight grilled flavor that the meat leant to the bread. He had smothered the entire thing with ketchup, much to Momma and Daddy's dismay. If he'd known, he would have eaten the entire hot dog—he'd have eaten a hundred hot dogs. Just thinking of it made Jamie's stomach contract, and he nearly doubled over with a cramp that ripped through his gut.

"Nothing to be done about that now, love." Mallorie's tone softened. "We need to hurry to the Burg. They're closer to your world; they might have something that is suitable, but we must go."

Jamie nodded, his legs still a bit shaky.

"Which way?" he asked.

The beetle fairy buzzed off, and Jamie followed. The night was quickly fleeing the sky; soon the sun would rise again, and another day would pass. Jamie took a deep breath, trying to control his emotions. He walked through the shin-high grass, where tall wild-flowers jutted up in sporadic bursts. Around the periphery of the meadow, Jamie saw great oak trees. As the sky lightened, more became apparent. There was some sort of structure in the distance.

"I see it!" Jamie cried excitedly.

Mallorie flew in a figure-eight pattern before him.

"You don't know what it is you see, love," Mallorie sang. "That's not the city, not quite yet," she continued. "But we must pass through this settlement in order to get to what's beyond."

Jamie kept walking. As the sky brightened, it became clear that the settlement, as Mallorie had called it, was a collection of tents, some striped and some silky white. Jamie squinted.

"It's a circus?" he murmured, unsure of what he was seeing.

"We are closer to your world now. The mist is thinner here. You won't be able to see through the veil yet, but soon enough, child, you will," Mallorie buzzed in his ear. "This place is built of nightmares of a different kind. Us fae stay away from this place.

It is where I will leave you. It is where you will join the Burg and where, perhaps, your journey will end."

Jamie stopped, staring at the scene that was unfolding in front of him. The circus grounds spread out in either direction as far as he could see. He saw an impossibly tall Ferris wheel, so tall it disappeared into the clouds; its cars were rusty and swung back and forth in the breeze. Jamie shivered. He hadn't thought of the beetle fairy leaving him, and he felt a great emptiness as he looked at Mallorie hovering in front of him.

"I'll take you as far as the gates, but then you must continue on your own. Our kind do not go inside. You must enter on your own," Mallorie said softly.

"But I can't do this without you. I can't," Jamie choked.

"You must, love," Mallorie whispered. "It's your only chance to leave our world. I don't know if you will be successful, but if you stay here with us, you will die. Your Lairdbalor will find you, and when he does, what remains of you will become a nightmare creature of its own making, leavings for the dwarves. Or, if you somehow manage to elude him, you will grow too old to walk, too old to speak. Your flesh will become the food for this world."

Jamie shivered. He shook his head, hoping against hope to wake from this place.

"What if the Burg can't save me? What if nothing can?"

"You're the only one from your world to ever make it this far, love," Mallorie said gently. "I don't know what will become of you. But you cannot turn back, and you cannot stay still—you must keep walking."

Jamie nodded. He forced himself forward, walking in silence, the beetle fairy in front of him, quiet. The tents glowed in the sunrise, and Jamie could not help but draw a breath in at the sight of the airy material soaking up the streaks of gold and pink, the entire field looking as though it were on fire. Suddenly, from behind him, there was a faint sound. Jamie stopped, straining to make it out. It was someone whistling, like in the movies, where men could whistle entire songs and not just one long tone. Jamie looked back, but he saw nothing.

"Do you hear that?" he asked.

Mallorie paused, circling back.

"What?" Mallorie asked, her voice on the edge of worry.

"It's a song. Someone's whistling a song." Jamie motioned behind him. "Back there."

The sound grew louder, the tune familiar. Jamie had heard it before—Daddy played it on the little radio in the kitchen when he cooked dinner. The notes danced around. It was jazz, Daddy had told him. Gershwin, Daddy had said. Jamie strained to remember what else Daddy had said about the tune. He had been curious about it, why Daddy liked it, why it went on for so long when most songs ended long before—this one seemed to last forever. It lasted the entire time it took for Daddy to cook the mushrooms and add the sour cream to the pan for his pasta sauce. Daddy was able to heat the water and boil the noodles, all in the time it took for this one song to be done. And now, here it was—a crystal, perfect whistle, the tone piercing the stillness of the meadow, growing louder and louder. It jumped impossibly from note to note. Jamie began to hum along as he recognized the melody.

"Jamie," Mallorie said carefully. "Jamie—stop it, Jamie."

"Stop what?" Jamie asked, annoyed. The sound was so happy— it was the sound of dinner being made, of Daddy happy in the kitchen, of a good Saturday night. It was the sound of his old life, and he didn't want to stop it.

"Jamie," Mallorie repeated. "Jamie, remember the bogle?"

"This isn't a bogle. It's just a song." Jamie hummed louder. He heard the irrationality of his words, but he was overwhelmed by the sheer joy of the tune. The notes skipped down his spine, and he would have danced if he hadn't felt so deliciously tingly. The melody changed—Daddy called this part the bridge.

"No. It's not a bogle. You're right, Jamie," Mallorie said. Something about the way she spoke made Jamie look up and meet her tiny, beady eyes. "This is far worse than a bogle."

Jamie shook his head. The melody grew louder still, the notes tripping over each other in a climb, and two competing strands now emerged—the whistler managed to create both. Jamie closed his eyes, letting the sound wash over him.

"Jamie . . . Jamie." Mallorie was directly next to his ear, her voice eerily calm. "Jamie, run."

Jamie snapped awake—the perfect whistle now was a series of discordant notes, broken and tuneless. It pierced his ears and reverberated in his head. The soft, disconnected feeling broke. Jamie looked behind him and saw the gelatinous body moving through the field with improbable grace. The rotting top hat caught the sunrise; the monocle reflected the light, making it blinding to look at. The Lairdbalor made a grand gesture with its mauled flipper of an arm, and then it started to sing.

"Embrace me, my sweet embraceable you. Embrace me, you irreplaceable you . . . "

The sound was horrid and grand in equal measure. Jamie was transfixed. Mallorie flew in front of his eyes, blocking the Lairdbalor from view.

"Run!" she keened.

Jamie obeyed blindly. He turned from the monster and ran as fast as he could toward the circus tents. Behind him, he heard the Lairdbalor's tinny voice.

"I want my arms around you . . . Embrace me, my sweet embraceable you. Embrace me, you irreplaceable you . . . "

The song grew louder, and Jamie could swear he felt the hot breath on his neck. He focused on the iron gates in the near distance. He knew without anyone telling him that he needed to enter under that arch. Bilbo let out a high-pitched squeal, his claws digging deep in Jamie's hair. The squeal helped to block out the wretched sound behind him.

"My sweet embraceable you . . . "

As the iron gate grew nearer, the sound cut out. The only noise was Jamie's rushed breath in his ears and the sound of tall grass being crushed under his feet. Jamie desperately wanted to look back—where was it? Was it right behind him? Would the rotting fabric of its flipper arm reach out at any minute? But Jamie raced on; a stitch developed in his side, but still he ran. The pitch of the meadow changed and the flat ground now sloped downhill. His feet flew out from under him, and he fell hard, his chin hitting the ground first. His flesh tore, a searing pain he barely noticed in his mad scramble to regain his feet. The iron gate was only a dozen yards away—he could reach it; he was almost there.

The sunrise reflection from the tent tops was blocked, and the Lairdbalor loomed over him like a great and terrible shadow. Jamie fell back. He opened his mouth to scream, but no sound came out. Bilbo's squeal intensified, and he clawed at Jamie's head in a panic—Jamie could feel the scratches. He looked up. The creature was larger than it had been in his previous dream visit. It was as big around as a dozen men standing together—and taller than Jamie remembered, tall enough to block out the sun. It smelled of things long dead.

"Hello, Jamie," it said, the brass tone of its voice filling the meadow.

"Please. I just want to go home," Jamie sobbed.

"Home. We all want to go home, Jamie. Tell me about your home, Jamie—are you happy there?" The slitlike lips didn't move; the sound resonated deep within the creature and then resounded like a symphony into the open space.

Jamie nodded.

"They were going to send you away, Jamie. Surely you remember that?" The Lairdbalor looked upward to the sky. "Such a sunrise, Jamie, such a sunrise. I've always greatly preferred sunrises to sunsets. The coming of light, a reprieve from all those things that scare us so at night. Isn't that so, Jamie?"

Jamie nodded, numb with terror. His mind was racing. Send him away?

"Yes, child, they were planning on sending you away. Your parents hadn't quite settled on how to tell you yet, bless them. Think back, Jamie, you saw the signs. You heard them talking when they thought you were asleep—think back, Jamie."

Jamie pulled himself off the ground, wiping the congealing blood from his chin. He shook his head, trying to block out the terrible voice. But an overheard conversation from Momma and Daddy's room resonated in his head, an argument they'd had after Mr. Kevin had stopped visiting. Money. It was too expensive, Daddy had said. Momma had been crying, saying she didn't know how to keep him safe. Jamie had covered his ears with his pillow— he hated it when they argued about money. He had hugged Bilbo close and repeated the lines to his book.

Thank goodness you're not something someone forgot . . . like a rusty tin coat hanger hanging in space.

He looked up at the Lairdbalor, his eyes filled with tears.

"You scared them, Jamie." The voice was a note that filled the sky. "Hush, child; it wasn't your *meang*. You aren't to blame. But you scared them. They feared you, *feagal bhalaich*. Do you remember why, Jamie? Do you remember why?"

Jamie shook his head. Momma and Daddy weren't afraid of him, they weren't. They were his parents; they loved him. Momma would hold him in her arms. Daddy would squeeze him so hard his breath was knocked out. He would lift Jamie up on his shoulders as they walked around the zoo. They weren't afraid of him.

"Lie! It's a lie!" Jamie screamed at the top of his lungs.

He shoved past the monster, letting his anger and fear guide him. The Lairdbalor moved easily aside as Jamie hurdled past. As he approached the circus gates, he saw there were words scratched into the black iron.

Clann is aingeal.

Jamie paused, glancing behind him. The Lairdbalor stood where he had left it.

"It's dangerous to confuse children with angels, Jamie."

The clear sound echoed around the meadow, catching an invisible point and bouncing back, clear as a bell.

"Go now, but think on what I've told you. When you remember, we will meet again. Find the ticket booth; the hapless *na dùil* who seek to help you are waiting. It's not their fault, Jamie. I do not blame them or you. Go now." The Lairdbalor turned and, with incongruent agility, moved seamlessly across the meadow, growing distant.

Jamie took a deep breath. His heart was racing. The idea that the Lairdbalor had let him go was even more horrible than the alternative. Mallorie was gone. He took a deep breath and stepped through the gate.

FOURTEEN

INSIDE the gate was much like outside the gate. The air felt the same, the sunrise reflected off the tents, but he was absolutely alone save for Bilbo, who shook at the nape of Jamie's neck. Gently, Jamie lifted the little rat off his neck and held him cupped in his grown-up hands. Jamie stroked his soft fur until Bilbo stopped shaking. Jamie cooed at him, singing the same song that Momma used to sing to him.

Hush, little baby, don't say a word.
Momma's gonna buy you a mockingbird.

The mere act of singing the words made the Lairdbalor's words feel unreal, disconnected. Suddenly, Jamie realized what the Lairdbalor's visit must have meant. He looked down at his body—he was, as far as he could tell, the same height, but the thick patch of golden hair on his chest was thinner now and the skin tighter. He saw creases across his belly. Jamie had no idea what it meant, but he knew he had aged, at least a bit. Every attack meant lost years, meant more time passed in his world, more time that his Momma and Daddy had to forget.

Like a rusty tin coat hanger hanging in space.

Jamie shook off the despair. There was no little beetle fairy to urge him on now, no one to answer his questions or fly circles around his head when he lost his way. Bilbo looked at him imploringly.

"C'mon, Bilbo. Let's go home."

He walked forward, looking from side to side. No one occupied the many tents—the entire scene was abandoned. Signs marked every tent. A large, garishly painted sign read "Spiritualist! Fortunes Told and Made!" Jamie stared at the sea-green tent, the entrance flapping in the wind. Looking around first, he stepped toward the tent opening, curious. He reached toward the tent flap, and for the first time he noticed that his hand had spots, like freckles, but broader and flat. He looked closer and discovered the freckles extended up his arm and onto his shoulders, which had myriad splotches. They looked like the freckles on Momma's shoulders; he stared in fascination. A crisscross of fine lines also marked his hands. Transfixed, he flexed and clenched his fist, watching the lines and splotches fold and change.

Snapping to attention, he completed what he had started and pulled the sea-green tent flap aside, revealing a space entirely empty except for a table with two chairs neatly tucked in. On the surface sat a large crystal ball that reflected the sea-green light from the tent and something more—it seemed to emit a light of its own, rainbow refractions spread across the room. Jamie held his hand high, letting the light dance across his skin, fascinated.

On his shoulder again, Bilbo nervously washed his face. Jamie stroked the little rat's head and took a step into the tent, the flap closing behind him. Jamie walked with the confidence of one who's already seen his own death—he crossed the room knowing there were far worse things than the unknown. Following a compulsion that he was sure the beetle fairy would disapprove of, he sat in one of the chairs. It was a cheap, plastic garden chair, the type that sits on every lawn of every house in particular neighborhoods. Jamie's grown-up body didn't quite fit. He stared across at the empty chair, almost expecting to see somebody. Something about this place made him feel as though he had always been here and as though he would never leave. He felt as though he had been alone forever; it was a feeling deeper than despair—it was inevitability.

Jamie switched his gaze to the crystal ball, the rainbow streaks of light blinding him momentarily. When he looked again, the colors swirled, beginning to form shapes. The shapes became people, and the people grew faces—with a start, Jamie recognized himself, not as he was, but as he had been. He saw his shaggy blond hair and seven-year-old face, large brown eyes and gap-toothed smile. Jamie ran his tongue over his teeth; they were all there now, and he suspected they were the real things, no baby teeth left.

He saw himself sitting on a bed in a room, but no room that he had ever been in. The walls were blank, and the single window had bars on the outside. The door had an electronic fixture on it that blinked green. Seven-year-old Jamie sat on a plain bed with a metal frame, no sheets or blankets. Those, he saw further, sat in a neatly folded pile next to him. Seven-year-old Jamie sat quietly, head down. Grown Jamie reached to the crystal ball and ran a finger down the side, sending a ripple through the image. Seven-year-old Jamie looked up as though he had felt a strong breeze.

"Where are you?" Jamie mouthed at his child self.

The image looked up at him, unseeing.

"I don't know," it mouthed back.

Jamie felt cold inside. His stomach clenched, and his breath was tight in his chest.

The image changed. Jamie watched as seven-year-old Jamie transformed to a somewhat older version of himself. His hair was still shaggy, but pimples dotted his face, and his arms and legs were entirely too long for his skinny body. He wore ill-fitting jeans and a T-shirt with "Ramones" written across it. Somewhat-older Jamie looked up, and his deep brown eyes were the same, full of sadness and intensity. He sat in an office with two chairs, and across from him sat a man that looked a bit like Mr. Kevin, although Jamie was sure he was not. Still, this man had a chart and a clipboard and was waiting for somewhat-older Jamie to speak; he did not. Grown Jamie ran his finger over the image, again sending ripples that made his younger self look up. Still unseeing, the figure mouthed, "I don't know."

Jamie looked away. He didn't know what it meant, but he wanted to escape this suddenly stifling tent, the sun beating down on its surface. But to leave would mean to leave himself. It would mean that no one bore witness to what he might have been, what he didn't know then or now. If the beetle fairy and wood elves were right, these images were never to pass, the years already gone. Instead, Jamie had been here and Momma and Daddy had been alone.

They feared you.

Jamie shook his head. It couldn't be true. What cause would they have to fear him? What was a seven-year-old capable of?

Dangerous to confuse children with angels.

It didn't make any sense, but Jamie had no beetle fairy to ask. Still he stared at the image. The colors swirled and began to form another, angrier image; lines of a drawing, black and messy, swirled in a mad circle, and at the center, only darkness. Jamie saw his own hand—his smaller, younger hand—the child's fingers clenched around a crayon, the effort threatening to break it in two. Jamie had a faint memory of the drawing—everything seemed so very far away in this place, as though he had been gone for years instead of days. He reached out and ran a finger down the smooth side of the crystal ball. A ripple ran through the scene, but the manic scribbling did not stop. Suddenly, a deep tug ran down the line on his forehead, the icy patch where the Asrai had raked her claw across his skin. He jumped up, the chair falling backward to the ground. Still staring at the ball, Jamie backed out of the tent, pulling the sea-green tent flap aside and stepping out into the sunshine.

Bilbo scurried to his shoulder, his tiny nose buried in Jamie's ear. Jamie stroked the little rat and looked around. The wood elves' book, still strapped to his back, was heavy, and the makeshift harness bit into his skin. Jamie grimaced as he adjusted the weight, hoping that the vines wouldn't break. No living things were around, or at least obvious. Jamie sighed. Constant fear had numbed his senses; he was hyperaware and at the same time so deeply jaded. He began to walk, although he didn't know what he was looking for. The Lairdbalor had said to go to the ticket booth. It seemed counterintuitive to follow the instructions of a monster that was created of the worst parts of himself, a monster that was hunting him. *A monster that let me go*, the voice whispered in Jamie's ear. Why? Jamie asked himself as he walked past still more empty tents. He had no desire to look inside—he was afraid of what he would find.

He reached the foot of the impossibly tall Ferris wheel. Jamie looked up, squinting against the blinding sun. The top of the Ferris wheel melted into the clouds. It was abandoned, like everything else. As Jamie stared at the peeling red and blue paint, the entry gate swung open, banging against the rusted metal barrier where an ancient line once stood. Well over a hundred red and blue carriages hung from the metal frame, each dusty from disuse, swinging lightly in the breeze. Jamie was awed by the sheer scope of the thing. He took a step closer, Bilbo chattering in his ear in his rat-speak. Jamie ran a finger down Bilbo's back.

"It's okay. I'm just looking, just looking," he whispered.

Jamie stepped through the entry gate, which slammed shut behind him. He jumped but did not panic—he could easily step over the thigh-high barrier. He stood almost directly beneath the structure and looked up again. The sight made him dizzy. Suddenly, the metal skeleton began to move, and an ancient and eerie music tinkled to life, triggered by the motion. The cars swayed back and forth, and Jamie jumped back so as not to be hit. The speed increased, the blue and red cars swinging madly as they circled. Jamie drew a sharp breath. At the very top, the sky became clear, and the carriages appeared to fly of their own will. As suddenly as it began, the giant iron beast screeched to a halt. A faded blue car swung back and forth in front of him. Jamie knew he was meant to enter, and he also knew that if he did, he would never descend from the clouds above. It was oddly compelling—the idea that this could be it, the end of this wretched journey. He had no idea what was at the top: if the Lairdbalor was waiting with a cup of its rose-scented tea; if Momma and Daddy would appear like in those cartoons of heaven where people lived on top of clouds; if everything would suddenly end and his body, his mind, all his collected parts would simply scatter and be no more. That—that was the possibility that brought him a step closer to the faded blue car.

On his shoulder, Bilbo let out a wild squeal. Jamie absently stroked the rat's soft fur.

"You should stay here, Bilbo . . . " he murmured.

He scooped up the little rat in one hand and, never taking his eyes off the faded blue carriage, gently placed Bilbo on the ground. Bilbo would be fine; he belonged here. He could leave this place, find Mallorie, live in the forest—he would be fine. Jamie took another step toward the carriage, ignoring Bilbo's panicked squeals. Jamie placed a hand on the gate, the blue paint chipping off on his palm at even that gentle touch. It swung open easily—he was meant to enter. He would sit and let it carry him to the very top, and then it would be over. All this—the uncertainty, the hunger, his too-large body and too-long hair, the lost years, the aching longing for Momma and Daddy, the nagging fear that everything the Lairdbalor had said was true, that he was destined to be alone in his world, that Momma and Daddy didn't want him, that they feared him, that he was dangerous, that he was not meant to be—it would all be over. He would sail over this circus, over the forest, over the wood elves' path, over the clearing at the bottom of the very long hill. He would rule over it all for the briefest of moments, and then it would all be over—and he could sleep.

As Jamie moved to the carriage, a voice broke through the deep fog of his thoughts.

"Wouldn't advise it, mate—this ride's out of order. Down for maintenance."

Jamie swiveled around, his head spinning. He couldn't see the source of the words, although he looked carefully—another beetle fairy? Something even smaller? He saw nothing. At his feet, Bilbo hopped up and down frantically. Jamie's head cleared, and he backed away in horror from the empty carriage. Now he saw that it was rusted nearly off its hinges, the seat stained and torn. He looked up—the clouds circled the top of the structure, and they were turning black with rain. Jamie scooped up Bilbo and stumbled back. The gate was closed, but Jamie stepped clumsily over it. Once back on the dirt path, he breathed a big sigh, a weight lifting from his shoulders.

"Hello!" Jamie yelled. "Hello? Who are you?"

He looked around—no one and nothing moved.

"Are you the Burg? What are you?" Jamie asked the empty space. There was no answer.

"I'm going to find the ticket booth," Jamie said. "Hear that? I'm going to the ticket booth."

With that, Jamie started to walk, not looking back at the rusting Ferris wheel, which had resumed its manic spinning, the tinkling, broken music trying desperately to keep up. Jamie was afraid that if he did look back, he wouldn't be able to resist again.

A wooden sign advertised a freak show in big, ornate letters. It had been painted many years ago, bright golds and reds now faded to the color of crushed autumn leaves. The mustard-yellow tent flap blew open just as Jamie passed, revealing a wooden proscenium stage lined with floor-level gaslights. Wooden folding chairs sat in anticipatory rows. The dirt floor was barren of footprints or any indication that anyone had entered in a very long time. Jamie paused, and Bilbo climbed back into his hair. Jamie shook his head.

"Hello?" Jamie called out. "Anyone in there?"

In response, tinny piano music began to play. There was no instrument that he could see, but it seemed to come from all around. The curtains on the stage rustled, and a figure emerged. It was small, the height of a child, the height Jamie had been once. It walked matter-of-factly across the stage to a set of stairs that led to the dirt floor. Jamie couldn't make out if the figure was male or female, or if, indeed, it was even human. To his surprise, its shape looked very human indeed. Perfect creamy-skinned hands and fingers, perfect human legs—it wore a long nightshirt, the type that you wore in the hospital. Jamie could see the strings that tied it shut in the back. It was the face that Jamie couldn't look away from. The features were all out of order: The nose was almost entirely nonexistent, a slit slightly to the left of its expected location. The eyes drooped downward, heavy lids obscuring the irises. The mouth was pulled down as though by an invisible string. It walked directly to Jamie and stopped. The creature, which stood as high as Jamie's waist, looked up at him, and he could see unsettling pale-gray eyes beneath the sagging skin.

"Hullo."

The voice was light, feminine.

"Hello," Jamie stuttered. "Are you the Burg?"

"Oh, heavens no. Are they here? What a hoot," the creature said. "What are you? What nightmare did you come from? Are you our new addition? What's your irregularity?"

"My what?" Jamie asked, surprised. "I . . . I'm not a nightmare. I'm trying to get home. I'm supposed to find the Burg—they're going to take me home."

"Hmm. Mental affliction. Not too showy, but a good 'un nonetheless. Well, come on in. I'll show you around."

The creature's voice was light and friendly. Jamie smiled despite himself.

"No, really. I'm not crazy. I've traveled here from a long ways away. I fell down a hill, and a beetle fairy brought me here. I'm to meet the Burg. They're going to take me to the city. I have this book; I took it from the wood elves. I think it might tell me how to get home."

As Jamie indicated the text slung to his back, Bilbo emerged from his hair and stood on his shoulder. The little creature grinned, the crooked mouth forming a bizarre half grimace.

"Ooh! Can I pet it?" she asked with genuine sweetness.

Jamie bent down, and Bilbo crawled into his hands and leaned into the creature's touch. Tiny, child's fingers hesitantly stroked the little rat's fur.

"Ooh, so soft," she cooed. "We don't get animals much here. Used to have an elephant, but haven't seen it for a while—not much of one for cuddling. For a good long spell, there was a pack of dogs roamed these parts, but nightmare dogs aren't much fun either. What nightmare are you, little guy?" she asked Bilbo.

In response, Bilbo nuzzled her hand. She regarded Jamie curiously.

"What are you really?"

"I told you—I'm human. I'm here by mistake."

The creature laughed, a light, airy sound. "Doubt that. Nothing's a mistake here. No, if you are telling the truth and you really are human, there's a reason you're here and not there. You just haven't figured it out yet."

Jamie shivered. "Are there others here? Others like you?"

"Not like me, but yes, there are others. Children are afraid of anything too very different, but we're all different in our own way." She turned her attention back to Bilbo and sighed deeply. "Usually, the animals end up in the forest—this is nice."

"Can you tell me where the ticket booth is?" Jamie asked softly.

She looked up, hooded gray eyes sharp and piercing.

"Ticket booth? We'll take you, but are you sure you really want to go? The two of you could stay here. It's not so bad here, you know. The others aren't so mean, they're just a bit shy, not so sure of newcomers."

Jamie smiled gently. "I'm sure it's a good place, but I have to try to get home. Momma and Daddy have been looking for me for a very long time. When I arrived here, I was about your size."

"I'm Sariah," she said simply.

Jamie held out his hand. "Jamie."

She took it, and they stayed that way for a long minute, her small hand in his.

"Sariah, can I ask . . . what are you? You're a nightmare? What sort?" Jamie asked cautiously, nervous about offending.

"I'm same as the others in this tent. Human oddities. I came from the hospital. A little boy saw me in the bed next to his. He was there for an illness. I was there a lot—I died there eventually, although I was a bit older than this. He saw me and thought that maybe his pneumonia would turn him into me. He dreamt that night that his face melted, his nose was cut off, and his mouth was pulled into his neck. He woke up screaming, and my face has never left his imagination. I am what he sees even now that he's an old man. He knows now that I wasn't a monster, but he can't help but still be afraid . . . " Her voice trailed off, her eyes focusing once again on Bilbo.

"Are you a ghost?" Jamie asked, his mind spinning.

Sariah laughed—the sound belonged on a playground, in a field on a summer day.

"Heavens no! I'm just a memory. Everything in this world is composed of memories—we remember things oddly, highs and lows."

"I'm sorry," Jamie whispered. "I'm sorry he couldn't have remembered you more kindly. He obviously never spoke to you."

Sariah looked up at him.

"Thank you for that, but I'm not sad. It wasn't the little boy's fault—it's not his fault now. We can't blame ourselves for our childhood fears. I created my own fair share of nightmares in the time I was alive. I feared death, I feared a particular nurse at the children's hospital toward the end of my life, I feared the dark, I feared crickets." She giggled again. "Can you imagine? Crickets of all things. They used to sing outside my window at night, and all I could hear was screaming. I'm sure they're somewhere in the forest, screaming obscenities." She looked up at Jamie. "Our fears are nothing to be ashamed of. They're not made of malice—they're instinct."

Jamie nodded. Bilbo suddenly ran up the length of her arm and sat on her shoulder. Sariah exploded with laughter, the sound like water flowing in a clear creek.

"We can take you to the ticket booth if that's what you want. But you're welcome to stay." Her voice was hopeful.

Jamie smiled. "Thank you. I'm afraid I'm not made for this world. I'm growing too old to be here. In a few days, maybe less, I'll die here—my body is aging. I have to get home as quickly as I can."

Sariah shrugged. "Well, all right then, let me get the others. They don't like to be left out of an adventure. We get so few of them here."

She ducked back into the tent, Bilbo still on her shoulder. Jamie felt a stab of apprehension. The little rat had never willingly left with anyone else. Maybe he was better off here, Jamie thought sadly. Bilbo wasn't aging as Jamie was—Bilbo was, after all, a nightmare of sorts himself—and he made the little girl so happy. The sun was high in the sky. Jamie breathed in. He was worried;

another night out here and he would age further still, and he wasn't sure how much longer he would be able to go without eating. Miraculously, he wasn't thirsty—he suspected it had something to do with the little blue bottle of lake water—but the hunger cramps were circling his stomach. He knew they weren't as strong as they should be; the shifting of time had left his body in a terrific state of confusion, and it had most likely lost its mode of measuring needs.

Sariah had disappeared behind the curtain. After a rustle of activity, she emerged at the head of an unlikely pack of oddities. One little creature's spine was so bent, he walked nearly folded in half. He looked up at Jamie, a grin on his tiny face, brown eyes bright with excitement.

"Human? Really?" he asked curiously.

Jamie smiled and laughed. The others were a collection of physical afflictions: a teenager, almost a woman, with a stump for an arm, a smooth, white hook of bone protruding from the stump; a little boy—smaller than Jamie had been before the very long hill—his face and arms a matted mess of burn tissue that created rivers and caverns, a winding map over his bare scalp, circling one apple-green eye. He, too, was fascinated with Bilbo, and little coos emitting from him. He regarded Jamie shyly. Jamie nodded toward Bilbo.

"It's okay. You can pet him. He's my friend."

The little boy ran a hesitant finger down Bilbo's back, then jumped, his scarred face expanding in a wide grin. Sariah took Jamie's hand and looked back at the others.

"Let's go, friends—Jamie needs to find the ticket booth, and we could use the fresh air. Been ages since we had occasion to go out."

She spoke with authority. The others followed, their faces anticipatory.

"If you don't mind my asking," Jamie said to Sariah, "why don't you leave the tent more often? Are there others here besides you?"

Sariah swallowed and paused before speaking.

"Yes, there are others—these tents all house nightmares. It's why I wouldn't feel right about you being out here on your own. We're not the worst of the bunch by far. Have you seen the Ferris wheel?"

Jamie shivered. "Yeah, I saw it."

"You can guess at what created that," Sariah continued. "Over there"—she indicated to her left—"that's where the Fire-eater used to be. Nasty sort, that one."

"What nightmare was it?"

"Lord knows what would create that," Sariah replied. "There are different sorts of nightmares in this world, Jamie. We're a sort of memory, and as such we are really rather harmless. I'll probably fade away from this place when the old man dies or when his mind deteriorates and he forgets me. I will cease to be a nightmare. Same with all of us." She indicated her ragged troupe, following close behind. "Richard there"—she nodded toward the little boy with the burn scars—"he's a combination of something a little girl saw in a movie and a child she saw once on the play yard. He's already less substantial than he was when he arrived—she's starting to forget, you see?"

Jamie regarded the little girl curiously. "Can all nightmares be forgotten?"

"Not all," Sariah answered. "Some are made of sterner stuff. Some come from the core of a person, and some turn into a monster of their own creation. Some build on themselves and become far more terrifying than they ever were in your world. The Fire-eater is like that."

"It's all so complicated," Jamie murmured.

"Fear is a complicated thing," Sariah said.

The little girl's hand felt solid and cool. Jamie couldn't help but marvel at how big he was—only a day or so ago, he was her size.

"Sariah, can I ask you something?" Jamie hesitated, not sure he wanted the answer.

"Of course."

"Is there any way for me to go back to the way things were? I mean, will I ever be a child again?"

Sariah stopped walking. The troupe behind her halted awkwardly. She looked up at Jamie, taking him in with her deeply hooded gray eyes.

"I'm not really the expert. I can only tell you that you can't unsee what you've seen and you can't unknow all you've learned.

Even if your body went back to that of a child, there are some things you can't undo. I can't see why you'd even want to try."

She started walking again. Jamie walked silently beside her. He thought of the drawing he'd seen in the crystal ball in the sea-green tent. He remembered that day. It hadn't been too long before the day he had fallen down the very tall hill. He'd been angry, although at what he couldn't remember now. It was Saturday, and everyone was supposed to be home, but Daddy wasn't—he was working. Momma had been frustrated; she'd said she wasn't, but Jamie had known better. Her voice changed when she was frustrated. She said things very slowly, each word overpronounced, the way they talked on *Sesame Street*, which was for babies, and Jamie was most certainly not a baby. She had talked to him in the frustrated voice, told him to do something—what was it? Jamie strained to remember. Turn off the television? Whatever it was, she had said it in the frustrated voice. Jamie had gotten angry. He had stomped off to his room, taken his crayons and paper from his desk, and lying on the floor, he had drawn the circle. Each rotation of the black crayon made him feel calmer, more at peace, and as the emotions swirled and spun inside him, he just kept drawing, round and round, round and round. He was almost done; he could feel all the anger nearly out of his entire body, only a little bit left in his fingertips. He felt a cloud lift, and he was almost ready to come out of his room, almost ready to be happy again. The door had opened— Momma's voice wasn't frustrated anymore. Jamie stopped drawing. Everything was okay now. He turned to look at her, all the sick in his stomach calmed. Momma, however, stared at the drawing and didn't even finish what she had been saying, which Jamie suspected had something to do with lunch, so he rather wanted to hear it. Instead, she stared, her eyes growing dark. A hand went to her mouth, and she backed out of the room, slamming the door as she went. Jamie had started crying—it was all so confusing, the look on her face—and she had locked him in there. He went and beat on the door with his fists. She hadn't answered, but he heard her talking to someone even though no one else was there that day. Daddy had come home and taken Jamie from his room. He'd had to pull him out from under his covers, where Jamie had gone to hide, convinced that he would never eat any lunch and no one would ever let him out again. Daddy had made him a sandwich and sat at the kitchen table with him while he ate. It was a terrible sandwich. Jamie didn't like peanut butter, only jam, but he hadn't said anything. He'd just scraped the terrible peanut butter off the roof of his mouth with his tongue, washing it down with gulps of milk.

Momma had gone into his room. When Jamie had been released from his terrible lunch, he had found his drawing missing, and the floor smelled of lemon cleaner. Jamie didn't understand, and not understanding made him cry again. He'd spent the rest of the afternoon under the covers talking to Bilbo. But seeing as Bilbo was a stuffed rat back then, he hadn't had much to say.

Here on this dusty walkway in his oversized, grown-up body, Jamie wondered what in that drawing made Momma act the way she had. He could see now that she was scared—scared of him—but why? What had he done? What could he have possibly drawn? His memory matched what the crystal ball had shown him—a black circle, round and round, round and round. He had heard Momma and Daddy talking about it days later—the terrible drawing, what had it meant? Why had he done it? Should they call someone? Would Mr. Kevin come back? Jamie hadn't understood. It was a black circle, round and round, round and round.

He'd been surprised they took him to the Getty that sunny day when he fell down the very tall hill. Jamie hadn't expected them to want to do anything fun with him after the drawing incident, but he liked the Getty. They had hot dogs in the cafeteria, and sometimes, if he was really good, Momma would buy him a little finger puppet from the gift store. On that particular Saturday, Jamie had had his eye on a tiny red bird puppet whose beak you could move with one finger. Daddy had said next time, and Jamie had felt a kind of deep-bone sadness. He knew Daddy wasn't happy with him, but he hadn't known why, and Momma was still too quiet. They had left soon after that. Jamie had suspected that he was in trouble, at least a little bit, and was rather glad that Momma had wanted to walk back down the hill rather than take the train. A longer walk meant it would be longer till he was actually in trouble.

All this played in Jamie's head as he walked past the empty tents. Sariah hummed a little melody, her small voice sweet and melodic.

"Do you know the Lairdbalor?" Jamie asked her suddenly.

Sariah looked up at him, her hooded gray eyes studying his face carefully.

"You brought it with you, I know that. I know that it's following you. But it doesn't frighten me—there's little it can do to us, insubstantial as we are. No, your Lairdbalor feeds off things that have more weight in this world. We're little more than whispers." Sariah offered him a half smile and shrugged.

Jamie was confused—nothing here seemed to fit with anything else.

"I don't understand. The beetle fairies, the wood elves—they're different from you?"

Sariah nodded. "Oh yes. It's as I said before—fear is a complicated thing. Some fears are more pervasive, some are more real, and some transcend the barrier of childhood and haunt you all your life. Some are just bad memories that your grown-up eyes see the reality of eventually—such as it is with us. The ones who live in the forest are far more substantial. Same with the Burg, but they rarely come here." She paused, looking up at the perfect blue sky. "It's nice to have visitors."

Jamie just nodded. They had been winding their way through the tents for what seemed like a long time. He wondered how Sariah and the others would ever find their way back. The only marker was the giant Ferris wheel, which always seemed to be in the same spot, about two tents away, behind them and slightly to the right. After two days and nights in this world, Jamie realized that this was just the way things were here. All the doubt and fear he would've felt even a day ago was washed into a quiet sense of wonder.

He had gone to a circus once, although it hadn't really been like this. Momma and Daddy had taken him, and he sat on a narrow bench in a giant tent with a stage and several different circles in the center. He didn't remember much—it was right before he started kindergarten, and five years old was hardly old enough to remember anything at all. He did remember, however, that there weren't any animals; instead, there were people dressed as animals and others in all manner of strange costumes. It had been horribly disappointing. They climbed up terrifically tall poles and leapt over each other on a giant trampoline. Strange music played. Jamie had been transfixed until a creature that resembled a giant frog crawled onto the stage. When it moved, Jamie could see it was a person in a costume. But the arms and legs protruding from the underside of the bright green costume looked like bones, and the strange dancing made it appear as if the frog was having a convulsion.

Jamie knew what a convulsion was—he had seen one in a video that Ms. Hamilton had shown them during First Aid Week. The little girl in the video fell out of her desk and shook with such ferocity that her eyes went entirely white. The narrator—a faceless voice that sounded like he was reading a bedtime story—told all who watched the video that the little girl might bite her tongue or hit her head, and to make sure neither happened. In the video, the teacher had run to the little girl, turned her on her side, and put a thin book in her mouth to bite down on, while the other students had lined up by the door, politely standing aside as a man in a dark-blue suit entered the room. He was a paramedic—Jamie hadn't known what that was—and he took the little girl away. After a moment, the class in the video sat back down and resumed their math work.

Jamie had been horrified. The paramedic had taken the little girl away—she was probably dead, her tongue bitten off and her neck snapped. Jamie had felt panic rising up in him. He'd raised his hand to get permission to use the restroom, but when Ms. Hamilton asked him what he wanted, the only sound that escaped from Jamie's throat was a high-pitched scream. He hadn't even known it was coming from him. It was disconnected; it belonged to someone else. It belonged in this nightmare world, not his first-grade classroom. The other students had run to the door, with none of the orderliness that they had just seen in the video. Ms. Hamilton had screamed too—screamed at him to stop. Finally, she had grabbed him by the shoulders and shook him. Jamie screamed only louder, his worst fears now true—she was trying to kill him. Her long fingernails were digging into his shoulders; he looked down and saw them covered in shiny red. He wrestled away and fell back. The shock of the fall made him stop screaming. It was then he realized he'd wet himself. The other kids were being pulled into the hallway by some other teacher. Jamie sat in his own mess, tears streaming from his eyes and a river of snot from his nose.

Jamie had sat there by himself; Ms. Hamilton had left the room. After what seemed like hours, Daddy had walked through the door and scooped up Jamie in his arms, ignoring his wet pants and snot-stained face. His backpack and homework were scattered on the floor, and Jamie tried to tell him that he would get in trouble, but Daddy had kissed his forehead and whispered that no one was in trouble. He'd carried him out the door, and Jamie had let himself go limp, his head against Daddy's chest. He hadn't paid much attention to the words that Daddy said to Ms. Hamilton and the principal, Mr. G, as they left. Later that night, after Jamie had had a bath and his favorite dinner and was in bed with Bilbo pretending to be asleep, he heard Momma and Daddy in the other room. Their conversation was muffled as though they were trying to be quiet, but Jamie could hear most of it.

"Why would they show that to children?" Momma had asked.

"Inappropriate," said Daddy.

"He's sensitive; he can't be the only one," Momma had said.

Jamie had wondered if sensitive had been what caused the little girl's seizure in the video. He'd stayed awake most of the night just in case he was more sensitive in his sleep, just in case his eyes rolled back into his head.

In any case, the green frog at the weird circus looked like it was having a seizure. Its bones shook in all directions. It leapt impossibly high in the air, grabbed onto a pole, turned upside down, and the audience clapped. Jamie hadn't clapped—he sat stock still, the image of the little girl with the white eyes superimposed onto the scene in the center of the crowd. Jamie hadn't realized he was shaking until Momma yelped in surprise. A puddle had spread from his pants, spilling over the side of the narrow bench. The little boy on the other side of Daddy had looked at him with disgust and pointed. Jamie had known he couldn't take it back; he couldn't change it. Momma had pulled him down the row, apologizing to all whose feet they stepped on. Once outside, she had pulled him to the bathrooms that looked like tall telephone booths from the old movies. She'd had a wild look in her eyes. Jamie couldn't tell if she was angry. He hated not knowing if she was angry. He had tears in his eyes and a knot in his throat, making it impossible to ask.

Momma had taken a deep breath and then knelt down in front of him. Her eyes had softened a bit.

"We'll go home. Okay, buddy?"

Daddy had joined them, holding a pile of sodden napkins. He'd just shaken his head at Momma, and they had gone home. No one spoke of it again. That was shortly before Mr. Kevin had made his appearance. Jamie didn't understand what it all meant. He didn't understand why everyone had been so quiet, but he had known that he'd ruined the circus and couldn't help but wonder if it would have gone differently if it had been a proper circus with elephants and not people dressed as frogs who could jump impossibly high in the air.

This circus looked like it was the sort that had animals once. Jamie adjusted the book on his back; the homemade straps were cutting into his shoulder.

"Here we are."

Sariah pointed about three tents away; Jamie saw a wooden structure, its red-and-white paint peeling, the front boarded up messily, big rusted nails sticking out. As they approached, Jamie saw there was a bit of a clearing here, in which an ancient cotton candy stand stood crookedly on one and a half broken wheels.

"There's no one here," Jamie observed.

"Not that you can see," Sariah replied, looking around. "We can't stay here—we need to get back to our tent."

Jamie felt a familiar stab of panic in his gut. "But what now? Where do I go now?"

Sariah squeezed his hand. "This is as far as we've ever traveled. I'd wait here. If someone is coming for you, then they'll likely be along shortly. But we don't know any further than this." She turned her attention to Bilbo. "I'm especially sorry to leave you," she whispered and looked up at Jamie, a sad half smile on her face. "We don't get many animals here."

The others crowded around. Little fingers stroked Bilbo's head and back. Eventually, they all backed off, standing silently behind Sariah. Bilbo gave Sariah one last nuzzle and scampered off her shoulder, down her arm, and up Jamie's, resting on his shoulder.

"One thing," Sariah said as she started to turn around. "You'll want to leave before nightfall. This place is different at night—it's not safe, not like now. Even if your Burg don't show, you want to keep walking, reach the other side, and keep going."

"Thank you," he whispered.

Sariah nodded and grinned. She was missing a tooth right up in the front, and a wave of sadness washed over him. She'd told him she died around this age, never knowing her adult teeth, never knowing a life where she wasn't the source of other children's nightmares. The others gave him little waves, and he waved back. The tall girl with the bone-hook arm regarded him deeply, breaking away from the others and crossing to him with fast steps. Jamie jumped back a pace, her movement so sudden and unexpected he wasn't sure how to react. She reached Jamie and looked him in the eyes, and he realized how very tall she was, as tall as a grown man. Her eyes were a copper brown. She leaned in toward Jamie's ear, and in a raspy voice unaccustomed to speech she whispered, "Don't believe what it tells you."

She pulled back and stared at Jamie again. Behind her copper eyes, a fire burned, casting constantly moving shadows.

"I hope you get home," she whispered, the words an obvious effort.

Jamie nodded, speechless. She nodded curtly and then turned abruptly and, with small, fast steps, rejoined the others as they walked out of sight around the side of a tent. Jamie wanted to cry out, to run after them. He didn't want to be alone here. Bilbo stood on his shoulder sniffing the air.

"What now?" Jamie murmured.

FIFTEEN

JAMIE wanted to call out, to run after the children, to beg them not to leave him here all alone. But he knew better—creatures from this world were not inclined to stay in any spot just for the asking. He looked around at the empty space. It appeared to be a kind of eating area or event square. Old picnic tables lay haphazardly about, and a popcorn cart on its side reminded Jamie of the gnawing hunger in his gut.

"I really should be much more hungry," he said out loud.

Two days of not eating back in his world would have made him very sick; Jamie knew this. Here it was an inconvenience and very uncomfortable, but compared to the other horrors he had encountered, a minor distraction. He walked to the ticket booth. His bare feet hardly felt the pebbles underneath—another minor distraction. Jamie peered into the empty space: nothing but dust inside. A once-brightly painted sign advertising two tickets for fifty cents hung crookedly over the awning of the small booth. Jamie turned in a slow circle. The book hanging from his back had become a familiar ache, and he adjusted the strap slightly, grimacing at the effort. Bilbo pawed at his ear with his claws. Jamie stroked him absently.

"I don't know what to do," he said softly.

The sun was high in sky; it must be midday in this world where time never seemed to work the way it was supposed to. Hours sped up and slowed down, daytime changed to nighttime without reason, and the stars could be plucked from their perch in the sky and destroyed for the sole purpose of scaring a little boy. Jamie sighed deeply. He wanted home so badly he thought he might just burst. He wondered how far he was from Momma and Daddy. Was he still at the bottom of that very long hill? If he did get back, would he just scramble up the side and be home again? Would he emerge in some unknown part of the world? A crowded square in China? A forest in deepest, darkest Peru like the bear in his stories, the bear that was left alone without anyone he loved, something someone forgot.

Jamie sat down at a dilapidated picnic table, the wood separating in long, disorderly strips. Paddington wasn't supposed to be a sad story—he knew that. It always made him cry nonetheless, and Momma would pull him close and stroke his hair. When he was younger, she would make a soft shushing noise in his ear and whisper that no one would ever leave him behind, his home wasn't going anywhere. Later he learned that he was too old, even at seven, to cry at such things, but he still read the bear story to himself when no one was around. It still made him cry.

Maybe he'd always known this would happen. Maybe it was his fate, like the three sisters in the Greek stories. They had already woven the thread of his disappearance, his death, and were poised and waiting for the moment to snip the last strand—maybe they already had. Maybe he had been working toward this moment his entire short life. Like Sariah, he would become a nightmare in this world, a cautionary tale told by parents to their children. The boy who fell down a hill and disappeared. Every time a hiker found bones or a grown man who had his same chocolate eyes surfaced, his story would resurface too, and once again, his nightmare would gain a bit of substance. He would stay semisolid for eternity, like the boy who disappeared from the mall while his mother shopped or the girl who was snatched while walking home from school and dumped in a latrine in the woods. She stood chest-high in that stinking waste until a hiker found her days later. She screamed for help that she surely, at least one time, thought would never come. Jamie wondered if she ever considered stopping, dropping below the surface, and holding her breath until everything went black and the putrid horror of that moment faded and she went on to the next world. Maybe she was here, somewhere in this circus, under one of these tent flaps, his memory making her a bit less translucent than she was a moment before. Maybe she hated him for it.

The little girl had been in the news for weeks—her disappearance, her rescue, her recovery. Then, gone. Jamie had asked Momma about it, but she hadn't answered his questions; her eyes red and dry, she had said that it was too much to even think about. Daddy had told him that if anyone ever tried to make him get into a car he was supposed to scream and run. Jamie had nodded, but Daddy's answer hadn't made any sense. He wasn't asking about the car, he wanted to know why—what about that little girl made the man in the car choose her? Was it the way she walked? Her dress? How was Jamie to stay safe if he didn't know why? He didn't know her name. Maybe all the lost children were here somewhere, waiting to be forgotten. Jamie's eyes were dry; there were no more tears left. He felt as empty as he had when the Lairdbalor had stolen his insides. But this was far worse—he'd been dreaming then.

Bilbo ran down Jamie's arm and rested on the cracked picnic table, sniffing the air anxiously.

"Maybe we're right where we're supposed to be," Jamie said, afraid of the words. What if he were right?

Bilbo scuttled to the end of the table, looking around.

"I know. It lied," Jamie said quietly. "It said there would be someone to guide me at the ticket booth."

Suddenly, Jamie giggled. It all seemed so absurd; he had actually believed the Lairdbalor, and part of the emptiness he felt right now was due to the fact that it had lied. No one was here. No one would ever be here. Jamie had believed it—a creature composed of the worst parts of himself, a literal nightmare, and he felt betrayed when this monster had lied. That lie felt more visceral than the potential of what the Lairdbalor could and would do if Jamie didn't figure out the wood elves' book and go home. Jamie could spend an eternity in a half-life at the bottom of the Lairdbalor's endless gullet, not too different from the little girl in the latrine, except no one would hear his screams for help. Yet it was this lie that felt like a bigger betrayal. Jamie laughed louder, the sound echoing off the dying landscape. The sound grew and grew; his gut shook with the effort. Bilbo stared at him, his beady black eyes unblinking. On top of everything, my only friend here is a stuffed rat. How old am I? Jamie wondered. By the look of his hands and skin, he knew that he was no longer a child, not even a teenager. He was a bona fide grown-up, not as old as Daddy perhaps, but he soon would be—the next attack, the next moment he dozed off, any little thing, and it would leap again and again and again, until there was nothing left of him but bones.

Jamie stopped laughing abruptly. There was nothing left of anyone in the end. He realized that was what had always bothered him, the thing that people never understood about him, his darkness, his horrible drawings, his fear and his utter isolation. That was it. There was nothing in the end, so how could everyone act so normal? How do you go on about your life? Go to school and pretend that what happened in history books and what was in your lunch sack mattered, go home and pretend that what time you went to sleep and what time you awoke mattered? How can you pretend that any of it made a difference? No, the only part that counted was what you saw when you opened your eyes at night, after you'd fallen asleep and your mind was free. That was what was real, that was the thing that at any minute could rear up and overtake you, negating all the things you believed to be real and true. There was no Momma and Daddy, there was nothing. The realest part of any one person was his or her fear. Jamie could see clearly now. He remembered what was in that drawing on that terrible night that seemed to be a lifetime ago. An endless black circle, the center dark as night, it expanded out from the paper and onto the floor. The center scraped through the paper, the crayon and marker cutting into the whisper-thin edges of the intended surface. But that wasn't what had scared Momma—what had scared her was the movement. The center swirled and brooded. It ebbed like the ocean at night, not all at once and not when you looked at it dead on, but when you closed your eyes, when you looked even a bit away. She saw it as Jamie had intended—she saw the vast darkness, the endless night that lay beyond—and it had scared her. Jamie saw it all the time. He saw it in the blankness of strangers' eyes and in the cruelty of other children; he saw it in corners of his room and in clouds in the sky. He'd spent much of his seven years trying to figure out how no one around him saw it too, how they acted so frustratingly normal all the time when there were unspeakable horrors hiding everywhere. There were people who would bomb and destroy ancient ruins, people who would kill children in unimaginable ways, people who withheld the best parts of themselves, people who had no idea of the monsters that lay just under their own surfaces. Jamie saw it all, and in a rush of release and light, he felt it all lift for the tiniest fraction of a second, hovering over him like a wretched buzzing cloud. His body released a lifetime's worth of tension, his pores expelling the ugliness like steam. He thought he might float. He was surrounded by a thousand sensations: the soap and lotion of the crook of Momma's neck; Daddy's aftershave; the feel of Daddy's strong hands on his back; Momma's fingers in his hair; new bedsheets at night; a bath drawn to just the right temperature; a glass of perfectly cold water; the smell of white flowers that bloomed only at night; the few precious moments every morning before he fully awoke, when he was in the in-between, before the ugliness of the day became pressing.

And then as suddenly as it had lifted, it came crashing down again. The awful weight of knowing, the crippling effects of seeing things as they really were, it all seeped back into his pores, back into his eye sockets and mucus membranes. He felt the familiar swirl of barely contained panic in his gut and knew—he knew that this was the way things really were. The shock forced Jamie to draw in a sharp breath, and he realized he was gripping the edges of the splintered picnic table so tightly that strips of ancient paint were dissolving in his hands. His head was inches from the weather-beaten surface, and he could smell the disuse and decay.

Bilbo chittered in his ear, the noises alternately calming and frantic. Go back, stay—none of it mattered. We are all swallowed by the darkness in the end. Jamie closed his eyes and let his forehead hit the wooden surface. He would sleep, sleep perchance to dream, for in this sleep of death, what dreams may come . . . The words rolled in his mind like a storm cloud. He'd heard them before, maybe read them in a book. He hadn't known what they meant, but now he did. He could almost hear the Lairdbalor's tinny voice telling him that the only honest actions we take are those outside of our control. Sleep is the ultimate equalizer—all living things find common ground in the subconscious, the place where nightmares wear top hats and the books hold no words.

Jamie sucked his breath in tight. His throat was raw, his body weak. Maybe I'm dying, he thought without alarm. As he prepared to draw another weighted breath, something boomed and flung him backward. He landed against the ticket booth. Bilbo's panicked claws pulled on his hair as the little rat scrambled madly back into his nest. Jamie tried to open his eyes but found them crusted shut. The smell of burned hair and flesh surrounded him. He coughed out the scratch in his throat. Everything felt as though it were coated in a thick smear of soot. Jamie wiped his eyes, forcing them open. The picnic table where he'd been sitting was a smoldering heap. The overturned popcorn machine burst into flame as though it had been struck with a fireball, and the fire cycled into the sky, black smoke rising from the cylinder that had once held the oil. Jamie scrambled to his feet with one hand on Bilbo and ducked around the back of the ticket booth. Another explosion, this time from inside a crooked puppet theater on the far side of the square. The rotted wood sprayed outward, and Jamie ducked back just in time as a wooden plank laden with rusty nails sailed past. Jamie rubbed his cheek, his reverie entirely gone; his only thought was escape. He looked back in the direction the freak show children had gone. On the other side of the square was another, larger walking path. He remembered what Sariah had told him—don't stay overnight, get out no matter what. Jamie took a quick breath and then ran with all his strength. He stared straight ahead, keeping his focus on the path, as another cracked picnic table exploded in pieces behind him. Jamie ran past the smoldering popcorn cart, a pillar of black, oily smoke spiraling into the sky. From the corner of his eye, he saw another spray of sparks and heard a resounding rumble. Jamie had almost made it to the path when pain bit sharply against his shins. He didn't realize he was falling until he was already down, his face dragged across the rough ground, small stones tearing his skin. Bilbo was screaming, an unearthly squeal rising from his tiny throat. Jamie lay stunned for a moment, unsure of what to do next. The weight of the book on his back was a comfort of sorts—it was the only place his body didn't feel raw and exposed.

"Stayyyy for the show!" a voice boomed.

Jamie's first thought was that it was the Lairdbalor—the voice had the same tinny tone, but it was discordant, where the Lairdbalor was perfectly on pitch.

"Stayy! Just getting the crowd warmed up. The main attraction is next up! Not the same without an audiencccccccccce . . . "

The last consonant was drawn out like a snake. Jamie snapped out of his daze. This wasn't the Lairdbalor; this was something different, something just as terrible, but nothing that had come from him. The nightmare of another child, one whose fears had created something so visceral and real that even nightmares feared it. This was the Fire-eater, the one the freak show children had warned him about. In sudden terror, he realized that they had likely not made it back to their tent—they were out here; they were exposed. He forced himself up and looked in the direction of the voice.

The creature was too tall. It appeared to be on those stilts that Jamie had seen on circus shows on television, and its movements were stilted in the same way as the clowns and jugglers who stood on the wooden flats hidden by long, filthy Coca-Cola red pants. Its face was contorted, half melted away, the skin frozen in a perpetual wave, pulling the flesh away from the eye socket, making it bulge as though about to burst from its casing at any moment. The other side of the face was perfection: high cheekbones framed an aqua-blue eye, sun-kissed skin. Golden hair hung down next to the unscathed face; on the other side, a mass of swirled flesh replaced the hair. It wore an odd mashup of material—overall straps connected to bright clown-blue and canary-yellow strips of cloth, a swath of fleece roughly stitched to a stretch of bright purple velvet—a patchwork of color and texture.

Jamie stared at the creature, his panic subsiding. He found no fear in his gut, only a strange pity.

"What nightmare are you?"

The creature pretended not to hear him and awkwardly stamped forward.

"Don't leave before the main attraction! Just getting warmed up!" it bellowed.

It pointed its long finger at the ticket booth behind Jamie, which exploded into flame. Jamie ducked and covered his face as debris sprayed the area. He stood, feeling a sharp pull down his spine. Jamie looked up at the monster without fear.

"I need to leave this place. I need to go home. You're not here for me, I didn't create you." Jamie spoke carefully, his voice unwavering.

The Fire-eater looked down at him, the good side of its face twisted in disbelief.

"But we have a show! A show! Must stay for the show!" The bellow turned to a whimper.

"No!" Jamie roared.

The intensity of the sound resounded deep in his throat and rose out from his mouth. All trace of the child he had been was gone—he would not meet his end at the hands of another child's nightmare.

"I'm leaving," he stated firmly and walked toward the Fire-eater, who stood unsteadily on its stilts.

The creature began to mouth words of protest, but Jamie brushed past, adrenaline pressing him forward. On his neck, Bilbo clung to his matted hair, his squeals turning to rapid cooing sounds. Jamie walked into the pathway and looked back at the bewildered monster.

"I'm leaving," Jamie repeated. "I need to go home."

With that, he turned and began to walk away. Behind him, he heard the disfigured giant scream in frustration. A fireball coursed past, narrowly missing Jamie's head and exploding against the metal awning of the abandoned cotton candy cart a few feet beyond.

Jamie turned abruptly and, in the same tone Daddy used to admonish him when he was very angry, said, "You will stop this nonsense and go away now. I'm leaving—you are not my nightmare."

Jamie turned and walked deliberately past the incinerated cotton candy machine. Another fireball flew past, and the silky fabric of a lime green–and–white tent burst into flame, smoke pouring into the air. Behind him, the creature laughed, a loud, raucous sound entirely full of malice. Jamie stopped in his tracks as the flames jumped from one tent to another and looked back. The monster grinned, half its face contorted into a grimace. Jamie had a spark of realization that while this monster might be too afraid to actually touch him, it could certainly destroy all that lay around him.

"Bilbo, hold on," Jamie whispered as he ran toward the fire.

At the end of this path, he somehow knew, was the way out of the circus. Jamie saw the rusted arch and the flat land beyond. What lay beyond that, he couldn't say. But in that moment, he knew that he needed to run, that he would not die here, not at the hands of another child's nightmare, not after all he had been through, not now.

A tent of faded sky blue melted to the ground as the fire spread. It jumped the path, and now both sides were burning. The smoke was blinding, and Jamie coughed as the cinders clung to the inside of his nose and coated the inside of his mouth. He ran through a line of fire, narrowly missing a flaming beam that crashed to the ground and splintered. There was a stabbing pain in both his legs where the fire burned his flesh, as though a thousand knives were being dragged down his skin. His lungs tightened; he ran blindly and knew he would not be able to go much farther. Ahead of him another tent exploded in flame, the licks of orange cinder raining down on the path. The entire circus was in flame, the path a blackened tunnel. Jamie stumbled forward, his face stinging from the barrage of fiery rain. With enormous effort he reached out, his arms lost in the blackness, and crashed into the rusted iron exit gate. Jamie clung to it as his legs went numb. The iron had absorbed the heat from the fire, and it seared its imprint into Jamie's hands. He fell back with shock and pain. Beyond the gates, he saw the flat land of the countryside—no smoke, for that was all contained in this part of the world. On painful hands and knees, he crawled to the gate and collapsed, and then, with effort he never conceived of, rolled into the clear air.

His lungs screamed; he hacked black phlegm out onto the dirt. His ears rang from the explosions. Smoke rolled in great black waves from the fire, stopping abruptly at the exit and turning back on itself. Jamie felt the little rat burrowed into a knot of hair at the back of his neck, barely breathing for terror.

"Shhhh," Jamie whispered. "It's over now, we're out."

Jamie rolled onto his back, plucking the shaking ball of rat from its nest on his neck and placing it on his bare chest. Bilbo's fur was crusted with ash; Jamie brushed it free, aware of the searing wounds on his hands. Deep red marks crossed both palms, the pattern of the iron gate. Jamie heard a terrible screaming, a tearing of metal, and the din of something thought to be forever solid crashing down. Jamie sat up, the effort making his head swim. The Ferris wheel had folded in on itself, crashing down as the entire circus burned. The smoke obscured the clouds, and faded red and blue carriage seats flew outward as though being tossed. Jamie shuddered. The children in the freak show had surely burned. Could a nightmare die? Truly? He thought of Feidlimid and the other wood elves. Knowing what he knew now, he wondered what became of them—did they simply change form and keep on living? Was there a world beyond where nightmares went to die?

"I'm sorry," he whispered. Bilbo nuzzled his stomach.

SIXTEEN

"YOU can't burn a memory," said a voice from behind Jamie. "This is a show the Fire-eater is putting on for you—the longer you watch, the longer it will perform. Best to keep moving."

Jamie bolted to his feet, looking around wildly and ignoring the ache of his muscles. There was nothing behind him. Jamie squinted and realized he could not see as clearly as before—everything was just a little bit blurry around the edges.

"Here."

The voice sounded annoyed. High pitched and flat toned,it reminded him of the electronic voice that came from Daddy's computer.

"Here!"

A cockroach the size of his singed palm crawled up to Jamie's toe. He jumped back, suppressing a deep urge to squash the creature.

"I am not the one you want to destroy," it stated matter-of-factly.

Jamie cleared his voice, controlling his initial impulse. Talking cockroaches, he thought darkly. Why not—after all, everything here is made of something terrible. It was only a matter of time before cockroaches appeared.

"I'm not sure what you are implying. I'm rather surprised at your reaction, given that your companion is also labeled as 'vermin' in your world." The insect sounded like a very small, very disappointed grown-up.

Jamie shook his head.

"I'm sorry," he coughed, his voice catching on the soot still stuck in his throat. "I'm sorry," he repeated. "I didn't expect to see you . . . what you are."

"What I am?" The insect sounded indignant. "The bats said you are in need—were they wrong?"

"The bats didn't tell me what you looked like," Jamie interrupted.

"Is that important?"

The insect paused, and to Jamie's great shock, it spread great black wings and sailed into the air, circling his head like the beetle fairy had.

"You fly," Jamie croaked, barely containing his disgust.

He had not been afraid of many insects, but cockroaches had always made his skin crawl. He didn't see them very often, but they were the one insect that could be killed with impunity in his house. Momma would catch and release crickets, moths, and all manner of beetle, but cockroaches were smashed on sight. Jamie had asked her why, and she told him how they carry disease and they would make him sick.

"I am no more likely to make you sick than any other creature. Your own kind is responsible for most of the illness in your world," the cockroach reproached. The winged insect flew right up to Jamie's face. "I was told you want our help. I was told the Laird-balor is hunting again."

"Yes." Jamie took a deep breath. "I'm sorry, really I am. I was just taken aback. I didn't expect you to be what you are."

"Well, now you know, and that's that," the cockroach replied. "We should leave—Fire-eater took a bite in there, no time to waste. Come along."

Jamie looked down at himself. He was a mass of dried blood and soot. He felt terrible, and more than anything he wanted to curl up somewhere soft and sleep. He wanted this to be over.

"I'm sure you do, but the fact remains that this is not over. You need to get to the city if you want any chance of reentering your world. The Fire-eater can't cross the boundary, but as long as he knows you are watching, he will continue this temper tantrum. We are wasting time. Come along."

"You can read my thoughts?"

"Yes."

"Not everything here can do that," Jamie stated flatly as he started walking after the insect.

"No. My kind is more substantial than the sort that exists in other areas. The ones in there are different." It buzzed back a bit indicating the smoldering circus. "The Fire-eater is an exception, but the others don't really exist in the same manner as you and I." The cockroach recited the information in the tone of a tour guide who despised facts he was forced to recite.

"Memories," Jamie said. "When the one who created them forgets, they disappear."

"Yes," the cockroach replied and then, inquisitive with a touch of concern, asked, "You met others in there?"

"The children. They led me a ways through the circus."

Jamie felt numb—everything hurt, and now it hardly registered with him that he was talking to a cockroach.

"Unusual," the insect commented.

"Why weren't you there to meet me?"

Jamie hadn't meant to sound so accusatory—he was just so tired of not knowing why anything was the way it was here.

The cockroach responded flatly.

"My kind can't go in there. You should have been informed."

"The bats," Jamie snapped. His frustration was entirely irrational but uncontrollable in this moment. "The bats don't talk to me at all—they spy on me and tell everyone else everything about me, but they don't tell me anything at all. They don't tell me what direction to walk, or how to avoid being burned alive by some other kid's nightmare, or where you'll be, or who to trust. They don't tell me anything."

"The fact remains that my kind cannot go in there any more than the beetle fairies could," the cockroach said firmly. "It's a different part of our world. For their part, the creatures from the circus can never leave. It's just the way things are. You can pass through because you are not one of us—at least not yet."

Jamie sighed.

"I'm sorry," he said simply. "Do you have a name?"

The cockroach glided back and, to Jamie's repressed revulsion, landed on his free shoulder.

"I have a title. You may call me Custos," it replied. "My job is to watch over those who cannot do so for themselves. I will get you to the city. You'll be able to see your world in parts—the skeen is thin, so you can see what has passed in all the time you've been gone. We need to travel quickly. The Fire-eater took a bite, and your time is short here."

Jamie sighed. He suspected as much. Even through the smoke and ash, he felt a tightening in his shoulders and chest. His face felt drawn. On the exposed skin on his hands and arms, he saw a network of fine lines and freckles, splotches of color that worked their way onto his wrists and fingers. He had lost years in the fire, though how many he could never be sure.

"The Lairdbalor told me those seeking to help me would be at the ticket booth," Jamie admitted.

Custos took to the air again, while Jamie kept walking. "The Lairdbalor speaks in riddles," it observed.

"The Fire-eater," Jamie answered, suddenly realizing the Lairdbalor's dark joke.

"You must never trust any creature from our world too much," Custos responded. "The Fire-eater isn't at its nature destructive, just impulsive. I don't know the manner of nightmare that created it, but like all things in our world, it operates with little regard to others."

Jamie looked back. They had gained a little ground, but the smoke still rose in the sky, encased by the invisible ring surrounding the circus.

"You're out here near the circus a lot?"

"It's my job," Custos stated. "My job is to keep watch, to let the others know when one is headed their way. The bats carry my messages to the city. I live in the waste yard, which you must pass through before the city limits."

Jamie sighed.

"How much longer can I make it here? I'm older than I was even this morning."

"I can't give you an answer. Your kind lives a long life—your hair is not gray, your beard is not white." Custos flew ahead. "Follow. Up here, do you see?"

Jamie squinted, the images ahead of him blurrier still. There appeared to be mountains but made of a substance that he couldn't determine.

"What is it?" he asked.

"The waste yard. Where your kind throws away things to be forgotten. It is the gateway to the city, and we must pass through. I am well accustomed to it, but you must listen to me. It's not safe to stay long, not for you."

"There's no other way?" Jamie asked, already knowing the answer.

"No. I'll guide you through, but you must listen to everything I say—this is the place where things are forgotten, and you are no exception."

"A rusty tin coat hanger hanging in space," Jamie murmured.

The waste yard rose rapidly in front of them. Mountains that reflected the afternoon light shifted and fell, rising and reappearing out of nowhere.

"What is it made of?" Jamie asked, mesmerized.

"Lots of things. It's best that you pay as little attention to the waste yard as possible—follow me and listen to my voice. There are those here that will take you if they have the chance. You've met them before—the bats informed me." Custos flew in a steady line, its voice robotic and level.

Jamie was confused.

"The wood elves? Why would they take me?"

"No," Custos responded flatly. "Dwarves. They have been seeking you for some time now and will take any chance possible. They tried to take you back in the forest but were too late. You have something they want."

"The book?"

"Yes. You took the book, and they want it."

"Were they the ones who destroyed the Holding? The ones who killed the wood elves?" Jamie asked, hoping he wasn't pushing too far.

"No. And if you offend me, I will tell you. Speak your mind always." Custos's tone was sharp. "You need to understand, Jamie, there is no true death in this world, not for our kind. The Holding is already rebuilt. Elisedd is back with her students. The only thing missing from their reality is the book, which you took. Quite the disruption."

Jamie gasped. "I thought it would tell me how to get home. It's all about humans, I thought."

"It's no matter. One way or another the book will return to them, and perhaps it will be useful to you before that time."

Custos paused and swiveled around to face Jamie.

"I don't know . . . " Jamie began.

"I am not the Scire—you need the Scire to understand the book. I am Custos; my job is to lead you through this place."

Custos turned sharply and began flying once again.

Jamie whispered, "What if it—"

"It is not my place to know if the book will be of any use to you. Perhaps it will not. Perhaps it will be the thing that gets you killed. Perhaps it will get you home. You need the Scire. Come, we are nearly there. The sun will fall soon, and it is far too dangerous to be in the in-between at nightfall."

Jamie glanced behind him. The massive Ferris wheel looked impossibly far away, but it was standing tall once again, the top disappearing into the clouds. The smoke had dissipated, and Jamie could see the setting sun reflecting on the multicolored patchwork of tent silks. The cockroach had said it was odd that others in the circus had spoken to him. Everything was odd here. A question clung to the sides of Jamie's throat. Unsure of how to say it, he choked it back; however, even unheard questions were clear to the creatures of this world.

"Time, Jamie, is eternal here. Everything happens all at once and over and over. It folds in on itself and stretches; things happen again and again. Do you understand?" Custos's voice was controlled and level.

"No. This already happened? What does that mean?" Jamie felt the frustration he had battled ever since he had fallen down the very steep hill.

"This scene has played out since eternity. You have always been walking across this stretch of land; you have always been near to entering the waste yard. You have always been here, and you have always been trying to get home. Do you understand?" Custos spoke slowly, as though to a child, but Jamie wasn't a child any longer.

"No, I don't. What does it mean?" Jamie choked. He couldn't fully grasp what the cockroach was saying and was afraid when he did, he would finally lose all hope.

"No matter. When the time has come, you will understand. For now, we are about to enter the waste yard."

Custos stopped and turned. Jamie looked up. The mountains of constantly shifting substance loomed directly overhead.

"I repeat, you must listen to my voice. Do not give any mind to the things you hear and see as we pass through. We are going to move quickly, and you must not address any of the creatures inside—you must not engage with anything. They will try to keep you here—it is in their nature. Too long in the waste yard and you will forget why you are here; you will forget everything that pulls you home. Do you understand?" Custos's voice was firm and demanding.

Jamie nodded and stroked Bilbo's fur. The little rat clung to his matted hair.

"It's okay, buddy," Jamie whispered.

CUSTOS turned and entered the waste yard. Jamie followed, his heart beating rapidly, missing a beat here and there, making it hard for him to breathe. That was new, and Jamie wondered if it was a symptom of his newly old body or simple nerves. Custos flew very close to Jamie's face, directly in his eye line. Jamie could see why: the debris was in endless motion, even though there was no detectable breeze. A foot farther away and Jamie would have lost sight of the cockroach altogether. Despite Custos's warning, Jamie couldn't help but look at the bits and pieces that swirled and massed around him: gum wrappers and bits of holiday wrapping paper, a mobile flyer with one wing missing, the packaging from a toy car, a half-eaten sandwich. A doll missing an arm and an eye sailed past Jamie's head, and he jumped to the side to avoid being hit.

"Do not move off the path—no matter what," Custos barked, its voice sharp and clear.

Jamie nodded. As the swirling debris grew thicker, he focused on the black-brown body of the roach, the motion of its wings, the slight hum in the air. He realized that he was holding his breath. Slowly and deliberately, Jamie took in air and let it out again. Overhead, a mountain of debris rose to the clouds. Jamie glanced up and quickly back ahead. Its magnitude was incomprehensible. There was a screeching sound, metal on metal, and the mountain collapsed on itself. A blinding cloud of crumpled homework papers, broken pencils, half-colored drawings, bits of brightly colored paper that used to be worth some class reward, empty glue bottles, and bright emerald glitter all blew past in a busy cloud. Jamie almost lost sight of Custos and hurried forward. Behind him came a hum, the high-pitched sound of a child singing a song she didn't quite know. Jamie desperately wanted to look back.

"Keep your eyes on me. Do you understand?" Custos snapped with the assuredness of a drill sergeant.

Jamie nodded again, trying to block out the noise. From his right came a terrible scream, the sort of sound that rips a tear in the world. Utter anguish and loss.

"My baby! My baby!" the voice wailed, neither male nor female, inhuman and born of desperation.

Jamie closed his eyes, trying to block it out.

"Look at me! Look at me now!" Custos roared, the tiny insect's voice filling the space.

Jamie snapped his eyes open. For a terrifying moment, the roach was gone and he was all alone. Then Custos came into focus, solid black, hovering in space.

"Come. Now."

Jamie again nodded and followed. The wailing finally dissolved into sobs that shook an entire mountain to the ground. The waste swirled around Jamie's feet. Wind forced the bits of lost things together, and they formed an enormous cloud. It swirled upward into the sky. The sound that emanated from the funnel was the sky being torn in two—the very heavens screamed in pain, and the cloud grew, picking up everything it touched. Only a hundred yards or so before them, the funnel cloud began its terrible journey through the impermanent land. It destroyed everything it touched and absorbed the damage. Still they walked into the horror. Every fiber in every muscle in Jamie's body fought against the instinct to run as fast as he could away from the funnel cloud—this storm of all the lost things, all the forgotten things, all things neglected and wasted. A storm of the deepest sorrow; a storm that knew only rage and loss.

Custos flew on, and Jamie held to his words. But he remembered other words that Custos had spoken: "You must never trust any creature from our world too much." Jamie's stomach dropped, his unreliable heart beating so hard it might burst through his chest. Another step and another, the sound deafening, a scream that absorbed all other sound. Jamie realized that he was screaming along with it, his mouth open, the sound sailing up and amplifying the massive funnel cloud that spun and blocked the sky. Do not trust any creature from this world too much. Jamie kept his eyes fixed on Custos and wondered if this was the moment he died, if this was the moment he always died—for all at once he realized what the roach had been telling him. All moments were the same; they were happening all at the same time and separately. He was always here and always home in Momma's arms—there was no separation. His terror was always tangible. He was never safe; he was never in danger. He was all things at the same time and at the same time not. He was everywhere and nowhere; everything mattered and nothing was on purpose. It was all the result of a terrible storm, a horrible screaming cyclone that ate the sky and plunged the day into night. It was always this and nothing else.

He stared up at the cloud, forgetting Custos, forgetting everything except the feel of the eternal stream of bent harmonicas, broken violin bows, stuffed bears with torn-off heads, maps to nowhere drawn on bits of cardboard. Jamie closed his eyes and let his scream join the chorus. The sharp scent of rose tea filled his nose, and Jamie breathed in sweet relief. This is where it all would end.

Arms pulled him back—he was being dragged away from the storm, his feet barely cooperating.

"Noooo," he whispered, suddenly so weary that he couldn't stand the thought of another rescue.

Hands pulled him back, but Jamie gave in to the blackness, closed his eyes, and slept.

SEVENTEEN

HIS dreams were fitful and restless, images of Daddy and Momma, too far away to hear him, looking in the wrong direction. He ran through a dimly lit cathedral, the ceiling made of irregular blocks of stone held together with thick gray mud. At the front, a dying Christ hung from a wooden cross and blood dripped to the ground, thick and pungent. The air smelled of iron and metals long left to rust. The Christ's eyes followed Jamie as he ran—eyes that grew glassy and unseeing. Jamie searched the pews but no one was here anymore—he knew no one came here anymore, and no one ever would again. He would die here, alone but for the dead body of someone else's god. He ran through a field filled with sun-kissed wheat that hit against his bare legs and arms, cutting like a knife, streaks of blood staining the perfect gold. He ran down an empty street, devoid of people. Suitcases full of clothes, books, and photographs lay strewn about as though thrown from the windows; broken doors lay discarded against dirty brick tenements. Glass from shattered windows crunched under Jamie's bare feet, cutting them to the bone, leaving a trail of gore as he raced down an abandoned alley. Strange symbols adorned the walls, a convergence of lines and angles that looked familiar but that Jamie couldn't place. He heard the memory of crying, the echo of gunfire. He ran down his street, his own house at the end. Cars drove past him unaware that he was there. His bare feet burned with the heat of the fall sun on the black asphalt. He saw his front door, Momma's nondescript white car parked in the driveway. He ran faster, desperate for reprieve. As he reached the house, with its patchy front grass and pink plastic lawn flamingo hiding in the overgrown ivy, he found he could not stop. His feet carried him past the tan house where the little boy had disappeared so many years ago. He ran past and still on and on.

Slowly, Jamie became aware that he was lying on his back with a rough woolen blanket draped over him. Jamie blinked awake and looked around. His vision was blurrier still, the edges foggy and faded. He reached up and felt his beard, which now reached to his chest. He ran a hand over the sparse, coarse hair. How old am I? he wondered with dread. Bilbo. Where was Bilbo?

Jamie shot up, the blood rushing to his head, and everything went black for a minute. Then colors began to fade in, and he focused as best he could on his surroundings. He was in a cave of some sort, the walls made of bits of plastic milk cartons and fruit snack wrappers, broken trains and foam swords with the handles broken off, too-small Halloween costumes and socks with holes in the toes. The floor was lined with notes from teachers, greeting cards from grandparents, and photographs of smiling families in front of places Jamie had never seen before.

A scuttling on his arm brought Jamie's heart to his throat. Bilbo was climbing up his arm, his tiny claws drawing blood in their frantic effort. Jamie grabbed the little rat and pulled him to his chest.

"Bilbo, thank god."

He had no idea where the rat had come from or where they were. Bilbo frantically washed his paws over and over, his beady eyes searching Jamie's face.

"Where are we? How much time passed?" Jamie asked, knowing the little rat could not answer.

He was covered to the waist with a light-beige blanket stitched together of old dress suits. Jamie swung his legs off the side of the cot he was laying on, the type they had in military television shows, low to the ground and stiff as a rock. Jamie carefully stood, not wanting the rush of blood to his eyes again. His back ached, and his shoulders held a pain worse than before, a deep-bone pain. With a start, he realized the book was gone; the straps that had cut into his skin for so long were missing. Now he realized exactly where he was and who had taken him. Now it was gone, and he would never find the answers it might have held.

"Your book is right there, waiting for you."

A voice, a perfect brass tone, curled out from the dark corner of the room. Jamie spun around, looking for the source.

A figure emerged from the corner of the cave, dressed in light linen robes, its face obscured. As it approached, Jamie could see the pale skin, dark eyes, and beard. It was tall—taller than Jamie, even in his adult form. Filthy bare feet stuck out from underneath the hem of its floor-length robe. Jamie sucked his breath in tightly, afraid to speak.

"There is such a thing as Cotard's syndrome in your world. Have you heard of it, Jamie?" the figure asked.

Its voice was the consistency of maple syrup, clear and smooth. Jamie was frozen, any terror he might have felt in that moment drowned out by an intense humming in his ears, high and piercing.

"It's the cells in your ears dying, Jamie—nothing to be afraid of. Happens to your kind with age, although, not usually all at once. For most of your kind, it's a ring here and a tone there. You will never hear those exact sounds again—isn't that fascinating? I find so many things about your kind fascinating. So fragile and so resilient."

The figure approached closer still. Jamie sat frozen, staring, waiting for the new horror that was to come.

"As I was saying, Jamie, Cotard's syndrome is particularly interesting. It makes your kind believe they are dead. Some react with fear; some believe they are surrounded by ghosts; others still believe they are walking among the living, unnoticed and ignored. Most report that, with time, the delusion passes. They begin to see themselves as alive once again, but never quite the same. I imagine that nothing would be quite the same after that, would it?"

The dwarf approached Jamie, who instinctively shrank back onto the cot.

"No need to be afraid, Jamie. You're home now—if you want to be, that is. Tell me, do you believe you are dead?"

Jamie found his breath, and in a very small voice asked, "What are you? You look like the dwarves, but . . . you're . . . you're not, are you?"

The words gave him courage. If this thing was going to kill him, it would have already done so, and if it changed its mind, there was little that Jamie could do to stop it.

"Smart boy, my dear *gaolach*." The figure stood woodenly in front of him.

"Lairdbalor," Jamie said, the word boring a hole into the back of his throat.

"*Tha gràdhag, tha.* You're nearly too smart for this place—nearly, but not quite, are you?"

Jamie stood, his feet unsteady, the patchwork blanket falling to the ground.

"But you're not here, are you? If you were, you wouldn't need to use the dwarf, would you?" Jamie's voice was strong, stronger than his heart or shaking hand. Bilbo clung to his hair, nearly convulsing with fear. "Don't be afraid, Bilbo. It's not really him, is it?" Jamie turned to face the dwarf. "You can't get to us here, can you? That means there must be a way out."

Jamie began pacing around the cave, but every corner seemed sealed.

"*Ciùin, eudail.* A bit of gratitude wouldn't hurt. Your guide led you straight to the heart of a storm. You would not have survived—maybe you didn't and now you're finally dead? What do you think, Jamie? Are you walking among the living? Or are we all ghosts? Or are you home asleep and having the nightmare of your life? What do you think?"

The Lairdbalor inside the dwarf's body moved slowly forward, the dwarf's face frozen except for the lips.

"Did you kill him, the dwarf, just to get to me?" Jamie asked as he examined the wall for cracks and weaknesses.

"Heavens, no—I am no *ùraind*. There is no killing something that lives in the in-between lands. The dwarves walk in the mist between the night and day; they collect the dead, but they are not among them. But even if I had harmed this creature, it would be no loss to the others. They are not so sentimental as us, Jamie."

The Lairdbalor sat down on the cot, and Jamie could almost see the decaying topcoat settle around it.

"Why do the others in this land fear you?" Jamie asked, running his hand over the walls, which appeared to be held together with a thick layer of dried glue.

"Oh, *bhalaich*, they fear me for the same reasons you fear me. They fear what they will be once they have seen what I have seen. They fear the things inside them that are too terrible to put a voice to. They fear what they are capable of." The Lairdbalor stood and stared down at the wood elves' book. "Inside all of us lives a darkness too terrible to ever truly know. Some see it every so often, when they shut their eyes, in the split seconds of impulse before reason takes over. They see it in moments of rage or oppor-tunity, or maybe in passing fantasies. My only *eucoir* is bringing that darkness to the light. Some things are best unknown, *bhalaich*. Some things are best left in the dark."

The Lairdbalor turned to face Jamie.

"Do you know, *bhalaich*, why the dwarves want this book? Do you know why they still pursue you even though your presence in this world should not be a concern to them in the least? Do you know?"

Jamie stopped searching the wall and turned to face the creature. "No."

"Then why do you protect it so tightly?" the Lairdbalor asked, its voice echoing around the small cavern.

"I don't know," Jamie answered honestly, the response bringing an unexpected lump of emotion to his throat. "It might have the answers that will get me home. I want to go home."

"And what if it does not?"

Jamie shook his head.

"It has to," he responded, fighting the impulse to scream and tear at the dwarf's face. Irrational as it was, Jamie felt nothing but barely contained rage in his sinewy arms, emanating out his fingertips.

"Your path home is not inside this book, Jamie. It is somewhere else, a place far more deadly than an enchanted book." The Lairdbalor picked up the book and leafed through the pages slowly, each blank as they had been before. "Have you asked yourself, Jamie, what it is you really want? Have you asked yourself if you *should* go home?"

"I have to," Jamie said, the rage dissipating into despair. "I can't stay here. I'll die here. I'm older every moment." He looked down at himself. "My beard is gray, and I feel my body is older than even before you took me here. I have to get home; I can't die here. I have to see Momma and Daddy. I need to go home."

"Many years have passed since you fell down that hill, Jamie. What if your parents are dead? What if they died of grief when you weren't found so many years ago? Or worse yet, what if they were relieved?"

Jamie exploded. "Shut up! Shut up! Stop! I don't believe you!"

He shut his eyes and conjured the image of the hook-arm girl's amber eyes, her quiet words: "Don't believe what it tells you." He forced himself to remember Custos's warning as they entered the waste yard about not trusting any creature from this world too much.

"You don't need to believe me, love—let me show you." The Lairdbalor set the book down and crossed to Jamie, who stood immobile. "Let me show you what would have happened, Jamie. Let me show you the darkness you're hiding inside."

His voice rang like the high note of an invisible orchestra, echoing off the walls of the chamber. The irregular rhythm of Jamie's heart picked up, and his breath shortened.

"That's age, *bhalaich*. Your heart weakens with age. The bodies of your kind lose their rhythm as you grow older, and soon other things will begin to fail inside your body. Your mind will grow dim, and you will forget what it is you seek. You will forget there was ever a world other than this."

"No! I won't stay that long. I will leave here. I will go back to my world. The book . . . even if the book is useless, I'll find a way."

"Let me show you, *bhalaich*. Let me give light to the great darkness of your life, and maybe you will see that you are in exactly the right place, the best place for you. Maybe you will see that you belong in a world composed of nightmares and fears. Maybe you will find peace."

Jamie shook his head. Tears streamed down his face, and he sunk to the floor, pulling his knees to his chest and rocking back and forth, murmuring no, no, no.

"Let me give you a reason for your suffering, love—let me dispel the storm and give you a method to your madness. Let me lift you from your sulfurous and tormenting flames. Render yourself up, love—let me show you what things in heaven and earth you have yet to dream of. Let me show you."

The Lairdbalor knelt down to Jamie, lifting up his face with two cool and infinitely gentle hands. Jamie nodded, an imperceptible surrender.

Jamie looked into the night-black eyes, blackness devoid of stars, deepest space capable only of taking away and never giving back. He felt the motion of walking down a hallway, and on either side he saw rows of lockers like in a secondary school. Jamie stared further into the eternal night and felt cold metal in his hands; he saw blurs of faces running past, screams that made no sound, and still he walked on. Hands grabbed at his arms, but he shook them off with little effort.

Jamie stared still further into the void. A door swung open, and he entered a room full of surprised faces, the features blurred and dull. He raised the cold metal in his hands, pointing it here and there, here and there, his mind perfectly blank, an impact knocking him back again and again. The blackness he was filled with was soon replaced by a rush of senses—a bitter, metallic wave hitting his nostrils; the screams around him suddenly shattering and real; the emptiness suddenly and irreversibly gone. *I didn't mean to*—Jamie heard his own voice over and over, felt the cold metal against his chin, a surge of pressure, and then he saw the blackness of the dwarf's eyes, the perfect unsustainable darkness once again.

Jamie slammed back, breaking the connection.

"No! No! No! You lie!" he screamed, his voice raw with the effort.

"Perhaps. Such an unhappy child, so many worries, so much pain. Everyone remembered it the same way: such an odd boy, always alone, no friends." The Lairdbalor looked at Jamie with such abject sadness that it brought tears to his eyes.

"But I didn't do that! I'm seven years old! I didn't do that!" Jamie choked out.

"No, *bhalaich*, you didn't do that, and you never will. You were never seventeen in your world. You never attended that school. You were only a memory in the minds of a few, the boy who disappeared so many years ago. You were a what-if, a fear passed on to your classmates by their mothers. You were here and you were safe, and as such, so were they." The Lairdbalor's voice was gentle.

"But I would never . . . I would never," Jamie sobbed, rocking back and forth.

"Maybe. Every life has a thousand paths, as complex as the lines that now mark your hands. Every life has a way of diverting the worst parts of ourselves, but they always resurface. Look again."

Jamie shook his head but felt himself drawn to the dwarf's night-black eyes. He stared, desperate for redemption. There was concrete beneath his feet, the night around him punctuated by streetlights and the occasional passing car. Jamie walked swiftly, with purpose. Ahead of him was a man walking with his arm around a woman in a bright dress. Looking around and seeing no other living beings save for the cockroaches that see all, Jamie in one swift motion shoved the couple into an alcove, not quite an alley, and in one swift motion opened both their throats. The bright dress turning steadily crimson. Then he was walking once again, hardly a drop of blood on him.

"No, no, no!" Jamie cried, his whole body shaking so much he could hardly speak.

"Shhh, love, shhhh . . . You were never twenty-five in your world, love. You were never so full of rage and hatred that you set out to destroy anything that crossed your path. You were here, *bhalaich*, you were here."

The Lairdbalor's brass voice rang like a discordant song, wrapping itself around Jamie's body, calming his convulsive shaking.

"I didn't! I didn't! I wouldn't! I've never hurt anybody. I wouldn't," Jamie sobbed, snot pouring from his nose, dripping to the floor, where a black-and-white photograph of a man with his arm around a little girl in front of a tree as big as a house stared up at him. "I didn't . . . I would never."

Jamie looked up once again, the dwarf's face stone but for the deep-black eyes. They held all the sadness and compassion of a lifetime. Once again, Jamie stared into their depths, hoping for validation, a release. He sat alone in a room, surrounded by decay and rot. A molding mattress pressed against a corner. An overhead light cast unnatural shadows, and the ever-present cockroaches lurked around the periphery. Jamie sat in the center of the room, his hair thinning, his body stripped of its healthy weight, leaving only the bones covered by flesh. He played with a flash of metal in his hands; it caught the overhead light, sending artificial rainbows into the corners. He drew it up and down his wrist, daring for the courage to apply his withering strength. When he finally did, the crimson black wave seeped out from the neat, exact cut. It poured out onto the floor, scattering the cockroaches. Jamie slumped over, his sparse, greasy hair matting in the spill. His eyes were closed, his face calm, but the expression did not sit well on such a face—deep crevices still held their shape. He was far too old for his true age, and he had already seen too much.

"Jesus, Jesus, Jesus . . . " Jamie covered his eyes, his body ice cold, the spot on his forehead where he'd been touched by the Asrai colder still. "No, no, no, no, no. . . " It couldn't be true—his life had not been wasted; he had not killed and destroyed. He did not die alone in a squalid room surrounded by the Burg. His life had not been a source of horror to others. It had to be wrong.

"Come, *bhalaich*—you were here. Your face is unlined; your heart is clear. Your mind is strong. You have never killed. You have never been so full of hatred and self-loathing that you caused harm to any living creature. You are kind, *bhalaich*. You are good. You were here, *bhalaich*, you were here. You were saved from your fate. Your journey has been the light you sought in your other life, the thing you never could quite find, the one thing that might quell the darkness. You were always meant to be here. You are safe."

Jamie looked up and, in a voice that shook as much as his hands, asked, "What of my parents? What happened to them?"

"What do you think, love? So much *bròn*—their *smalan* was such that they claimed they never had a son. They denied you were theirs. They left you." The Lairdbalor's voice had a discordant edge.

Jamie shut his eyes, his mind spinning. He finally looked at the Lairdbalor.

"How do I know you are telling the truth?"

"What cause would I have to lie?"

The voice held danger, a host pushed to the limit of his hospitality.

"None of these things happened. I didn't do any of this. I am seven years old despite this body, despite everything, and I haven't done anything. Why show me? You can't get to me here, can you? You're speaking through this creature, but you don't know where I am, do you? You're too weak to catch me, aren't you? You need me to give up. You need me to stop caring."

Jamie's voice gained strength, and his tears and shakes calmed to a tremble. He suddenly knew that he was right, that he was stronger than the Lairdbalor, that he was beyond its grasp. This creature was only a proxy, a pretend villain.

The dwarf stood, and the Lairdbalor laughed, a bellowing, terrible sound. Jamie pressed back against the wall. There was another sound too—outside the structure was a terrible scream, deep and guttural, like a thousand voices pointed at the sky, each releasing the gut bottom of their souls. It roared closer, and every hair on Jamie's arms stood as though charged with electricity. The Lairdbalor reached inside the dwarf's cloak, pulling something from a hidden pocket. It looked like a broken school ruler, split so that the sharpened end was as deadly as any weapon. Jamie edged around the room. The Lairdbalor stopped his terrible laugh, highlighting the growing cacophony outside, the roar of things being uprooted, the sound of destruction.

The dwarf and Jamie lunged at the same time. Jamie grabbed the edge of the sharpened wood, and it sliced his hand from thumb to wrist. He instinctively fell back. Jamie rolled to the side as the dwarf stabbed the stake down, missing Jamie and hitting the floor, tearing a hole in the paper lining. Again the dwarf lunged. With his good hand, Jamie grabbed the wood elves' book, thrusting it in front of him. The stake stuck deep into the pages and refused to budge. The dwarf tugged, but without a handle to provide leverage, its effort was wasted. And it seemed to be growing even paler. As Jamie wondered how that was possible, the dwarf's skin took on a gray pallor and the night-black eyes rolled back into its head. The storm outside roared still closer, and the dwarf reeled backward, unable to keep its balance. Jamie jumped to his feet and, holding the book before him as a sort of shield, took a step toward the dying creature.

"Why kill me?" Jamie whispered, the shock of the attack wearing into betrayal.

"I won't, *bhalaich*." The voice was losing its brassy tenor—it sounded rough, the words strained. "I cannot kill something that exists in the in-between, and you have been walking that line for some time now."

Jamie shook his head and knelt in front of the dwarf, whose skin was steadily turning from clear ivory to a muddy gray.

"What is it you want?" Jamie's words were barely audible.

"You still carry the fear from your world—you still fear death. You still react as you did as a child, and you are no longer a child, *bhalaich*. You have to decide, Jamie," the Lairdbalor croaked, its host swiftly losing the ability to transmit the message. "You will never know if I am right. You will never know if others are safe from you. You have to decide."

With that, the dwarf began to fold inward, the skin turning a burned, ashy black, flaking away and collapsing. The hair, the cloak—everything burned to cinder in a fireless blaze; within seconds, all that was left was a pile of soot. Jamie stared in shock at the remains of the dwarf.

"Where are you?" he screamed at the ceiling.

His cry was answered with a scream that engulfed everything around him. The tornado ripped through the structure, the paper floor and piecemeal walls lifted and torn to shreds. Jamie was thrown through the air, and he wrapped his entire body around the book and held as tightly as he ever had. The little rat at the base of his neck was encased in a mass of matted hair; Jamie could feel the roots being tugged straight out of his head. It occurred to him that he was flying in slow motion. Indeed, the overwhelming roar of the funnel cloud was softer, a mere hum, and the objects that flew past him swirled lazily through the space: a book with all the pictures cut out, a broken pink crayon with the wrapper peeled away, an action figure dipped in some sort of ink so that it was impossible to tell who he might have been. Jamie looked around him in wonder. I'm in the eye of the tornado, he thought, but not a real tornado—surely a real tornado isn't like this. Though maybe it is, he thought again. How would anyone know? It's a nightmare a child had once, and this is the center, which isn't really so bad after all. Even the worst nightmares hold a bit of reprieve.

A large plastic horse with chipped paint and broken bits of springs and metal mountings flew from the side of the funnel cloud and collided with Jamie. The impact sent Jamie flying, and he tightened his grip on the book as he was thrown back into the storm, the noise once again deafening. The wind felt as though it would pull him into a thousand pieces. Suddenly, he collided with the ground. He rolled several times, his body still wrapped around the book, the little rat clinging to Jamie's neck. Jamie landed in a pile of discarded comic books, the pages sticky with ancient candy. He looked up to see the tornado moving swiftly away, the cloud that followed it blocking the night sky.

EIGHTEEN

TENDERLY, Jamie pulled himself up off the ground and looked around. He was not surprised to see that day had fled and night had overtaken the sky. The cloud of the storm was settling, and he was surrounded once again by endless mountains of discarded things illuminated by the starlight. To his right was a pile of doll heads, various sizes and colors, all ripped from their bodies by force, jagged plastic stems substituted for what had once been necks. Directly in front of him lay a bicycle, a two-wheeler with a twisted frame, probably thrown from the tornado. Jamie had never ridden a two-wheeler by himself. Daddy had kept trying to show him how, but Jamie had never done it, partially because he was scared he'd fall and have bloody knees, but on a deeper level, he really just didn't care. He liked his scooter—it was fun, and he felt like he was flying when he rode fast down the sidewalk. The bicycle looked cumbersome and entirely too complicated, plus he really didn't want bloody knees. Regarding it now, laying in a pile of forgotten possessions, toys, and ideas scribbled down on bits of paper, Jamie smiled. His grown-up eyes saw how simple it really was, and he wished he would have let Daddy show him. He'd never have a chance now. An adult is supposed to already be able to ride a bicycle—no one would offer to hold the back of the seat and run alongside while he pedaled. It was a thing he would never learn, a moment he had lost.

How old is Daddy now? Jamie wondered. Jamie himself was at least as old as Daddy had been only a couple of days ago, but so much time had passed. Daddy and Momma would be old now, their hair gray, their skin wrinkled, an entire life passed by without ever showing their son how to ride a bike or cook a meal or do his own laundry. An entire life passed by without any answer as to what was at the bottom of that very long hill. Jamie sighed. He needed to keep moving. Too much remembering, too much regret—it all weighed on him. It collected in piles like the discarded plastic trucks and one-armed metal soldiers that lay in heaps around him. What direction to go in? Jamie supposed it didn't really matter. What mattered was that he kept moving—kept thinking and not just remembering. As long as his feet were moving he was trying, and that should count for something.

Jamie took a step, and then another. He stroked Bilbo's shaking form through the mass of hair that surrounded him.

"It's okay, buddy. I think that was the worst bit, at least for now. Don't be scared. We can't be scared, we can't be," Jamie murmured.

Bilbo's shaking subsided a bit. The little rat pulled himself out of the mat of hair he had formed, and Jamie released a sigh of relief as the pressure at the base of his skull ceased.

"C'mon, Bilbo. Let's go home."

Jamie began walking down the rough path between the piles of memories and broken playthings. The night sky was bright with stars, and as he walked, he tried to find the patterns in them. They were entirely different from the stars back home. There he could find Orion—the three belt stars all in a row—and the Seven Sisters, which looked like a clump of light on the horizon line. He also could spot Cassiopeia, which looked like a W low in the sky and Momma said was supposed to be a throne. But here it was different, and it changed every time you looked away. Jamie kept a vigilant watch as he walked, but anytime he needed to check to make sure he wasn't stepping on a bit of machinery from a broken train engine or an orange plastic racecar track, he had to look away; whenever he looked back, the stars had reconfigured, an entirely new sky with entirely new patterns.

It's the same with life, mused Jamie. Anytime you look away, all the things you think you know reconfigure and sort themselves out in a different way. The world keeps moving whether or not you are in it. The people who love you, the places that held a spot for you, the things you did that only you could do—all these things get overtaken and a new pattern is forged. All things keep moving forward with or without you. So it must be back in the real world, Jamie thought darkly. How long had they looked? How long had Momma and Daddy cried before there were no more tears to be shed? How long did any of his friends remember him? His stars had shifted dramatically since he had left. Maybe he had no place left at all; maybe he was the one who flew from the sky, dissolving in a brilliant flash of light before hitting the earth. Maybe he was dead—maybe he had been all along.

Jamie hated to think that death was like this. He didn't believe in heaven exactly, but he didn't think this was the alternative. He had a friend in his first-grade class, a little girl named Sarah who wore pink-framed glasses and had skin the color of milk chocolate and who liked to talk about God and heaven. She was a Christian, although Jamie still wasn't sure what that meant. Heaven, according to Sarah, was a world made of clouds where the good people went when they died, and it was right above the clouds in the sky. Jamie had asked her what about the days when the sky was clear, and she had called him stupid.

"The clouds are always there," she had said in a matter-of-fact voice. "They are always there—just sometimes they're higher up than other times."

Jamie had secretly wondered if she had meant outer space, which would make everyone in heaven an alien, since technically they didn't live on planet Earth. However, he hadn't asked because he didn't want to be called stupid again.

Looking at the shifting stars right now, Jamie realized that Sarah was very wrong; heaven had nothing to do with stars or God. It was a world like this one—maybe a bit less frightening, maybe not. It was at the bottom of a very long hill, and people weren't always aware that there was anywhere else they could be. Some were good and some were bad, but it was the place where people went at the end of their lives, when their bodies on Earth were all used up. Maybe it was a place where the dreams were pleasant ones—a place where there were no Lairdbalors or Fire-eaters, no towering Ferris wheels or dwarves with pale skin. Maybe it was a place where no one could die again and no one felt lost. Maybe it wasn't. Maybe it was a place where the children from the freak show weren't frightening and no one was scared.

Jamie kept walking, and his mind swirled with questions that he knew had no answers. The Lairdbalor had showed him so many things, but what to trust? The only truth Jamie knew, the only reason the images had not already driven him mad, was that he had not done those things. Even if it were true that he might have someday done them, now he never could—time had passed, and the people he would have harmed had lived instead and gone on with their lives. They had done all the usual grown-ups things: They had jobs, husbands and wives, children, dogs. They watched television and read books. They lived. Jamie had not harmed them, nor would he.

Unless . . . That simple word clung to the back of Jamie's mind and refused to release its talons from the inside of his skull. Unless it could still happen. You're only seven, the idea whispered. If you go back, you could still do those things in ten years, twenty years, thirty years if you live so long. You could still kill; you are still a monster. Jamie shook the thought to the very back reaches of his mind. He didn't know the answer. Unless Jamie had been forgotten, and no one would remember him if he returned. Unless no one waited for him—he was a rusty tin coat hanger hanging in space, a lost thing, a nightmare that had long since been forgotten by the children he had once known.

And the dwarf—Jamie had destroyed a part of this world. What of that? Was there a price? The Lairdbalor would never have harmed the dwarf if it hadn't been for Jamie. And in that moment, he had most definitely wanted the dwarf dead, he wanted the Lairdbalor dead. A phrase rolled around in Jamie's head, a phrase from the courtroom television show that Momma and Daddy watched sometimes. Malice aforethought. He had made Momma write it out for him, and she had explained that it meant you wanted bad things to happen to someone and then you took steps to make sure they did. Jamie had been seven and had nodded understanding, but only in this moment did he really comprehend. He knew he was capable of killing anything that stood in his way here in this world. Suddenly he knew it, and he knew that the Lairdbalor was right. He was capable of terrible things. He was a bogle, a nightmare waiting to be thrust into the light. He existed in the in-between, capable of great harm but impossible to kill. His body was numb; his ears buzzed with the swan song of the dying sounds, parts of his childhood that would never be heard again.

Jamie walked numbly on, the path winding through the piles of trash, the book sitting heavily in his arms. He kept an eye out for a bag, anything that might fit it. He didn't see anything, so he kept carrying the heavy book, shifting his grip to try and ease his aching arms and shoulders.

A scuttling noise was coming toward him. Jamie resisted the urge to hide in a pile of discarded baseball cards, the edges dog-eared and stained with soda. Whatever it was, it was going to find him no matter what he did. If it wanted to finally kill him, it probably would, so there was no use hiding or pretending that he had any control of the creatures in this world. He reached up and stroked Bilbo's head.

"Hang on. We can handle this," he said softly, not sure if he believed himself.

The scuttling became louder, the sound of a thousand tiny legs moving all at once. Jamie fought the knee-jerk panic in his gut. It was a horror movie sound, a sound that invoked the worst kind of images and carried the residual scent of death and rot. Jamie stopped walking and stood his ground. Whatever it was would meet him here, and he would not hide from it—he was tired of hiding. The sound came closer still. Jamie swallowed down the scream that rose in his throat, a hard, scraping lump that left a burn. Louder still, and Jamie closed his eyes; he murmured the words to the song Momma used to sing him when he cried.

Hush, little baby, don't say a word.

Momma's gonna buy you a mockingbird.

Closer and closer—it overtook the night. It roared as loud in Jamie's imagination as the tornado. Overhead, the stars shifted again, reconfiguring into another senseless order that would soon be disrupted.

And if that mockingbird don't sing . . .

Jamie sucked in his breath as something skittered across his foot. The sensation was light, barely perceptible, but it triggered every nerve in Jamie's body, and he froze in pain of anticipation.

"You have been very difficult to track. Please do not stray again. We do not have much time before the storm returns."

The curt, high-pitched voice nearly knocked Jamie back with relief and confusion. He looked down to see Custos standing on his bare foot. Beyond him were a thousand shiny black bodies, all standing at attention. None more than two inches in length, they regarded him with black eyes and entirely blank expressions.

"If you are injured, you will need the Medicus, which are not here. They are in the city, as are the Scire, who can read your book. We are Custos, and you must follow, swiftly," the cockroach stated curtly.

With that, Custos took to the air, and the entire army of cockroaches, stretching out as far as Jamie could see, surged forward, directly into the mountain of metal soda tops and gum wrappers with jokes printed on the inside. The sheer mass of them forced the trash to part, forming a new path. Custos flew to Jamie's eye level.

"Follow. There are more of us to protect you now. Follow." The voice was cold but not unkind.

Jamie nodded and followed the herd of insects. The scuttling was overwhelming, but now that he knew the source of the sound, it did not seem nearly as fearsome. The cockroach army forged through piles of overdue library books and plush animals with tears down their stomachs. They pushed through plastic giraffes and hippos with black mold growing on their brightly painted sides. They trekked through spilled juice boxes and pencils with missing erasers and shirts with grape jelly stains. Jamie stepped carefully, not wanting to accidentally squash one of his protectors, but the cockroaches parted around his feet in perfect rhythm, as though they knew exactly the angle and pitch of his every step. They traveled as a mass with one mind; only Custos flew, staying at eye level, a few feet in front of Jamie.

In the distance, Jamie began to see lights—the steady glow of office towers and the fast-moving flashes of headlights sailing across the sky. A wave of relief crashed over Jamie. This was home. This was the city, those were cars, those were buildings—he had made it home.

"No. You have made it to the city, which is not the same as in your world. There are places where the skeen is thinner—we will show you these places—but there is no entry to your world from here, only a window."

Custos did not look back, and Jamie tried to swallow his excitement.

"You must pass over the bridge to the city. You must go alone—we cannot follow you there. We are Custos, and our place is the waste yard. You will be met by the Urbis Incola if you make it to the other side," Custos said in a voice devoid of emotion.

"If?" Jamie said, his heart racing.

"Yes—if. You might not. You are the first one of your kind to travel this way, and I do not see how you will make it. But Custos does not cross the bridge, so there is no way we can determine your success."

The voice delivered the news as though it was instructions for crossing the street, simple and matter of fact. Jamie sucked in his breath.

"There are so many of you. What happened to you in the storm?"

He had wanted to ask before, but the sheer uniformity of the march had not inspired him to ask questions.

"You were taken by the funnel cloud. We could not stop it. I feared you had died, but your thoughts were still loud enough to hear, even muffled as they were. I called the others, and we searched. The dwarves are in the waste yard—they were looking for you, although it seems they have stopped." Custos halted its flight abruptly and pivoted back, hovering inches from Jamie's face. "Why is that?"

The cockroaches at his feet ceased their collective movement and stood at attention. Jamie took a deep breath.

"The Lairdbalor killed one."

"I suspected as much," Custos replied. "Good."

With that, the formation began to move again. Custos asked for no elaboration on Jamie's answer and once again flew in front of him, leading the charge to the city lights that looked so much like Jamie's world that he could not help but feel something like hope.

"What is the bridge? Why is it dangerous?"

"Trolls," Custos answered without looking back.

Jamie had read stories about trolls under bridges, but they were children's fairy stories—even at seven, he didn't believe in trolls.

"What . . . "

"I cannot tell you more; I do not know. We do not cross the bridge. We are Custos, and our place is here, in the waste yard," Custos repeated robotically.

"Can the bats help?" Jamie asked, not really expecting a reply.

"They have not before," Custos answered. "But I suppose they are capable of it."

Jamie shook his head. Everything was a riddle. An army of cockroaches was leading him to a bridge guarded by trolls. If he survived, he would meet still more cockroaches, who might be able to teach him to read a magical book. He giggled at the absurdity. Bilbo nuzzled his neck. Another absurdity, Jamie thought as he ran his finger over Bilbo's soft fur—a pleasant one, but an absurdity nonetheless. How will I explain to anyone where I've been? he thought as the city lights grew nearer. If I make it back and am asked, how am I to tell? I am a grown man, almost an old man, and all I have are stories of fairies and elves, dwarves and trolls, talking cockroaches and toys that come to life. I'm mad, he thought with a loose grin—perfectly mad, and not likely to make it past this step.

On the upside, he thought ironically, if I die at the hands of bridge trolls, I won't have to explain at all.

Suddenly the bridge loomed in front of him. Jamie had seen it before, though he could not place where. The land surrounding it was green and lush, perfectly manicured, beautiful in its precision. Beneath it stretched a pond with clear water and brightly colored koi swimming in circles. At its base sat dark-green shrubs trimmed into ovals and smooth, pleasing shapes. The wooden bridge rose so steeply that it was more ladder than steps. The top was narrow and not too high. Jamie could see the other side easily. It let out onto a lush green lawn adorned with rounded pond rocks and flowers of the deepest reds and oranges arranged in intricate patterns. And Jamie could also see there were no trolls underneath, and he laughed, a nervous release. The stars shone brightly overhead. Jamie remembered Feidlimid the wood elf plucking the star from the sky and tossing it into the meadow to scare the gnights— so simple. Jamie wondered if he, too, could pluck a star from the sky and toss it like a pebble—if he could make it skim the water's surface and send the koi scattering. He laughed at the thought.

The army of cockroaches had halted and was rapidly turning and disappearing back into the waste yard that sat in stark contrast to the beautiful garden in front of him. Only the flying Custos, Jamie's original guardian, remained.

"I do not understand your reaction, but I suppose it is not important for me to understand," Custos stated as it hovered.

Jamie shook his head.

"I don't see any trolls," he said simply.

Custos did not respond; instead, it flew a few feet beyond, and Jamie followed. With its whole body, it indicated the bridge, picturesque in the starlight.

"The Urbis Incola are on the other side, if you arrive. That is all I can tell you—it is all I know," the cockroach stated.

"You said others have not made it across the bridge," Jamie said, determined to get as much information as he could before he was left alone in the night once again.

"Yes, I said that."

"None like me—you said that. But who then? Who tried to cross?"

"Others from this world. Others sometimes need the safety the city can provide. There are many places to hide in the city, especially if you are being hunted," Custos responded, but then it paused. "You are being hunted, Jamie. You need to hide, but do not hide too long. You need to gather strength and leave this world." The voice almost sounded emotional but then reverted back to cold logic. "You must cross the bridge—there is no other way. Others have tried swimming across the water only to find themselves back at this point. The trolls may not be present to your eyes, but make no mistake they are here. The bats might help, but I have never known them to. They do not interfere with anything from this world; they only pass on messages."

Jamie started with a sudden thought. "They brought me water once. I was thirsty, so thirsty I didn't think I could go on, and they brought me water."

Custos paused, surprised. "Did they? Unusual."

Jamie looked at the cockroach. Its form held no disgust for him now.

"Thank you," he said.

Custos stared at him with tiny black eyes.

"It is my job."

With that, it flew off back into the waste yard.

NINETEEN

JAMIE regarded the bridge. The water below it reflected the starlight, and the koi swam in continuous circles, following each other's tails. Jamie stepped forward and reached up to his shoulder, where Bilbo was perched, nervously washing his paws.

"Hold on, Bilbo. I don't know what will happen here," Jamie said softly.

It struck him as a funny sort of thing to say—he had never been able to anticipate what was going to happen in this world. Bilbo responded by crawling to the back of Jamie's head and burrowing in his cave of matted, filthy hair, making him wince. The book was heavy in his arms. Jamie turned and took a last look at the waste yard, looking for something in particular. As he scanned, he was surprised to see exactly what he sought. A stained, candy-pink backpack with cartoon ponies in purple and turquoise stuck out from the bottom of the nearest pile of refuse. Jamie was nearly sure it hadn't been there before—he would have stepped right over it. In any case, Jamie was happy to see something that would make climbing the bridge a bit easier. He pulled the pack from the pile and shook it free of the bits of paper and string that clung to the sides. He recognized the ponies; they were the sort of thing the girls in his school loved, and many had plushy versions they brought for show-and-tell. Jamie never brought anything for show-and-tell, not after the time he had brought Bilbo—back when he was stuffed—and he had "disturbed" the other children. At least that was what Ms. Hamilton had told him. Jamie had stopped bringing anything to the Friday afternoon sessions after that. With a smirk, Jamie couldn't help but imagine what they'd think of Bilbo now.

Jamie stuffed the book into the pink backpack. It barely fit, but by shaking the bag and allowing the canvas sides to slowly worm their way around the book's edges, it eventually slid in. Jamie slung the backpack on his shoulders. For a moment, he was acutely aware of what he looked like—a grown man with a beard to his chest, wearing a length of cloth around his waist and a child's pink backpack. He was the man Momma would have told him not to stare at.

Jamie turned back to the bridge, illuminated in a spotlight glow from the stars. He took a step toward the structure. He could see the other side clearly, but still Custos's warning was solid: trolls. Jamie knew enough of this world to know that he should never underestimate its monsters. As he approached the steps, it was clear that he would need to climb the side like a ladder, as it rose straight up to the sky. From this angle, it looked immeasurably taller than it had from a few feet away. Jamie was sure it was no illusion. Things in this world had a way of changing size and shape. He reached out and took hold of the splintering wooden steps. The wood was warm, as though it had been sitting in the sun, but there was no sun in this place surrounding the bridge. Jamie had a strange thought that it must always be night here. He pulled himself up to the first step. The steps were narrow, and it was impossible for him to get any higher without falling backward off the bridge. Jamie stepped back off onto the grass and reconsidered. The railing, he realized—he would have to climb the railing in the steepest places; the steps were far too narrow to hold him.

Jamie took hold of the railing and again pulled himself onto the first step. Keeping his body slightly slanted and stepping carefully up to each step while simultaneously hanging onto the railing and progressing hand over hand, he began his awkward ascent. The bridge stretched up and up—it had grown even since he had begun climbing. Jamie took a deep breath; he could not give up now, although his muscles were strained to the point of shaking. He knew that one lost hand, one misstep, and he would plummet back to the ground, which looked unnaturally far below him now. In reality, Jamie thought, he should be only a foot above the grass, but that space had stretched too, and Jamie could see the tops of the trees surrounding the bridge. A fall from this height would surely kill him; if it didn't kill him, it would knock out an ankle or knee, and without the ability to walk, he was as good as dead. Jamie continued his climb, hand over hand, careful feet on the shallow steps. At one point his left hand slipped, and Jamie hovered in midair for a split second before he regained his grip. Shaking more than ever, he continued, up and up—now the tops of the trees were far below him, the water nearly unrecognizable, the air cold and thin.

Finally, the slope began to lessen, and Jamie was able to step more freely. He breathed a sigh of relief and let go of the handrail. The bridge before him was as flat as the bridges he had driven across with Momma and Daddy on their few car trips. He could no longer see what lay on the other side—it was obscured by a muddy darkness that swirled like smoke around the periphery of the bridge. He had not forgotten the Custos's warning—a monster the likes of which he had not yet met lived here and was waiting for him to get near enough to make its presence known. Jamie took step after careful step, barely breathing. The warm, pulsing presence of the little rat on his neck was a comfort.

Out of the darkness stepped a figure, waiting in the distance. Jamie shuddered, knowing that he had no option but to keep moving forward but not knowing what to expect. His body tensed, and he walked slowly toward the dark shape.

"Bilbo, I want you to know that you're my very best friend, the best one. I wouldn't have made it nearly so far without you. I'm sorry if I can't get you home, but I want you to know I tried," Jamie said softly to the little rat on his neck.

Bilbo responded by poking his wet nose into Jamie's skin.

Jamie's eyes were dry, weary, and strained. He had been close to death many times in this world, but at no time did it seem so certain. He felt the touch of his mother's fingers in his hair; he heard her soft voice in his ear.

Hush, little baby, don't say a word.

He felt Daddy's arms around him, the warmth overwhelming, overtaking all fear and sadness. In his mind's eye, he saw their faces in the distance. The details were already beginning to fade—how was that possible? He had been gone only a few days. How could he forget so soon? Jamie took a long breath; the figure shuffled closer, any defining details still obscured. Jamie realized his hands were shaking, not from effort this time, but rather from the unknown. Overhead a bat flitted by, low enough to stir the breeze and make Jamie look up. He knew he could not count on any help from these creatures, but they had offered it once— maybe they would once more.

The troll steadily approached on slow, shuffling feet. Jamie stepped forward, trying desperately to control his breathing.

"Hello there, young person," the voice rang out across the expanse, the voice of an old man, cracked with age and time.

Jamie stopped, confused. It was not malicious or frightening; rather, it was kind, the voice of the old man next door who raked leaves in the front yard and had once given Jamie a tiny flag on the Fourth of July. It was the voice he imagined that his grandpa might have one day but did not have quite yet. It was kind.

"Nice of you to climb all the way up here to see me," the figure said as it finally came into focus.

The old man before him had wispy white hair that barely covered his wrinkled head. He wore tan slacks and a button-up shirt with a pattern of blue lines, and over that a cardigan of some sort of off-brown wool. His shoes were dark leather loafers, the sort that could be slipped on and off easily. His face was round like an apple: fleshy cheeks and overgrown eyebrows the same color as his hair. He smiled, his teeth the too-perfect tone of dentures, and his skin had liver spots that could be mistaken for freckles.

"Surprised, aren't ya?" the figure said, his voice amused.

"Are you a troll?" Jamie asked, realizing how little sense it made.

"Yes, well, there are many kinds of trolls, aren't there?" the old man responded. "Now tell me, where are you on your way to?"

Jamie breathed unsteadily. This creature did not appear in the form he had imagined from his fairy stories, but it was clear he was in charge of this bridge, and everything Jamie had learned about this world had taught him never to trust appearances.

"The city. I have to go to the city. I have to find my way home," Jamie said firmly, careful not to sound rude or short.

The old man nodded.

"It's that way a bit, the city anyhow—can't vouch for the other." He paused, grinding his jaw a moment before looking up, his eyes a vivid blue, devoid of the cloudiness of age. "You know what your prospects are there? Home, I mean—not the city."

Jamie shook his head. "I don't understand."

"I forget you're but a child—your body is deceiving. I apologize. Let me speak more plainly," the old man replied carefully, like a teacher explaining a lesson. "Your prospects, what you expect to see when you go home. Have you considered it?"

"I want my parents."

"Well," the old man said, shaking his head meditatively. "That might prove to be a problem. You have any idea how many years you've been gone, son?"

Jamie shook his head again, refusing to let the old man's words pull the tears that rested in the corners of his eyes down his cheeks.

"You look to be in the range of forty-something years old, but I'm a lousy guess at age now. Older I get, the younger people look, so you might just be older. Hard to say. Your parents are likely dead, son," the old man said in a matter-of-fact voice that was not devoid of sympathy.

"No," Jamie burst out, finding his voice. "They're not dead. Let me pass on my way."

"Pass on your way?" the old man said, amused. "Do I look as though I could stop ya? Although please might be a nice touch."

Jamie paused, sensing a trap.

"Please let me pass on my way."

"In a moment. Let me just take a good look at ya."

The old man leaned closer. Jamie could smell the stench of decay—old skin and bits of things that had long gone bad. He stood still, determined not to run, not to panic. He would pass by, he would go to the city, he would go home, and he would find his parents. The old man reached a withered hand out and placed a single finger on Jamie's hand. The skin blistered and shriveled under his touch. Jamie cried out and jumped back, aware of how defenseless he was. The old man laughed.

"Yep, about forty-something. Well, except for that bit."

He laughed again, a rolling chuckle. Jamie looked at the spot on his arm. It had wrinkled and shriveled like the old man—that spot was a million years old and it sagged inward, in contrast to the rest of Jamie's body. He realized in horror what this thing was, and the memory of this fear hit him like a wave. His nightmare, one that he had almost forgotten: being made to lie down on his grandmother's nubby-cloth bedspread, too young for preschool, barely old enough to hold memory. Grandma's ancient breath rolling over him through her open mouth as she slept. It had smelled of old things—bits of food eaten long ago, rotten teeth, and air trapped too long in aging lungs. Jamie had held his breath, sure that if he inhaled her ancientness, he would wake up aged beyond his years.

Jamie squinted at the old man. This was his nightmare—this creature was feeding off a fear that was particular to Jamie, and something did not quite sit right. The fingerprint left by the Asrai drove an icy pick into his skin, the pain radiating outward, making it difficult to see. A wave of realization washed over him; Jamie knew what this was, and it was no troll.

"Bogle," he murmured, trying to sort out his vision through the blinding pain in his head. "You're nothing but a bogle."

The old man laughed, a low chuckle, dangerous in its control.

"Smart one, aren't ya? Come here, son, let me tell you something."

He leaned in toward Jamie, the smell of rotting flesh rising like a wave. Vomit rose in Jamie's throat. The old man opened his mouth, and his denture-perfect teeth were now rotted stubs, and bits of dead things hung from the edges. A forked tongue shot out and waved back and forth in front of Jamie's eyes. Jamie screamed, and the overwhelming smell of death overtook him. He fell to his knees, retching from his empty stomach. The nausea passed, and everything in Jamie's vision went white. Oh god, he thought, I can't pass out now, I can't. This thing, this bogle, is ready to take me. The grainy snow passed, and the pain in his forehead subsided. The smell of decay and rot vanished, replaced with the scent of night jasmine. Even the bile that Jamie had spewed all over the splintery wooden bridge was gone, dissolving into the grains of wood like water in a sponge.

He looked up and was not surprised that the old man had disappeared. The bridge was empty but for wisps of fog and the stars overhead. Jamie looked at his hands. The aged spot where the old man had touched him was gone, but it was replaced with more lines and liver spots like those that had patched the old man's face. Jamie's shoulders were stiff, and his back ached under the weight of the wood elves' book. Bilbo clung to his shoulder, nervously sniffing the air.

"Bogle. It was a bogle, nothing more."

Jamie murmured the words and stroked Bilbo's fur, but he knew it was much more than that—the bogle had taken still more years. He could see it in his skin, feel it in his bones; his beard reached the middle of his chest, and its streaks of gray were more pronounced. Many more attacks like this one and there wouldn't be anything left to take. Jamie pulled himself to his feet, wincing at the ache in his knees. His skin clung to his bones like leather, lined with age and taut around his neatly defined muscles. He looked behind him—still nothing—and proceeded forward once again. Another bat sailed overhead. Jamie looked up, grateful for the company. The bridge stretched forever into the night; there was no downward slope that Jamie could see. He would walk this bridge forever and never reach the end, and every attack, every minute, he aged—and his parents aged too. Maybe it was as the old man had said. Maybe they were dead; maybe they had long forgotten him.

Maybe there was no redemption from this place, no escape from the bottom of that very long hill. He was the reason the wood elves had all been murdered. He had brought nightmares to a nightmare world, and perhaps it was only fitting that he would die here on this bridge. Bilbo nuzzled his neck. Jamie reached up to feel the little creature's soft fur.

In the distant fog, a shape began to manifest, and with it came a sound, the tone of a bow being pulled across string. The hollow intonation rang into the night and, not finding any surface to bounce off of, sailed away. As Jamie approached, he saw the figure was wiry and tall, a man with chocolate skin and chiseled lines that created chasms in the otherwise perfect smoothness of his face. His salt-and-pepper hair hung back from where his hairline once had been. Another old man, Jamie thought. This old man was playing a violin at a ferocious rate, the music spilling out so rapidly it was difficult to hear a melody. His eyes were closed, and he seemed rooted to the spot where he stood, his upper body moving ever so slightly to the tune. An open case lay in front of him, and scattered quarters and dimes lined the bottom. Jamie knew what was expected of him and smiled at the absurdity; money was a thing that was a vast mystery even back in his previous life. His seven-year-old self had played with coins with a vague notion of their worth; never having been asked to use them for their practical purposes, he had never learned their exact value.

There was no graceful way to step past the figure, and Jamie knew that a creature that had made itself seen would not easily be ignored. As he approached, the music slowed, losing its frantic beat and finding a gentle, rhythmic tune. The notes dipped low and then soared to such a height that Jamie held his breath—the stars caught the sound and, for a moment, Jamie could almost hear them sing in response. The rawness of the string and fiber vibrating through the polished wood stole all the air from Jamie's lungs, and every muscle in his body relaxed. A warmth washed over him; his aching back and muscles lulled for a moment in the resonance. On his shoulder, Jamie heard something like a purr and realized that it was coming from his rat—a low rumble in Bilbo's throat, a sound of utter contentment.

The icy finger mark on Jamie's forehead suddenly stabbed inward as though a shard of ice had been driven into his skull. Jamie was pulled forward as though by an invisible thread. Jamie knew he couldn't stay; the Asrai, true to their word, were pulling him past this man, this moment. Jamie wondered how long he had been standing there. It seemed he might have always been there, swaying in place for eternity. A sense of belonging radiating out from his chest, and for once—the first time in a long time, since before the very long hill and before his overwhelming unhappiness threatened to swallow him, before the time he thought so very much about everything, before time itself—he thought he might have felt like this, no memory but acceptance and warmth.

Still, the ice pick in his forehead ached, breaking his reverie, and he stepped unwillingly toward the man, who played on. Jamie shuffled his feet, caught between the searing pain in his head and the lull of utter contentment. The tune changed as Jamie stepped forward—the tempo increased, the notes became darker, more intense. The stars above resonated in response, but their light flickered, making the night darker than before. As Jamie came alongside the man, his eyes flew open, and the milky white clouds of the blind stared wildly at him. The tempo increased, the notes rose to a heartbreaking pitch, and Jamie ached deep in his gut. The invisible string of ice that originated from his forehead continued to pull him forward. The man dropped the violin, the instrument and bow clattering to the ground—still the humming from the stars above continued, as though they had absorbed the music and now they cast it out along with their light. Jamie jumped past and tried to run, but his feet refused to move faster than a walk. The man stood still, staring out at Jamie, and pointing at him with one leathery finger. He mouthed a word that Jamie could not make out; he could see, however, that the man's mouth was a black hole, devoid of teeth or tongue. It was a void, an unfillable black space—like the Lairdbalor's gaping mouth and the infinity beyond its corners. Jamie pulled his feet along but they moved slower still, stuck in place. The only thing moving him was the searing frozen pull that emanated from his forehead.

Jamie turned his back to the man and, with all the strength he had left, dragged his leaden feet, one after the other. He heard the creaking of the wooden bridge behind him and the pressure of feet on its rotting surface. He heard his heart beating. The stars hummed the violin song, the notes dipping so low they scraped the bottom of a man's soul with the perfect simplicity of their tone. Jamie wanted desperately to look back, but he knew he would see others behind him, and his feet still moved so very slowly. He wondered what they were—others like the violinist? In his imagination, he saw rotting bodies with flesh hanging in ragged pieces, the undead of the comic books he had read back when he had been seven. He wondered if they were creatures that had come from the water below, malformed mermaids with shrunken heads and claws that scraped the wooden surface as they pulled their formless masses closer, faster than Jamie could escape. Were they shadow men, shapeless creatures that existed only in the night? Darkness incarnate, creatures that moved along the walls and were as much a trick of the eye as they were nightmare? The not knowing drove men mad, never certain if the shapes that danced in the corners of their eyes were real or delusion. Or maybe it was nothing at all, and Jamie was fleeing from an old man playing the violin. He had finally lost the ability to recognize true danger and, as a result, saw it in all things, even a blind old man on a bridge. It's a bogle, it's a bogle, Jamie thought desperately though he knew he was wrong. Trolls. What was it the bogle had said? There were many kinds of trolls. Jamie suspected that whatever he might see if he could work up the courage to look behind him would be the thing that would scare him the most. He closed his eyes and pulled one foot in front of the other, methodically and slowly. The rustle behind him increased. He could feel breath at his neck, and then just as suddenly it pulled away, sucked back. Only the throbbing in his forehead remained steady. Jamie could feel the creatures, whatever they might be, getting closer. He stifled a sob composed as much of fear as it was of the utter anguish of uncertainty.

He tried to visualize Momma's face only to find the picture grainy and unreliable. The features weren't right; it was the

composite of too many memories, too old and unused. Jamie tried
to smell her soap-and-lotion skin. He tried to focus on the softness
of her neck, the lull of her voice when she sang. The notes were
discordant and wrong, the smell false. Jamie sucked in air—the
memories he had of his life were failing. They were already too old
and too far away. They had become unreal, and his life in his world
was stale, unused, wasted. Jamie let the sob tear from his throat. It
carried anger at his life lost, his memories stolen from him, the pain
in his body and heart, and the curse of knowing that he had never
been anything but a source of pain and loss. He stopped moving and
fell forward, and as he did, he felt a thousand fingertip touches at his
back. Jamie covered his head where the throbbing intensity of the
Asrai's finger-touch ached with an intensity that hardly seemed real.

The tapping of fingertips became caresses along his back,
beckoning him back, pulling at his wrap, stroking his bare skin.
Jamie lifted his head, and an inhuman howl rose from his throat.
He felt himself becoming part of the mist, dissolving back into
the night, only a note in the old man's song. A scream filled the
night as though a hole had been ripped across the sky. The pressure
on his back, the sensation of warmth and dissolution, ceased
abruptly. Jamie was encased by a thousand wings. Pinched faces
screeched past his, and Jamie realized what was happening. He
was encased in bats—the creatures had surrounded him and the
high-pitched screams they emanated filled his head. His feet came
unstuck from the wooden surface, and Jamie pulled himself erect.
Bilbo once again encased in hair at the back of his neck. Jamie ran,
the bats following—like the cockroaches, they seamlessly swirled
around him, enfolding him like a cloak. Not caring if he careened
off the edge, Jamie ran as fast as he could, every last bit of strength
propelling him forward until, without warning, he fell through
the air, his feet still pumping uselessly. A thousand prickly, hairy
bodies and coarse-textured wings surrounded him, and he fell
blind, with no concept of how close or far the ground might be.
The impact was softened by the mass of bodies surrounding him,
but it still knocked the wind from his chest. Jamie lay coughing as
the cloud of bats swirled back into the sky.

Stunned, Jamie looked back. The steep slope of the bridge rose behind him; beneath him was the soft grass of the clearing. Jamie laughed in utter disbelief. He had made it across. He pulled himself up, feeling a wrenching sensation in his shoulder. The pink pony backpack was still firmly attached to his shoulders. Jamie stared at the sight in front of him. The sky was beginning to lighten a bit—another reminder of lost time. The office towers rose so high they were lost to the rapidly fading night sky. Sporadic lights from windows gave the illusion of a thousand eyes looking in all directions. A paved city street stretched out in front of him, clean white paint marking the lanes. No cars in sight—the roads seemed entirely for show. In fact, there was no sign of life anywhere. Jamie remembered the Custos had told him that the Urbis Incola would meet him. He choked back a quiet laugh. He had heard that before, and he would not wait here for them. If they did live here, they would find him—everything always did. Jamie pulled Bilbo from the back of his head, wincing at the raw patches of skin on the back of his neck. Bilbo was shaking, his head hidden in his paws.

"It's okay, Bilbo—we made it. We're in the city. Whatever happens, it can't be worse than what's already passed."

Jamie wasn't sure he believed himself, but he wasn't sure he cared anymore. He was closer to home, he was closer to finding out whatever was in the book, and he felt a gnawing sense of hope. Afraid to let it settle in too tightly, he took a breath and placed the rat on his shoulder, adjusted his backpack, and walked down the street.

TWENTY

THERE was no reason to use the sidewalks in this uninhabited city. Jamie walked down the center line, enjoying the sensation of doing something that would normally be so obviously dangerous. It reminded him of street fairs. Daddy took him to the farmer's market on some Sundays—the street would be closed down, and Jamie could walk right down the middle line. He smiled at the memory. Daddy always bought him a tomato from the bin and then laughed as Jamie ate it like an apple. He loved the way the inside squished up in his mouth, the skin rubbery and soft.

As he walked, Jamie looked down the side streets. Lamps hung high over the pavement, casting pools of light that faded as the sun overtook the night. Time passed so oddly here, Jamie mused. In his world, the dawn seemed to take forever to pass; here it took minutes. If the sun decided it wanted to rise, it just did it, pushing the night out of its way. Jamie had no way of knowing how many hours the night had taken, but it had seemed interminable. The days were worse, but maybe this would be the last day; maybe he would find his way home. There was still no sign of the Urbis Incola. Jamie realized that he was looking for cockroaches, but he really had no idea what they might appear as. Nothing was as he expected it to be. The streets were lined with small markets, offices

with peeling signs, signs that life had existed here at one point—
or maybe it never had. Maybe this was the nightmare of a child
somewhere, lost in his or her memory, a city long forgotten and
abandoned. Maybe it was the sum total of all men's nightmares—
that one day all human life would disappear. Structures that held
so much importance, the places that controlled their livelihoods,
all these things would simply dry up, and the city would be given
back to the creatures on whose eradication so much time had been
spent—the cockroaches, street cats, spiders, and rats. Jamie reached
up to stroke Bilbo's head. The little rat had seen so much, and none of
it was his fault. He had lived a thousand nightmares simply by merit
of loving Jamie. The heaviness in Jamie's head repeated that truth to
him over and over. The icy patch on his forehead had calmed, and
now it felt no colder than an autumn breeze.

Jamie walked on. The sun reflected off the metal-and-glass
towers. Jamie squinted, and a comfortable warmth hit his bare
skin. He stopped and looked around him; to his right was an office,
the sign hanging half to the ground, the door chained shut with
a heavy silver chain. Jamie could make out the print on the filthy
window glass.

Nico's Travel Palace

Brochures lay scattered on a faded carpet. Jamie wiped a patch
of the window with his hand and peered further in. They advertised such places as Peru, Argentina, Paris. Jamie looked deeper
still, fascinated by the utter ruin of the place. On a stand near the
window was another dusty rack of brochures, and they all read the
same thing: "Home." Jamie shook his head, and looked back. Each
was different, as far as he could see, the dirt and neglect obscuring
the images, but they all showed different houses, children's bed-
rooms, a tree decorated with bright lights, a green yard with a
swing. So intent was his examination that Jamie did not hear the
footsteps approaching from behind.

"So sorry, so sorry—not expecting customers so early. Let me
open up the shop, and we can talk about where it is you want to go."

The accent was thick, like that of the old lady who lived on the
next block who passed out powdered sugar cookies on Halloween.

Jamie spun, his heart beating madly against his ribs. The man looked like he belonged to the voice: thick gray-and-black beard and hair that fell to his shoulders in the same alternating waves of gray and black. His face was lined, and he wore a thick black turtleneck sweater that hugged his large frame. Jamie started to respond, but the figure passed straight through the closed door, a single fluid motion that caused a flurry of wind inside the musty shop. Ancient brochures fluttered off the filthy desk, and then stillness.

Jamie shook his head, looking around him. Dark clouds were starting to overtake the sun; he could feel a flush of goose shivers on his exposed skin. Taking one last look at the Travel Palace, he reached up and ran his finger down Bilbo's silky back.

"Okay, Bilbo, let's find home."

Jamie walked down the center of the street. He knew better than to call out—creatures of this world had a way of finding him when they wanted to, and making a ruckus hadn't helped him yet. The sun brought sweat to Jamie's brow, and in wiping it, he realized how caked with dirt he was. He smiled at the thought of what he must look like. He was glad none of the windows offered a reflection; he didn't really want to know.

A movement in the distance made Jamie jump. He walked faster toward it—a shadow, low to the ground. He jogged the rest of the block, anxious to find the Urbis Incola, anxious to find home.

Sitting in the center of an abandoned four-lane intersection was a white cat with tawny spots of red and gold. One spot covered its back haunch, another the opposite shoulder. The tips of its ears were soft black, and two matching spots on the top of its head gave the impression that it had an extra set of eyes in addition to the vivid green ones that stared Jamie down as he approached. Jamie stopped a couple of feet from the cat. It stared at him interestedly, with the amused air that cats always seemed to have toward humans.

"Hello," Jamie said, unsure of what to do. "Are you the Urbis Incola?"

The cat continued to stare and then leaned over and began licking a white paw, obviously unconcerned with Jamie.

"Are you—are you really here? Or a memory?" Jamie asked.

The cat looked up from its paw and stared at him as though considering whether to answer. Then with a full backstretch, the cat stood, turned, and sauntered down the street. Jamie followed. He had no idea if it was the right thing to do, but walking blindly was just as likely to be effective, so he figured he might as well follow a cat. The cat didn't look back at Jamie but kept its pace a few feet in front of him. Jamie walked on, watching both the cat and the buildings that lined the street. The creature stopped in front of a large, block-wide building with a thousand windows that rose to the sky. Jamie looked at the overhanging marquee sign, which appeared to have been carved from stone. Cecil Hotel. Jamie looked to the cat, who was sitting inside the open front doors. Jamie took a deep breath and followed. The doors were heavy glass with a golden metal trim. They were both open, waiting for Jamie to enter. The lobby was filled with an incongruent mix of furniture. An old-fashioned settee-style sofa leaned against the wall. Silver metal folding chairs formed a circle to his left. A sofa like the over-stuffed one in Jamie's own living room sat directly in the center of the room. Jamie had to step around it to reach the front desk, where the cat now sat on the counter, regarding him impassively. Jamie looked around. Chairs with red-and-gold cushions lined the opposite wall. One had a broken leg and threatened to fall over entirely; the others had tears through the fabric as though a giant paw had scratched its way across, shredding the aged silk covers. The walls and floor were creamy-white marble but stained with disuse. Jamie could see spiderwebs and smears of dust; fingerprints lined the walls as though someone had walked along the periphery, dotting their prints here and there. Jamie shivered—so someone else was here, and that someone had hands like his. The floor was littered with trash, bits of wrappers, and dry leaves.

An old newspaper blew by, and Jamie reached down to grab it. He had never read the newspaper in his old life—he had been seven, and the events of the world made little sense to him—but there was something he wanted desperately to know. He looked at the top where, in tiny print, the date was usually stamped. He knew what year it had been when he fell down the very long hill, but what year was it now? To his great disappointment, there was no date, and the articles weren't the usual sort either. They were mostly pictures of different rooms—bathrooms that consisted of only a sink and shower, the curtain pulled tight around the space; a dreary bedroom that held a bed and a rusty heater barely attached to the wall. Jamie realized they must be images from the hotel. He stared as the images changed in front of him, the black-and-white print shifting; now a man sat on the bed, and in his hand he cradled an object that was obscured by the folds of his clothes. Jamie squinted and the man held the object up to his head: a small, dark handgun. Jamie let out a silent cry as the man pulled the trigger, and charcoal-colored ink sprayed across the page. He dropped the newspaper, and an invisible wind blew it away. Jamie looked up, his heart pounding, skipping beats. The cat regarded him still. Jamie stepped forward to the white marble countertop, and the cat licked a paw, jumped down on the business side of the desk, and strode through an open door. Jamie looked to Bilbo, who sat on his shoulder sniffing the air.

"Hello?" Jamie ventured.

"Just a minute!" sang a woman's voice from the back.

Jamie jumped back, the unexpectedness of the sound making his heart beat even faster—it was difficult to take a full breath. From the office door walked a woman, young but still an adult. Her skin was the color of toasted almonds, and her black eyes slanted just so, like the cat's. Her straight black hair was sopping wet, as were her clothes. A simple black skirt, cream T-shirt, and dark-red sweater clung to her body, dripping water onto the marble floor.

"Hello," she said sunnily as Jamie stared. "You'll be wanting the rooftop then? Yes?"

Jamie stood silent.

"I don't know." He looked around. "What is this place?"

The woman laughed. Her teeth were straight and bright, perfect white.

"The Cecil of course! Pardon our mess. We're redecorating— have been for quite some time." She paused, looking confused for a short moment. Shaking it off, she brightened once more. "I think the rooftop has the best view. I'll get you a key."

She disappeared through the office door, leaving a puddle in her wake.

Jamie turned. He wanted to leave this place—he wanted his guides.

"You checking in?" a man's voice growled from the corner.

Jamie turned in the direction of the sound. A man sat in one of the shredded red-and-gold chairs. Black hair and eyes gave his pale skin a bluish hue; he wore jeans and a simple button-up shirt, but his bare feet were caked in something that looked like mud but was too dark and tinged with red to be so. Jamie shivered, and Bilbo curled up in his cave of hair at the base of Jamie's neck.

"No," Jamie said firmly. "I'm leaving."

He turned to the door and started to walk, feeling a vibrating in his ears.

"It's starting to fall apart. It knows you're here. Maybe it's time to run."

The man drew out the last letter of the word like a hiss, making Jamie's breath quicken. He broke into a sprint, bursting through the glass-and-metal doors. Out on the sidewalk, Jamie paused, heaving to catch a breath. Something slammed into his chest, shoving him abruptly away from the door and knocking him off his feet. Before Jamie could register the impact, a rush of air poured over him, knocking him flat on his back and sucking the breath from his lungs. As it dissipated, he sat up, coughing, his empty lungs desperately searching for a breath.

"Never follow cats," a robotic yet annoyed voice intoned from the street.

Jamie pulled himself to his feet, looking around frantically.

"Who is that?" he barked, his empty lungs still making his speech ragged.

What had looked like a bag of rubbish leaning against the neighboring building was now moving slowly across the street. Other bits of trash—food wrappers, old receipts, stained paper coffee cups—clung to its side. Jamie watched with apprehension.

He had been expecting more cockroaches; it had never occurred to him that the Burg took different forms in the city.

"You have been looking for us," the mass stated, stopping in front of Jamie.

The bag rustled, and the creature looked up at Jamie's face. It was composed entirely of waste, much like the papier-mâché creatures Jamie had made in school out of glue paste and newspaper, except the features were not rigid. They changed as the trash settled, two holes for eyes and a mouth that changed form as the bits of wrappers and old coffee cups shifted. It was fascinating and impossible. Jamie stared, speechless.

"Never follow cats," the creature said again. "We are Urbis Incola, here to guide you in the city."

"What is this place?" Jamie asked, indicating the Cecil Hotel behind him.

"A place where nightmares collect, in your world and ours," the Urbis Incola stated. "I advise stepping away from the periphery, unless you want to be hit by the jumper again."

Jamie looked up at the Cecil looming overhead and stepped into the street, the Urbis Incola following. The cat reappeared in the doorway and stared at him through the foggy glass. Jamie shivered slightly.

"What is the jumper?"

"Pauline is her name, if you care to know. She'll have another run at it here in a minute. Just wait," the creature said passively.

Sure enough, a rush of air shot down from the top of the building, slamming into the sidewalk and flooding out with such force that the Urbis Incola's exterior shifted almost entirely, its face morphing and reconfiguring. As Jamie watched, other figures formed behind the original. Bits of newspaper and trash sorted themselves together, various sizes and shapes. They stood impassive as the leader addressed Jamie.

"We should go. Things will start to break down soon; it is best not to be near the Cecil. Come."

The creature shuffled into the street, turning to the left. Jamie followed, Bilbo on his shoulder again. Behind them came the others, the soft rustle of paper the only indication they existed at all. They walked without discussion. A thousand questions swirled in Jamie's head—the empty storefronts, the abandoned towers, the cat, the girl with water running from her hair and clothes. As they walked, a window shattered from the outside in, glass spraying the ruined interior of a restaurant of some sort. Jamie jumped back, but the Urbis Incola did not stop its pace.

"What was that?" Jamie exclaimed.

"Things are starting to break down. We don't have much time. Night will be here soon. Best to follow. Try not to look," the creature droned.

Jamie shivered. Bilbo holed up in his nest in Jamie's hair.

Jamie looked up at the towering buildings and heard a hiss in the air and saw a bright flash of light growing closer and closer. With a spark of panic, he realized what the object was, and in an instant that felt a million years long, he watched the splintered windowpane hurtling directly toward him. The Urbis Incola whipped around and slammed into Jamie; he fell backward just as the razor-sharp glass imbedded itself in the pavement. Jamie felt tiny whispers of glass in his bare skin. The Urbis Incola stood over him, unfazed.

"Best to follow. We should hurry. It's already starting."

The creature shuffled down the street again, and Jamie followed on unsteady legs. The ground underneath them rumbled. Jamie knew what an earthquake was; he remembered being in a few of them with Momma and Daddy, and every time the house shook for a few moments. Once a framed picture had fallen to the ground, the one of Momma and Daddy at their wedding. Jamie loved that picture—they were looking at each other, and Momma had a ring of flowers in her hair. Jamie thought she looked like a fairy princess. Daddy had a beard that lined only his jaw and lip; he looked tall and incredibly important. This quake felt like the one that had overturned the picture, but it lasted so much longer. A signpost on the corner to Jamie's right fell over, crashing into the sidewalk. The Urbis Incola walked on, unimpressed.

Jamie followed, his heart skipping beats as a brick wall lining what had once been a patio café collapsed to the ground with a deafening rumble. Bricks rolled across the street, and Jamie winced with pain as one of them hit his bare toes. Up above, a window shattered, the sound bright and crisp. Jamie instinctively covered his head as tiny bits of glass rained down. The Urbis Incola walked on, not reacting to the increasing destruction.

"Best not to look. It is reacting to your presence," the creature informed him calmly.

"But how?" Jamie asked as a set of concrete steps leading to an office tower crumbled before his eyes.

From all over the city, Jamie heard the tinkling shatter of broken glass, the thunder of collapsing brick and mortar, the echo of impact on the asphalt streets. The sun was obscured with dust, the blue sky barely visible. A building with neat rows of glass windows to his right swayed back and forth, rocking off its foundation. The Urbis Incola turned back and faced Jamie.

"Run," it advised.

Jamie looked up as the tower came crashing straight down, a storm of glass and concrete pelting the street. He ran as fast as he could, dodging desperately to avoid the ragged chunks of ruins on the street. Something hit the back of his head; for a moment, everything went white and fuzzy, like the static on the television. He tasted blood in his mouth. He stumbled, and a piece of glass on the sidewalk drove deep into his foot. The pain cleared his head, and he ran faster, ignoring the stabbing ache.

The Urbis Incola had disappeared. As Jamie looked wildly from side to side, a newspaper box ripped up from the ground and hurtled itself across the street. A steel pillar melted into a puddle of metallic liquid. Jamie ran on as a cracked letter W, nearly as tall as himself, sailed through the air and slammed into the street before him. The asphalt cracked and buckled. Jamie fell forward, clawed his way back to standing, and ran on. The pain in his foot was unbearable. Jamie coughed out the black dust that surrounded him in waves.

"Best to keep moving."

The monotone voice came from somewhere in front of him. Jamie limped toward it.

"Help me!" he cried.

"You must keep moving, Jamie. Best to keep moving," The Urbis Incola repeated. Something wrapped around his arm from within the near dark of the city's collapse and pulled him forward.

"We are almost to a safe place, Jamie. You must keep moving."

The voice was in his ear, and Jamie could feel the gentle sensation of the swirling trash against his arm. Behind him, another tower crumbled, glass and black smoke rising like a mushroom cloud. Jamie's cry caught in his throat; he ran as best he could, leaning on his guide. A wall of dust and debris swept down a side street, hitting Jamie full force and nearly knocking him over again. Only the support on his arm held him upright. From the swirling remains of a parking tower, Jamie saw faces—pale skin and night-black hair and eyes obscured with rough-hewn cloaks. His breath caught.

"We need to hurry, Jamie. Just a bit more."

The calm voice forced Jamie to look forward and ignore the pain in his foot. A thunderous crash behind him sent a spray of rocks flying, embedding themselves in Jamie's hair; he heard Bilbo let out a frightened squeal, and a sharp tug on the back of Jamie's neck spurred him forward. On the edge of his hearing, the low chant of the dwarves rang in his ears. He remembered the pile of ash in the waste yard and wondered what revenge they would exact.

"I was attacked by a dwarf in the waste yard. It's dead now I think, I don't know how. They've followed me here." Jamie's voice was strained with barely disguised panic.

The Urbis Incola pulled him down the cracked street.

"Jamie, no one can kill a thing that lives in the imaginations of others. It is beyond your grasp. The dwarf was destroyed, but it is not gone." It spoke clearly into Jamie's ear. "Nothing here can ever truly die. Not even you. It just becomes trapped, as you will before too long. Here. You must get inside quickly."

Jamie looked up at a massive structure, all angles and jutting edges, long rectangular windows and unexpected crevices.

"What?" he murmured.

"The Scire are waiting inside. They do not leave the building. You will need to enter. You will be safe inside, at least for a time." The Urbis Incola motioned with a mass of fluttering trash.

"You're coming with me?" Jamie asked.

A rusted metal bus bench flew down the street and barely missed his head. Jamie ducked and ran up the irregular, angular steps. The creature held its ground and shook its head.

"We are Urbis Incola. It is our job to guide."

Jamie started to object, but when he looked back, the creature was gone—in its place, a flurry of trash. A wave of water raced down the side street facing the building. Six feet at its shallowest place, it crashed into the buildings on either side, breaking glass and gaining momentum. Jamie ran up the steps, past a large, tan stone fountain. Everything about the structure shifted every time he looked away. The angles changed ever so slightly, the steps stretched a bit farther on, and at one point, the fountain was replaced with a massive overhang from which hung a row of black metal bells. Bilbo clung to his hair and emitted a high-pitched hum. On Jamie ran, up the steps and through a large stone arch that rose from nowhere. A statue of a figure in a robe, its features muddled in the ironwork, loomed over the gateway. As Jamie stumbled through it, the statue grew and leaned farther out.

No doubt I'm seeing all the nightmares that surrounded this place, Jamie thought to himself. With his adult eyes, he could perceive a child's fear of this massive building, with its irregular shape and looming arches. It held no fear for him now. Jamie pushed himself through the entryway into a dimly lit room, and heavy wooden doors shut behind him with a boom. He breathed a sigh of relief as he heard the wave slam into the doors. A trickle of water seeping under the closed entry was the only evidence of the tumult outside.

He was in a cathedral—a massive room with rows of wooden-backed benches, the only light coming from chandeliers of triangular black metal that hung from the vaulted ceiling. Despite his pain, despite his racing heart, Jamie sighed in awe. The pews stretched to the front and wrapped around the sides of the room. Behind and above him was a massive system of bright silver organ pipes. Jamie almost forgot everything happening outside, almost forgot everything that troubled him. It seemed that if he could just sit for a minute in one of those clean wooden pews and stare down the long aisle, then he could rest, and maybe that would be enough—enough for a lifetime. He walked slowly, dragging his injured foot behind him. At the front of the room, a black iron Jesus hung from a wooden cross. Jamie shivered at the sight, the nails in Jesus's feet a sharp reminder of his own piercing pain.

Agnostic—Daddy had once explained when Jamie had asked what religion they were—not Christian, not Jewish, or any other religion for that matter. We're somewhere in-between; that was what Daddy had said. Jamie knew a bit about the in-between now and understood what he'd been trying to say. There is a place where all things converge and everything is true. Jamie had been a child when Daddy had told him this and had thought that in-between was the same as nothing at all. But here in this great hall, with a storm behind him and a dying god in front of him, he realized that it was the opposite of nothing—it was the sum total of all things, the place where anything was possible. As a child, Jamie had been content to snuggle into Daddy's arms and feign understanding, satisfied to wait until he was a grown-up. But here he was a grown-up, facing Jesus hanging from a cross in an abandoned cathedral. He understood now, and at the same time nothing made sense—least of all this. In-between. Jamie's strength failed, and he collapsed into a wooden pew.

"Bilbo," he whispered. "What now?"

"I should look at your foot."

A voice spoke gently from behind him. Jamie whirled around to see a childlike figure even younger than he had been before the very long hill, a million years ago.

"Are you the Scire?"

The figure nodded. She had bone-white skin and long golden hair pulled back at the neck. Her eyes were a pale gray, and her robes matched her eyes perfectly. She looked little more than a shadow—perhaps she had been standing there all along.

"I will look at your foot," the golden-haired creature said again, her voice little more than a whisper.

She lifted his bloody foot, caked with the ruin of the city. She looked up at him with impassive eyes.

"You have a length of glass stuck in your foot. I will need to remove it—it will hurt."

Her gentle voice sounded apologetic. Jamie just nodded. She ran a finger down the length of his foot and stopped where the searing pain started. She dug through the flesh with her fingers. Jamie had to bite his lip to keep from passing out from the pain of it, but the pressure released, slowly. She held out a shard of bloody glass, an inch in length, for his inspection.

"It's good to remember such things."

Jamie took the shard without question and held it in his hand for a moment before letting it tumble to the marble floor. His foot throbbed, but each pulse lessened the dull ache.

"What is happening?" Jamie asked, his voice soft, his eyes searching hers.

"Everything is ending, Jamie," the Scire answered. "You will have to make a choice soon, but before you do, you need to see. You need to decide what it is you want."

"I want to go home," Jamie choked.

"Perhaps. You are no longer a child, Jamie—the things you wanted then may not be the same. It is important to see the difference." She laid an ice-cold hand on Jamie's. "You have the book."

Jamie nodded and pulled out the wood elves' book. The Scire sat next to him on the polished wooden pew. The fingerprint spot on his forehead dropped several degrees, bordering on ice. The Scire looked up at him, staring at the spot, her brow slightly furrowed.

"There's not much time left," she said.

Jamie placed the book on her lap, and the Scire opened it. The blank pages stared up at them. In Jamie's ear, Bilbo's anxious wheezing increased, and he retreated to his cave of matted hair. She ran her finger down the page, turning to look at Jamie.

"I understand you were shown some things—is that right?" the Scire asked.

Jamie nodded, remembering the endless night of the dwarf's eyes.

"Those things are here, as are others. Do you truly want to see, Jamie?" she asked, her gray eyes reflecting like silver.

With great effort, Jamie nodded, every muscle in his body tense.

The Scire turned a page, and a cavity opened where the pages met the binding. Jamie saw foggy images almost like on television, but these figures were drawn with a dark pen. As soon as they were created, they were undone, action that began and concluded in moments.

"Do not look to see, Jamie—look to understand."

Jamie blinked hard. The images on the page morphed, and he saw a story unfold. A figure walked down a hallway. Kids—not children but not adults, their faces contorted in fear—shrank away from him. In the figure's hands was a long, cylindrical machine, a machine with only one purpose, only one goal. Jamie closed his eyes.

"No, no, no! I already saw this. I know these things, horrible things, I did."

The icy hand once again touched his.

"Look, Jamie. You must see everything if you see anything at all."

With great effort, Jamie opened his eyes. As tears streamed down his face, he watched the muzzle of the gun raise and lower, dark blood spreading across the page. The image faded, and he saw the figure—hood over his face and eyes, head against a wall—and the spot on Jamie's forehead burned ice into his skin. The Scire turned the page. The same figure sat in a crowded classroom, hood over his head, obscuring his eyes. Jamie watched the black ink embed and disappear as it drew countless figures around him that stood and fell back, ran for the walls—something was in the hallway, something they were running from. The figure in the center stood, hood still covering his face, and crossed to the door. He held it shut. Behind him, figures forced open a window. The door rattled—something on the other side was attempting to force it open, but the hooded figure held it fast. Behind him, screaming forms climbed up and out until the room was empty. At that, with no other option, he stood back. The door burst open. The muzzle of the machine raised and lowered, knocking the hooded figure back, black ink staining the page.

Jamie shook his head.

"But I . . . that wasn't me. I was the one who . . . " he stuttered.

"Were you?" the Scire asked. "This is a thing that never happened, Jamie. You have to choose the reality you will take with you if you choose to go home. You can be a killer or the savior of so many. You choose."

Jamie shook his head, not understanding. The Scire turned another page. A man as old as Daddy walked down the street, arm around a woman in a coat that Jamie knew was brightly colored, even though the black ink created only monotones. Jamie could almost feel the fabric under his fingers, the curve of her hip as she moved—the sensation was so real that he felt dizzy. A force from behind propelled him forward; the woman hit a brick wall with a cry of pain. The man spun. A hooded figure raised an edged line that even in dark ink reflected the moonlight, but no dark blood spilled from the man's throat. Instead he reached up, grabbed the figure's wrist, and pushed him back until the edged object fell from his grip.

"I wasn't the man . . . I was the other. I killed them," Jamie pleaded with the child for understanding, his voice raw.

"This is a thing that never happened, Jamie—which other will you be? What do you choose? Are you a killer?" she asked, her gray moon eyes unblinking.

"What do you choose, Jamie?" she whispered again. "This book contains all the secrets of every man in your world. It has been written for an eternity and will continue to be so. Everything that is and could be is here. There is no understanding; there is only choice. You have a unique gift, Jamie—you can see all the possibilities of your life as it was, and now you get to choose."

Behind them, the great wooden-and-iron doors rattled.

"It's all ending, and our time here is at its close. Remember,

Jamie, every life has a thousand paths. The worst parts of ourselves are only possible because of the great light we also carry. You choose which path to follow. You choose the reality that will be written here."

With that she stood, placing the book on the bench.

Behind them the doors rattled, and a heavy crash came from somewhere in the distance. A flurry of dust rushed under the heavy framed door. The Scire looked to Jamie and then walked toward the front of the cathedral, where the iron Jesus hung from his wooden cross. Overhead, the black chandeliers rocked back and forth, casting shadows on the walls. Jamie stood, desperate for an answer.

"But the dwarves, what of them? It's them outside, isn't it?"

The Scire answered without stopping her slow ascent to the front of the hall.

"Them and others. Your presence in our world is much like a splinter in yours. You do not belong here, and there are forces who will do anything to remove you." She stopped and turned back, regarding Jamie with her clear gray eyes. "Have you considered why so many have helped you in your journey, Jamie?" Her whispery voice was challenging but gentle.

"The Lairdbalor—they were afraid of the Lairdbalor," he stammered.

The Scire pondered his answer.

"Your Lairdbalor is only possible because of you, Jamie. You are as much it as it is you. Many in this world fear him, but no more than they fear the disruption you bring with you. Your presence has already caused much disruption, but you're not at fault—not exactly. You cannot apologize for things you cannot control."

Jamie's head swam.

"But the things that happened—the wood elves, the Holding—I did that?" He felt suddenly sick to his stomach.

The Scire nodded.

"There's no cause for distress. As others have told you, Jamie, you cannot kill a nightmare—fear has a way of rebuilding itself. The wood elves, my cousins, are in their Holding as we speak, trying to understand the mysteries of your kind. All the things that were destroyed in your wake have been rebuilt. It is as if you were never there, and the same will be true with the city. But we must expel you from our world. Some of our kind think that will happen only when your bones are picked clean of their flesh, when your soul is no longer bound to your body. Others look to deliverance, but for that to happen, you must decide to relinquish control over your fate. You must stop looking for patterns. You must choose what part of yourself to embrace."

The wind outside blew the heavy framed doors wide open. A storm of rubbish and debris spewed into the cathedral, and a terrible howling cycled outside, the sound of a dying city. The ground shook with the impact of the destruction. Jamie looked to the Scire, who now stood in front of the black iron Jesus. She looked up to the ceiling and spread her arms open wide. An iron chandelier dropped, narrowly missing Jamie's head—he ducked and, grabbing the book, fell into the aisle.

"Your fear keeps you here, Jamie. In a world built of fear, it is no easy feat to choose—but choose you must."

The Scire's whisper sailed through the chaos, floating in and out of Jamie's ears. The massive pipe organ ripped away from the wall as the entire structure shuddered from an unseen impact. It teetered precariously back and forth and then, with a magnificent scream, hurtled to the pews below, cracking the expanse of the stone floor. Jamie looked wildly about, but the Scire remained still, arms outstretched. Long iron tears ran down the length of Jesus, forming a charcoal lake below, pooling around the Scire's feet. The ornately carved face lost all features, caved inward, and collapsed.

From a side door, Jamie heard a clear brass note. The fingerprint embedded deep in his forehead drove an icy stab clear back to the base of his skull. Jamie saw only gray static; his head rang. He fell forward, the little rat at the base of his neck pulling hair from his head in chunks. Cool, smooth hands surrounded him. Jamie was lifted, turned on his back, and carried by a thousand silky hands. The roar of the city increased, and under it all, Jamie heard the rhythmic intonation of the dwarves' chant. The symphony was punctuated by the ringing clear tone—a melody, a laugh, a song. His eyes cleared as the silken hands lowered him to the ground. He looked up to see rows of identical faces—bone-white skin and impossibly clear gray eyes, golden hair tied back so that only fine wisps framed their childlike faces—the Scire surrounded him. The chanting intensified, the words unknown and familiar, and the clear tone sang out over the din of the collapse happening all around.

"It's time, Jamie."

The Lairdbalor's words were gentle but commanding. Jamie sat up. He was at the front of the cathedral, and around him the bright polished pews lay in disarray. An army of pale-faced dwarves with night-black hair and eyes walked toward him, their rough tunics barely obscuring their passive faces. The Scire backed slowly away, and the Lairdbalor shuffled forward with unfathomable grace. Its black eel skin reflected the light from the swaying chandeliers. The tattered topcoat held an unreliable air of dignity, and the top hat rested lightly on the slope of his head. Jamie's head was empty of thought—only instinct remained. The dwarves marched forward. To Jamie's horror, as their robes touched the Scire, the golden-haired creatures collapsed into piles of ash.

"You choose either to die here or embrace your fears, Jamie. It's time," the Lairdbalor said.

The entire structure shook. Across the ceiling, a crevice grew into a crack. As Jamie watched, the ceiling splintered in two, the metal and stone crashing downward. Jamie's ears rang with the deafening impact, and his head throbbed. Most of the dwarves were trapped under the wreckage, but not all—not all. Jamie watched more and more pull themselves from the tangled pile and march forward still, the Scire turning to ash in their wake.

"Do you choose to end your life in this world or come with me, Jamie? Do you choose to become your fears? Do you choose to make the two halves of yourself whole? Soon the choice will be made for you, and you will forever be lost to our world—you will live your life over and over, a nightmare that ends with your death for eternity." The Lairdbalor's voice rose in perfect clarity above the din.

"But what is left for me at home?" Jamie whispered.

"I cannot answer that. *bhalaich, tà sùil.*"

The Lairdbalor moved forward as the dwarves progressed steadily, ash swirling in their wake. The remaining Scire picked up the impossibly large book and held it out to Jamie.

"To remind you," a Scire said to him in a soft voice.

The numbness in the core of Jamie's body was replaced with something else—sterner stuff, something greater than nightmares and fear. He reached out to grab the text and looked into the clear gray eyes once more.

He walked toward the Lairdbalor, and as the creature opened its great expanse of a mouth, Jamie did not hesitate. The darkness swallowed him, engulfing him in a perfect night.

JAMIE sat in perfect stillness, perfect silence. The chaos and destruction were gone, replaced with a velvety blackness. Only the feel of the book in his arms and Bilbo's wet nose at his neck reminded him that he lived at all. His mind was clear; his heart beat in even, steady beats. He felt a downward motion, as though he were drifting. A voice from inside his head echoed through the expanse.

"*Is coileanta, bhalaich, is coileanta,*" it whispered. The darkness moved around him like gentle hands, caressing. "It's time to go home, Jamie. Open your eyes."

TWENTY-ONE

THE sunlight burned his eyes, and Jamie stumbled back.

"Watch yourself!" a voice behind him called, and Jamie jumped, not sure what manner of creature it was. He spun to see a grown-up in a steel-gray business suit, his hair bald except for wisps around the sides, his eyes pinched and angry. Jamie stared at him, not sure how to react.

"What are you?" he whispered.

The man shook his head and kept walking. Jamie turned in circles. Men and women, dressed in various states of formality, walked to and fro. A younger girl, a teenager maybe, wearing a bright-blue hood over her brown skin, stopped and regarded him with sad eyes.

"Do you need help?" she asked.

Jamie stared at her, trying to understand what was happening and what these creatures were, what nightmares they were made of. He looked up at towering office buildings reflecting the setting sun; the sidewalks were whole, no glass littered the street, nothing had been destroyed.

"I need to go home," Jamie croaked.

The girl looked at him curiously, and an older man approached, wearing the kind of button-up shirt that Daddy wore. The man looked to the girl with a warning in his eyes.

"You okay?" he asked, but the question wasn't directed at Jamie.

With shock, Jamie saw that the man feared for the girl's safety. He feared *Jamie*. The realization struck him as sharply funny, and he laughed—a child's laugh—not understanding what they could fear from him, not in this world. The girl nodded, not taking her eyes off Jamie.

"I think he needs help. We should tell security," she said quietly to the man.

Jamie laughed again—security? He backed up away from the two, not sure what they were and not trusting their voices. He was suddenly aware of a weight in his arms and looked down to see the wood elves' book. But it was no longer impossibly large—it was the size of any normal book and had a heavy leather cover, stained and tattered. His other hand was wrapped around a creature with gray-brown fur that used to be tawny, its glass bead eyes unseeing. Its tail had the slightest crook to it from where it had been caught in Momma's vacuum cleaner. Jamie let out a sob.

"Bilbo—no, no, no, no, no!"

All the emotion and terror Jamie had been holding in for an eternity poured out of him. All the confusion at the bottom of the very long hill; the pain; the unknown; the dreams; the spot in his forehead that was still degrees colder than anywhere else on his body; everything. The beetle fairy; the children in the freak show; the tall girl with the hook arm; the vision in the dwarf's eyes; and the end, the golden-haired creatures turning to ash; the perfect night. It all came crashing down, and Jamie howled with pain. His body ached with loneliness, with loss. He longed for Momma's arms so much, every cell in his body cried out for it. The soap-and-lotion smell of her neck; the feel of Daddy's arms around him, so tight he couldn't breathe. He stumbled backward, looking wildly around, and backed into a cylinder that overturned, bags of loose trash fluttering in the breeze. Jamie fell to his knees pawing at the pile.

"Help me! Help me! Help me!"

The trash did not respond—no shifting face appeared, no guide rose from the rubble. He was aware of the growing crowd—eyes boring into him, every sort, old and young—and Jamie felt their fear rolling off them in waves. A cockroach, long and black with a perfect brown-red shell, scurried from the waste. Jamie jumped for it.

"Help me! Custos! I need your help! I don't understand, where am I? What do I do?"

He was mad with grief and confusion—this wasn't what was supposed to happen. He wasn't home; he wasn't anywhere he knew. He was all alone, wrapped in the tattered remains of the Asrai's cloth, which in the light of the world lost its magic and looked like a filthy, torn sheet. Clutching a stuffed rat and a book, he wasn't a child but a grown man, with matted hair to his waist and a beard streaked with white that covered his sunken chest. He was a monster.

A man in a gray-blue uniform approached him. Through his hysteria, Jamie had a recollection—this man was a police officer and would help. He turned his head upward to the officer as he approached, a small black object in his hand.

"Help me, help me, help me," Jamie murmured, his voice fading as his eyes closed, an immeasurable tiredness overtaking him.

"HE'S coming around," a woman's voice stated calmly.

Jamie did not want to open his eyes. The blackness was interrupted by flashes of light all around him, a methodical beeping to his right, the sound of metal curtain rings being pulled to his left, and the feeling of pressure on his arms and chest.

"Sir? Can you hear us? Can you open your eyes?"

The voice was gentle, soft—it reminded Jamie of Momma when she would whisper to him in the morning, when he didn't want to get up to go to school and would lie in bed, eyes squeezed shut. Momma would come in and whisper in his ear.

"Wake up, Jamie. Wake up, baby boy."

Jamie would hold it in as long as he could and then start to giggle; at that, Momma would kiss his face, starting with his forehead and down his cheeks, ending with his nose. By then,

Jamie would be giggling uncontrollably. The warmth of the blankets and Momma's lips on his forehead—Jamie would wish for the day to never begin, to stay in just that moment. But it would pass; he would open his eyes, and the spell would be broken.

"Sir?" the voice said again, and he felt another pressure on his arm.

"Are we running fingerprints?" another voice asked, this one a man. It was also quiet, not scared like the people in the street had been.

Where had they taken him? He wondered if it was the hotel with the girl and the water and the terrible man in the chair, and with a start, he jerked up, his eyes open, looking around frantically. His rat was gone; his hand was empty.

"Sir? Calm down, sir, calm down. You're okay. You're okay now."

The owner of the first voice was a woman who looked somewhere between Momma and Grandma's age. Her coarse black hair had streaks of bright white; her chocolate skin was lined with age. Her dark eyes were gentle, and Jamie's breath immediately slowed, his heart calmed.

"My rat," Jamie rasped, his throat so dry he could barely get the words out. "Bilbo, where's Bilbo?"

The woman looked confused, and Jamie was hit with a stab of panic. She didn't know where Bilbo was—he was gone.

"Your things are right here, sir. Everything you came in with is right here. Is this your rat?"

She reached inside a plastic ziplock bag that lay on a little table next to him and pulled out Bilbo by the tail. Jamie nodded frantically. He clutched the little rat to his chest and felt tears well up and escape from his eyes.

"My god," the male voice intoned.

The woman shot a look at the source of the sound. Jamie looked too. The man was younger—not a teenager, a young grown-up— with black hair and sun-kissed skin. He looked at Jamie with a mix of amusement and sadness. Jamie looked away. He liked the woman better; she reminded him of Momma.

"Ricardo, why don't you go let the desk know that our guest is awake?" she said to the man. It was more an order than a question.

Ricardo turned and walked out. Jamie examined the space. He lay in a bed with silver metal railings, and tubes ran from his arms to bags hanging from matching metal hooks. A rectangular window ran the length of the room, and outside Jamie could see night sky and a glimpse of the moon. The room was dimly lit except for a bedside light; the walls a soft beige. A bathroom split off the side, separated by a white door with a shiny metal handle.

He realized with a start that he was in a hospital, like the one in the show that Momma and Daddy watched. He wondered what had happened to him. He looked down at himself—he was wearing a pale-green gown, and the Asrai's wrap was gone. His skin was clean; his beard was gone—not entirely, but cut short, as was his matted hair. He ran a hand over his head—his hair was as short as it had been on the day he tumbled down the very long hill. Where will Bilbo hide? he thought idly and looked down at his stuffed rat, feeling a pang in his heart. He knew this would happen; he knew it all along, but he missed the wet nose on his neck, the scratchy paws on his shoulder.

"Sir? You okay there?" the woman asked. "I'm Selma, I work here. Do you know where you are?"

Jamie shook his head.

"I suspect not. You were pretty out of it when you arrived. You are at Mercy Medical Center. You collapsed in the street downtown, and they brought you here. You've been out for over a day—exhausted is my guess, dehydrated too, malnourished, and basically in need of a little fixing up." She smiled at him, revealing perfect white teeth. "Do you know your name, love?"

Jamie felt warm—her voice washed over him, and the kindness brought tears to his eyes.

"Jamie. My name is Jamie Peters, and I fell down a hill a long time ago. I need to go home. I've been trying to get home."

Selma poured a glass of water from a small pitcher. Jamie gulped it down. She took the glass away and poured another, which he also poured straight down his throat.

"Okay, Jamie, okay, easy—try to sip this next one. Your body is pretty fragile still."

She handed him another glass, which Jamie obediently sipped.

"Let's get you sitting up a little, can we?" she said as she placed a cool hand on Jamie's shoulder to pull him forward, and with a button, she raised the back of his bed. Jamie looked around, surprised, and Selma smiled. "There. That's better, isn't it?"

She pulled a rolling stool over to the bed and sat next to him, regarding him with curious eyes.

"Well, Jamie Peters, we'll do our best to help you, but we'll need more information. I'm a counselor here at Mercy. You can tell me anything. Let's start with what you were doing downtown."

Jamie shook his head.

"I had to get to the city. The skeen is thinner there, but everything fell apart. There was a cat . . . " Jamie found his words rambling, the story convoluted in its telling. "I had to get back. It's all in the book—look in the book." He motioned to the bag on the side table that held the shreds of the Asrai's cloth and the wood elves' book.

"Can I look in your book, Jamie?" Selma asked, reaching in the bag.

Jamie nodded eagerly. She would see what it was, and his story wouldn't sound so wild; it would make sense. With hesitant hands, she took the book and opened the cover. A darkness passed over him, and he swallowed hard, looking up at Selma who was staring down at the book. The first page was blank, as was creamy page after page. She flipped through to the end and then looked up at Jamie with questioning eyes. Jamie's stomach dropped. Of course the pages would be blank—he needed the Scire to read the book. His hands trembled as he stared down at the blank space.

"Do you know your phone number, Jamie? Is there someone we can call? Do you have an address?" Selma asked gently, breaking his reverie.

Jamie brightened.

"Yes, I know my address." He had memorized it, saying it over and over—Momma and Daddy had said it was important in case he ever became lost, like he was now. "It's 11705 National Boulevard."

Selma smiled.

"Okay, Jamie Peters. Let me go see what I can do about getting you home. In the meantime, I'll check and see if you can have some dinner—are you hungry?"

Jamie nodded, and his stomach, knotted and tight, growled at the mere suggestion.

Selma left. Soon after Ricardo returned with a tray of food that Jamie ate so fast, Ricardo laughed and brought another, telling Jamie not to let anyone know. Jamie smiled. A series of other people came in and out, some in long white coats, some in regular grown-up clothes. Some smiled and talked to him; some did not. Jamie grew tired and slept again, this time clutching Bilbo tightly to his chest. He knew now that just because he wasn't real didn't mean he wasn't alive. In his dreams, he floated endlessly in the night; perfect stillness. He felt the whisper of Momma's kisses on his forehead and tried to suppress the giggle, but morning came anyway. Jamie was brought a tray of pancakes and bacon. He ate it all and drank the orange juice. There was a cup of black coffee on the tray as well. He regarded it with suspicion—the smell was acrid and strong. The sun rose in the sky, and Jamie could see the tops of trees from his window and birds flying by. He longed to get up but had been warned to stay put, and the wires in his arms prevented him from standing. He wondered when Momma and Daddy would arrive. Selma returned in the afternoon, after Jamie had finished a grilled cheese sandwich. Other people, of varying ages, were with her, all carrying clipboards and concerned looks on their faces.

"Hello, Jamie. We've been trying to get to the bottom of who you are and where you belong," Selma said kindly, but there was an edge to her voice.

A man with salt-and-pepper hair and dark tan skin sat on the edge of Jamie's bed, placing his clipboard on the side table.

"Hello, Jamie. I am Dr. Kelson. You can call me Bill. Selma has been filling me in. When you arrived, we ran some tests, and they just came back. We need to discuss them with you."

Jamie nodded, stroking Bilbo's head.

"First off, how are you feeling?" Dr. Kelson asked.

"I like the grilled cheese, but they shouldn't give me coffee. I can't drink coffee."

Dr. Kelson laughed softly.

"I'll let them know. You're looking much better—do you feel better?"

Jamie smiled. "Yes. Thank you for cutting my hair."

The team chuckled collectively.

"Well, we didn't have much choice, Jamie," Selma said. "We had to check for any cuts or abrasions on your head, and you had quite a rat's nest going."

Jamie nodded.

"It's where he hid." He pointed to Bilbo. Dr. Kelson gave him a strange look.

"Thing is, Jamie, when you arrived, we ran your fingerprints and a sample of your DNA to try to figure out who you are."

Jamie interrupted, knowing that he was being rude.

"DNA? You can do that?" he asked, secretly wondering if he had had a surgery.

"I do apologize. Your consent was waived as you were brought in unconscious and without any identification." Dr. Kelson paused, looking at Jamie curiously.

"No," Jamie said, shaking his head a little. "DNA? Like in the movies?"

Dr. Kelson glanced at Selma, his brow wrinkling just slightly. "Well yes, I suppose like the movies. It's something we've been able to do for quite some time now." He spoke carefully, and Jamie could see frustration underneath Dr. Kelson's carefully measured speech. "It wasn't intrusive—just a little saliva from your mouth," Dr. Kelson answered patiently.

"You can do that?" Jamie repeated in wonder. In the crime shows on television, the ones Momma and Daddy watched when he was in the bath, DNA was a mysterious and scary thing, and it took a long time to know what it meant.

Dr. Kelson smiled. "Yes, we test it right here at the hospital and can usually find out who a person is pretty quickly." He paused, his face concerned. "Thing is, Jamie, you weren't who we expected you to be."

Jamie nodded, suddenly understanding the looks of confusion on their faces.

"I've been gone too long. Time works differently where I was."

"How long do you think you've been gone, Jamie?" Selma asked quietly.

"Days and nights. Time passed in waves and slowed down and sped up all at once. The Lairdbalor stole years, but I suppose that was my choice . . . " Jamie's thoughts wandered; all the events of the last few days blurred together, confused and jumbled.

"Jamie Peters, you were reported missing fifty-two years ago," Selma said, fear in her voice. She was waiting for him to react.

Jamie smiled, trying to put her at ease.

"I fell down a hill. I've been trying to get home. Time is different there. I was seven. It's okay . . . it's okay," he spoke soothingly to the crowd surrounding the bed, trying to calm the emotions that passed over their faces.

"Where have you been, son?" Selma asked, taking a step to him and grasping his hand. Her skin was warm, and Jamie squeezed back, the kindness overwhelming him.

"Trying to get home. Can someone please call Momma and Daddy?"

TWENTY-TWO

LATER that day, the wires and tubes were removed from Jamie's arm, and he was allowed to walk himself to the bathroom, carefully. He was supposed to take things slow, as Selma and the others kept telling him, but Jamie couldn't stop the buzzing in his head. It was difficult to keep his eyes open when he lay down. His dreams were muddled, mixes of images and emotion; the only image that was clear was the Lairdbalor. But it held no fear for Jamie now. Its black eel face and wretched clothing seemed as much a part of Jamie as his newly shorn hair.

Ricardo showed Jamie how to shave with a sort of electric razor that looked like nothing more than light passing over his skin. Jamie marveled at the sight of his adult face. The team had stood nearby when Jamie first entered the bathroom, expecting him to panic when he caught sight of his reflection, but Jamie knew. He had always known he was not a child any longer. He had tried to explain the last fifty-two years. Selma had sat quietly and patiently and listened, a small light blinking on a tiny handheld box that she told him meant he was being recorded. It had come out in the wrong order; saying it aloud made it sound like nonsense, a child's imaginings. Dr. Kelson had asked him if someone had kept him, how he had eaten. Jamie didn't have an answer for him. He hadn't eaten and hadn't really needed to—time worked differently in the otherworld, and it hadn't been much of a bother, not in comparison to everything else.

Jamie spent a great deal of time in the bathroom staring at his grown-up face. He wondered what Momma would say when she saw him. Lines crossed his forehead. He could see gray even in the short hair, and his eyes looked old in a way he couldn't describe. Another full day passed, and Jamie grew anxious. He felt better—he wanted to go home. More than anything, he wondered where his parents were. It occurred to him that they might be coming from far away. Fifty-two years. Maybe they lived in some other city, some other state. An entire lifetime had passed since that day on the hill; they could be anywhere by now. Funny, he hadn't even considered that in all this time he had been looking. He had known that years were passing, but still the only place he could imagine them being was his little home with the brick patio out back, the creaky wood floors and bright yellow walls. Now, as he lay in the hospital bed, he realized how absurd it was that they should stay in the same place while the rest of the world had moved on.

He talked to Bilbo, silently praying that he would become real again, crawl to his shoulder and nuzzle his neck, but knowing that, too, had passed. He looked in the wood elves' book and thought about what the child had told him. He dozed, and in his sleep the Lairdbalor appeared, staring at him with gelatinous eyes from behind the impossible monocle. He didn't speak; he didn't need to. Jamie tasted the sweet rose tea in his mouth, and felt the sensation of falling.

When he awoke, Selma was standing over the bed.

"Jamie, you feel up for a walk?" she asked. "I brought you some things," she said, indicating a small pile of clothes. "These should fit."

Jamie nodded and went to change in the bathroom. He dressed in the same type of scrubs that the nurses who checked on him wore. Jamie stood for a moment, enjoying the sensation of the fabric against his skin. He slipped on the pair of shoes that Selma had brought. His feet were rough and ill-kept from an entire lifetime without shoes. The canvas shoes squeezed uncomfortably, and Jamie grimaced. Before he walked out into the hallway, he grabbed Bilbo from the bed. Selma gave him an understanding nod. He walked down the hallway, his jaw a bit ajar. Faces passed him, staring. Jamie tried to smile back—none of these creatures were bogles. It all seemed so simple here, no hidden monsters, just people. Selma led him around a corner and into a courtyard. To Jamie's surprise, it was warm. When he looked up, the sky was a perfect blue framed by a clear glass ceiling. In the corner stood a small chapel that had little stone benches for people to sit. A tiny stream ran through the space. Jamie watched it, enchanted. As he stood motionless, a black beetle, its wings reflecting the colors of the sky, buzzed down and dive-bombed his head. Selma ducked and waved an arm.

"I hate those things!" she exclaimed.

Jamie smiled and held out his hand, where the little beetle fairy lit, wings fluttering in the sun. Selma stared, her eyes wide.

"Well!" she exclaimed.

"Some things are the same in this world and the other," he said simply. "Although I expect you don't talk here," he said to the beetle fairy, which as predicted, did not respond. Instead, the little insect took to the air, skyrocketing upward and out a tiny slit in the glass ceiling.

Selma sat on a stone bench and patted the seat next to her. Jamie sat, breathing in the scent of the green.

"I like this," he said softly.

"Thought you might. Every floor has its own biodome, but this one is my favorite. We're on the top floor, so here you can see the sky. So many things have changed, Jamie, I can't imagine. We've tried to keep your room as simple as possible, but we will eventually need to reintroduce you to the world. This place though, well, it always feels timeless to me." She paused. "Listen, Jamie, I need to tell you something, and I hate to have to say it now, but I don't want you to find out by accident. Your story has already leaked out of the hospital— out front, the news crews are already lining up."

"For me?" Jamie asked, honestly surprised.

Selma gave him a gentle smile. "Of course for you, little boy.

It's a miracle that you're back, wherever you've been—it's a bona fide miracle."

Jamie took a deep breath.

"Selma, where are my parents? Why haven't they come yet?" He dreaded the answer but knew it was the reason they were in this peaceful place.

"I don't know a better way to tell you, so I'll just say it." Selma paused, her lip trembling slightly. "Jamie, your parents died a little over two years after you disappeared."

The air sucked from Jamie's lungs; he held Bilbo to his chest, hands shaking. The words were frozen there, and yet he had known it—at least, a small part of him had known it. They hadn't come. A day had passed, and they hadn't come, and they would have. Jamie gasped for breath, his eyes dry but his chest heaving. He had known there was a reason. He had known they would be there if they could.

"Jamie?" Selma prompted gently. "I'm so, so sorry. It was an accident, just a terrible accident. Their car was hit, and from the reports, they died instantly. No one suffered; there was no pain." She paused. "Jamie, what can I do?"

Jamie shook his head. Two years after he had disappeared.

"I was still in the meadow," he whispered. "I fell asleep. I woke up, and I was already taller. They were already dead by the time I started looking for them."

Selma placed her cool, leathery hand on his. "If I could undo this, I would. I would move mountains to undo this."

Jamie squeezed her hand, his eyes burning, his chest and gut empty. He clutched Bilbo to his chest. "Momma, my mother, she used to repeat this bit of a story to me: 'Thank goodness for all the things you are not, thank goodness you're not something someone forgot...'" Jamie paused, searching for the words. "I can't remember the rest."

Selma's eyes were full of tears. "Left all alone in some punkerish place, like a rusty tin coat hanger hanging in space."

"That's it," Jamie said, his face turning to stone, his heart beating slowly, like something already dead.

"I used to read that to my own children," Selma answered softly.

"They showed me so many things, in the otherworld." Jamie looked to Selma, his eyes pleading with her to understand, to believe him. "They told me my parents wanted to send me away. They told me I was dangerous. They told me my parents didn't want me."

Selma ran her free hand down Jamie's face, stroking his cheek with her thumb.

"Oh, dear one, no—your parents were desperate for you. When you are ready to, you can read the reports. They loved you, Jamie. They loved you so very much, and I know they want you here and would want you to make a life for yourself."

Jamie laughed, a caustic, desperate sound. "I don't know." He turned to Selma. "There's no reason for any of it, is there? It's all just *ainstil.*" The ancient word came from a place deep inside of Jamie, its meaning never more clear. "I think I'd like to go back to my room now," he said. His body was humming, as though a wiry static had entered every molecule of his being.

Selma nodded. "Of course."

She took his hand but said nothing as she led him out of the courtyard and back to his room. Jamie curled up on the bed facing the window, Bilbo at his throat. When he closed his eyes, he saw the Lairdbalor, heard the perfect brass pitch of his voice.

"*Tà sùil, bhalaich,*" the monster intoned.

"Why?" Jamie asked the vision.

"Some things just happen, Jamie. There are no whys. Paths collide, children get lost, stars are plucked from the sky. You need to open your eyes."

DAYS passed. The doctors came and went, and Jamie stared out the window, not noticing or caring. Selma sat by his bed and tried to get him to talk, but Jamie just stared, stroking Bilbo's stuffed head, thinking about how he missed the silky fur and how desperately he needed to talk to someone who understood. His dreams were full of darkness, the sensation of falling, the faint taste of sweet rose tea. Had the Lairdbalor known all along what had happened to his parents? Were all the things it showed him false? Jamie played out the images in his head: walking down the hallway, the cold metal object in his hands, holding the door shut, the force of the blast knocking him back; the couple in the street, the feel of the woman's hip; the old man crouching on the floor, blood pouring from his split wrists. Other images surfaced too—the ones he had been shown in the circus: the little boy locked away in a hospital, cold sterility and stale air. What did it all mean? Questions swirled. Were his parents lost in a circus tent somewhere, hiding from the Fire-eater? What nightmare had they become? Could he return? Would he find them if he did? He had no idea how—hurling himself down another very long hill seemed unlikely to succeed. What if it wasn't all false? The image of the old man, blood spilling from his open wrists, played at the corner of his imagination. Most things existed in the fog, but some were crystal clear.

He remembered a passage of poetry Momma used to like. He had asked her once to read it for him, and she had; in his memory he could still hear her soft voice, her golden-red hair framing her face, her fingers in his hair as he sat on her lap, the book spread out before them.

There is really no death,
And if ever there was it led forward life, and does not wait at the
end to arrest it,
And ceased the moment life appeared.
All goes onward and outward . . . and nothing collapses,
And to die is different from what any one supposed, and luckier.

Jamie supposed the passage should make him feel better—the idea that his parents were somehow still with him, alive somewhere and waiting for him. It was the last thought that haunted him. He knew it to be true—death was different from what anyone supposed, but not luckier. Jamie had seen too much of what lay beyond this world to know better. He had seen where nightmare and pain live. He knew what caused the swirling thoughts late at night, and where all the fears existed.

He knew it was possible to be trapped, dying the same death over and over, living the same pain for as long as anyone remembered, and memory is long. Jamie wondered, what if he locked himself in the tiny bathroom and opened his wrists, watched the blood pool at his feet? Where would he go? Would he find them? Would his bones be enough to bind him to them in what lay beyond?

Selma had left a file folder full of aged newspaper clippings on the bedside table. Jamie regarded them impassively. One evening after she came to tell him he was going to be moved to a "more comfortable place" where he could "find his way again," he picked up the pile of papers. With a feeling of utter numbness, he started leafing through a thousand stories about himself, featuring photographs of the hill at the Getty, police dogs, and officers in uniform.

Search on for Missing Boy

No Leads in Child's Disappearance

Mountain Lion Spotted in Los Angeles Hills Raises Questions about Missing Boy

Jamie scanned the headlines. There were grainy photos of Momma and Daddy—they clung to each other, standing behind microphones. Jamie's school pictures lined the articles, his tooth missing, his eyes bright, a smile on his lips. The dates on the articles became further apart—time was passing, no one was looking anymore.

A Year Apart: The Disappearance of Jamie Peters

The *New York Times* article was long. It showed pictures of his parents sitting side by side on the sofa in his home, holding a tattered backpack that had been found at the bottom of the hill. Jamie ran his finger over their faces, his disemboweled gut aching with loss. The next stack was worse.

Tragedy: Parents of Missing Boy Killed

This article he read. A truck had hydroplaned and jumped lanes, running their car off the road. The randomness of the accident seemed to have shocked the reporter, but Jamie's heart was static. Everything was random. There was no order; if not them, then someone else, and on and on.

What Happened to Jamie Peters?

A ten-year follow-up: Jamie's first-grade school picture showing him in a line with other children with missing teeth and smiles who had not yet known horror.

In an article dated a few years later, a man in prison had confessed to killing him, and it seemed no one had much of a counter-argument. The man had confessed to a great many things, however, and Jamie was still missing, a freak case, no sign of where he had gone or what had happened. And then nothing. Jamie and his parents disappeared from the news, something someone forgot, a rusty tin coat hanger hanging in space.

"They thought you'd been kidnapped, especially after they found the backpack."

Selma stood in the doorway, her voice gentle and unobtrusive.

"I'm glad you're looking at it all. You need to process it," she said quietly, crossing to Jamie's bed. "Can I sit?"

Jamie nodded, a searing pain in his chest.

"Where were you, Jamie?" Selma leaned in, her voice urgent. "All those reporters downstairs, all of us, everyone who worried about you all these years, we want to know—where have you been? You don't need to protect anyone any longer. It's okay."

Jamie looked at her, his eyes full.

"I was at the bottom of that hill. I was stuck in a nightmare. I was trying to get home."

Selma's brow furrowed slightly, trying to understand. "You know you're moving this afternoon, right, Jamie?"

He nodded. "Where am I going?"

"A care center near here. It's a very nice place. You'll have help there—they're going to teach you how to operate in the world. You'll have your own little apartment. They'll help you get used to, well, everything. Fifty-two years brings a lot of changes," she said gently.

"Do I have to?" Jamie asked, his voice very small.

Selma reached over and took his hand. "I'm afraid so, dear, at least for a little while. Wherever you've been, you need to relearn our world."

Jamie looked out the window—everything was so horribly wrong.

"I don't have any money. I'm a grown man, but I don't know anything here. What am I supposed to do? How does this work?"

He looked back at Selma, his eyes desperate.

The corners of Selma's mouth twisted into a gentle smile.

"Your parents and lots of others created a fund a long time ago, Jamie. It's been waiting for you. You're lucky—you have bit to get started with."

Jamie nodded absently.

"Selma, where are they buried?"

Selma sat up, the concrete question a relief. "Well, I looked into it. They weren't buried—they were cremated." She paused. "Do you know what that means Jamie?"

Jamie shook his head, frustrated at his lack of understanding.

Selma took a deep breath.

"It means they were turned to ash, like the ashes you find in a fireplace. They were scattered over the ocean." She examined his face closely. "Are you okay, Jamie?"

He nodded again. The image of Momma and her beautiful golden-red hair and Daddy with his impossibly strong hands flying over the water made him smile, even though his eyes burned with tears.

"I would like to go there—can I?"

"Of course. I can take you," Selma answered and squeezed his hand.

Jamie looked into her gentle brown eyes and fell into her arms, sobs escaping his lungs. Her arms folded around him, and a hand stroked his head, fingers in his hair. His grief came in waves, a howl of loss and rage escaping his mouth. She rocked him back and forth, humming a soft song. When he was drained of all emotion, Jamie's eyes closed, and gentle hands laid him back on the bed and pulled the covers up tightly around his chest. He slept a perfect, dreamless sleep.

JAMIE sat on the rocks overlooking the water. He often came here as the sun was setting; he liked to think of what his parents would have said about the colors of the fading sun on the water. Weeks had passed. In the otherworld he would have been reduced to bones, but here he was getting stronger every day. His skin and muscles defied a man nearing sixty years old. The center allowed him a relative freedom, but Jamie looked forward to the day when he was on his own, when he didn't have to be wary of a curfew or have worried clinical observations of his every move. The deep salt ache for his parents still brought tears to his eyes, but he could see through the fog; he could see the world they would have wanted for him.

The reporters and storytellers still chased him. He didn't mind them much—they were curious, and he tried to show them kindness. It was nice not to have been forgotten, not to have been relegated to some punkerish place. Still, as he looked out over the darkening water, he thought about what would have been. The same what-ifs swirled. Would he have been in that car with his parents? Would they have even been on that road? Would something else equally chaotic have happened instead?

Jamie would never know, and in the moments here as the sun sank from the sky, he let those thoughts take flight. He could almost see them chasing each other like fireflies over the water. The darkness and the light that existed in the core of his being sat on even ground in this time and regarded each other without judgment. Soon enough life would start again, and he would have to make the myriad decisions that determined what world he lived in. But for this one long moment, he closed his eyes, the taste of sweet rose tea on his tongue and the perfect pitch of tenor brass filling his ears.

ACKNOWLEDGMENTS

THIS book would not exist without my husband, who has supported me through every inspiration, rewrite, frustration, and success. I am equally indebted to my son, because while this book is not a mirror of him, his spirit is intrinsically woven into every inch of the story.

Thank you to Todd Bottorff and Turner Publishing for seeing the potential and possibility in *The Lairdbalor*. A million thank yous to Stephanie Beard, Caroline Herd, Maddie Cothren, and Jon O'Neal, as well as my entire editing team. I am so honored to work with you.

A special thank you to Leslie Ellen Jones, who not only edited my terrible commas but also provided invaluable feedback before I ever sent this story out into the world.

John Vise is the artist behind *The Lairdbalor*. On a summer night in New Orleans, deep in Frenchman Street, I found a craft fair and John's brilliant work. Thank you for the nightmares and inspiration.

The incomparable Daniel Pollack provided the soundtrack by which this book was written. I binge listened to his Rachmaninoff, Chopin, and Liszt, among others. The emotion that Daniel conveys though a piece of music cannot be expressed in words.

I am incredibly fortunate to have a supportive and loving family. No writer is an island; everything is possible only because of the foundation on which I stand.

Finally, this is for all the millions upon millions of people out there who suffer from anxiety. It is a difficult world to navigate, there are monsters everywhere you turn, and the fact that no one can see them but you makes it particularly unbearable. I hope I have given a window into that nightmare, and for those trapped in its depths, a sense that you are not alone.

ABOUT THE AUTHOR

KATHLEEN KAUFMAN is a native Coloradan and long-time resident of Los Angeles, California. She is a University of Southern California alum, teaches high school English, and is a writing and composition adjunct professor at Santa Monica College. In addition to writing, Kathleen is an avid amateur photographer and has published work in *The Huffington Post* and other publications. When not writing, she probably has a camera in hand or is curled up with a good horror novel. Kathleen currently lives in Los Angeles with her husband, son, terrier, and a pack of cats.

CPSIA information can be obtained
at www.ICGtesting.com
Printed in the USA
BVOW03*1333150917
494999BV00004B/10/P